Praise for Amanda Prowse

'The queen of domestic drama.'
Daily Mail

'Powerful and emotional family dr[ama]
that packs a real punch.'
Heat

'A great read full of family atmosphere.'
Wendy Holden

'Captivating, heartbreaking, superbly written.'
Closer

'A page-turner, difficult to put down, brilliantly
written in an accessible style and language…
I cannot speak too highly of this book.'
LoveReading

'Full of raw emotion, this sensitive exploration
of mental illness is a real tear-jerker.'
Sunday Mirror

'Prepare to work your way through
as many tissues as pages.'
Cosmopolitan

'A fast, unputdownable read.'
Red

ALSO BY AMANDA PROWSE

Novels

Poppy Day
What Have I Done?
Clover's Child
A Little Love
Christmas for One
Will You Remember Me?
A Mother's Story
Perfect Daughter
Three-and-a-Half Heartbeats
The Second Chance Café
Another Love
My Husband's Wife
I Won't Be Home for
Christmas
Anna
Theo
How to Fall in Love Again

Novellas

Something Quite Beautiful
The Game
A Christmas Wish
Ten Pound Ticket
Imogen's Baby
Miss Potterton's Birthday
Tea
Mr Portobello's Morning
Paper

Something Quite Beautiful

AMANDA PROWSE

HEAD of ZEUS

An Aria Book

Typeset by Palimpsest Book Production Limited, Falkirk, Stirlingshire

Printed and bound in Great Britain by
CPI Group (UK) Ltd, Croydon CR0 4YY

Head of Zeus Ltd
First Floor East
5–8 Hardwick Street
London EC1R 4RG

WWW.HEADOFZEUS.COM

Contents

Something Quite Beautiful

For my readers who every time they fall into a page with my words on it, form a literary bridge from my mind to theirs... how I love these little walkways where we meet no matter the weather!

One

The small, square blacked-out windows on either side of the wagon were set too high to offer a view. A minor irritation for many, but for the three prisoners ensconced inside, it was the start of their punishment. They sat in individual cages in the back of the truck, separated by half a metre.

The diminutive Warren Binns was quiet, thoughtful, as he tried to calculate if they would pass his native Sheffield on their way North. He took a deep breath, trying to breathe in a clue as to his whereabouts, hoping for a whiff of something familiar, something that meant home. There was nothing but the stench of sweat that emanated from all occupants of the van. It was cold outside, but with the heating on full blast, they were uncomfortably hot inside this airless metal box. The enclosed space reeked of misery and desperation.

Warren closed his eyes and pictured the terraced house in Weavers Row. He wondered if he would ever get the chance to unlock the front door again, now that the key nestled somewhere among his bagged and tagged belongings, attached to the key ring his mum had bought him; a picture of a large trophy inscribed with the words Number One Son. A little sliver of cut and shaped brass that meant so much more than the sum of its parts. Warren clung to the knowledge that, somewhere, he belonged and was loved. Weavers Row was the one place on the earth that he could reach into the fridge or run a bath without consideration or needing permission. He not only missed the occupants of Weavers Row, but also the little life that he had led inside his childhood home. He longed to walk through the green front door after a day at college or a shift at the quarry and make a brew in the tiny kitchen, before collapsing in the lounge and warming his feet in front of the three-bar electric fire. Stretching out in the sturdy framed chair, on the sagging cushions that used to belong to his grandad and had the perfect dimensions for an afternoon snooze. He pictured the swirly patterned carpet that had worn to nothing where it was most trodden, and the crowded cupboard under the stairs, which smelled of olden days and memories. He had hidden in it as a child, playing among the meters and the old Quality Street tins full of delicate, glass Christmas decorations and tinsel in gaudy shades. In later years he hung his leather biker jacket here – on a hook next to the hoover – and stowed his toolbox on the floor, his mum's shopping trolley stacked on top of it. What would happen to his stuff, now that they knew he wasn't coming home. Would they throw it away? He shook his head; it didn't really matter, not in the grand scheme of things.

Warren pulled at the bar that was joined by chain to the loops around his ankle and succeeded in pulling his manacled hands to within four inches of his face. He laughed; the itch on his nose would have to stay put. His feet, similarly anchored inside their rubber sandals were hot and itchy against the vinyl matting.

'What's so funny, Bud?'

Warren stared straight ahead, ignoring the posh, chinless twat sat to his right. He wasn't anyone's bud. The guy didn't take the hint.

'Oh, I see, the strong silent type. It's all good. I'm Henry, in case anyone is interested.'

'No one is interested, so shut the fuck up!' A burly skinhead growled in a cockney accent from behind Henry's head.

'That's good advice from your friend.' The portly, sweating security guard perched on the narrow bench between the cages looked Henry in the eye.

'He ain't my fucking friend!' It was torturous enough to be so physically confined, knees pressed against the metal screen in front of him, shoulders horribly compressed inside the box, without being lumped together with a long-haired dickhead who sounded like he had swallowed a silver spoon.

The guard pointed at the skinhead, noting his tattooed neck and misshapen nose. 'Name?'

'Keegan Lomax.' The guard nodded as if cataloguing him. One to watch.

Henry was not going to shut up any time soon. 'Keegan, as in Kevin? I've never been a football fan, more of a cricket man, but wasn't he a footballer? God I *hope* he is or I'm making a complete tit of myself. It could have been worse, you might have been called Beckham or Redknapp, they're footballers, aren't they? And I'm sorry to say, boys, that this is where my footy knowledge ends. Although if I *did* have to support a team, it would probably be Barcelona, it's one of my favourite cities in the whole world. I think there is nothing better than a stroll down las Ramblas, a cold beer and a plate of tapas in the sun, bliss!'

'What bit of *shut the fuck up* did you not get?' Keegan spoke through gritted teeth as he stamped his shackled feet.

'Alright. Let's calm it down a bit, gentlemen.' The guard raised and lowered his palms as though placating an animal.

Warren smiled wryly to himself. He wasn't sure where he was heading, but it would be an interesting journey if nothing else. He was glad of Henry's diversion. Amy's tear stained face sat behind his eyelids with every blink, the way her mouth had crumpled as she tried to speak, her large eyes brimming. She looked like she was drowning with the effort of trying to contain all that she wanted to say, aware that the clock was ticking, unaware of how long they had to say goodbye, minutes? Seconds? *When... when will I see you again, War? Where are you going now and how soon until you come home, and... and how will I know when you are coming back, how will you let me know?* She had smiled, trying to be brave as her chest heaved in an effort to stem the sobs. Her small hands fidgeted with a rose-printed hanky that she twisted and untwisted around her fingers. It was this memory that would jar Warren from sleep in the middle of the night and greet him upon waking each morning. He had not been able to answer her, could not find one single word of solace or comfort. He had tried, but the barriers he had constructed around his heart and mouth in the preceding months were so strong that it was impossible to break them down. Even at that moment, when a peg on which to hang hope would have made the impending years so much easier, he found it impossible to utter a single word of optimism or love. Instead he had nodded. It was probably for the best, better for her that she didn't wake each day with a lift in her heart that today might be the day that he came home. Better for everybody.

'How much further is it? I'm getting *terribly* bored.' It was as if Henry was immune to the reaction he provoked.

'A good few hours yet.' The guard kept his answer short and vague.

'Well, in that case, can I interest anyone in a game of I Spy?' Henry wasn't giving up.

'Fucking perfect.' Keegan banged his shaved head on the cage in front of him.

'All okay back there?' The driver slid back a small Plexiglas panel to speak to his colleague.

'Fine, mate, we're just debating football and wondering how far it is to Glenculloch.' There was the faintest smirk about his face.

Warren stiffened and turned his head to look at Keegan, whose eyes were wide. It was the first mention of where they were heading. Warren had heard bad things about this place and judging from Keegan's expression he guessed it was the same for him. He tried to recall what he'd heard while he was on remand. Even Carl, a serial offender who had seen it all, had turned serious when he explained the rumours surrounding Glenculloch. 'It's an old MoD site, submarines or something nuclear. It's at the bottom of a mountain on Rannoch Moor. They say it's run by a woman who thinks she's God. Everything that happens there is in her hands – reform you, kill you, whichever. It's off the radar for obvious reasons – officially, it doesn't even exist. I know a screw that went up there, and I'm telling you it's in the middle of shitting nowhere. And I mean shitting nowhere!'

Three hundred miles away, at the bottom of a mountain on Rannoch Moor, Matthew Shackleton stood behind his desk and pulled his navy v-necked sweater over his starched white button-down shirt. He was a bit chilly, and hated to start his working day without making himself as comfortable as possible. He wore the same thing every day: one of six identical jerseys – three in blue and three in green – along with a pair of expensive chinos that hugged his long legs, and leather deck shoes that would have been more appropriate strolling along a dock. He patted the parting of his hair to ensure it was straight, and surreptitiously used his fingertips to check on the thinning spot that had appeared on his crown. He knew it was to be expected – on the wrong side of fifty he had anticipated a little wear and tear – but it was still a grim daily reminder that he was on the descent. He buffed his round tortoiseshell spectacles with the soft cloth from inside his glasses case. Pushing them on, he began to sort through the mail.

This was Matthew's third career. When, after serving as an army Captain and later as a warden at Belmarsh prison, a friend had suggested semi-retirement in an administrative role in the wilds of Scotland it had sounded like an adventure. But had he known what life at Glenculloch was going to be like, he might have thought twice. He remembered the day he arrived four years earlier, and how, as the car approached, he leant forward in his seat, narrowing his eyes to better study the vast metal and concrete box that loomed before him. It resembled a giant slanting triangle; modernist, smooth-surfaced and most incongruent to the Scottish wilderness. It could almost have been dropped there by an alien hand.

'I can't see any windows.'

His driver, one of the guards with whom he had made awkward small talk since being collected from Edinburgh Airport, shook his head. 'No, you won't, there aren't any. Sunlight is a privilege that needs to be earned.' He chewed his gum, open-mouthed, and sniggered.

'Is that right?' Matthew lowered his head and tilted his neck, trying to get the best view from the windscreen.

Matthew dragged his thoughts back to the stack of manila envelopes in front of him. A postcard sat incongruously on top of the pile. It depicted a mountain scene; a towering hunk of snow-capped granite that nudged the bright blue skyline. Mount Domett, wherever that might be. He pulled the card closer to decipher the tiny script in the bottom right-hand corner. New Zealand, fancy that. It was from someone called Nicholas, Nicholas Patterson.

'Morning, Matthew.' A tall, brisk-looking woman in a tan cashmere coat strode into the office.

'Good morning, Edwina. Bit nippy today.' Matthew shivered involuntarily and rubbed his palms together.

'Yes. Better double-check on any frost warning tonight.'

'Already done it. You're worried about the fruit trees, right?'

'And the bougainvillea. I've fashioned some rather nifty covers from old fleecy blankets that ought to do the trick. I've already double-mulched the roots. Trouble is the main beds don't get the morning sun and are more vulnerable to frost.'

'Righto, I'm on it.'

Edwina smiled as she removed her coat and hung it on the wooden coat stand, placing it next to Matthew's mackintosh. She knew he would be. They made a formidable gardening partnership. Edwina knew that she had met her green-fingered match when during a sudden, violent storm last spring, she had ventured outside in the early hours with her pyjama bottoms tucked into her wellington boots. Armed with a head-torch and a handful of twine she was intent on placing carrier bags over delicate flower heads and tying up any wandering stems. Matthew's outside light had flicked on simultaneously and there he was, with a Drizabone over his nightshirt, a rather natty sou'wester and the same intention. Undeterred by the driving rain and cracks of thunder, they had toiled merrily, determined to preserve what they had worked hard to achieve.

The two were colleagues and neighbours, living side by side in the grounds of Glenculloch in identical one-bedroom cottages, the only original buildings that pre-dated the facility. The houses sat with their back walls against the new structure, meaning their view was unobscured by their ugly workplace. Edwina loved the peace and quiet; the big, bruised sky; the rocky outcrops that sat in jagged contrast to the soft heathers sprouting at their base. To her it was the romantic landscape of adventure – though she knew that Matthew felt differently, and rather missed city life, with its constant hum of traffic, where you could buy fresh bread and good wine from the local deli and see the latest flicks on a rainy afternoon with a bag of popcorn.

But then, their taste was certainly opposed. Matthew's cottage was crammed with vintage chaise-longues, fussy gilt-framed prints and curios that reminded him of his grandmother and echoed the classic 'stately home' interior he tried to emulate. Edwina was most particular about the objects that surrounded her. Her walls were painted in muted neutral shades and she favoured pale over-sized sofas and pine wood furniture with clean, elegant lines. When choosing anything, from clothes to furniture, she asked the simple questions, is it practical and does it look attractive? There was no room in her life for ugly clutter. During her sixty years on the planet she had learnt the importance of beauty. The memory of her mother hovered; despite sharing many words of wisdom, she could only ever picture her in the kitchen, her hands immersed in either suds or dough, *Look, Edwina May, this is just an empty old jam jar ready for the bin, but watch what happens when I pop some bluebells in it – it becomes something quite beautiful...*

'You have a postcard.' Matthew interrupted her reverie.

'Oh, splendid!'

She reached out her hand and strode towards his desk like a child being offered sweets, afraid the offer might be withdrawn. She studied first the picture and then the text, scrawled by a biro on the other side. Turning it over twice more, she scrutinised the picture and then the words again.

'Well well, Nicholas in New Zealand. How wonderful.' She beamed at Matthew, who smiled back; he loved to see her this happy.

'Is he a friend of yours?'

'Yes.' She nodded.

Matthew swallowed the curious mixture of interest and jealousy that rose in his throat. He had hoped for a bit more.

Edwina walked into her small office adjacent to Matthew's desk. It was a grey room with little in it to admire or lift the spirits; it was in fact similar to the inmates' rooms, bland and impersonal. That was with the exception of the large cork board that held pride of place behind her work space. It hung like a fine work of art, a brightly painted and magnificent collage that brought all the corners of the world into this windy, damp corner of Perthshire. The snowy peak of a Patagonian mountain was partly obscured by the outstretched arms of Christ the Redeemer as he watched over Rio. A pale, stone fort in Jordan overlapped a dense Finnish forest. She selected a fat-headed pin from the small, square box and tacked the picture of Mount Dommet in between a spouting geyser in Yellowstone National Park and the Nynäshamn docks just south of Stockholm.

'Coffee?'

'Please.' She nodded.

Matthew placed the stack of mail in the wire basket on the corner of her desk. He avoided touching the bulky green filing cabinet that sat against the wall. Once, he had placed the mail basket on top of it and Edwina had been so furious that he had thought he might get the sack. She was clearly a woman that liked things kept just so. She obviously had a system, and he was not about to interfere with a woman and her system, especially a woman like the formidable Edwina Justice, who was rumoured to have left her last job as head warden at HMP

Marlham because she refused to work within the guidelines for prisoner punishment.

He popped an espresso in a little china cup in front of her and folded his arms over his chest. As usual he took up only the minimum of space; he was, in every detail, neat.

'We have three new inmates that arrived late afternoon yesterday. CCTV report shows that one of them, Warren Binns, spent a large part of the night pacing, but the other two seem to have slept straight through. The induction room is booked for nine-fifteen. I've emailed you their files and I've notified Angelo.'

'Thank you, Matthew.' She smiled at him for the second time that morning and gratefully sipped the strong coffee.

Edwina clicked open her desktop and entered today's password. This daily rotation of letters and numbers, issued by Whitehall, was the only contact she had with the Ministry of Justice, other than her annual report. She rather liked the autonomy, though it had taken her a while to digest the reality of the job when it had first been offered four years ago, in a dimly lit basement beneath the Royal Courts of Justice. It had been a lot to absorb and she had been more than a little distracted by her future employer's brash manner.

'So let me get this straight, you are saying that I wouldn't come under any jurisdiction?' she asked quizzically.

The Minister for Penal Reform smiled and loosened his tie. 'Exactly right, you'd be invisible. You'd be the boss, answerable to no one. No one. There's an election looming and the PM wants to get tough and remove these little shits from the streets, so we are throwing the rule book out and giving you complete free reign to do as you see fit. Not that we'll be phrasing it exactly like that you understand, heaven forbid we offend the PC brigade.' He laughed and winked at the IT guy on the computer. Edwina felt excluded; did he think *she* was the PC brigade? He continued, 'This place does not exist, if you get my drift. What happens up there really will be up to you. Reform them, kill them, whichever. You'll be God. Imagine that.'

The minister leant forward, placing his elbows on his thighs and forming a pyramid with his fingers, through which he spoke. 'Now, I expect you're wondering about finances. Well, this is one of those problems we believe can be solved by throwing money at it. We give you a handsome budget, a very handsome budget, and what you do with it is up to you. No questions asked. You could get yourself a hot-tub, a chocolate fountain and a lifelong subscription to your favourite magazine; let the little fuckers eat dust for all we care. We are running out of ideas and it's time to get radical or sink.'

Edwina smiled at the simple clarity of the man's suggestions. It was clear from his expression that he genuinely considered this to be the route to happiness for her – probably for all women – after all, what more could she possibly want other than a hot-tub, chocolate and a magazine full of pretty pictures? At least she was used to it; operating in a man's world where she was at the top of her game was full of challenges like this. She chose, as ever, to ignore his asinine suggestions.

'So I'm to be your guinea pig?'

'We prefer the term "pilot project".'

Her next question seemed naive in retrospect, 'If this place doesn't exist and there is no monitoring of data, no quotas, no KPIs or benchmarks for improvement, and no departmental visits, how will you know if it's working?'

'You will tell us.'

Edwina had hardened a great deal since then. Now, scanning the list of new inmates, she registered only the first line of each case note, no longer tutting at the horror of their crimes. Warren Binns, seventeen – Murder. Keegan Lomax, sixteen – Murder. Henry McFarlane-Hunter, seventeen – Multiple Murder. She didn't even register surprise at their young ages, or sadness at the waste of their lives. It was all quite routine at Glenculloch, and she had learned in the four years that she had been running the site that it was not always advisable to be too forewarned. Too much information might mean she ignored that gut feeling, gave in to a preconceived idea based on the facts. There was a danger that the details of a case might skew her judgement and Edwina relied very heavily on her instinct, the feeling in her stomach, a little voice on her shoulder.

'I wonder why you were up all night pacing, Mr Binns, what have you got on your mind?' She voiced her thoughts, and then shook them away. Better to get the induction over with first.

Turning away from the screen, she savoured her coffee and looked up at the cork board. It had been lovely to hear from Nicholas.

Angelo the Italian man-mountain collected the new inmates and marched them in single file to the induction room – although, thanks to the shackles of handcuffs and leg restraints, each attached to another inmate via a looped belt chain, it was more of a shuffle than a march. It was a chance for all three to take in further details about their environment, and Warren tried to drink it all in. To his left were what looked like the accommodation cells – identical seven-foot cabins consisting of a bed, sink, urinal and a small mirror, as well as a door-less cubby for storage under the sink. Warren thought longingly of all his stuff crowding the cupboard under the stairs at home, but personalising your room with posters and knickknacks was clearly forbidden. All the cell doors were open – obviously privacy was not a consideration here – and looked like they were on some sort of automatic timer system. He hoped the doors closed at night.

Grey was the interior design colour of choice, the walls were pale dove-coloured moulded panels and the whole structure was without windows. He craned his neck and looked up into a high, angular ceiling, as tall as a cathedral, where three square panels cut into the roof let in some natural light. These were covered with a gauzy film meaning that sunlight was dappled, leaving marbled white pools reflected on the opposite walls. A shiny chrome walkway ran around the outside top of the main area, which reminded Warren of the fire escape in the tenement opposite his terrace. Along this walkway, behind darkened glass walls, were the administrative offices and meeting rooms, the clockwork heart of Glenculloch.

Warren gazed in all directions at his new home, overawed by the enormity of the proportions; it was part warehouse, part bunker. Unlike the house in Weavers Row, there was nothing soft, every object and surface was hard and angular, functional and monochrome. The floor, coated with a white rubber matting that curved in a lip up the first four inches of every wall and door, was clinical in its cleanliness. There was not a speck of dust nor twist of litter, nor a whiff of cigarette smoke nor odour of food; it was sterile, hygienic and soulless. With the exception of a few oversized potted palms that sat in huge steel containers which were bolted to the floor, there was not a splash of colour anywhere. In their regulation electric-blue tracksuits, the inmates would find it very hard to hide.

Angelo stopped at a door on the ground floor beyond the recreation area and ushered them inside a small lecture theatre containing a whiteboard and twelve desks. Like the cells, the room was windowless with harsh strip lighting that was an inadequate substitute for sunshine. He released them from their belts, but left their handcuffs on, and the boys took their seats centrally, behind three of the desks.

Henry laughed loudly. 'This is like prep school for baddies!'

'I swear to God if you start with your bollocks again, I will not be responsible for my actions. Do you hear me, posh boy?' Keegan feared what a loose cannon like Henry might mean for the group. He had heard some bad things about Glenculloch and didn't want to blight his time so early on.

'Are you always this grumpy?' Henry looked genuinely offended.

'Shut the fuck up!' Keegan growled in Henry's direction.

Angelo stood in front of the trio, his voice barely more than a whisper. 'If I were you, I'd pipe down, all of you. The Principal is on her way and you don't want to start off on the wrong side of her. Trust me.'

'Yeah, of course I'll trust you, why wouldn't I, bro?' Keegan raised his cuffed wrists in the guard's direction. But when he turned to Warren he looked genuinely scared. 'I've never seen the Governor before in any nick I've been in.'

'Lordy do, how many have you been in?' Henry smirked.

Keegan ignored him.

Angelo leant closer to Keegan. 'This is unlike any other correctional facility. And whether you trust me or not, *bro*, doesn't really matter, so take it as a warning. Do not get on the wrong side of the Principal.'

'This is like lesson 101, scaring the new kids!' Henry smirked again.

Angelo walked over to the desk at which Henry sat. 'If I wanted to scare you, I could, believe me. I'd give you some basic statistics that might make you very scared.'

'Well, I'm not so sure about that. I've heard that seventy-nine per cent of all statistics are made up on the spot!' It was as if Henry couldn't help himself.

Angelo licked his lips and leant closer to Henry. 'Here's one that isn't made up. Of the three hundred and thirty inmates that have entered Glenculloch in the last four years, we've had no recorded deaths and none have been released. And yet we are now down to two hundred and eighty-eight. Now, I ain't no Vorderman, but that don't add up. So, as I say, don't get on the wrong side of the Principal. In here, she makes the law, she is the law. You could do a lot worse than listen to your friend.' Angelo nodded his head in Keegan's direction.

'He is not my fucking friend!' Keegan grimaced.

'Good morning, gentlemen.' Edwina Justice strolled into the theatre as if it were a boardroom, her heels clicking on the shiny floor. The four stared at her in silence. She looked immaculate in a navy skirt that sat just below her knee. Warren noted her cropped greying hair, the pearls that sat on her earlobes, her smart white cotton shirt and navy blazer. She looked rich.

'Morning, Angelo.'

'Morning, Ma'am.'

Edwina stood with her hands on her slender hips and addressed them. 'Gentlemen, do we need these handcuffs? Are any of you going to threaten violence? Or can we ask Angelo to remove the offending articles?'

The three looked at one another. What was the catch?

'You' – Edwina pointed at Warren – 'are you able to control yourself if we remove your ironware?'

Warren nodded.

'And you, Mr...?'

'Lomax, Keegan Lomax.'

'Thank you, Mr Lomax; can I trust you have enough self-control not to behave in an unruly fashion if released?'

Keegan nodded.

'That's excellent. Angelo, do the honours please.'

Angelo made his way along the desks; one by one he released the boys from their restraints. Each rubbed at the skin on their wrists and flexed their fingers to restore feeling. Angelo took his place at the back of the room.

'My name is Edwina Justice and I am the Principal here at Glenculloch. I trust that your first night was comfortable. I can imagine that you are all feeling slightly unsettled by the journey: it's a long way and not the most luxurious of transport.' There was a pause while she surveyed each boy and they studied her in return. 'The purpose of this meeting is to teach you the ground rules for your time here. I think it would be most unfair to expect you to operate within a system that you do not fully understand. This morning I will explain the house rules and you will be permitted to ask me a question each. Just one.' She raised her index finger to emphasise the point. 'It can be anything, on any topic, but I would advise you to ask wisely as the chance to ask a question again might not occur for a very long time, maybe years. Is that clear so far?'

'Yep,' Keegan answered.

'Crystal,' Henry responded as he drummed the desk with his fingers.

'For the record, gentlemen, if ever I speak to you or ask you a question, you will respond in full sentences followed by Principal or Ma'am and without finger drumming or other distraction. So "crystal" and "yep" would not be acceptable. You weren't to know, but now you do. Please sit up straight.'

Warren Binns was the only one not to have to readjust his

posture. The Principal picked up a marker pen and approached the whiteboard.

'Glenculloch is run on sound principles. The system is straightforward, designed to punish those that deserve it and rehabilitate those that don't. It's quite simple really. There are six rules and only six rules. I expect you to learn and live by them. No more, no less. By following the rules, you will carve a path of discovery for yourself, break them and you will find that pathway blocked by a whole heap of trouble. Is that clear?'

She scanned the three and pointed at Warren. 'Is that clear?'

Warren remembered the earlier instruction. 'Yes, that's clear, Ma'am.'

The Principal nodded, satisfied. She removed the lid from the marker pen and starting writing on the whiteboard.

1. *Always tell the truth.*
2. *Always display good manners.*
3. *Never swear.*
4. *Work hard.*
5. *Respect yourself.*
6. *Respect others.*

She turned to the group and watched as the boys read each rule. 'If anyone is unclear on what any of these rules mean, then please raise your hand now so that I may offer further explanation.' No one raised their hand. She waited for another second, looking at each man in turn, before interpreting their silence as understanding.

'Excellent. May I remind you that these are not optional, they are mandatory.' She paused again, allowing this information to sink in as each one read and re-read the six rules by which they were expected to live. 'I would now like to take your questions. You first, Mr Lomax.'

Keegan coughed and shifted in his seat. He hadn't wanted to go first; he felt embarrassed, awkward and didn't want to be judged. This setting reminded him of school, an environment in which he had far from flourished. He tried to ask the question that was battering the inside of his lips as though he could care less about the answer. 'I'm personally not fussed, but I've heard that we don't get any visitors here, that no one gets any visitors, ever, and I was just wondering if that's true, but as I say, I'm not really bothered about it, Ma'am?'

'Thank you for that, Mr Lomax; it's a source of great debate. The answer to your question is yes, that is true. There are no visitors to Glenculloch, we are an invisible site. I believe it's for the best, no distractions and no disappointments. This is to allow a clear, focused and uncomplicated rehabilitation programme that is open to all who reside here.'

Keegan shook his head and wiped invisible sweat from his forehead. He raised his top lip and eyebrow simultaneously, a look that said *whatever...* An image of he and Joanna crept into his mind, sat side by side on the sofa, their thighs touching, her hand sat inside his, her beautiful fingers interlaced with his own and the feel of her nails against his palm. He would have to think very carefully about exactly how that felt and catalogue every minute detail, storing it away for recollection whenever he needed it.

Edwina Justice turned to Henry. 'May I have your question please?'

The boy was agitated, edgy; his tone antagonistic. 'Hi, I was just wondering, what would happen if we *did* kick off? I mean, you've taken off our restraints, which is really cool, but there's three of us and only two of you. And not being sexist or anything, but I fancy my chances against you, even on a bad day.' Henry pointed at her and then Angelo as if trying to fathom the maths; maybe he was the only one aware of the odds.

Henry laughed, and Edwina recalled the first line of Henry's report: *Psychopathic tendencies – on the night in question, Mr McFarlane-Hunter blocked all exits and locked the doors before setting fire to the home of his ex-girlfriend, killing both of her parents, her grandmother and three siblings. Tests for narcotics and alcohol proved negative. Has shown no empathy or remorse.* She fixed him with a stare before speaking. 'Angelo, would you be so kind as to show the gentlemen our deterrents?'

The guard stepped forward from the back of the room and stood next to the Principal. Facing them, he carefully lifted the hem of his shirt. Nestling against his hard, muscled stomach sat a snub nose revolver. Edwina continued as though Angelo had revealed something innocuous. 'Every inch of this facility is under the watchful eye of cameras and in this case it is not merely an expression, I do mean every single inch. We carry state of the art integrated tracking and warning alarms, meaning that all staff are monitored by the main Ops room every second that they are on site. There is not one angle, one nook or one cranny, with the exception of my office, that is not monitored twenty-four hours a day, three hundred and sixty-five days of the year.' She pointed to her own gun, hiding beneath her blazer and next to her tailored shirt; it sat snugly in a leather holster that ran across her back and under her arm. 'This is the Smith and Wesson three five seven calibre Magnum. FBI studies show it to be fatal in 98.7 per cent of cases if an adult male is hit in the head or torso. It is the weapon of choice for all guards and Glenculloch personnel who, incidentally, are all ex-military: expert snipers or Special Forces-trained, myself included. Everyone at Glenculloch may discharge their weapon as and when they see fit.'

Henry visibly shrunk; he didn't fancy his chances after all. The Principal turned to Warren.

'May I have your question please?'

Warren had several things he wanted to ask, but the words leapt from his mouth that had been swirling around his head since he had heard the Principal's speech minutes earlier.

'I... I would like to ask' – he swallowed, trying to remove his tongue that had stuck to the dry roof of his mouth – 'who is it that decides those that deserve to be punished and those that don't?'

'Me.' Edwina wasted no other words on Warren's enquiry.

Henry coughed. 'Hi, Henry McFarlane-Hunter again.' He waved with an elaborate hand gesture as though miming a rainbow. 'It may just be me, but I am not sure that can be right, there *must* be some board or outside influence. I mean, who is your boss? I'm not even *entirely* sure how long my sentence is. It wasn't that clear with the whole, judge summing up, mother howling, keys jangling thing going on in the court. Would you care to clarify?'

Edwina Justice paused and stared at Henry. 'Certainly. All prisoners at Glenculloch are sent here for twenty years. They will all serve their full sentence, unless I deem that to be inadequate and duly increase their tariff, which is not uncommon. As I say to all newcomers, you should expect to be here for at least twenty years. Thank you for your question, although uninvited.'

'Jesus Christ, twenty years? I think I might die before then of boredom and enforced politeness.' Henry slouched back in his chair and rubbed his hands over his face and raked his chin.

'Angelo?'

'Yes, Ma'am?'

'Could you please restrain Mr McFarlane-Hunter and take him into solitary confinement. I want him placed on a strict calorie reduction liquid diet and in total isolation for forty-eight hours.'

Henry scraped the chair backwards and tried to stand. 'What the fuck? You can't...' Henry didn't get a chance to finish his sentence; Angelo was on him in seconds. Warren and Keegan were both startled at the speed in which the enormous guard managed to cover the room. Both jumped as the sound of Henry's head smashing against the top of the desk rang out. Neither envied the familiar snap of metal against his wrists, which were bent up behind his back. Two snakes of bright-red blood ran from his nose and into his mouth, which was hanging open in shock.

Edwina wiped the board clean, seemingly oblivious to the scuffle behind her. She was glad of the diversion of the board. It was necessary to retain absolute control, but that didn't mean she wanted to witness control being taken. She closed her eyes and delivered her words, concentrating on keeping the quaver from her voice.

'Mr McFarlane-Hunter, you had already broken rules two and six and now apparently rule three also. Make it seventy-two hours, Angelo.'

'Yes, Ma'am.'

Henry was strangely silent as he was dragged from the room. Edwina turned to face the remaining two newcomers who sat in stunned silence. She noted Warren's ashen complexion and trembling hands.

'Thank you for your time today, gentlemen. I will send someone in to escort you back to your rooms presently.' With that she swept from the room as if she had been addressing the WI.

Two

Warren manoeuvred his plastic tray through the crowd and took an empty seat on the bench opposite Keegan. After six months in Glenculloch they had become firm friends.

'Good afternoon, how goes it?'

Keegan lifted a spoonful of gravy-soaked potato and allowed it to slop back down onto the tray, causing a satisfying splat. The machine that issued their food at the press of a button had messed up again. He rubbed his head, scratching at the stubble. 'Oh, just frigging perfect. I don't know what's worse, the lumpy, sauce-smothered shite which hides God knows what or the fact that I have twenty years to get used to eating it.'

Warren grimaced and nodded. 'At least it's better than being hungry – and I've had a bit of that in my time.' He pictured his younger self, curled tightly on the bare mattress of his bed, wearing his school uniform for warmth and with a towel draped over his torso as he tried to ignore the gnawing pain in his stomach. He would imagine chips that dripped with salt and vinegar, steaming battered cod that would scald his fingers and smear his mouth with grease, plates of ketchup-doused sausages, fried eggs sprinkled with salt, hot buttery toast and heaps of apple crumble and custard. He remembered trudging to school in those same clothes that had kept him warm at night, trying to concentrate on what was being taught while ignoring the taunts of his class mates, *Rubbish Binns, Looney Binns, Stinky Binns*.

Keegan caught Warren's eye momentarily; it was rare to offer this kind of insight in prison, it didn't do to give too much of yourself away. The less people knew about you, the less chance there was of them exploiting any weakness.

'Have you seen Hooray?' Warren gave Henry his newly acquired nickname.

Keegan shook his head. 'Not for a couple of days, I heard he wasn't too well.' He tapped the side of his head.

'Oh.' Warren didn't know what to say, he hadn't warmed to the bloke, but wasn't about to enjoy his misfortune. 'That's not good.'

'No,' Keegan concurred, 'that's not good at all.'

As he spoke, he became aware of a burly West Indian man listening in on their conversation. Bo had a reputation as a gossip and a fearmonger. Keegan and Warren generally tried to stay away from him. Now he squatted down at the end of their table and rested on his haunches, his wide thighs splayed under the regulation blue trousers. He looked like he was relishing what he was about to say.

'I don't want to be the bearer of bad news, but I'm afraid your friend ain't coming back.'

'Is that right?' Warren noticed that Keegan made no attempt to deny their friendship this time.

Bo looked to the left and right, checking no guard was within earshot. 'I expect he is one of the disappeared.'

'The what?' Keegan laughed at the kid who was, in his opinion, another nutter.

'You can laugh, but I've been here since the beginning and I'm telling you, my friend, that for all her cool politeness and fancy shirts, Justice is a cold, cold bitch. I bet she told you

you'd do twenty, but the truth is no one here will do twenty, you'll do forever, trust me. One bloke trashed a plant in the recreation area and got an extra five. I'm not lying, five years for a plant!' He sucked his teeth. 'But that's not the real worry, it's the ones that disappear you should be concerned about. She kills them or has them killed and there ain't fuck-all you can do. She is the law in here, completely untouchable. She removes their file, bangs shut that drawer and it's like they were never here; gone. I'm tellin' you, man—'

'I might be wrong, but isn't that Henry over there?' Keegan used his spoon to point over the soothsayer's shoulder. All three turned, and, sure enough, Henry, who looked a little worse for wear, unshaven and as if he had lost some of his sparkle, sidled onto an empty bench with his tray.

'He's not disappeared! Just a bit late for his dinner!' Keegan chuckled.

Bo shook his head. 'He may have turned up and you can mock all you like, but when there is fuck-all between you and the nose of that Smith and Wesson, I bet you won't find it quite so funny.'

Keegan leant closer to Bo. 'Here's the thing, mate, there's been rumours and hearsay at every children's home and nick I've ever set foot in and it's usually done to scare the new kids. But I ain't a new kid and you ain't scaring me or Binns, so fuck off.'

Bo raised his palms. 'I don't want no trouble with you, Keegan, not in here, but I'm *telling* you. I took the joinery class; I was there when they took delivery of a stack of rectangular wooden boxes; they came in on a big truck. I couldn't figure out what they were at first, but it soon became clear, they were coffin boxes.' Bo's hand shook as he pointed a finger towards Keegan. 'And the worst thing about them boxes is not how you end up in one, but the idea that no bastard would give a shit, no one at home would be told, no one would mourn you or miss you. You'd be shoved under the moor with the soil rattling against the lid and no one would even know let alone care. It's not a good way to end your time.'

The two men pushed their trays away as the troubled Bo wandered off; both had rather lost their appetites.

'Actually' – Warren coughed – 'he *did* scare me a little bit.'

Keegan laughed. 'Well, don't ever tell him that!'

'As if.' Warren smiled. 'Do you think its true, Keegan?'

Keegan hesitated, chewing the inside of his cheek. He placed his clasped hands on the table in front of him. 'I dunno, mate, this whole place is fucked that's for sure. And it shits me up because it's not like anywhere else and so I don't know what to expect. I'd heard something similar before I even got here. Apparently a couple of boys who were in rooms just down from me have gone, vanished, and no one mentions them, like they were never here, as if they're scared to mention them. It's like no one is supposed to have realised, or remembered them. It's weird shit definitely. I don't know what's going on, but I'm not going to go around asking questions, I'm keeping my nose clean. I've been thinking about it and in twenty years I'll be thirty-six, that ain't too old, I'll still have time to have a life. I can still get my car, cruise around, go down to the coast, hang out.'

Warren nodded, his mum was thirty-six, it seemed old to him, too old to start a life, to catch up.

'What classes are you taking?'

Keegan shook his head. 'Well, definitely not joinery, I don't want to see those bloody boxes!' He grinned. 'Nah, I'm not taking any. I've decided to pass, can't see how map-reading or bookkeeping is going to help me in here. I'd rather hit the gym than fill my head with all that useless shit. You?'

'I'm taking both of those – map-reading, bookkeeping, and also horticulture and computing.'

Keegan smirked. 'That's why you're such a weed, Binns, you should ditch a class and come to the gym – it'd do you more good!'

Warren shrugged. 'Maybe. Or I could keep hanging around with you; your biceps are the size of my bloody waist.'

'Ah, so its protection you're after. And there was me thinking we was mates.'

Warren smiled, acknowledging the admission.

'Is it true El Dictator drops by those classes unannounced and sits at the back, snooping?' Keegan obviously had his ear to the ground.

'Yes, but it's more like she's checking on things, she makes notes. Not really snooping...'

'Christ, Binns, don't defend the cow, you saw what she did to Hooray, she's a fucking psycho. What sort of bird would want to be trapped up here with a bunch of crims? She's got to be some sort of freak and definitely a dyke. And what are you taking all them classes for? It's a mug's game, completely pointless. You'll be a right old brainbox by the time you leave here – shame you'll be too old and messed up to get a job. No one is going to give you a job, Binns, not when you tell them where you did all your learning; this is hardly university, is it? You should do like me, keep fit and think about all them honeys that will be waiting.' He rubbed his hands together at the prospect.

Warren studied the tray in front of him. 'I can't do that, it'd drive me mad not to have something to do – I mean, with my brain. I know it probably won't help me and maybe it won't mean a job on the outside, but at least if I'm learning things then this won't of all been a waste.'

Keegan shook his head. 'What's a waste, mate, is that I have a hot bird fuck knows where, doing fuck knows what with fuck knows who, while I'm forced to sit in this shithole!' Keegan threw his spoon down and pushed his thumbs into his temples as if to relieve some unseen pressure.

'It won't do you any good thinking like that. That's why I take the courses; I figure I may as well. It's good to keep busy. It stops you from thinking too much.'

'Christ, you sound like my nan! Nah, I've thought about it and I ain't gonna bother. You're no different to me; one of us may know how to switch on a computer and grow beans, but we are both fucked.'

Warren smiled grimly. He was right.

'If you could have one day back, just twenty-four hours, what would you do?' Keegan leant forward.

Warren sighed. 'I don't know...' There were so many things he would like to cram in, it was difficult to know in which order to place them. Besides, it would depend if it was a day that Sheffield Wednesday were playing.

Keegan was almost whispering now. 'I don't have to think about it. I'd get me the biggest bucket of fried chicken that you have ever seen and I'd take my bird to the pictures. We'd watch a really good film, like *The Godfather* or the first *Die Hard* and we'd eat so much chicken that we could hardly move. Then I'd go to a swimming pool and swim twenty lengths until I was exhausted, then we'd be collected by motorbikes, I'm thinking a couple of big, fat Harleys, and we wouldn't bother with helmets, we'd be driven up the Embankment really fast back to my swanky flat—'

'Do you have a swanky flat?' Warren was intrigued.

'What do you think? Course I bloody don't! But this is my perfect day and before you say it, yes I know that driving without a helmet is not a good idea and I'd probably catch a cold if my hair was still wet – Jesus! You are my nan!'

Warren laughed. 'I can't help it, I just have a more practical mind!'

'Practical or boring?'

'Both probably.'

A few hours later, in the early evening, Warren lay on his bed, staring at the concrete ceiling with its strip light, and considered Keegan's words. He knew exactly what he would do with his twenty-four hours: he'd rock up at Weavers Row and put the key in the lock, just like any normal day. He'd have a cup of tea and some toast and spend time in the front room chatting to Amy, catching up, maybe explain why he was convicted and give her some advice about how to have a brighter future than him. He thought about the next twenty years, doing the sums over and over. He was seventeen, so in twenty years he would be thirty-seven and that was nearly forty. Forty. A whole lifetime spent in this shitty cell, breathing second-hand air that had already been breathed by more than three hundred stinking blokes, without feeling a breeze against his skin or the sun on his face. He wanted to open a window; not necessarily to escape, but to drink in deep gulps of air unfiltered by a pipe and vent. And Amy, sweet, sweet Amy. By the time he got out she would be beyond his reach: married, maybe with kids. It was unthinkable. She would have a life that excluded him, a life in which he didn't figure. The Warren-shaped wound in her mind and heart would have healed over like skin and it would be as if he had never existed for her. Without warning a sharp pain spread across his chest. It felt like a band being tightened and caused him to cry out, he could feel his heart racing. He slammed against the metal-panelled wall and placed his hands against his breastbone. He bucked and pummelled on his bed and started shouting, 'I can't breathe! Help me, I can't breathe!' He kicked out, and heard the metallic ring as his foot made contact. The ceiling seemed to be getting closer and Warren sweated profusely as he fought for breath. The light above his cell door flashed red and emitted a whining pulse.

It was only a minute or two before a guard and a medic were by his side.

'Relax, just relax.' A gangly, bespectacled medic wearing white scrubs was trying to calm Warren down.

'I can't... fucking... breathe!'

The man took Warren's pulse and placed his hand on his chest. 'It's okay, Warren, you are having a panic attack and I know it's frightening, but it will pass and so the sooner we can calm you down, the sooner this will be over, there is nothing to worry about, try and breathe deeply, pal. It's okay, it'll pass. You are going to be okay.' The man's tone was measured and soothing, unlike the guard who stood by the open door with a suspicious expression and a finger that twitched near the inside of his shirt, just in case. He had seen and heard enough in his time to know that trust was not an option.

Warren slowed his breathing and tried to remain calm. Amy's face came into focus; she looked at him with indifference and without the faintest hint of recognition. *Forty... forty... a lifetime.* Warren felt a surge of energy that started in his feet and swept his body, he felt strong, empowered, but above all, he felt angry. With a roar he leapt from the bed and, using his elbow, he landed a blow in the solar plexus of the unsuspecting medic, who lurched backwards and crashed to the floor. He sat, dazed, his back against the wall, clutching his chest. The guard acted quickly. With his gun drawn and cocked, he sprinted forward and put the muzzle against the boy's temple. Warren could feel the cold press of metal against his skin. His stomach turned to ice as it shrunk around his bowel. He sank down onto the mattress. 'I'm sorry,' he wailed, calmer now that his breathing had returned to a regular pattern. 'I don't know what happened, I just felt so angry, I'm sorry.' Warren Binns was terrified. He did not want to die.

The guard kicked at his shins with the heavy toe of his boot and pointed with the barrel of his weapon. In seconds Warren was flat on the floor of his cell, his nose millimetres away from the medic's Nike trainer. He felt the bite of cuffs against his wrists. In a matter of minutes, and following a manacled shuffle of shame, Warren found himself entering a small dark hole on the ground floor. It was no more than a box; about six foot in width and four foot in height. It made him long for his cell, which seemed almost luxurious in comparison. For only the second time in recent years, but the second that night, he wept.

Angelo knocked and entered the Principal's office.

'What was it?' Edwina had been alerted that a siren had gone off and this nearly always meant trouble. She braced herself for the answer.

'It was Binns, Ma'am. A panic attack apparently, but then he lashed out and winded one of the medics. We've put him in solitary, he'll be checked hourly.'

Edwina nodded, thinking, *What a shame*. 'Thanks, Angelo, keep me posted.'

'Will do, Ma'am.'

Edwina rubbed at her temples and stretched her arms over her head. It had been a long day.

'Do you know I'm feeling quite fed up tonight, Matthew!' she shouted across her office, to where Matthew was sitting at his desk. It was unusual for her to utter anything negative, and even this she uttered with a vague hint of positivity.

'Well, we are all allowed off days, you more so than most. You've got a difficult job, it can't be easy.'

'It's not,' she concurred, 'but if it was easy, I wouldn't be interested. I'm weird like that.'

Matthew shook his head; he didn't think she was weird at all, far from it. He placed a mug of camomile tea in front of her, with a little shortbread square, the perfect antidote for her flustered pulse and a low blood sugar. He liked to do little things for her to make her life easier. He liked looking after her.

It was rare that she had days like this, days when everything felt a little overwhelming, leaving her wondering if she wouldn't be better off activating plan B, the life that she and Alan had planned, a life that she promised him she would still seek. They had spent hours over the years on country walks or over the breakfast table, describing a little villa in the Italian countryside, where she would hike and forage during the day, wearing a raffia hat and a loose linen dress, while he captured the sky in watercolour. In the evenings they would play backgammon and drink red wine. The plan had changed since Alan's death of course, but Edwina still envisaged sitting in her garden, watching the sun sink against the Tuscan horizon, eating fresh pasta with torn basil from her herb beds, topped off with a drizzle of her neighbour's home-pressed olive oil. Chatting to Alan's empty chair from the other side of a wicker table on the covered terrace, she would tell him all about the discoveries of her day, surrounded by sweet-scented lemon trees, potted olives and a vibrant trumpet vine that wound its way around the wooden arbour overhead. A neat border of boxwood and miniature cypress would form a pretty boundary to her land. She breathed deeply, and could almost smell the intoxicating scent of this imaginary Mediterranean garden, which would be bursting with heady perfume and vibrant colours after a day of basking in the hot sun.

She held the mug between her cupped palms. 'Thank you for my tea, this is just what the doctor ordered. And I'm sorry to sound a bit defeated. I don't know, Matthew, sometimes it gets to me; in fact most days recently, I think I'm tired.'

'Of course you're tired, it's inevitable; you have a great deal of responsibility, more than any other governor I've known. It's not like you have a team to shoulder the load, it's just you.'

'And you,' she interrupted, 'I don't know what I'd do without you, apart from go stark staring bonkers.'

Her acknowledgment caused Matthew's heart to swell. 'Well, yes, and me, but I'm more of the support act and you do an amazing job if you don't mind me saying.'

She smiled over the rim of her hot drink. 'I don't mind one bit.'

He blushed; it was rare that their conversation strayed outside of the perfunctory or garden matters, and it lifted his day. 'I worked at Belmarsh for three years before I came here and even though they weren't all lifers, it was far more depressing. It felt like a conveyor belt, the same faces in and out – and if not the same faces then the same type, they could have been the same person. Similar expressions, attitudes, it often felt pointless. It's different here. It feels hopeful.'

'Really?'

'Yes, really, you care about these blokes and I suspect that for many it's the first time in their life that anyone has. That's enough to make a huge difference, you know. You are governor and mother all rolled into one.'

'Oh, I don't know about that.' Edwina dusted shortbread crumbs from her shirt, glad of the task, awkward at the compliment.

'No, I *do* think that.' He was insistent. 'You would have been an amazing mother...'

Her sob came quickly and without warning. It strangled the breath in her throat and caused her eyes to redden as fat tears inched down her face. 'Oh goodness, look at me, silly old thing!' She grabbed the paper napkin on which her biscuit had been delivered and swiped at her eyes and nose. This was not the first time she had experienced this. There had been countless times over the last couple of decades when the new babies of family, friends and colleagues had been thrust under her nose and into her arms, their mothers standing and watching with acute embarrassment as Edwina cried wordlessly and noiselessly into their white cotton suits. It didn't matter what the occasion or environment, it was an almost instant reflex.

Matthew sank into the chair on the opposite side of her desk as if physically weakened. His hand flew to his mouth, as if trying to recall the words that had flown from his mouth and swallow them whole.

'Edwina, I am so sorry. I would not upset you for the world. I don't know what to say apart from sorry, I'm sorry if my words have offended you. I didn't think, I...'

She waved her free hand in front of him, trying to halt the flow of his apology as the other continued to mop at her tears. 'Oh God, Matthew, no, no.' She blew her nose noisily on the crumb-laden sheet. 'Offend me?' She shook her head. 'It's probably the nicest thing that anyone could ever say to me. Do you really think I would have made a good mum?'

He smiled at her across the desk. 'Yes. I really do.'

Three

Edwina read and re-read the notes on the screen in front of her, using her thumb and forefinger to circle her mouth as she did so. It was one of the habits that Alan used to tease her about as she studied on Sundays, lying at the end of the sofa with her feet on his lap. Today, as then, it helped her concentrate as she studied the facts and dissected the language, looking for an inconsistency, a reason. There was neither. She swallowed the bile that threatened to leap from her throat and took a sip of water from the glass that sat a fingertip away. This had happened under this very roof only last night. What had she been doing, sleeping? Feeding her plants? She shuddered.

She clicked the file shut and lifted the telephone receiver. 'Do you have a minute?' she asked before replacing the phone in its cradle. Minutes later, Angelo appeared in her doorway.

'Sit down, please, Angelo.' Her tone was weary.

He lowered his bulk into the narrow chair, reminding her of an adult visiting a primary school, trying to get comfortable on an unfeasibly small piece of furniture.

She pointed at her computer screen, which had, until minutes ago, given her all the facts. 'Thank you and your team for the report. I can see you've all worked hard to bring it together so quickly. It seems quite straightforward, sadly. What do you make of it?' She leant back in her chair.

Angelo shook his head. 'In my opinion, he did it, no question.'

She sighed and nodded; it was what she had expected to hear. 'It certainly looks that way. Why were events in the boy's room not detected last night?'

He raised his palms up to the ceiling in a gesture of open admission; he had nothing to hide. 'I've checked back over the footage, it looked like he was sleeping, his back was to the camera and he was lying still with his head under the top sheet – not unusual, and certainly nothing to arouse suspicion. As I say, the wardens thought he was sleeping. We can't go around waking everyone every hour; we'd have a mutiny on our hands.' Angelo shook his head again. The poor kid.

She nodded; she got that. 'Is there any supporting footage for what he claimed?'

Angelo looked at the floor and nodded. 'Yes.' He grimaced as he recalled the images that had forced their way into his consciousness.

'Then I don't think we really have a choice, do we?'

'I'd say not, Ma'am, not in this instance.'

The two sat in silence, contemplating the weight of the words that flew around the room as light as air.

'Bring him down to 2D. I'll meet you there.'

Angelo nodded and left. Edwina Justice removed her earrings and necklace, and placed them in a little box inside her desk drawer. She pulled the heel of first one shoe and then the other, easing her feet from their leather confines. She flexed her toes and rubbed at the arch of her foot before slipping her stockinged feet into flat black pumps. Pulling a tissue from the box on her shelf, she wiped away the residue of her lipstick and ran a corner over her eyelids to blot up any eye shadow. She used her palm to flatten the spiky tendrils of her short hair. It was all part of the ritual, she felt it humanised her and gave the exchange a level of reverence that she felt was necessary.

She took her time, not stalling exactly, but certainly in no great hurry to arrive. She placed her finger on the pad that read her biometrics, and the steel security door of room 2D slid open along its runners. Angelo stood in front of a small table with his hands clasped in front of him. There was a barely perceptible twitch in his left eye. Behind the table, with his legs shackled and his hands cuffed to his belt sat Robert 'Bo' Greene. His chest heaved inside his tracksuit top. The Principal cut to the chase, wasting time on preliminaries only caused unnecessary anxiety.

'When you came here, Bo, I explained the rules to you.'

'I ain't never broken any of the rules. Never. I never have,' he lied as he shook his head.

Edwina continued as though he hadn't spoken.

'The rules that we have in place are designed to keep everyone safe. I think it should be every inmate's right to expect others to respect them and to respect their safety. Every man and boy under this roof should be able to live within these walls without experiencing harm, regardless of the crime that they have committed before they arrived.'

'And I agree with you, Ma'am, I'm grateful that you keep me safe here.' Bo flicked his head to remove the sweat that streaked his brow. She watched as two fat droplets fell onto the tabletop.

She stood in front of the table and looked into Bo's face. 'I am not referring to you, Bo, I am in fact referring to Marcus. You know who I mean, don't you?'

'No, I don't know anyone called Marcus. I just keep myself to myself, keep my head down and do my time and follow the rules. I don't know anyone called Marcus.' He stared wide-eyed and stuck out his bottom lip; if he was aiming at an expression of innocence, it didn't work.

'I am going to ask you one last time. Is there anything that you would like to tell me about Marcus? Or, more specifically, about Marcus and you?'

Bo shook his head and remained silent. He attempted to shrug but his ironware made it nigh impossible.

Edwina placed one arm across her stomach and with the other propped on it she cupped her chin. 'Angelo, would you mind.'

Angelo stepped forward and held a photograph up, inches from Bo's face. It was a still, taken from the footage that had been captured a week earlier by the bathroom camera. The main security ops team had found it after combing through hours of footage. Bo swallowed. 'That... That's not me, I swear!' he stuttered. 'Well, it might be me, but I don't remember anything... we is mates, more than mates. If you get my drift.'

It was a few seconds before anyone spoke. The silence bore down on the trio like a stifling blanket.

'Have you seen Marcus today, Bo?'

Bo shook his head vehemently, indicating that what was to follow was probably the truth. 'No, I never saw him today. I didn't.'

Edwina Justice rested her knuckles on the small, square table. 'I have. I saw him just after breakfast.'

Bo shook his head again. 'No, I never saw him today, I didn't.'

Edwina ignored him. 'Or rather, when I say I saw him just after breakfast, I should clarify, I saw his body.'

Bo stared wide-eyed, his mouth fell open, his shoulders sagged as the breath left his body, he looked deflated as though punched in the gut. 'Oh man! Nah, nah, nah. You are fucking with me, man! That ain't so, no way. No way!' He was shaking his head furiously now.

'I was called to his room at a little after seven-thirty. It was distressing for us all and certainly not something I shall forget in a hurry. Marcus had taken the bed sheet from his mattress and shredded it; he then stuffed those shreds into his throat until he suffocated. He left a note for me, explaining that you had raped him, on four separate occasions over the last fortnight and that you had promised to rape him again and that if he told, he could expect worse. He pointed out that he could not envisage worse. He was not prepared to let you control him and so he killed himself.'

'I never... I... swear I would never do that!' Bo could not think fast enough to utter the words that might have helped.

'You swear to a lot of things and yet if you didn't do it, why would Marcus say you did? Why would he kill himself?'

'He was crazy! You can ask anyone, he was proper mad! He has stitched me up, I ain't done nothing I swear!'

'We have the footage, Bo, captured on tape, of you doing exactly what Marcus said you did, right before he killed himself.'

'You fucking bitch! You nasty dyke! I want my Brief and I want him here now, do you hear me? I want him here now!' Bo was screaming now, though the quiver of fear in his voice was unmistakeable.

'I wonder who Marcus called out for, I wonder who he wanted?' Edwina turned to Angelo and gave an almost imperceptible nod. 'You have no right to stay here and moreover I do not want you here. I can only keep the people in my charge safe by dealing with people like you, Bo.'

'I never did nothing! I'm sorry! He was up for it, I'm telling you, man! I never did nothing!'

Edwina Justice turned and made for the door. Bo's tone changed instantly.

'I know a little bit about you, you're a widow, right? Well, your bloke had a lucky escape. And thank fuck no kids. You are a heartless bitch, do you hear me? A cold, heartless bitch!'

Edwina chose not to respond to the succinct summary of her situation and character. The very word, widow, for her conjured elderly crones sat in the Mediterranean sun, clad in black and sweating over a rosary under smoky candlelight as their eyesight faded and their pulse grew weaker. She wasn't like that, had never been like that. She surreptitiously rubbed her thumb along the underside of the thin gold band on the third finger of her left hand, proof of their commitment, she saw him wearing his best suit and reeking of lemony scent, mouthing the words *'til death do us part...* Losing her husband, her love and her hope at the age of forty had shaped her, but not broken her. Not quite.

More hurtful was the reference to her never having children, *no kids*, those two words offered so casually as though ticking a box. *No kids*. His cool delivery of the phrase suggested that it was by design, a blessing, a decision she had made, allowing her to focus on her career without the diversion of motherhood. This she knew was the most popular interpretation of her childless state, but it was, however, so far from the truth. Not becoming a parent would always be her greatest sadness. When Alan died her hope of becoming a mother had died with him. She knew she had been pushing her luck leaving it that long to try for their much-wanted baby, but time seemed to have crept up on them. The years of grieving that followed his passing left no room for dating. She could not bear the idea of being in the company of any man that wasn't him, let alone go looking for a suitable father. This didn't stop her dreaming with alarming regularity of the baby that she would never have, allowing herself to picture a downy head and to feel the press of a tiny mouth against her cheek. Following this dream, despite her advancing years and redundant system, she would wake and feel the pull of her womb, the ache of longing for what she would never have.

Without turning her head, she walked from the room. It would be over in seconds. This wasn't the first and certainly wouldn't be the last, but the sick feeling in the pit of her stomach was just the same as it had been that first time. She closed her office door, unusual in itself and watched as the swell of the water in her glass shook in time with the tremor of her hand.

She never thought that she would appreciate the calm, unhurried manner in which Alan had died, slipping away with his hand inside hers, hearing her words of commitment and love whispered across his dented pillow. *You are loved... I love you... always...* she had coaxed, permitted, stroking his brow, wiping his mouth, performing small practical tasks to hide the fact that her heart was splitting like a ripe pomegranate, spilling and overflowing with pure and desperate sorrow. At the end, it had been peaceful and calm, quite lovely, and there for perfect recall before she fell asleep at night and when she woke in the morning. She shivered as she considered the confines of room 2D: the flat surfaces, the stark walls and the harsh lighting. For those who ended their days here, their experience would be the exact opposite.

Warren sat opposite his friend and pushed his spoon into a pile of meat and vegetables, bound by a thick, grey gravy full of little bubbles which, on closer inspection, turned out to be globules of grease.

Keegan toyed with the spoon and laughed, 'You must have a cast-iron gut, mate, I don't know how you can eat this crap.'

'You eat it too!' Warren countered.

'Yes, but the difference is you seem to enjoy it.'

Warren ignored his friend and piled his spoon high. 'You should tuck in; one thing I can tell you is that it is much better hot than cold.'

'I know. I'm just not that hungry. Something weird happened today...'

'What?' Warren barely lifted his eyes from his next mouthful of stew.

'About midmorning, a couple of Angelo's thugs emptied Bo's room. And I mean emptied, took everything, loaded all his stuff into a big black bag, clothes, toothbrush and all. 'Why would they do that?'

Warren shrugged. 'Maybe he's moved rooms?'

Keegan smacked his forehead in mock realisation. 'Oh yeah, silly me! He's probably gone into the east wing so he's got a better view of the pool!'

'Ha ha, you know what I mean, another room, maybe his needs a repair or something.'

'What other room, Binns? All the accommodation is on this one floor. No, he's gone. *Gone.* If you get my drift.'

'He'll probably turn up; you know what they say about bad pennies...'

'Do you think he's in solitary?' Keegan didn't look at Warren as he spoke; unlike his friend, he had never experienced it.

'Possible, but doubtful. That's not what happens, you don't take nothing with you, well, I didn't, and when you get out, you go back to your room, so all your stuff is pretty much as you left it.'

Warren remembered waking in the middle of the second night, lying on the bare floor of that metal box in the pitch black. He held his hand up in front of his face, but couldn't see anything. Then he placed his hand over his face, and it petrified him – he couldn't be one hundred per cent sure that it was his own hand. He screamed and placed his arms by his side. His thoughts wandered. Was this his coffin? Was he dead? Of course not, because he was thinking and aware; he could feel the cold wall where it touched his bare skin, and the droplets of condensation that dripped onto his face from the shallow roof. Or maybe he was dead and this was hell. It certainly felt like hell. Maybe he was destined to pay forever for taking a life, and this was how he would spend eternity: trapped without light, without noise and punished by his own imaginings, a brain whirring with thoughts that he couldn't switch off. Warren shivered and tried to rid his mind of the memory.

Keegan was still talking. 'And I'll tell you who else has gone AWOL, you know the sobbing Irish bloke?'

'Who, Holy Joe? He's a top man, in a couple of my classes.'

'Yep, him, he used to go on and on, didn't he, crying over who was looking after his *poor motherless kids*' – Keegan did his best Irish accent – 'all that praying to God for one more glimpse of his daughter's face, he used to drive me mad! Well, him, think about it, when's the last time you saw him around?'

Warren thought. 'I haven't thought about him til you mentioned it, but it must be a couple of weeks since I saw him last.'

'Exactly. I walked past his room earlier, and there's a new kid in there, no trace of Holy Joe, nothing. There's something up, Binns, and I don't want to sound like Bo, but I don't think either of them are coming back any time soon.'

'Oh shut up, Keegan, if you start believing that crap, there's no hope for any of us!' Warren threw his spoon down onto his tray, his appetite gone.

Keegan looked his friend in the eye. 'I'm just saying we need to be careful, that's all.'

Henry was walking along the dinner bench as if to join them. He jumped down behind Warren with a thud. 'Have you heard?'

'About Bo?' Warren asked without thinking.

'Bo, no, why? What's wrong with him?'

Warren shrugged, regretting having mentioned it. Henry continued unfazed. 'Nope, about Marcus, the kid a couple of doors down from me.'

Keegan and Warren stared at Henry, waiting for the story but unsure whether, if it came from Henry's lips, it should be discounted.

'He's only gone and topped himself.'

Four

Keegan and Warren sat side by side on a narrow wooden bench in the communal atrium just as they had done twice a week for the last eighteen months. It was Free Time, which meant that they were free to wander the atrium, or free to sit in their rooms. It wasn't much of a choice. To the right of them, a game of basketball was in full flow, scrutinised as always by the watchful eyes of the security guards, and the cameras that blinked in every corner and on every post. The pair watched the action in silence as the ball bounced back and forth between two teams of five men, swooping and ducking as their trainers squeaked on the shiny surface. Officially, anyone could participate, but the standard was so high that it deterred any but the most athletic from volunteering their services. Both men sporadically turned their faces towards the covered glass roof; it was the closest they would get to fresh air. It was a moment of calm before the storm.

Keegan spotted him first. 'Oh God, here comes Hooray, where can we hide?'

Warren, as ever, had sympathy for the underdog. 'He'd seek you out wherever you went. He's alright though – not like us, granted, but not any harm. I feel a bit sorry for the bloke, I can't imagine he fits in anywhere.'

'You *are* turning into my nan! And the reason he doesn't fit in anywhere is because he is a complete and utter dickhead.'

'Hey, bros!' Henry appeared with a book in one hand and

the other raised in the high-five position. They both declined the offer of a slap on the palm, and Warren visibly cringed. Keegan laughed as if Henry had more than proved his point.

'Still with us, Hooray?' Keegan winked at Warren. How long it would take before Hooray finally lost his marbles was a regular topic of conversation.

'Yep, all present and correct, just doing my thing, hanging out. Who's a complete and utter dickhead?'

'Oh, one of the guards.' Keegan smirked, he hadn't realised Henry was close enough to hear.

'What are you reading?' Warren used the question as a diversion tactic.

'It's *The Anglers Guide to River Fishing.*' Henry held up the cover, on which a large salmon jumped in an elegant arc, diamond droplets of water glinting from his pearlescent scales.

Keegan laughed. 'Well, that'll be useful in here, did they not have one on bird watching?'

'Ha! Funny man, and talking of birds, I want a word with you, Binns!'

'Oh, er, right. Fire away – although I should warn you I don't know much about birds.'

'No, that's the one class you're not taking, right?' Keegan grinned. 'Wildlife studies? He's taking everything else though, he's a proper swot!'

Warren shook his head. It was pointless trying to convince Keegan to enrol on anything, he had given up trying over a year ago now.

'Ah, but I do not, in fact, refer to the feathered variety.' Henry clarified.

'Well, in that case, you must want to talk to me, cos when it comes to the fairer sex, I am more of an expert than Binns.' Keegan laughed.

'Thank you for the offer, Keegan, but it's Warren I need to speak to. The question I have for you is this: who's Amy?'

Warren felt his pulse quicken. *How the hell...?* He shrugged, hoping his silence would be enough to shut Henry up. It wasn't.

'Come on, man, spill the beans – sharesy is fairsy. All we have in here is the joy of talking about it, so give!'

'I don't know what you're talking about.' Warren turned his attention back to the game of basketball, motioning to Henry to move aside and stop blocking his view.

Henry wasn't done. 'You are not getting out of it that easily. I walked past your room yesterday and peeked in, you were kipping like a baby and you started moaning, then... drum roll please... you called out *Amy*! Lucky, lucky Binns, I thought. I hope Amy is as good as he is making her sound. We could all do with a little slice of Amy around here, if you get my drift.'

The flash of crimson behind Warren's eyes clouded his view and his judgement. Fists clenched, he leapt on Henry, who screamed as he hit the floor with a bone-shattering crack. The guards appeared immediately, and by the time anyone realised what was happening, Warren was flat on the floor, his arms and legs bound with plastic cable ties that bit into his flesh and Henry, groaning loudly and clutching at his shoulder, was being carted off to the sanatorium on a stretcher, his arm hanging limply at his side at an odd angle. His book lay abandoned on the floor. Warren's breath came in shallow pants. *How dare he, how fucking dare he?* He was vaguely aware of Keegan's voice telling anyone that would listen that he had been provoked.

'Henry started it, I saw everything! Warren's not a scrapper, he's my mate! Henry's been asking for it, really winding him up for a long time now, in fact since we arrived. Any man would have done the same, I swear! Warren ain't that sort, please, just let him calm down here, we can sort this out, there's no need to take it any further. He's my mate, please...'

Warren bucked and twisted, trying to loosen the ties at his wrists and ankles but the more he pulled the deeper they cut. He listened to the tone of Keegan's voice and couldn't place the emotion. It was only later, as he lay, still bound, on his bed and replayed the scene in his head, that he realised his friend had sounded frightened.

Warren was woken by the sound of his door being slid open. His eyelids were heavy, his head pounded and he felt exhausted. He had lost all sense of time; he might have been confined to his cell for minutes or hours.

Angelo stood in the doorway. 'Let's get you up, Binns. Someone wants a word with you.' He snipped the plastic ties and Warren lay for a minute, allowing the blood to flow back into his limbs. His whole body shook at the thought of going back into solitary. He didn't know if he could hack it. He closed his eyes, fighting the desire to beg, knowing it made little difference, not now it had been escalated. What was it Bo said, *I've been here since the beginning and I'm telling you, my friend, that for all her cool politeness and fancy shirts, Justice is a cold, cold bitch...*

'Should I bring anything with me?' For some reason, an image of Bo's belongings in a black bin liner flashed into his mind.

'You won't be needing anything.'

Warren felt his bowel spasm and fought hard to control the desire to relieve himself. It was his turn to be frightened. Suddenly the idea of solitary did not seem so bad; he guessed that there were things at Glenculloch that were far, far worse.

He pulled on his bright-blue tracksuit bottoms and matching jacket. He looked in the small rectangular mirror over his sink and raked his hair with his fingertips. The purple bruises on his knuckles stood out, marking him as an aggressor, he could only think what this might mean. His heart beat loudly in his ears.

Clad in the usual restraints for arms and legs, Warren followed Angelo's slow progression to the Principal's office in something like a trance, his teeth chattering and his legs swaying as if with a will of their own. The adrenalin of the encounter with Henry had subsided, leaving him weakened, reflective and strangely tearful.

Angelo knocked on the door and entered. The Principal sat behind her desk with a silver pen in her hand.

'Thank you, Angelo; you may remove Mr Binns' ironwear.'

Angelo sat him in a chair and unlocked his handcuffs and leg-irons, before leaving him alone with the Principal. Warren didn't want him to go, figuring that at least with a witness, she was unlikely to harm him. Her words from his induction day nearly two years earlier floated into his mind: *There is not one angle, one nook or one cranny, with the exception of my office, that is not monitored twenty-four hours a day, three hundred and sixty-five days of the year.* This is where they would do it. Warren gulped.

It felt like an age before she placed the pen on the desk and spoke. 'Are you afraid of me, Mr Binns?'

He nodded. 'Yes, I am... Ma... Mrs... Principal.' His teeth shook in his gums. Warren did not want to die.

She leant back in her chair and studied him. 'It's good that you are afraid, to know fear is what allows us to know peace. The fear of the fear can keep it at bay.'

He had no idea what this meant, but nodded nonetheless.

'How is your hand? It looks rather nasty.'

Warren looked at the grape-like lumps on his knuckles; he flexed his swollen fingers, which throbbed.

'It's okay. Thank you, it looks worse than it is.'

She breathed deeply. 'Is there anything you would like to say to me, Mr Binns?'

Warren looked at his feet and shook his head. 'I'm sorry about what happened in the atrium. I'm really sorry. It all happened so quickly. He went too far, he did, but I know what he's like; I should have walked away, cooled off or something. I've known him since day one and I shouldn't have resorted to violence, I know that's not the answer. I should have just walked away. Is Henry alright, did I hurt him? His shoulder looked pretty messed up.'

Edwina Justice did not respond to his question, it was as if Warren hadn't asked. 'You are right; you should not have resorted to violence.'

Warren stared at his feet.

The Principal sat upright in her chair as though this required her full attention. 'I would like you to tell me about the murder you committed and I would like you to give me a bit of background as to why. Can you do that?'

He nodded.

She gestured towards him with her palm, inviting him to begin.

Warren took a deep breath. He didn't know where to start. It wasn't easy to talk about this stuff, and he had tried to bury certain details, many of which had resurfaced earlier with Henry's words.

'It's hard to know how to start really, Ma'am.'

'I'm sure it is, but please do try.' Her voice was clipped and matter-of-fact, as if she was asking for his address rather than forcing him to pick open the stitches on a painful wound and relive the agony of that day, that moment.

Warren wriggled in the seat, but his discomfort was nothing that a physical shift could cure. He could see that he had no alternative but to talk.

'I... I grew up in Sheffield on the moors. It was quite bleak, but I loved it. I used to walk for miles, I was always out somewhere and at night I would sit looking out of my bedroom window and I could see the lights of the city twinkling down below us; they looked like stars that had fallen. I loved going to school, I know a lot of kids hate it, but I didn't. I loved it. I mean, I didn't really have friends and I was laughed at and all that, but I wanted to learn whatever they could teach me and I got lunch every day and that was nice. I used to watch the clock go round, waiting for lunch time.' He felt his cheeks redden at the admission. 'We were quite poor. We were very poor. It was just me, my mum and my nan in the house and then just me and my mum after my nan passed away. I never had a dad, but that was okay, because I'd never had one. I didn't realise how poor we were until I saw how other people lived, if that makes any sense. I kind of looked after me and my mum and then Amy came along, that's my baby sister.' He looked up and smiled as he said her name. 'There was still no bloke on the scene, but Amy was like a brilliant new present, I couldn't believe that something so small could take up so much space, but she did, and noisy, cor, she went from bawling all night as a baby to singing all day as a toddler, she hasn't shut up yet I don't think!'

Edwina swallowed the bubble of envy that rose in her throat. *You lucky thing, Mr Binns, your lucky mum! Oh to live in a house where a baby filled it with noise and a toddler filled it with song!*

Warren continued, unaware of the effect of his words. 'She brightened up the place and was sharp as a button, smart, a proper little mimic. All she ever wanted was for me to read books to her; she liked that better than anything. She used to follow me everywhere, whatever the weather. I used to say she drove me mad and try and make her go back to the house, but I liked it really. She'd make me presents, like a picture of an owl made out of pasta that she stuck on with glue, and cards with sweet wrappers stuck on the front. I put the owl one up on my wall. She was like my own little fan club and she relied on me, so even though neither of us had a dad, it was like she did in some ways, because she had me and I told her I would always look after her.' Warren paused and exhaled, he looked at his fingers which lay knitted in his lap. 'And then when I was fourteen things changed a lot for me, for us. My mum hooked up with this bloke, Dave. He was alright at first and it was nice to get things, I must admit. He used to bring us sweets and he bought me a pair of football boots and I was dead chuffed, I'd never had a pair before. He bought Amy a pram for her dolls and that made me really happy, cos she never had stuff like that either. They got married and I was happy to have a dad at first, it was a really good day, my mum laughed all day long and I had to wear a suit. I thought it was the start of something really good, but he turned out to be a lazy pig, a really nasty piece of work. By the time I realised what he was really like it was too late. My mum had kind of shrunk, she just went quiet, and he called all the shots, even though it was our house, where we had always lived way before him, it was like he owned the place. We were all frightened of him. He started to knock my mum about and then started on me, and I could have coped with that, I did cope with that for a number of years.' Warren closed his eyes briefly and saw the fist coming towards his face;

his mum's voice in background, softly begging, *Please, Dave, leave him alone... no... no more...*

'I planned on leaving. I worked hard at school so I could get taken on in an apprenticeship, I was doing okay. I was just going to disappear one day and leave him wondering where I'd got to, not that he'd have cared. I wanted to take Amy with me, I was trying to work out how I could do it, just waiting for the chance. I think about that now and I can see that it wasn't practical. I don't know how I would have looked after her and done an apprenticeship and we didn't have anywhere to live, plus of course my mum would probably have come and got her back. But, it was weird, it was like I couldn't think straight and in my head, I convinced myself it was all possible and I was just waiting for the right time to escape. One day, I came home from college early and...' Warren swallowed the sharp pull of tears that slid down his throat. He exhaled through bloated cheeks, trying to keep it together. 'I'm sorry.'

'That's okay, Warren, you take your time.'

'I came home early and he was laying face down on the sofa. I could smell the drink on him, but that wasn't unusual, he went up the club most lunchtimes and got pissed and then he'd sleep all afternoon until he could go back to the club and drink some more. I thought he was on his own, I was going to tiptoe up the stairs past him and leave him to it, but he wasn't.' Warren paused to swipe at the tears that now coursed freely down his cheeks, angry and embarrassed. 'He wasn't on his own. He was on top of Amy. I could see her little hand sticking out from under his fat gut; she was still holding her blanky, gripping it tightly. She'd painted her little fingernails and the polish had worn off; I could see these little blobs of pink, sparkly paint, hanging onto her blanky. She was seven years old' – his mouth was contorted with crying now – 'I didn't think about what to do, I just did it. I ran to the cupboard under the stairs and grabbed the chisel from my toolbox. I went back into the front room and I reached under his gut and I stuck it in him, up under his ribs, just once, but I stabbed him hard. I meant to kill him, I did. I wanted him dead and that's what I told the judge. She was seven and she was the only thing in our shitty little family that wasn't broken, she was the only thing that was perfect and I had made a promise to look after her. But I broke that promise, I broke it, because I didn't keep her safe, did I?' Warren's face was red and blotchy, and he hung his head to wipe furiously at his eyes.

The Principal didn't say a word, and so Warren carried on, injecting a false note of brightness into his voice as if trying to lighten the mood. 'So that's it! And now I'm here. And when Henry said something not very nice about Amy, I couldn't handle it. I don't mind a joke or the piss-taking that you expect in here, but not her, nothing about her. She's just a little girl and she's already been through too much.' He fought to get his breath under control.

Edwina Justice swung her leather swivel chair around and contemplated the collage on the corkboard behind her. The two sat in silence.

It was some moments before she spoke. 'I think when the very worst thing that can happen, happens, it puts your whole life in perspective in a way that's impossible for others to understand.' She pictured the moment Alan's hand had gone limp inside her palm, she had squeezed it tightly and then tapped it with her fingertips, trying to bring him back. His eyes stared ahead, his jaw slack and she remembered asking him, *Where have you gone?* To which, of course, he didn't reply.

Warren listened.

'I haven't experienced anything like you, but my husband

died; he got sick very suddenly and died within two weeks. That was nearly twenty years ago. We had so much yet to achieve and I watched all our hopes and plans disappear in a heartbeat. It shocked me then and it shocks me now. I miss him every single day, I still expect him to phone me or to walk through the door, and every time I remember that it is never going to happen, I start to grieve all over again. You would think it might get easier, but it doesn't. I used to wonder what the point of carrying on was. It all felt so pointless when the person I wanted to live with was no longer here, the person who gave my life meaning, who welcomed me home. But then I realised that life is precious and you have to carry on, no matter how hard or how hurt or how much you long to disappear. You have to carry on, because life is precious.' She turned the chair to face Warren. 'Do you understand that?' He nodded. She continued, 'I believe some people are born bad...'

Warren heard his stepdad's words, *You useless little bastard, just like your shit of a father...*

'And I believe some people simply find themselves in bad situations.'

Warren nodded again, not trusting himself to speak, he got it, he was born bad. He half wanted it to be over, *Go on get out your gun, just shoot me, I know I'm a useless little bastard and I know I failed, I broke my promise. I said I'd keep her safe and I didn't. He hurt her and I wasn't there to stop him...*

'You must miss your sister very much?'

He nodded. It was the first time he had allowed himself to think about her in a very long time. 'I do. I miss her every day. And my mum. But at least I know that they are safe now, that he's not there to hurt them. He'll never hurt them ever again, and that makes it kind of worth it.'

Edwina Justice leant forward on her desk. 'I understand that sentiment. I have worked with offenders my whole life and I have a knack for seeing beneath the veneer, Mr Binns. It's nothing you can be trained for, but it is more of a gift or a curse, depending on how you look at it. I can tell when a person is lying. I can tell when a person is so full of evil that the only answer is to lock him away for a very long time. Unpleasant though it is, it's how I keep others safe, and keeping everyone safe has to be my priority. And then occasionally I can see that a person who is good has done bad things, sometimes to protect himself, sometimes to protect others, sometimes to survive. I am rarely, if ever, wrong.'

Warren stared at the woman sat in front of him. Where was this going?

Edwina Justice turned in her chair and reached under her desk. Warren gripped the arms of the chair and closed his eyes; he did not want to stare down the barrel. He remembered the feel of the guard's Smith and Wesson against his temple. He trembled as he waited for the tell-tale click of the gun being readied. This was it. *I'm sorry, Amy, I'm sorry I let him hurt you. I'm sorry I let you down, Mum. I love you both so much, I always have and I always will. Be a good girl, Amy, carry on reading. I love you...*

The Principal almost whispered, 'Please, open your eyes.'

He slowly opened his eyes and blinked away the sweat that had fallen from his brow. He noticed a large khaki rucksack that sat on the desk between them.

'Do you believe in second chances, Warren?'

Warren shook his head. 'No. No, I don't.'

'You don't?'

'No.' He shook his head again.

'Why not?'

'Because I've never been given one and so I don't think they exist.'

She smiled, unable to fault his simple logic. 'What if I was to tell you that they do exist, Warren?'

'Then I probably wouldn't believe you.'

He held her gaze, maybe second chances existed in her world of blazers and pearls, but not in his. He had spent the best part of his life wishing: wishing for hot food to materialise in his hands, for a thick duvet to magic itself from thin air, and for a drunken bastard to fall down a hole, break his neck and never be found. He had given up wishing, his wishes never came true.

Edwina Justice stood and held the rucksack in her hands. 'Stand up, Warren.'

He stood, slowly.

'I want you to take this.' She placed the pack in his hesitant hands. 'In this rucksack are a new passport, a change of clothes, some sturdy boots, waterproofs, a tent and some money, a lot of money, enough money for you to start over. Your new name is Zac Porter. This is your second chance.'

Warren ran his palm over the nylon fabric. It took a moment for his brain to understand what was being said. What was the catch?

Edwina walked over to the large green filing cabinet and twisted the middle handle. The three deep drawers were no such thing; they were in fact a door. Using both hands, she heaved the door open.

Zac peered through it and blinked. It was the first time in eighteen months that he had seen the outside world. He was looking at a beautiful garden. Flowers of every colour fought for space along crowded paths. Trees were dotted among the expanse of grass. His eye was drawn to a square of pale shingle bearing a cluster of bright-blue china pots, holding neatly trimmed green shrubs. Low, square-cut hedges surrounded bushes of roses, and heavy bowers of bloom-laden branches shook in the gentle breeze. It was breathtaking.

'You have earned your sunlight, Zac. Go far far away and make a wonderful life for yourself, become all the things that I know you are capable of. You are a wonderful boy, who tried your best. You saved Amy, you set her free, and because of you *she* has a second chance. Never forget that. I want you to remember the rules that I have taught you. Abide by them and use your skills. Your life is out there waiting for you, the life that you should have had. You must give yourself the life that you deserve. Don't waste it, Zac, don't waste one minute and remember that life is precious.'

Zac smiled at the Principal. 'Is this what happened to Bo and Holy Joe?'

'Now, Zac, I told you a long time ago, you only had that one question!'

'Okay, I'm sorry. But could you tell Keegan...'

'No. I can't.' She held up her palm, interrupting him, 'because Warren Binns doesn't exist anymore and Mr Lomax has never met or even heard of Zac Porter. It's how it has to be. You understand that, don't you?'

Zac nodded, he got it. He smiled at her. 'I don't know what to say to you. I don't know how to thank you, for everything you've done. Thank you, thank you for believing me.'

'There are just two things I ask of you, Mr Porter.'

Zac looked at the smiling face of his benefactor, still unused to his new name. 'Anything, I'll do anything at all.'

'The first thing is to always make time to appreciate something beautiful, no matter how small.'

Zac nodded, he would learn what that meant and he would do it.

'And secondly, when you are settled in your new life, wherever that might be, please send me a postcard, so I can stop worrying about you.'

Zac smiled at her and nodded. Edwina Justice extended her arm in the direction of the garden. He stepped forward and hesitated, before putting his arms around her and holding her close, the way a boy might hold his mum. Zac placed the rucksack on his back and stepped over the threshold, into the light.

Five

Matthew Shackleton flicked the switch on the coffee machine and buffed his spectacles with the soft cloth from inside his glasses case. Perching them on the end of his nose, he began to sort through the mail.

The colourful edge of the postcard peeked out from beneath the stack of manila envelopes. It was a bustling market scene in Kerala. He pulled the image closer to his face to decipher the tiny script at the bottom right-hand corner, India, fancy that. It was from someone called Zac, Zac Porter.

'Good morning, Matthew.'

'Good morning, Edwina. It's going to be a hot one today.' He fanned himself and pumped the cotton of his shirt to circulate the air.

'Yes. Better make sure the watering is heavy, I'd go large on the sprinklers.'

'I'm on it, don't worry, are you worried about the fruit trees?'

'And the bougainvillea. We can try out our new tubing system; if we've done it right, it should irrigate them just so, but you can't be too careful when it's this hot. I think early evening might be a good time, we don't want to scorch those leaves.'

'Ooh no, heaven forbid. Let's start at dusk, we need to tidy a couple of the beds and I think a few slug pellets wouldn't go amiss.'

'Good idea. I need to give the roses a bit of attention too; there were a couple of aphid eggs on my Champagne Summer variety.'

'The little rotters.'

'My thoughts entirely.' She smiled at him.

'I was wondering' – he coughed – 'I was wondering...'

'Yes, Matthew?' she urged. There were three new inmates to be inducted, a busy day like any other, and she wasn't big on patience.

'I was thinking that maybe you might like to join me for some supper when we've finished. My little salad garden is doing very well; I've got baby spuds, radishes and whatnot. There's nothing quite like home grown with a decent steak and a large glass of red, sitting in the garden on a warm evening. Plus I'm a bit stuck with the crossword and you know what they say, two heads and all that...' He looked at the stack of mail on his desk, avoiding her stare. He felt the creep of an awkward blush work its way up from his neck.

Edwina was stunned into silence. She pictured Alan. It wasn't a memory, but was a new image. He was mouthing words to her, smiling. *I want you to be happy; I want someone to welcome you home. You have to carry on, no matter how hard or how hurt or how much you long to disappear. You have to carry on, because life is precious...*

She took a deep breath. 'No.' She shook her head.

Matthew looked mortified. 'Oh! Of course not! I'm so sorry, I just thought...'

She interrupted him, 'I mean no to the crossword – can't stand them. I think it's a slippery slope, one minute you are doing the crossword and the next you're reaching for a tapestry kit and after that it's surgical stockings, vitamin tonics and *The People's Friend*. I mean, yes, yes to dinner, absolutely, that would be lovely. But definitely no crosswords. Shall I bring backgammon?'

'Backgammon?'

'Yes. I'm a fiend; some would say the queen of backgammon, virtually unbeatable.'

'Well, we shall see about that.' He smiled.

'Yes we will,' she countered as she walked towards her office.

'By the way, before you rush off, you have a postcard.'

Edwina turned and reached out her hand, striding towards his desk, grasping the offering with eager fingers. She studied first the picture and then the text, scrawled by a biro on the other side. Turning it over twice more, she scrutinised the picture and then the words again.

'Well well, Kerala. How wonderful.' She beamed at Matthew who smiled back; he loved to see her this happy.

'Is it from a friend of yours?'

'Yes.' She nodded and strode towards her corkboard, in search of a pin.

The
Game

The Night Before

It is easy to tell when applause is real and when it's not. Polite applause is awkward, embarrassing; no one really wants to continue, but equally, no one wants to be the first to stop. Those that are being applauded know the difference too; they can see it and feel it. You can't fool anyone and you can't fake it. Real applause lifts you up, like wings do, and sends you soaring. It is infectious, loud and energising. This was just like that.

Three hundred pairs of hands smacking their palms together without reservation or restraint, it sounded like thunder, like horses' hooves cantering along cold, hard soil, a thousand football trench rattles all blended together for five minutes or so. Someone then decided that it wasn't enough; they started to whoop and holler. Someone else considered this to be a great idea and they too started to shout out, giving a word to the shout, 'More! More!' This became the chorus, a crescendo building and building.

For Gemma Peters, standing centre stage in her green velvet gown, fake pearls and stiff lace collar, it was a strange experience. It looked like they were clapping in slow motion; she could see the slow raise of an arm before it landed in a slap of congratulations across her dad's back, and she could see her mum bringing a tissue up to her eye to blot away a stray tear while carefully balancing her oversized handbag in the crook of her chubby arm. One of the English teachers, a tall bloke in a knitted tie, was trying to catch her eye. She looked at him and he winked, raising his clenched fist. He mouthed the words with one hand now placed over his heart, 'Well done!'

Her friends, Alice and Victoria, jumped up and down with their arms linked, reminding her of denim pogo sticks. She smiled at them. There were very few people in the crowd whose opinion mattered to her, but these were two of them. Her eyes sought Luke: he stood out, the shape of him, his particular shade of hair and stance were achingly familiar. *Look at me, see what I did?* He looked away.

Glancing at the three hundred faces smiling, nodding and commenting from the sides of their mouths to their loved ones, she felt elated. It was a wonderful feeling and one that she knew would not last. Gemma predicted that once her costume had been hung back on the rail in its plastic wrapper and the make-up removed, these same people would walk past her in the street or sit next to her on the bus and not give her a second glance. She would be back to ordinary. This was her one moment to be amazing.

She breathed deeply, taking in the odour of sweat and the unmistakeable tang of the school hall. As the heavy, rust-coloured, patched curtains hit the wooden floor a cloud of dust swirled around her feet, the particles of *Carousel*, *Charley's Aunt*, *Hamlet*, a thousand other productions and a little bit of everyone in them. Her drama teacher, Miss Greg, stood at the bottom of the stairs. A nervous, mouse-like woman who hid behind oversized glasses, she shocked them regularly by standing up and shouting loudly in the character of whoever they were discussing. It was easier for her when she was being someone else; Gemma understood this.

Miss Greg threw her arms around Gemma, crushing her

cheekbone into the gold-coloured chain from which a second pair of glasses hung against her pink jersey. With her guard down and fuelled by elation, she hugged the girl and grazed the top of her head with a kiss.

'Oh my goodness, you were absolutely magnificent! Really incredible, Gemma! Well done you!'

Gemma could see the glimmer of tears behind her glasses. She hadn't realised that it had meant so much to her.

'Did you hear the applause? Did you hear it? They were going crazy! Isn't it wonderful?'

Gemma nodded but didn't speak, feeling deflated, disappointed.

She made her way backstage, accepting the hand squeezes and impromptu hugs that were showered upon her. As she navigated the narrow corridor, walking between the usually empty, locker-lined walls, people she had never seen before, parents of other kids probably, darted out, content to let her pass only once they had given her a compliment or touched her. It was a strange experience.

Her mum and dad, Jackie and Neil, were facing the door in the changing room, waiting for her, as she knew they would be. A little welcome party of two. It was funny to see them standing in front of the row of pegs that was usually cluttered with PE kit, uniform and girls squabbling or preening themselves before going back to lessons. They stood close together; her dad wasn't tall and her mum's head reached up to his shoulder. They were always close together like that, either on the sofa or in the kitchen. He would wash while she dried or sometimes they swapped, just to get a bit of variation and always with the burble of local radio as their background noise.

Her mum rushed forward, pulling her daughter into her. She wanted to be the first.

'I can't tell you how proud I am of you, baby! You are so clever, Gem, I can't believe what you just did! How did you remember it all? You were absolutely brilliant! People were nudging me and saying, "Is that your Gemma? What a clever girl!" And you are. You really are.'

She smiled at her mum, knowing she wasn't clever. Anyone could learn lines, take instruction on where to stand and how to speak, but to her mum it would have seemed amazing.

This she knew because her paintings from nursery were still Sellotaped to the kitchen cupboard doors, and her 'A'-grade book review on *The Diary of Anne Frank* was only ever a fingertip's reach away for when anyone visited. The fact was, everyone in the class had been given an 'A', in recognition of how they had dealt with such a sensitive subject, but that wouldn't have registered with Jackie. She had always been like that; everything Gemma did was greeted with 'Incredible!' or described as 'Brilliant! Unbelievable!' Gemma knew the last bit was the truth: 'unbelievable'. She had looked up the word in the dictionary and knew the definition by heart: 'too unrealistic or improbable to be believed'.

She worked hard to achieve fairly average results, but the fact that her parents always saw her with her nose in a book meant that she was gifted. Gemma had tried to explain this to them, but it was pointless, as though they couldn't hear, didn't want to hear.

Her statements always elicited stock responses:

'I'm not that bright.'

'Course you are, you clever girl!'

'I'm not in the top set; I'm only in the middle stream.'

'Only because those bloody teachers haven't got a clue, you're cleverer than all of them!'

Her particular favourite:

'I don't think I will go to university.'

'Course you will! Don't talk rubbish, you are going to Oxford, I can see it now! I'm already saving up for your bike, a red one with a little wicker basket on the front.'

So there was very little point. What her parents did not appreciate was that the empty, shallow, yet constant praising of her mediocrity meant her confidence was shattered and her self-esteem through the floor. They had over the years unwittingly recalibrated her to feel that all praise was unmerited so she was now unable to distinguish between real achievement and hollow compliments, and to try and improve felt fruitless. Gemma often woke in the middle of the night in a cold sweat. Her nightmare was always the same: the moment her parents pulled the sheet of paper from the envelope and saw the crappy A-Level grades that she was certain she would receive. What would happen then, when the bubble burst? If she pictured that moment she felt a swell of panic rise in her chest that made her want to scream.

Gemma's dad elbowed his wife out of the way. 'Let me get at her, Jacks. Come here, darling.'

He too crushed her against his chest and kissed the top of her head.

'Blimey, girl, who knew you could do that? Gem, you were absolutely bloody brilliant. I mean, you know I can't be doing with plays and all that, but I tell you what, I could sit through that again. You was marvellous!'

She closed her eyes and fell into her dad just for a second, inhaling the scent of his coat. It smelled like his aftershave and something else, a bit like the smoke of bonfires, and petrol, as if fuel vapours had permeated the fabric and now clung to the little fibres that tickled her nose. There was also the faint smell of dirt, not dirty, not body odour, but actual dirt, like soil. Gemma thought then that if she smelled her dad without knowing him, she would know that he wasn't a professional; no doctor or lawyer would smell that way. It was a working man's smell.

He released her too soon and studied her face.

'You look exhausted, sweetheart. Let's get you home and tucked up.'

Her dad made everything connected with home sound cosy and safe, he always did.

Her mum interjected. 'I've got some nice muffins that I can toast for you, a little bit of strawberry jam and a cup of tea and you'll be all set.'

Jackie was constantly concerned with food and its intake. If she was less preoccupied with it, Gemma thought, she wouldn't be so fat. But she never said this; she would never hurt her mum's feelings, not for the world.

'Stacey's in the car. I've popped the engine on so it's nice and warm for you, how long will you be, love? I'm parked right out the front. The VIP spot for the leading lady!' Her dad zipped up his padded car coat over his ample stomach and reached into the pocket for his car keys.

'Do you want Mummy to wait with you while you take your make-up off?'

'Course she doesn't, Jacks, she wants to see her mates for a bit, don't you, love? Or probably has to see the teachers or something.'

'Oh right, yes, good point, Neil.'

Gemma nodded. They did this a lot, had a complete conversation about her, debating what was right, what was wrong, where she could go, what she should do, say, think. And then a conclusion would be reached without her having said a single word or added a single opinion, as though she wasn't there at all but was in fact invisible, or mute. A mute opinionless nothing.

'Right then, see you in a bit. Hurry up though, it's bloody freezing out there.'

Her dad kissed her on the forehead as he walked past. Even though he was inside and in the warm, he rubbed his fat, hairy fingers together in anticipation of going out into the cold. The large gold wedding ring on his left hand, with its flattened shield and his and Jackie's initials engraved on it, glinted under the strip light.

'Actually, Mum, is it okay if I walk home? Some of us were going to get hot chocolate and hang out for a bit.'

Her mum bit her lower lip. Gemma could see the debate raging: her desire to toast her muffins was strong.

'Oh, Gem, it's already late now.' She looked at her watch. It was half past eight. Jackie stared at the door through which her husband had just walked as thought therein might lie the right answer.

'Maybe I should ask Daddy.' She did this, she referred to herself and her husband as 'Mummy' and 'Daddy', as though she were talking to a toddler who still hadn't quite got the hang of the words and so repetition was necessary to allow them to permeate.

Gemma looked at her with a hopeful, expectant expression.

'What will you do, phone when you want picking up?'

'I can't, I've left my phone at home. But I won't be on my own, there's loads of us.'

'Oh, Gem, I don't know.'

Phones were not allowed on the set and hers was nestling next to her lamp on the bedside table, on top of her homework diary and next to her hairbrush. It was switched off and locked in an attempt to dissuade Stacey from rooting through her texts. Fat chance.

Gemma could see her mum's cogs turning, thinking about

the hard work that her daughter had put into the production, weighing up the pros and cons. Yes, she deserved some fun time, especially after that performance, but it was a bit late for a school night. Her face broke into a smile as she reached the decision that Gemma should be allowed to do whatever made her happy; after all, she had been magnificent! Unbelievable!

'Oh go on then, but please, please, Gem, not too late, my little actress!' Her mum kissed her cheek as she fastened the buttons of her beige anorak over her wide bottom. She ambled off through the sprung safety door and out into the corridor.

Gemma watched her through the glass pane etched with safety wire, as if framed inside a crossword. She watched her disappear out of view, walking like a human puzzle, with her funny little waddle of a walk. It was the walk she had always had because of her size. Her dad and nan had told her that her mum had been slim before she'd had her and Stacey, but the most difficult thing for Gemma to imagine was not her mum slim, but how she would walk. She couldn't picture her striding; instead it was her shuffle that came to mind, and the great effort it took to make her body move, flat-footed and almost rolling on her foot with each step, lumbering and unwieldy, inelegant and ugly. It sickened her.

Standing over the white china sink, Gemma removed her stage make-up. Rubbing at her eyes, she watched as her face was transformed from beautiful. Thick black mascara slid down her cheeks, like liquid liquorice that stained the pale palette covering her bones. Gemma stared at the face in front of her with its smudged features, smeared crimson mouth and sunken eyes. She looked distorted, unrecognisable, as though someone else had snuck around the other side of the wall and was peeking through at her.

Blissful Ignorance

'Come on, Jacks, you're letting all the heat out!' Neil chided as his wife opened the passenger door and proceeded to rummage through her bag. Eventually, she plopped down into the seat of the white Ford Transit Connect and pulled the seatbelt over her shoulder, stretching it until it reached the clip.

'I was just checking I had my keys and that I've put the programme somewhere safe. I didn't want it to get crumpled. That'll go in her scrapbook. Shame they didn't do a picture of her, but at least her name is bigger than any of the others. It's very clear who the leading lady was, so that's good.'

They smiled at each other.

'Where's Gemma?' Neil squinted past his wife into the October evening.

'Not coming.'

'What d'you mean, not coming?'

'She wanted to stay for a bit, there's a crowd of them going out for hot chocolate. I said we didn't mind as long as she's not too late.'

'Gawd, she's got you wrapped around her finger, that one!'

'Hello, kettle, this is pot!' Jackie laughed.

Neil chuckled. He drove slowly along the dark roads; always cautious in the company vehicle.

'God, my stomach is jumping. Our little girl, eh? I find it amazing, Jacks. I was so crap at school, it just never interested me and yet there's my Gemma, up on that stage, a little slip of a thing, talking Shakespeare and making it sound so easy that even I understood it!'

Jackie squeezed his arm. 'I know. I was worried I wouldn't know what was going on, but I did, she made it sound so normal, just like talking. And you're right, it's a gift, that.'

'Oh it is, no mistaking it. She looked tired, mind.'

Stacey piped up from the back seat. 'Well, I thought it was the most boring thing I have ever seen, ever.'

Neil and Jackie exchanged a look; it was only natural for her to be a little jealous of all the attention her sister was getting.

'Now come on, Stace, don't be like that, we can't all be brainboxes.' Her dad winked at her in the rear-view mirror.

Jackie knew it couldn't be a picnic for her, being at the same school as her sister who found everything so easy. She thought that the teachers probably expected the same from Stacey, but that was unfair, she never compared them and didn't want others to either.

Jackie shifted to face her daughter, who had slunk down on the back seat. 'Tell you what, Stace, when we get in, I'll do a nice cup of tea and some toasted muffins with strawberry jam, how about that?'

Stacey groaned and pulled the hood of her sweatshirt so far over her head that it covered her eyes.

Neil pulled into the driveway of their semi-detached house in Ennerdale Close.

They had been over the threshold for a full five minutes when the usual discord began.

'I don't want to go to bed.'

Jackie Peters knew that these words were going to fly out

of her youngest daughter's mouth, but she dreaded them just the same.

'Stacey, you are going to bed. It is late and you've got school tomorrow!'

Jackie hated the ritual of the quarrel; it was predictable, yet despite the forewarning she still found it wearing each and every night, as if they were arguing on a loop. It was Stacey's nature to push against the boundary, knock over the barrier and shout her corner. Jackie imagined herself a couple of years down the line saying, 'No, *you can't go out dressed like that!*' Or, '*No, your boyfriend cannot stay over!*' She knew instinctively that these debates would be had with Stacey in the future, who was so unlike her big sister. She almost welcomed the prospect; at least it would be different subject matter.

It perplexed Jackie, who at the age of forty was always desperate to crawl into her bed as early as was logistically possible. But Stacey, at fourteen, would fight and argue for even a minute's stay of execution. What was so great about staying up anyway? She tried to remember if she had been the same at that age, but couldn't. She remembered being twelve, thinking that her life would change when she became a teenager, a word with such magical connotations, as though she would get to know the secrets of the universe, all would be revealed and the fog of muggy-headed confusion that she had existed in up until that point would be lifted. Of course it wasn't. On her thirteenth birthday she had been given a training bra, a book token and a Human League poster, hardly the secrets of the universe, but very much appreciated nonetheless. She shook her head as she imagined presenting Stacey with similar gifts: she'd think it was a joke and would surely peek behind her mum's back to find her 'real' presents. They had so much nowadays and, truth be told, she didn't know if they were any happier for it.

'It's not late, it's not even nine o'clock, and all my friends can stay up until at least ten! Demelza goes to bed when she wants!'

'Demelza's parents are divorced, it's different.'

'Why's it different?'

'Stacey, it just is and I don't want to talk about it anymore. Why do you insist on spoiling such a lovely evening?'

'I don't want to spoil such a lovely evening, but I want to know why it's different for Demelza because her parents are divorced. How does that matter to your bedtime?'

Jackie sighed; sometimes you just had to give your kids a life lesson.

'Okay, Stacey, here it is. What I'm trying to say is that not everyone is as lucky as you to live in a house where there is a mummy and a daddy who are married and love each other very much. Demelza's mummy is single and probably out every night.' She refrained from adding, '*With different men, while her daughter is left to fend for herself, no doubt foraging in empty cupboards for stray Pop-Tarts and then spending the best part of the night clearing up her mother's sick and restoring her pants from around her ankles when she comes in at 3 a.m. inebriated.*'

'She probably doesn't have a lovely shepherd's pie and Victoria sponge waiting for her when she comes in from school. Now, it's not Demelza's fault, of course, but that is why she can go to bed when she likes and why it is different.'

Jackie shook her head at the image of little Demelza fending for herself. This was not the sort of subject that she would have raised with Stacey ordinarily, but she was the kind of child that would only settle for the full facts. Jackie felt very sorry for these children from broken homes, knowing that it ruined them for life. She had to admit to feeling a certain sense of smugness that she had it all.

'Demelza's mum isn't like that.'

'Well, with all due respect, Stacey, you don't *know* that.'

'I know Demelza's allowed to stay up till ten because that's when her mum finishes at the hospital. She's a doctor and she's famous, because she discovered that children who live near electricity pylons can get cancer. And the queen gave her a medal because she is the cleverest professor in England. And they are vegetarians.'

Jackie was at a loss and fell back on her stock phrase, as she always did in moments like these. 'Do I need to get your father?'

'I don't know, do you?'

'Don't you cheek me, Stacey Louise! Just get up those stairs now!'

She hated having to yell at her, but it was part of the ritual. Until her mother had really lost her rag and shouted in anger, Stacey would not budge. It was almost as if she wanted to see her like that. It wasn't over until the fat lady shouted.

Stacey stomped from the room. Jackie plopped down on the coffee-coloured Draylon sofa and stared ahead, watching as Stacey stood on the bottom stair and stuck her tongue out, wiggling her bum in an exaggerated fashion. Jackie huffed and puffed as if oblivious to what was occurring on the other side of the sitting room wall, but she wasn't. As ever, she could see her daughter's image reflected from the glass in the front door onto the television screen. It made her laugh; it was so child-like and innocent and Stacey always thought she was getting away with it. She buried her head in her magazine, taking in the headline about a love-rat who had done the dirty on some hapless pregnant lady with none other than the poor lady's mother. Jackie tutted and read on with interest.

'Gemma?' She heard the front door rattle shut, but it wasn't Gemma, it was Neil.

Her husband popped his head around the door. 'No, love only me putting the bottles out.'

She patted the space next to her. He had been washing up the cups. Wiping his hands on the front of his sweatshirt, he sat beside his wife on the sofa. The cushion sagged and she listed towards him.

'Stacey gone up?' he asked.

'Yep, but not without the usual palaver.'

Neil shook his head and laughed. 'And what about that other girl of ours, eh?'

'She was amazing, Neil, wasn't she?' Jackie knew that whenever she spoke about her eldest child it was with a tone of pride and incredulity, but she couldn't help it. How such a talented, beautiful girl had sprung from such a plain pasture as her was a mystery.

'I don't know how she did it, Jacks, I really don't. I mean, to learn all them words and make it so interesting. I felt so proud of her.'

'We both did, Neil.'

He nodded, acknowledging that he didn't own the lion's share when it came to how proud they were of Gemma.

'We should treat her, Jacks, what do you think?'

'I was thinking the same. What should we do?' She folded her magazine and shoved it down the side of the sofa cushion.

'Well, I know it's a lot, but she's been banging on about one of those iPod things for months. Shall we have a look in the catalogue?'

Jackie smiled and placed her head on his shoulder. Her lovely husband, always putting his family first, always. It would mean another few months without going to the hairdresser's, of buying everything 'own label' and scrimping on the meat, but Gemma was worth it.

'Yes, let's do that, Neil.'

Neil slid his arm across her shoulders. She leant on him and could hear his heart beating.

'Reckon she must take after her clever mum.'

'Oh, don't be daft, I'm not clever.'

'Yes you are; I hate it when you say that you aren't. You don't need fancy letters and exams after your name to be clever, and you are, you know. You're amazing and I love you.'

Jackie beamed, knowing that he meant it.

'Who's dropping her off?' he asked.

'No one. She's walking, there's a crowd of them apparently.'

Neil nodded. 'It's right that she enjoys herself, she deserves it.'

'Oh, I know. I just hope she isn't too late, I'm exhausted.' This she offered, confident of her husband's response.

'Tell you what, you go on up and I'll wait for her, she won't be much longer.'

'Are you sure, love?'

'Sure.'

Neil and Jackie Peters kissed, just a peck, but long and hard like it meant something. It was their way; they often kissed for the sheer joy of feeling the other's lips against their own, they always had.

Jackie watched as her husband pulled one of the tassel-edged cushions from behind his back and laid it on the arm of the sofa before placing his head on it. He always performed this little ritual when having a quick kip on the sofa, either on a Sunday afternoon after lunch or to recharge his batteries. He deserved it; he worked so hard. Jackie knew he would doze but would still hear the front door or even just her key in it; he was quite a light sleeper.

She watched from the door as his toes flexed inside his

socks. She had a tummy full of toasted muffins and all was right with the world.

'I love you, Neil.'

He opened his eyes and gazed at his wife, who hovered in the doorway. 'I love you too. I wasn't going to tell you, but I made my bonus again this month and I think I know what it's going on.' He smiled. 'I still can't get over it, Jacks. I mean, there's me, delivering parcels for a living, but for Gemma it'll be so different: Oxford University and then the world will be her oyster. She can be a lawyer or whatever she wants, but something important, something that matters.'

'She could be an actress!' Jackie added.

'Ooh no, I don't think so, that'd be a waste of that brain. Besides, have you seen half the things on telly now, they expect these girls to wear next to nothing and look like tarts. That's not for our girl.'

Jackie trod the stairs and cleaned her teeth, placing her toothbrush in the little china pot where the other three sat. She spent a few seconds prodding at the skin around her eyes, trying to work out why it was collapsing into something that resembled crepe paper, then she gave the already gleaming sink a quick wipe over with a damp cloth that she stored in the bathroom cabinet, along with spare loo roll and cans of deodorant and shaving cream. She came out of the bathroom and stood on the little square landing in her pink nylon nightie and peach-coloured towelling dressing gown, static making her fine hair stand on end. Her clothes were in a bundle over her arm; she figured that if she hung up the skirt, jumper and her all-in-one corset, they would do again for tomorrow.

Jackie bent her head around the bedroom door and looked in on Stacey. Despite her protestations, Stacey was sound asleep, oblivious, having nodded off with one of her magazines lying open across her legs. Jackie folded it shut and popped it on the floor. She clicked off the bedside lamp and placed a kiss on her two fingers before touching those same fingers to Stacey's little face.

'Night night, darling. Medal from the queen indeed. Whatever next?'

Stacey didn't stir, little Miss *I'm not tired* was out for the count.

Jackie's bed was calling to her. What with Gemma's performance and having to do an early tea and then getting everyone back to school, she was ready to hit her pillow. It had been an amazing day: all Gemma's hard work, all those hours of rehearsals had paid off. Jackie smiled; she was a very lucky woman. Two great kids and a devoted husband. She felt safe knowing that her husband was downstairs waiting for Gemma – on duty, if you like.

She crept downstairs to fetch her glass of water for the night and tiptoed through the lounge, trying not to wake her husband. He was already snoring, and his big hands were knitted over his stomach, meeting across the long, red, arrow-headed tail of his company's logo: 'Delivery Devils'. The room looked lovely and cosy in the lamplight; the Lladro ladies they had collected over the years stood with their parasols and full skirts, caught in mid-dance with their baskets of flowers at their feet. The cuckoo clock with its chains and pendulum ticked loudly, each tick and each tock bouncing off the magnolia woodchip. The electric fire with its redundant brass companion set looked cold and grey against its wooden surround, which was home to fourteen owls of varying sizes, each one reminding her of a different seaside holiday with the kids and none as precious as the first, given to her by Neil when they were in Broadstairs and she had been expecting Gemma. Everything was as it should be and in its rightful place. Pulling the door to, she climbed the stairs again.

Jackie pulled back the candlewick bedspread and tried not to notice as the mattress sagged under her hefty frame. She felt ashamed of her size, even though it was her own fault. She desperately wanted to lose weight, hating her body and the way it made her feel every single day, worn down by the constant comparisons she drew between herself and every other female she encountered. Comparisons that left her feeling stripped of self-confidence; it was an ugly way to live.

With the dawning of every new day, in the first seconds of waking, she hoped that it had all been a horrible dream and that she might see her hip bones jutting out above her pants and feel her sculpted thighs beneath her fingers, like she used to when she and Neil had first met. She longed to be his 'little doll' and not cuddly Jackie who had eaten his 'little doll' and wrapped her in a suit of dough. He said that he loved her no matter what and whilst she knew at some level that this was true, she still caught him looking at the firm bottoms and small boobs of the girls on television and it made her want to cry.

Jackie considered what getting his bonus for the third month in a row meant: a caravan holiday in the summer, so she would have to try doubly hard to shed some weight. She wouldn't let on, but she'd seen the brochure on the passenger seat in Neil's van, bless him. She knew it would be a big deal for him, he would be really excited and she would act surprised when he told her.

Despite being tired, Jackie didn't drop off immediately, not until she had mentally gone through everything that she needed to do the next day. It was a habit that she had got into, reciting the list in her head: *put the rubbish out, empty the laundry basket and wash the contents, get the chops out of the freezer, do the ironing, phone me mum, do a bit of a shop – we're running low on milk, collect the girls and take them swimming, make the pud for Saturday night's tea.*

Eventually she slept. The alarm clock that had been hers since she was a little girl ticked loudly, but the noise was so familiar that she was oblivious to it. She lay on her back and snored, her wheezing whistle reverberating around the room.

She didn't know what made her wake at 3 a.m.: maybe she always did but then usually went straight back to sleep; maybe it was the Neil-shaped gap in the bed that made her wake up properly, reaching for him, only to find that he wasn't there. Her mind worked quickly: if he hadn't come to bed and had been waiting up for Gemma…

Jackie didn't put her dressing gown on, which in itself was strange. She never, ever went beyond her bedroom wearing just a nightie; it clung to her, allowing her shape to be seen too keenly. She always hid her body, but at that time of the morning she didn't even think about it. Her clock had said three o'clock. Three o'clock! What on earth was going on?

She jumped out of bed quickly and went straight to Gemma's room. Jackie knew before she got there that Gemma wasn't in it, not because of any psychic ability, but because the room was bathed in a yellow glow. Gemma always drew the thick, floral curtains to block the light from the street lamp outside her window, but tonight, as Jackie stood on the landing, about to walk into her daughter's room, she could see that the curtains were open and she wasn't in her bed.

It wasn't enough for Jackie that she could see the bed was made and unoccupied, with the top of the duvet turned over and tucked in and the pillows plumped just so; she had to walk over to it and touch the flat duvet and place her palm on the cold pillow slip. Proof.

She turned to face the wardrobe and opened the doors, running her hands over the school uniform and home clothes that hung in two groups, segregated by a silver metal pole that held up the top shelf. Jackie bent down and peered beneath the clothes. A logical mind would have known that Gemma was not hiding in the wardrobe, but nothing about the situation at that time of the morning felt logical. Jackie stood up straight and placed her hand over her mouth, breathing deeply between her fingers before thundering down the stairs.

'Neil!' she shouted.

At the sound of his wife's voice he leapt from the sofa. He looked confused, as though he didn't know where he was.

'What, Jacks? Are you all right?' He looked at his surroundings; it was clearly strange to him that he wasn't in bed.

'She's not back!'

'What?' He rubbed at the back of his neck, which had been bent at an awkward angle, propped on one of their cushions. The fug of sleep clung to him.

Jackie watched as he shook his head, trying to make himself alert, as if his brain was lagging a few seconds behind anything that he heard or said. She watched as he sniffed the air and looked relieved that there was no smoke, no fumes and no fire.

'She's not back! Gemma's not in her room!'

Jackie was speaking very quickly and could see that he had forgotten why he was downstairs and what he was waiting for. She said it again more forcefully and this time she made it clear.

'Her room is empty! She's not back!'

'What time is it?'

'It's three o'clock. Three o'clock! Where is she?' She knew her voice was higher than usual, almost a screech; it was as if she couldn't control it, but she didn't want to panic, not yet.

'Jacks, calm down, just calm down, love.' He placed his hand on her shoulder. 'She'll have stayed at Victoria's. Maybe she couldn't phone.' He sounded rational and not at all anxious; it helped.

'Actually she did say that she'd left her phone here,' Jackie suddenly remembered.

It began to sound plausible: her mobile was at home and if she had arrived somewhere late, then she would have been too shy to ask to use the phone. This was possible, and Gemma was always polite; she might have thought it rude to ask to use a phone. *Oh, Gemma!*

'Well, there you go,' he countered. 'She probably thought it had got too late to walk home alone and didn't want to wake us. She knows how we feel about her wandering around after dark. She's a sensible girl; she'll have stayed at Victoria's. Don't worry. Come on, let's go to bed.'

'Neil, she's never done this before.'

'No, I know, love, but she's growing up, maybe we have to cut her a bit of slack.'

Jackie nodded at him, he was right; if she stayed anywhere, it would be with Victoria, although it was usually by prior arrangement. Jackie trusted her husband. He always knew best and sounded quite calm, and this calmed her. If he wasn't worrying, then neither would she, although that was much easier said than done.

They trundled up the stairs. Jackie stopped on the third stair.

'Have you left the lamp on, love? You know what Gemma's like about the dark.'

'Yep, the little one by the sofa.'

'Okay.'

Jackie wanted to make sure that if she did come in, she would be able to find her way.

She lay next to her husband and stared into the darkness, letting her eyes wander over the shiny floral wallpaper, shag-pile carpet and heavy pink velvet curtains that had been there when they moved in; they shifted slightly in the draught from the small top window that was always ajar. The white metal bed frame with its ornamental flower-painted china knobs creaked as her husband turned onto his side, trying to get comfortable. The photograph of the girls when they were little, sitting on their nan's sofa in their matching red and cream lace party dresses, hung above the bed; that had been a lovely day.

Sleep was slow in coming. No matter how she tried to distract herself, she felt ill at ease. Why hadn't Gemma phoned? But what could she do about it at this hour? The answer was nothing, absolutely nothing.

'I tell you this, Jacks, I'm not taking away from what she's achieved tonight, but I'll be having words with Gemma when she gets home. I won't have her worrying her mother like this, it isn't fair.' Neil's words cracked open the silence and sent her mind whirring again.

She pictured her daughter on the floor of Victoria's bedroom. They were probably still chatting about the play and goodness knows what else. Neil dozed by her side, but she lay awake for a while. It felt strange that there were only three people under their roof that night and not her proper little family all safe and accounted for. Jackie didn't like it. She didn't like it one bit.

Have You Lost Her?

Jackie woke with a start, proving that she must have dropped off at some point, but she didn't remember when. For a split second when her eyes first opened, she forgot why there was a twist of anxiety in her gut, a headache pawing behind her eyes and a lump in her throat. She quickly remembered. It wasn't much past six, but Jackie climbed out of bed, wanting to get the day started. She knew that until she had heard Gemma's voice, until she had done that, she wouldn't breathe again normally, her heart and lungs would be unable to find their natural rhythm, not until then.

She filled the kettle and pressed the little button to make it boil. As was her habit, while waiting for the click she took the J-cloth from the little gap at the side of the washing-up bowl, squeezed out the excess water and wiped down the draining board, then ran the cloth along the front of the cooker where the knobs were. She tried not to, but eventually she glanced at the digital time display on the cooker. Ten past six: was it too early to phone? She put two tea bags into two mugs and drummed her small, manicured fingers on the work surface. *Sod it*. If she woke up the Roberts household it would just be too bad. After all, it was a work and school day, they would have to be up soon enough.

She held the phone close to her mouth, awkward at having to call at this early hour.

'Angela?'

'Yes?'

'It's Jackie Peters.'

'Oh hello, Jackie, how are you?' Angela's manner was that of someone trying to be polite while at the same time wondering what the reason was for the early morning call from someone that she hardly spoke to. It had always been obvious to Jackie that the woman didn't like her, no matter how hard she tried to disguise it by shouting very loudly that, *'We must get together for coffee...'* Their girls had been friends for nearly six years now and Angela still hadn't got past the shouting about it stage. Jackie used to wonder what Angela would have done if she had said, *'Yes, lovely, let's do it now! What a great idea, Angela. Right now, let's get together for coffee!'* She never would of course and Angela knew it.

She and Neil always joked that the Roberts thought that they were in a different league, what with them having gone on two cruises, one Mediterranean and one Caribbean, and the fact that their three-bed semi was built in the 1930s, on a private development, whereas theirs was clearly ex-local authority, which, while they were exactly the same dimensions, meant a difference of about a hundred and forty thousand pounds.

'Yes, fine. Well, sort of. I'm sorry to phone so early—'

'It's not a problem,' Angela interrupted, her clipped tone suggesting otherwise.

'I just wanted to have a word with Gemma.'

Jackie knew she sounded apologetic.

'Gemma?'

'Yes.'

'Erm, did you think she was here?'

Jackie could hear her heart beating loud and fast in her ears;

her breath came in shallow pants and her response was at least a second slower than was normal.

'Is she not with you, Angela?' She spoke slowly; strangely, her voice was little more than a whisper, as though she didn't want her question to be heard because she didn't want to hear the answer.

'I don't think so, unless she came in with Vicks and they went straight upstairs. Would you like me to go and check?'

Would I like you to go and check? She had to refrain from shouting, *'Yes! Go and check now! Please, please hurry! Move your skinny, teaching assistant's arse up those stairs and then come back quickly!'* Instead, she nodded into the receiver and her voice was once again small.

'Yes, please, Angela. If it's not too much trouble.'

'Hang on a mo.'

Jackie would hang on a mo; she would hang on, standing on the lino on the kitchen floor but feeling as if she was sinking into it. Her nylon nightie clung to her bottom, her hair was flat from sleep, and indentations from the folds on the pillowcase were still visible on her plump, rosy cheek. She repeated a phrase in her head: *please be there, Gemma. Be there, Gemma. Be there safe and sound on Victoria's bedroom floor, wrapped in a sleeping bag on the blow-up bed. Please be there, Gemma.*

The truth was, however, that Jackie knew what Angela was going to say before she said it. She tried to enjoy the calm of the waiting moments, knowing that after this there would be no calm. Call it a mother's instinct or something else, but she knew and already her mind was trying to process the information, trying to think what came next.

How long she stood clutching the receiver between hopeful palms she couldn't say. Maybe two minutes, maybe less, more, who knows? These details would only become important later.

'Jackie, hi. Sorry to keep you.'

'That's okay.' Why she said that she didn't know, it was all far, far from okay.

'Had a word with Vicks, apparently she left Gemma at school after the play. Hope everything is okay. Not a problem is there?'

'I… I… don't know really. I need Neil.' She placed the phone back in its cradle and stared at the two mugs awaiting hot water. Her legs felt like lead.

Jackie eventually managed to rouse herself and go upstairs. She pushed on the bathroom door, which was unlocked. Neil was in his trousers, naked from the waist up, a slight bulge of fat sitting like a cushion above the tight black belt of his trousers. He was shaving, pulling his chin with his left hand into a taut and unnatural angle while scraping at the whiskers with the razor in his right hand. She had always liked watching him shave, finding it very intimate. He spoke to his wife's reflection as it hovered over his right shoulder.

'Did you speak to her?' His tone was almost jolly and she felt a surge of something that she couldn't readily identify, but it was close to anger.

'No. She's not there, Neil.'

'What?'

'I spoke to Victoria's mum and Gemma's not there.' She had to repeat it, as though he hadn't been concentrating or simply couldn't process what she was telling him.

'Not there?' Again it was as if he had misheard or doubted the information that he was being given.

She shook her head. 'No.'

There was a second of silence before he spoke.

'Well, where the bloody hell is she then?' He turned to face her as though she had the answer and he needed her to give it to him.

She stared at him. 'I'll phone around.'

Her adrenalin had started to pump as her heart pounded; her vision and hearing felt sharp. Neil looked vacantly at his wife. She could see that mentally he was where she had been five minutes before.

She called Luke's mother, knowing the two of them were close, but it was pointless, the woman could barely recall Gemma, let alone help with locating her. Next it was Alice's mum and she had the same conversation, as earlier. *Was she with them? Had they seen her?*

Jackie noted that Alice's mum sounded really upbeat and it annoyed her.

'She isn't here, but let me go and grab Alice for you. Have you lost her?' The woman, whose name escaped her, sounded as though she were trying to be funny, making a little joke. The question, however, reverberated in Jackie's skull. *Have I lost her? Have I lost her?*

'Hello, Mrs Peters.' Alice sounded coy, wary, as if she might be in trouble.

It was strangely comforting to be speaking to a friend of Gemma's, a connection of sorts.

'Hello, Alice love, do you know where Gemma is? Did you go with her for hot chocolate?'

'Mmmmno, we left her at school, she said she was being picked up.'

'She said she was being picked up?'

Jackie's stomach muscles contracted and she shook her head. Was it her that had got the plan wrong? Should she have picked her up? Is that what they had agreed? But if Gemma had been waiting, she would have called; she could have walked home by now.

'If you hear anything, Alice, give me a ring will you, love?'

'Yeah, course. Is Gemma all right?'

'Yes, yes, she's fine, love, don't you worry.' Her lie was swift and unconvincing to both of them.

Jackie became aware that Neil was standing by her side in their little kitchen; she didn't know how long he'd been there. He stared at her as she replaced the phone. The two were silent for a second or two. Who was going to say it?

'Shall I call the police?'

Jackie said it. She had said it out loud, the phrase and the act that they had both been pondering, dreading, delaying.

'Or maybe not.' She shook her head. Was it a stupid idea? 'It'll be embarrassing if we get them involved, I don't want to waste their time. Plus I don't like the idea of it, it's like we've done something wrong: how could we not know where our little girl is? I don't want to get into trouble.'

Neil squeezed her arm. 'You won't, Jacks. I think it's a good idea. I'll do it.'

'Neil…'

She heard the kitchen door open and jerked her head up to see her daughter standing in front of her. Jackie only hoped that her youngest didn't sense the wave of disappointment that enveloped her.

'Jesus, who were you expecting?' Stacey folded her arms across her chest.

Jackie didn't tell her off for blaspheming, which she would normally have done, but equally she couldn't answer her daughter. It wasn't so much who she had been expecting as who she had been hoping for, and it hadn't been Stacey.

Day One

Jackie and Neil Peters sat perched on the edge of their sofa. Shock rendered them pretty useless; they were fuelled by hope and nervous energy. They leant forward, almost sliding off the sofa, trying to pay attention, to hear every syllable and catch every nuance. Poised, like shaking leverets caught in the headlights, ready to bolt, to make tea or coffee, to answer the phone or the door should the bell ring. There were police in their house and the Peters were unused to dealing with the police, unsure whether they were clients or suspects. On this last point they were correct.

Neil exhaled loudly as though he had taken a deep breath. His wife sat silently by his side, wringing her hands and fidgeting with invisible bits of thread on her skirt. She stared at the cuckoo clock, preoccupied with the maths of the hours since she had last seen her daughter, as if mentally trying to resolve a problem on an exam sheet.

If Gemma leaves school at 9 p.m. and walks at an average of three miles an hour, where could she have got to by ten o'clock the next morning? Thirty-nine miles, thirty-nine miles... What, or more importantly where, is thirty-nine miles away from here? Somewhere like Colchester? How far is that? And what if she wasn't on foot, what if she was being driven. Driven where? By whom?

Block it out, block it out, don't think about that, don't think about it, Jackie, it will all be okay. Her self-soothing mantra did not help.

Stacey was at school; everyone figured it was best to keep things as normal as possible for her.

Detective Sergeant Gavin Edwards sat in the chair to the side of the fireplace. He was pumped up, newly promoted and without any of the cynicism that someone with more years under their belt might display. His colleague, Melanie Vincent, hovered by the door, allowing her eyes to appraise the house, the decor, looking for clues, anything at all. The introductions had been brief and curt; everyone was eager to get on with the job in hand. A list of all Gemma's friends and their parents and telephone numbers had been given to one of DS Edwards' team who at that very moment was double-checking for any information and confirming Gemma wasn't with any one of them. The school had been given a quick sweep and statements had been taken from those that had seen her leave the previous evening, for people had indeed seen her leave.

As far as DS Edwards and the team were concerned, the case of Gemma Peters was genuine and worrying, warranting the level of manpower and time that they were throwing at it. Her situation didn't fit either of the usual scenarios. She wasn't from one of the rougher estates or not so nice postcodes where children played truant, might sleep at the homes of any number of distant 'relatives' and were more often than not misplaced rather than missing. Neither had the report been filed by an estranged partner, whose access and visiting rights were sketchy and who felt the agreed rules were not being adhered to. This was no malicious call from a disgruntled parent. Usually and thankfully, such children turned up safe and sound before the ink had dried on the first page of the report.

Gemma Peters was different. She hadn't gone missing

before and appeared to be from a caring, stable family with a comfortable home environment; she was smart, doing well at school and popular, and this was entirely out of character. The fact that the last confirmed sighting of Gemma had been at 9 p.m. the previous evening was cause for great concern. The first few hours of a disappearance were crucial and the more time that elapsed, the less hope there was of finding that child alive. This was a cruel fact, but a fact nonetheless.

'So you noticed she was missing at three o'clock this morning?'

Gemma's parents nodded in unison.

'And you called us at a quarter to seven?'

Neil caught the look that the policeman threw at his colleague. Had they failed already? Why hadn't they called earlier? It hadn't seemed real, it hadn't seemed urgent, they were tired and it had been late. This reasoning sounded pathetic and inadequate in the face of what was happening now.

'We thought she was at her friend's.' Jackie was aware of her apologetic tone.

'Why? Because she told you she was staying at a friend's?' Gavin asked.

'No. No, she said she would walk home, but if she ever stays over anywhere then it's at her friend Victoria's and so when she wasn't home, we just assumed that that was where she would be.'

'So she had done this before, stayed at Victoria's without letting you know first?'

'No, never. She's not like that, she's a good girl.'

'So this had not been discussed and was grossly out of character?'

Jackie nodded, feeling every inch a suspect and not the parent desperate for answers.

'And this was at 3 a.m.?'

Jackie nodded again.

'And you called us at just before 7 a.m.?'

'It didn't feel like that long.' Her voice quavered.

'What did you do in the four hours between three and seven?'

'We were in bed, asleep in bed.'

'So, just like a regular night?'

Jackie nodded. The way he said it made it sound like they hadn't cared, hadn't noticed. She felt sick.

'Does Gemma have a boyfriend?'

Neil coughed. 'Well, no, not really a boyfriend, but a boy friend, if you get my meaning. Luke, he's in her class and I think they might be a bit sweet on each other, but not boyfriend and girlfriend in the sense you mean it. She's not a very worldly girl, only goes out with her mates at the weekends and is more interested in revising. She's going to Oxford.'

Gavin nodded. 'Does she ever stay at Luke's house?'

'Good God no!' Neil raised his voice. 'She's not that kind of a girl. What sort of parents would let a fifteen-year-old stay at a boy's house?'

'You'd be surprised. I understand how invasive this must seem, Mr Peters—'

'Neil, please.'

'Thanks. Neil, the reason I ask is to help build up a picture of Gemma, her friends, her lifestyle. It will help us fill in all the gaps and the sooner we can do that and locate her, the better.'

Neil nodded but continued to stare at his hands, which were locked in a pyramid resting on his knees.

'Could you describe Gemma for me, Mrs Peters?'

'Do you mean what she looks like?' Jackie was wary of getting the answer wrong.

'Not so much; we already have the photos you've given us and her physical details, but I'd like to hear how you would describe her as a person. Take your time.' He smiled at her.

Jackie pictured her daughter standing on the stage. She spoke quietly and looked at the carpet; it made it easier somehow.

'She's a very clever girl, top in everything, but she's not big-headed at all, she's quite shy actually. She's a kind girl, brings down her plates and cups from her room and her dirty laundry, I never have to ask her twice. She's very popular and beautiful, but I suppose you can see that in her pictures. Gemma's never been in trouble, never done anything but make us so proud. She is nice to her little sister and spends time chatting to her nan when she comes over. Oh no!'

Everyone watched as Jackie's hand flew to her mouth.

'What's the matter, love?' Neil coaxed.

'Her coat's in her wardrobe, she didn't take it in because of the play! I've only just remembered. She'll be cold.' Jackie's hot tears fell hard and fast, clogging her nose and throat as she slumped against her husband's chest. 'I want her home, Neil, I want her back!'

Eight Weeks

'It's bedtime, Stacey.' Jackie's voice was no more than a cracked whisper.

The girl nodded and stood, bending to kiss her mum on the forehead before wordlessly treading the stairs. Her deep sigh was as much an expression of relief at being able to escape the insufferable silence of her parents' pokey lounge as it was recognition of the tiredness that dogged her waking hours. When your sleep tumbled on a sea of nightmares and imaginings, it made functioning normally almost impossible.

Neil came into the lounge from the kitchen, drying his hands on a red-checked tea towel.

'Stacey gone up?'

Jackie nodded.

Neil sat by her side and removed the folded local paper from her lap. He ran his hand over his stubble, which now grew in yellowed skin. 'Are you sure you don't want anything to eat, love?'

She shook her head. Food had become tasteless and pointless; every mouthful felt like wet cardboard that choked in her throat. How could she be expected to eat food prepared in their warm family kitchen, by the loving hand of her husband, and served on clean white china, when her little girl might be hungry, scared, hurt?

Jackie picked at the already torn nails that had been ripped and bitten from the nail bed. The momentary flare of pain gave her something to focus on; the dots of blood that peppered the quick on each finger were strangely satisfying.

'It would do you good, Jacks, to get something inside you, even if it's just a bit of toast.'

'Would it, Neil? Just how exactly would it do me good to eat a bit of toast?' she snapped. 'Would it give me a night of rest or bring Gemma waltzing through the door?' Tiny flecks of spit flew against the sweatshirt that hung from Neil's frame. He was used to it, every suggestion was barked at or rebuked, and tears always followed this. It was exhausting for them both.

Jackie didn't bother with a tissue or hankie anymore; she had learnt they were pointless. It was easier to let her body shed its tears and allow them to soak into her hair and clothes, becoming part of the fabric, part of her, like a fountain on a timer. Constantly reaching for, refreshing or binning sodden loo roll or tissues only slowed the process.

Neil stood and ambled to the window. He did this a lot, staring out through the net curtains into the black void of night, hoping for a glimpse of something and grateful not to have to be in such close proximity to his wife. He was sick of bolstering her, he wished that she would stop crying, if only for a while. He longed for respite from the soundtrack of their misery.

'I'll pop out for a wander, see you in a bit.'

Neil collected his coat from the row of hooks in the hallway and closed the door behind him; he didn't know if she had heard him, it was hard to tell. Jackie's expression no matter what was happening or who was talking to her remained the same. Her eyes darted from beneath swollen lids, her teeth chewed at her bottom lip, which was sore, and her head almost lolled against her chest, as though keeping it upright required strength that she did not possess.

Neil spent his days and a large part of his nights wandering, looking and searching. His job took him all over the south of England, giving him the chance to peek up alleyways and peer into windows. He prodded at mounds in skips, looked under every mattress discarded on a country verge and stared into the murky depths of drains. It was madness, but it was how he now lived.

Jackie swallowed three shiny pink pills daily. *'Just to take the edge off.'* That was what the doctor said. She hadn't really understood what that meant, but she did now. They took the edge off her, leaving her less like herself, muted, and for that she was grateful.

It was as if she functioned on power-saving mode, with even the smallest chore using up her fragile reserves. A couple of minutes spent concentrating on a photograph of Gemma taken at nursery school, or trying to remember how they had celebrated her last birthday would leave her in a state of confusion; then a quick glance at the cuckoo clock would reveal that several hours had passed.

This worked in reverse too. Extreme fatigue would carry her to bed, where the duvet would envelop her in a cocoon of apathy. A deep, dark slumber would take over, offering relief from the wearying yoke of grief. Yet when her eyes darted open, her breath coming in shallow pants as the ghost of the nightmare returned, she would realise that it had been only minutes since the warm space had offered solace.

The phrase 'spending time' went round in her head. She concluded that if time was a currency, it was the emotionally stable that had the biggest reserves. When your mind flitted between distress and chaos, time was not yours to spend. It flipped you over and usurped you at will.

Jackie Peters was now a shell; all the marrow and matter

of her former self had been sucked out. In their place was a person she didn't recognise. The face that stared back at her from the mirror was only vaguely familiar.

She stared at this face to see if it would move or talk. It began to scare her; she could feel the cold cloak of madness wrapping itself around her in those minutes. There was something tempting about the idea of sliding into an abyss in which she could hide, just for a little while. The tidal pull of insanity within her was strong, but she would not give in to it, not yet. She needed to be strong for when Gemma came home; she would need looking after, and that was her job.

It was nearly nine o'clock. Jackie clicked the lamp on and ran her bitten nails along her teeth.

A Girl Is Found

Neil flicked the indicator and eased the van into the lay-by behind the all-day breakfast caravan and its oversized Union flag fluttering in the breeze. A large whiteboard was propped by the open hatch: the menu advertised numerous fried breakfast combinations. His mobile flashed from its plastic cradle on the dashboard. He took several calls a day on his hands-free set; it was usually the control room issuing new jobs, pick-ups within a short drive of the postcode in which he found himself. His day was without routine, he lived at the mercy of clothes manufacturers whose samples needed to get to buyers, householders who derived a good income from eBay, shipping all manner of junk across county borders, and retailers without their own logistics operations. This call, however, was not one he wanted to take whilst navigating roundabouts and traffic lights. It was DS Gavin Edwards.

'This a good time, Neil?'

'Yes, just pulled over. Everything okay?' Neil's breath came in short bursts, as it always did when Gavin called him. The excitement and expectant flip of his stomach that had been there in the first days of Gemma's disappearance was now replaced with a nervous bile, as if the news he was dreading was about to hit his brain. His hands shook against the steering wheel and he was sweating.

'Where are you, Neil?'

'Just off the A13.'

There was a pause. Neil held his breath, waiting. *Please God, no. Please let her be safe.*

'I haven't contacted Jackie, thought it best to speak to you first.'

Neil nodded, forgetting that he was on the phone.

'Can you meet me at Queen's Hospital?'

'Queen's? Yes of course. Is it Gemma? Have you found her, is she okay?'

He heard Gavin's sharp intake of breath, pictured him at his desk in his grey suit, pinching the bridge of his nose as he had seen him do several times before when concentrating.

'There's no easy way to say this, Neil.'

Oh God, oh no. Oh God, please no, not my little girl.

'But we've found a body.'

Neil opened the van door and was instantly sick on the ground. He remained hunched over long after his stomach had emptied itself, staring at the watery splat and wanting to stay there forever, not wanting to move or face what came next.

'Jesus, mate! Some of us are trying to eat – you fucking twat!'

Neil looked up at the two men in high-vis jackets, chomping on bacon butties and holding scalding Styrofoam cups of strong tea. They shook their heads in his direction. He didn't have the strength to respond.

The three men walked abreast along the wide corridor. Neil was conscious that his rubber-soled steel-toe-capped boots were squeaking with every step, heralding his presence. He wished he was wearing different shoes, like Dr Mitchell's or Gavin's, whose walk was stealthy in comparison. They walked a little too quickly, all three very keen to get the episode over with, for very different reasons. Neil could only think ahead to going home and telling Jackie. He started to rehearse the phrases in his head, not sure which he would choose, all sounding equally horrific, surreal.

'Oh, Christ, please give me the strength.'

'You okay?' Gavin placed a hand on his back.

Neil was perplexed, unaware that he had spoken out loud.

The trio stopped at an innocuous-looking door. The doctor gave him a brief flicker of a tooth-hiding smile, consolatory.

Neil exhaled. The idea of entering a mortuary was abhorrent to him. He didn't know what to expect and his gut heaved in nervous anticipation. He felt sick and confused. He exhaled again, trying to calm his pulse.

Gemma had spent a night at Queen's three years ago, when she'd broken her arm; it felt like minutes ago. And now here he was in the basement, a section of this disinfected building he had never considered before. A building where misery and joy, the entire human condition, was spread over eight linoleum-covered floors.

He had never seen a corpse before. His stomach knotted and he swallowed the nausea that swept his body.

'You okay?' Gavin asked for the second time.

Neil nodded. No one commented on the lie: he was far from okay. He thought of the day she was born, the moment he had been handed the tiny, wrapped, bloodied bundle. He had loved her, instantly and without measure; his little girl.

He stepped inside behind the doctor. His tongue stuck to the dry roof of his mouth, his vision blurred and his heart threatened to leap from his chest. The desire to run was strong. He swallowed, his breath coming in odd bursts. His eyes were drawn to the sheet-covered body.

He walked hesitantly towards the bed in the middle of the room. Neil was trembling, his limbs jerked involuntarily. His stomach muscles were tightly clenched.

Dr Mitchell held the edge of the cloth in his hands and hesitated. 'Are you ready?'

Neil nodded.

The doctor pulled the sheet away from the face and stood back.

Neil glanced at her face and looked away, only able to take small glimpses. She looked cold, her complexion bluish grey. He let his eyes follow the line from the soft brow, over the eyelids, along the nose and mouth. An ugly cut severed the colourless top lip on one side, which butterfly stitches did their best to hold together. The skin looked smooth, she reminded Neil of a mannequin. Her hair was matted on the crown and thick with clots of dark blood that was black and treacle-like.

Neil shook his head. 'It's not Gemma.'

Outside in the corridor, Neil leant against the wall, battling with the new image that would haunt his thoughts in the restless early hours, but also struggling with the shame at the sense of disappointment that engulfed him. He had wanted it to be over.

He cried. For only the second time since Gemma's disappearance, he cried.

'Could... could you get her a pillow? I know my girls are much comfier with a pillow.'

'Sure, mate.' Gavin patted his back. 'Someone will sort that out.'

Neil was late home, not that it mattered: things were exactly as he had left them that morning. The cold, silent, semi-dark rooms where his wife sat on the sofa, a fretful sentinel with one eye on the front door and an ear cocked for the telephone; and Stacey in her bed. He hated the way Jackie's body twisted towards the door and her hand flew to her breast every time his key was placed in the lock. He sometimes thought it would be easier not to go home at all, spare them all the disappointment.

'Any news?' This was her standard, futile greeting. Both knew that if there were any developments, he would not wait until he got home before putting her out of her misery.

'No, love.' He shook his head and placed his hands on his hips. 'No news.'

She rose to seek out the brief respite of her bed, where, if she was lucky, she might sleep for an hour or so.

'Don't forget to leave the lamp on.'

Again he nodded. It was the same instruction she gave every night, afraid that Gemma might not be able to find her way in the dark.

Jackie turned from the doorway and stared at her husband as he sank down onto the sofa. 'I'm worried you've given up on her, Neil.' She panted, open-mouthed, as if the effort of getting the words out had left her physically exhausted.

Neil shook his head slightly, blinking, gathering his thoughts.

Jackie stepped forward, back into the room, her fingers fidgeting against her face, hooking inside her mouth, pushing her front teeth. 'Because if you've given up on her...' She paused, trying to properly phrase what she had to say. 'I... I don't think I could cope.'

It took him a second to realise he was sobbing. It felt strange, embarrassing. This was something he usually did in private, as if it was shameful. Jackie felt something akin to relief at the sight of his tears. She placed the pads of her fingertips against his cheek and gently tapped the wet stubble. Neil caught her wrist and placed her flat palm over his mouth, pushing a kiss against it. The hand onto which he had slipped a thin gold band and from which he had lifted not one but two perfect tiny newborns. When his words came, they were barely more than a whisper. Jackie had to lean close to hear him.

'I loved her from the first moment I saw her. That very second you put her into my arms, I swore that I'd never let her down and that I'd look after her and keep her safe.' He paused to swallow the next wave of tears that clogged his throat. 'I see her every waking second and she is in all of my dreams, always just a little bit out of reach. I will only give up on her when we reach the end, whatever that is, but not until then, Jacks, not until it is over. Do you understand me?' He gripped her wrists a little too tightly.

She nodded. Yes, she understood.

The Unbearable Truth

It had been nearly five months since Gemma's disappearance. For Jackie and Neil it felt simultaneously like a lifetime and a matter of weeks.

Stacey leant around the fridge door. 'We haven't got any milk or butter, or juice or bread.'

She looked across the kitchen at her parents, who seemed fixated by the kettle. Her mum was wearing sweat pants that she had bought when she was fat; they now hung off her tiny frame. Her dad still had his pyjama top on under his jumper. They reminded her of zombies.

'I'll pop out later, Stacey.' Neil smiled. It was his new smile, the one where his mouth flicked up but his eyes forgot to crinkle.

The phone made them all jump. As usual there was a split second when they all looked at each other. Was this it? The call they had been waiting for? The call they prayed would never come? The call they expected and dreaded in equal measure? This expectant dread usually lasted for a second or two, until the caller was revealed as a family member or someone selling something they didn't want and couldn't afford.

Neil pulled the phone from its cradle and nodded into the receiver. His wife and daughter watched as his legs seemed to buckle under him and he swayed.

'What, Neil? What is it?' Jackie started to question him

while he was still listening to the words on the other end of the phone.

He held the mouthpiece against his chest as the strength finally left his legs. He slid down the kitchen wall until he was huddled in the corner.

'That was Gavin.'

'What? What did he say?' Jackie twisted her T-shirt against her throat.

'They've got her. She's at the police station. They've got her.'

Jackie lurched forward and fell onto her husband. 'Oh my God! Oh, Neil! Oh my God! I don't believe it. I'd nearly given up, I had! Oh my God. Let's go, let's go! Come on!'

She moved quicker than he had seen her move in months as she gathered up the van keys and raced out of the front door.

'Come on!' she shouted back up the hallway.

Stacey and Neil followed her outside and into the sunshine.

'I've already washed and changed her bed linen; I did that last week, that's weird, isn't it? As if I knew, cos I haven't done it for weeks! Her pyjamas are all fresh as well. I expect she'll want a good rest, won't she? We'll get her tucked up.' Jackie babbled through her tears with excitement and nerves.

Neil wasn't sure how to play it. He had tried not to plan for this moment, hadn't wanted to tempt fate. 'We'll have to see how she is, Jacks, take it slow.'

'Take it slow? How much slower can we take it? We've been waiting for nearly six months!' She clapped her hands together.

'I know, love, but you need to calm down a bit. We don't know what she's been through or how she is.'

'Don't!' Jackie held her hand up. She couldn't bear to think of those details, not yet. First she wanted to get her home and then they would deal with what they had to deal with.

'I'll have to stop off on the way home and get some food in.

I'll get her some soup and apple juice, all her favourite little bits and pieces.'

'God, there's been none of my favourite food in for months and Gemma appears and you are already getting her special treats in – it's not fair!' Stacey piped up from the back seat.

Neil and Jackie looked at each other and laughed. It was the first time they had laughed in a very, very long time. It felt good. He reached across and squeezed his wife's sculpted thigh beneath his fingertips.

Detective Sergeant Gavin Edwards and Detective Constable Melanie Vincent stood side by side in the foyer of Romford police station, waiting for the Peters family.

Jackie rushed through the main door, speaking as she entered. 'Where is she?'

Neil wasn't far behind her. He grasped Gavin's hand in a handshake. 'Thank you. Thanks, Gavin, for everything.' He beamed. 'Where is she?'

'Come this way, guys.' Melanie walked ahead and stopped at a bank of chairs set along the wall of a corridor. 'You can wait here, Stacey, okay?'

Stacey shrugged and sat in the middle chair, crossing her outstretched legs at the ankle. She pulled her phone from the pocket of her hoodie and ignored the rest of the party as they sidled past and into an empty interview room.

Jackie and Neil sat on the two chairs opposite the police officers. Over the last few months the line between law enforcers and friends had become smudged.

'I'm so excited! I can't believe it. Where is she?' Jackie fidgeted in her seat, grinning.

The two officers had never seen Jackie so animated.

'I need you to calm down a bit, Jackie.' Gavin gave a brief smile.

'You're the second person to say that to me!' Jackie nudged her husband.

Gavin looked at Melanie, nodding slightly, handing her the reins.

Melanie sat in the chair on the other side of the table. She linked her fingers and placed them in front of her, looking more formal than she ever had in their little lounge in Ennerdale Close.

'We have all worked hard, waiting for this day, Jackie, you know that.'

Jackie nodded, still beaming. 'Yes, and we are so grateful, Mel, really grateful!'

'We have found Gemma and she appears unharmed.'

'That's wonderful! Thank you, thank you so much,' Jackie interjected. Neil was starting to ask himself the obvious question. *If she's unharmed, then where has she been and who with?*

'We found her living in a flat in Paddington, with three other occupants. One of them is a man called Vassili Salenko; is that a name you know?'

They both shook their heads.

'The flat was raided on an unrelated matter and we found Gemma, going by the name of Jemima.'

'He must have taken her, that Vladimir or whatever his name is,' Jackie jumped in. Her smile had faded. Her chest heaved.

'Here's the thing,' Gavin cut in, his words coming slowly. 'I have spoken to Gemma at length and she is adamant that she went with him of her own accord.'

'What? Why? I don't understand.' Jackie shook her head as her eyes squinted in confusion.

'We're still not sure.' Gavin's tone was restrained.

'He's just making her say that! She's a schoolgirl, for God's sake!' Neil couldn't hide the edge of aggression in his voice.

'Possibly.' Gavin tried to throw the man a rope.

'You know what.' Neil stood and raised his palms. 'It doesn't really matter right now, who did what and who went where, we are just bloody glad to have her back. So if we can get her home, let her have a bit of a rest and then we've got all the time in the world to sort out what happened. You can talk to her to your heart's content, but we just want to get her back.'

'I'm afraid it's not that straightforward, Neil.'

'What d'you mean, not that straightforward? Course it is! Now, if you could please just let us have our daughter back!'

'She doesn't want to see you.' Gavin looked away, having delivered the cruellest blow.

'Don't be silly, Gavin, of course she does!' Jackie spoke to him as if he were a child.

Melanie stepped in. 'I'm sorry, Jackie, but she doesn't.'

Neil sank back down into the chair and both sat in silence, trying to digest the information.

Jackie spoke to her lap. 'He's brainwashed her or something. Why wouldn't she want to come home?'

Melanie swallowed the memory of her interview with Gemma. *'You have put them through hell, Gemma. They are nice people, would it hurt to give them one quick telephone call?'*

'Can I just see her, please, Mel? Please.'

Melanie hated the way Jackie was almost begging. 'She's not actually here, she's at Paddington Green, but they can only hold her for so long.'

Jackie placed her head in her hands and sobbed. 'I don't understand. I don't understand any of it.'

Neil rubbed her back as he tried to order his own thoughts.

★

They collected Stacey and the three of them made their way towards the van.

'Neil?' Gavin called from the top of the steps.

Neil walked back up to talk to him.

'This breaks just about every rule and if you tell anyone, anyone at all, I'll be in serious shit, but here is a mobile number for Gemma.'

Neil took the scrap of paper and pushed it into his jeans pocket. 'Thank you. Is it as bad as it sounds, Gavin?'

He looked into Neil's eyes. 'Salenko is a nasty piece of work.'

'How the hell has my Gemma got mixed up with someone like that?' Neil asked, not expecting a reply.

He walked back to the van feeling exhausted and beaten. They drove home in silence, not bothering to stop and pick up food.

Jackie would not have believed that it was possible to sink any deeper into despair, but this was a whole other level of sadness and confusion. She was gripped by a numbness that left her feeling blind and deaf, unable to see, hear or communicate with the outside world. She climbed the stairs and lay on top of the freshly laundered duvet on Gemma's bed, unable to cry, unable to sleep.

Neil flicked on the lamp and closed the front door behind him. He walked to the top of the close and turned left on the main road, out of earshot and out of sight. He held the scrap of paper in his palm and punched the digits into his keypad. He held the phone to his face and listened and then a mere couple of seconds later, there it was, sweet music that he had imagined he might never hear again. His little girl's voice.

'Heeello?' She sounded cheery, playful.

The tears that clogged his nose and throat made speech almost impossible.

'Hello?' she repeated.

Neil pushed the phone into the side of his face, trying to get as close to her as possible. 'Gemma?'

'Who's this?'

He hesitated, coughed. 'It's me, it's Dad.'

He expected her to hang up. He waited. The silence connected them, a thin sinew from one silent vocal cord to the other, stretching approximately twenty miles across the dark.

He spoke slowly, with caution, as if bent low with hand outstretched, trying to lure a mistrustful pet. 'Gemma, just listen, love. I'm not going to tell you what to do, but I just want to know that you are safe. I want to know that you are happy.'

'I am,' she whispered. It reminded him of when she was small and would whisper in the dark across the hallway, with bedroom doors open:

'I'm scared, Daddy.'

'No need, my little love, nothing to be scared of. It's just the dark and Mummy and I are right here, we're always right here.'

'I don't understand what's happened, I thought we were happy.' His tears ran down his face.

He could hear her breathing.

'You were happy, Dad, you and Mum, but not me.'

'I only ever wanted what was best for you, we both did. We love you so very much.' It was becoming harder and harder for him to speak with clarity. 'Could you give us another chance? Show us how to make you happy, because that's all we want.' It was his parting shot, to put her in control whilst trying to get her home.

'Well then, you should be pleased, because I am happy, Dad.'

There was the smallest of clicks and then, just like that, she was gone.

A New Life

Alyssa was thin, her ribs poked against her navy vest. And she was shorter than the platform-heeled sandals peeping out from beneath her tight jeans led you to believe. She swished her white-blonde hair over her bony, bare shoulder and held the smouldering cigarette aloft with her index and middle fingers; a slender white stick perched between two red talons. The long thumbnail of the same hand was hooked under her front tooth. Her kohl-rimmed eyes were narrowed against the yellow smoke that curled in front of her face. The bare inside of her arm revealed a tiny peppering of angry blue bruises. Gemma had to concentrate on the words; her English was far from perfect.

'The bathroom.' Alyssa waited in the open doorway and indicated with her cigarette. Her speech was heavily accented, her nonchalance doing nothing to help her enunciation. Gemma guessed correctly that she was from Eastern Europe and wondered if she and Vassili had arrived there together. Maybe they were related.

She cast her eyes over the cramped room, maybe six foot by eight in size. The lemon-coloured plastic bath displayed residual grime in various lines. A shampoo bottle of no recognisable brand was tipped upside down and rested in a well on the bath top intended for soap; the owner was clearly trying to eke out one final blob, big enough to work into a lather.

A large metal-framed frosted-glass window was covered with a dirty orange and green striped towel. The frame was rusted: Gemma doubted it had been opened in a very long time. The loo was filthy; months of neglect had left it encrusted with every variety of human waste. The whole room stank of urine and damp, not the most pleasant combination. Gemma tried to breathe only through her mouth.

The floor was covered in pale green lino, which seemed to highlight the splats of blood and streaks of wee that surrounded the bowl. Dark pubic hair had gathered in little nests that lurked in every corner and behind every pipe. It was disgusting. A white plastic-coated wire shelving unit was cluttered with matted combs, splayed make-up brushes, bottles of peroxide, tubes of cream, boxes of condoms, three disposable razors and tampons in various stages of wrap. She felt embarrassed to bear witness to such intimate items. There was a round mirror above the sink, whose hot tap ran cold and dripped constantly.

Gemma tried to picture having a bath in this room; she shuddered involuntarily, blinking away the image of the family bathroom at home, with its clean white sink and fluffy towels. She followed Alyssa as she sashayed down the corridor at a leisurely pace.

Gemma felt a mixture of excitement and fear. This was it, her new, grown-up, pressure-free life. The moment she had pulled her sweatshirt over her head and laced up her high-tops after the play, she had known that the time was right. Fingering the folded piece of paper in her jeans pocket, which had nothing more than an address and a telephone number scrawled in biro, her adventure had begun. He had said that it would be her 'get out of jail free card'. He was right, and now was the time to use it.

Vassili was where he said he would be, at the back of the

precinct, in a red car. Her stomach had flipped as she climbed into the passenger seat.

'You can always rely on me, Jemima. I am your friend now.'

She smiled. He still couldn't get her name right, but that didn't matter. Jemima, Gemma, whatever, she was free.

She swallowed the tears that threatened as his car crawled past her parents' house.

He patted her thigh. 'Don't cry, Jemima. I said I would look after you. I can find you work and you shall live with me and the other girls. We are a happy home, we look after each other.' He ran his thumb over her cheek. 'A very pretty girl like you, you will always find work. Don't look so sad. You want a cigarette?'

She nodded, took one from the packet he held out to her and sparked the flint.

'Have you told anyone?'

She shook her head, recalling how she and Vassili had met. She had been hovering on the pavement outside the station, her face tear-streaked, and he had been strolling in the sunshine, in his mirrored shades and leather bomber jacket.

'No, I haven't told anyone.' She pictured Victoria and then Luke. It amazed her how easily she could discard her friend and her lover, both of whom had meant the world to her. Especially Luke, who had taken her body and broken her heart.

'Here is your room.' Alyssa drew her into the present with her slow drawl.

After the bathroom, Gemma's expectations were not high and she was proved right. She pushed open the door, which she noticed had a big hole kicked into the bottom of it, the giveaway being the large imprint of a boot that had misjudged one of its blows. Smudges of polish and lines of black rubber indicated a man's kick. Gemma hoped he would not be coming back any time soon, whoever he was.

The first thing she noticed upon entering was how dark the room was, despite it being early afternoon. A thick woollen blanket covered in indeterminate stains hung over the window. It had been tacked up with rusted nails that had been driven through the fabric and into the plaster.

'Laurel has only just gone two days ago and so now room is free, for you. If you want it. Vassili has lots of little girlfriends, no pressure.'

The slope of the girl's shoulder against the doorframe and the way her eyes closed as she delivered the words told Gemma that Alyssa couldn't care less if she took the room or not. She half expected her to add, *'If not you, then someone else.'*

'Where is Laurel now?'

'She is dying.'

Gemma could not hide her shock; her hand flew up to cover her mouth. 'She is dying! Oh my God, that's terrible. Where is she? Why's she dying?'

Alyssa threw her head back and laughed, loud and open-mouthed, snorting through her nose, pausing only to regain composure. Her laugh quickly turned into a cough, which she allayed by taking a deep drag on her dwindling cigarette.

'Oh my God! No... No, I'm sorry, it is my bad English. She is not dying.'

Gemma exhaled with visible relief.

The girl continued. 'Laurel is not dying. She is dead.'

'Dead?'

'Dead. Yes.' Alyssa nodded and fished in her pocket for another cigarette.

'How did she die?' Almost as soon as the enquiry had left Gemma's mouth she regretted it, knowing that she did not want to hear how Laurel had met her end.

'She is killed by boyfriend, he is strangling her. It was a

money thing, you know.' Alyssa shrugged as though it was of little consequence.

Gemma stared at Alyssa. No, she didn't know. She was unable to hide her horrified expression as she tried to picture the faceless Laurel's last moments and replayed the nonchalant tone with which the information had been given.

Alyssa registered Gemma's reaction. 'But don't worry, it was not in this bed.'

She pointed to a soiled double mattress that lay bare on the floor. Gemma was once again relieved but also bemused.

'It was over there in the corner.' The girl finished her sentence as she jerked her cigarette towards the edge of the room.

Gemma swallowed the naked fear that leapt in her throat.

Turn Off the Lamp

Neil hated lying to his wife but knew that he was better off handling things alone; she was too fragile to deal with any more disappointment right now. He spent hours trawling the streets of Paddington, driving up and down the main thoroughfares and snaking along cut-throughs, circling housing estates and loitering on any quiet corner. And then one day, six weeks after being called in by Gavin and Melanie, he spotted her.

He had pulled up at a crossing and was thinking that it might be time to end his covert search for the day, when she emerged from a crowd and stepped off the kerb, walking across in front of him. She didn't say thank you as they had taught her, didn't wave her hand in recognition, but instead almost trotted over the black-and-white stripes. It took all his strength not to jump out of the van, shove her in the back and haul her home against her will, but he knew that if he did that, she would only leave again. He needed her to want to come home, it was the only way it would work. He also figured, correctly, that if he called her again, she would ditch the phone and he would lose the only means he had of contacting her, although the temptation to call the number that was indelibly etched in his brain was torturous.

He sat and stared as she walked down the opposite side of the road, his gaze following his daughter as she blended with the crowd. She looked taller and thinner than he remembered and was wearing clothes he had never seen before: high sandals and a short red leather jacket. He was only aware that he should be moving when the driver in the car behind beeped at him. Pulling away, he crawled as slowly as he was able, indicating left as if he was going to park and allowing the irate procession of vehicles behind him to overtake. He managed to stay a couple of feet behind Gemma's field of vision, when she suddenly stopped at a narrow wooden door between a fried chicken shop and a launderette. He watched as she pulled out a key and entered the building. Neil made a note of the address and, fighting every instinct in his body, he drove away, leaving his little girl in the squalid building with a man about whom he knew two things: his name was Vassili and he was a nasty piece of work.

Gemma threw the keys down on the kitchen table and fell into one of the chairs. Vassili closed the newspaper, pulled his cigarettes from his shirt, lit one and inhaled deeply.

'Jemima, we need to sort what will happen now for you.'

She shrugged. 'What do you mean?'

He leant forward and tucked her hair behind her ear. 'You know what I mean. What we spoke of before: you earning money for us, like Alyssa and Stasia. It can't be that you live here free, no one lives here free.'

Gemma tucked her arms around her trunk. 'But it's different. You love me and you don't love them.'

Vassili laughed. 'Yes, yes, that is true. But how can we run away together and live by the sea if we don't have money?'

She shrugged again. 'I could get a different job!'

He shook his head. 'You can't get a different job because we have to hide you from your parents and if you get a different job, I would never see you and that would make me so sad.' He turned the corners of his mouth down and pushed out his bottom lip.

'I don't know if I can do it, Vas.' She looked at the window, the brick wall covered in graffiti opposite made for a depressing view. Still, it wouldn't be forever, not much longer until they left London and went to the coast.

'You said you would do anything to make me happy, anything for us.'

She nodded.

'It would be so sad if we finished and you had to leave the house just because you would not commit to our love and to making me happy. There are bad people out there, Jemima, and I hate to think of you not being safe.'

She considered this and swallowed the swell of panic that rose in her chest. She had nowhere else to go.

'I don't want us to finish.' Her voice was small. 'I really love you.'

'Well, I don't want us to finish either. I love you too. It would make me so happy if you did this one thing. You shouldn't think about it so much, it is only doing what you and I do, but without the love. That should make it easy, no?'

'I'm not sure. I do want you to be happy and I do want us to be together.'

'Then it's easy, Jemima. You work for me and we save and then we go forever!'

'To our house by the sea?'

'To our house by the sea. Where we can sit in the garden and make barbeque and dance under the stars.' He gripped her hand.

She smiled. It sounded lovely.

★

Neil managed to stay away for two days. On the third, he finished his rounds and pulled up on the edge of the road around the corner from the chicken shop. He hadn't slept for two nights, mulling over the options, trying to decide what to do next. He had come up with a plan. He figured that if he could just get her to come home, they could work on her, persuade her and make it so comfortable that she wouldn't ever want to be anywhere else. He would tell her about the caravan holiday that they could book and the iPod they would buy her. She could leave school; do whatever. Nothing mattered more than getting her home and keeping her safe.

Gemma applied her make-up in the bathroom mirror. Alyssa watched and smiled, nodding her approval as Gemma painted her lips a glossy red.

'You look beautiful!'

Gemma smiled, embarrassed. 'Really?'

'Yes, really. And such a great little figure. This will be easy for you, Jemima.'

Gemma pulled at the short denim skirt that kept riding up and tried to make the gap between the over-the-knee boots and the skirt smaller. She swigged at the little glass of vodka that Alyssa had poured her; it certainly helped soothe her nerves and made the whole event feel like a bit of an adventure.

Neil sent a text to Gemma's mobile.

I am around the corner, Gemma, on the edge of Praed Street and Junction Place. I'm in the van and would dearly love to talk to you, Gem. If you don't want to come home, that's fine, but this is our chance to wipe the slate clean and start over. You would make Mum and me the happiest people on the planet. We love you and we miss you and nothing else really matters. Please, Gemma, come to the van. I shall wait for you. Dad x

Gemma stepped from the bathroom.

Vassili stood in the corridor and whistled. 'Wow! Jemima, you look so hot! Really hot!'

She looked at Alyssa, embarrassed by her boyfriend's attentions.

'Do I?' She wasn't sure.

'Ay ay ay, you are perfect and you shall earn so much money that it will only be matter of time.' He winked at her.

They had agreed not to tell Alyssa of their plans to leave London and go to the seaside. She felt her cheeks flush. Alyssa had talked her through the ropes; there was a long list of dos and don'ts. It was just business, a job. The secret was not to think about it too much.

Alyssa slipped a little white oval into her palm. 'Take this, Jemima, it will make it easier for you.'

Gemma popped the tablet on her tongue and washed it down with the last of the vodka. She was all set. Climbing down the stairs in her high heels, she felt invincible and sexy. This was life. This was living.

Vassili called from the top landing. 'I'll be waiting for you, hot chick!'

She waved up at him through the stairwell. She sauntered out of the front door and strolled along Praed Street, enjoying the looks that she got from every pair of male eyes and feeling a swell of excitement in her stomach that she had never experienced before. She crossed over and her phone buzzed in her bag.

There was a text from Vas: *Tonight, you are so beautiful.*

She smiled. Tonight she felt beautiful.

There was another text. She opened it and the breath caught in her throat. It was from her dad and he was close. Gemma looked up. There were two white vans in the road, parked one in front of the other, and a gap of three yards between them.

Gemma headed towards them and as she got closer she could make out the 'Delivery Devils' logo on the back door. Walking slowly, she tried to decide what to do for the best. It was confusing, her head swam. She loved Vassili and wanted the life he promised her, a grown-up life by the seaside. But going home to Ennerdale Close where there would be clean sheets, her little sister and hot water on demand, it would be so cosy. The memory of school life pawed behind her eyes, when all she'd had to worry about was writing essays and meeting her friends.

Gemma approached the vehicles and could make out the shape of her dad's head in the driver's seat. Her heart lurched and her stomach flipped. *Daddy...* She smiled.

Suddenly the passenger door of the first van opened and the driver leant across. 'You working, love?'

The man was in his mid-thirties, not badly dressed. He was holding a roll of bank notes.

Gemma was rendered immobile, unsure which path to take: back to safety and boredom or onwards on her adventure with the man she loved, a man who loved her.

'I said, are you working, love?'

Neil indicated and steered the van into the driveway. He put his key in the lock and watched as Jackie twisted her body towards the sound.

'Any news?' she asked in her usual strained yet hopeful tone.

Neil stood for a second in the doorway, casting his eyes around the room as if it was strange to him. He walked past her and reached down towards the lamp on its little table by the side of the sofa.

'What are you doing?' Jackie's voice was accusatory, incredulous.

'I'm turning off the lamp!'

'No you are not! You can't, you know how she feels about the dark, we need to keep it on just in—'

He shook his head, as his finger and thumb clicked against the little black bar. 'No, no we don't, not anymore.' He placed his finger over her lips. 'She's not coming home. She's never coming home, Jacks.'

Neil knew that he would take the image to his grave; his little girl climbing into the seat of the van behind him, looking like any other tart. A part of him had died.

He fell onto the sofa, too defeated to cry. Jackie wrapped him in her arms. He buried his head in her lap, gripping her clothes, clinging on for all he was worth, a man silently drowning in his sorrow. Jackie stroked the hair away from his forehead.

She spoke softly and slowly into the darkness that enveloped them.

'I wonder what I did wrong, y'know. I think about it all the time. I try and think about what I should have done differently, but the thing is, if you don't know that you are doing anything wrong, then you just keep doing it, don't you? I thought it was all about making her comfy, making her feel special, but I don't know anything any more. I keep thinking, Neil, about that night. All those people clapping and going crazy. I never knew I could be so proud. It was incredible, wasn't it?'

Neil sniffed and raised his head. 'It was, Jacks. She was unbelievable.'

Jackie smiled. 'Yes she was, unbelievable.'

The two sat in the dark, enjoying a closeness that had been missing for some time. They must have dozed off eventually and were woken by a small voice that cracked the darkness.

'Why... why are you sitting in the dark?'

Jackie gasped as a sob leapt from her throat. She reached out and clicked on the lamp and there she was, her little girl, as if magicked from the night, looking thin and bone weary, haunted and lost, as tears streaked her face, but home. Home where she belonged.

Home where she belonged.

Imogen's
Baby

This story is dedicated to Amy, whose bravery, grit, determination and inner light have inspired Imogen's story. I wish you nothing but joy for your future. Some people you meet, stay with you, leave an impression and teach you things. You are one such person, Amy Gilbert.

I don't remember one defining moment when I held a child or heard one cry and felt my womb pulse with longing, nothing like that. It's just always been there, that desire to become a mum. Like other aspects of my life that have always been there – proud of being a Scot, hating cheese, or wanting to live in a noisy community, a bustling street; I always have, for as long as I can remember. I love the signs of life, the constant squall and bustle of activity and the way it makes me feel, as if I'm connected to a bigger world, to people. That's very important to me.

So: yes, I think there has always been that need. I was like lots of other little girls – when not engaging in rough and tumble, I'd tenderly coo to my dolly and rock her to sleep. Her name was Baby Jean and I'd make up her crib and place her gently inside, tiptoeing out of the room so as not to wake her. Yep, I was just like every other little girl, I dreamt of becoming a mummy. Not that my mum, Isla, ever encouraged me in any way, not like some mums who buy you a pinny and start your training with mini-Hoovers and tiny saucepans, telling you to cook tea for your imaginary husband who is out at work. God, that's such an outdated mode, but nonetheless, I know some of my own friends who do this with their toddler daughters even now. But with or without my mum's encouragement, it was as if there was something hard-wired into my DNA, an in-built need. I never considered becoming a parent might not be an option for me, ever. Even though my own birth was... let's say tricky, and the tales from that fateful day have been bandied about more than a dozen times. I know all the gory details!

Despite this, I have always been willing to do whatever it takes to fulfil my dream, and why not? I don't think being single should be a barrier, not in this day and age when so many marriages end in divorce and couples who start off with the best intentions can still end up as single parents. What does it matter, so long as that child is loved and cared for? More and more people are choosing not to marry and that's fine too. For me, the most important relationship is the one I will have with my child. I'll keep him or her safe. I'll love my child unconditionally and I will help it to become the best citizen of the planet that it can possibly be. What is it they say? You don't know until you try. *Well, I am trying, I'm trying very hard and I'm not going to give up without a fight. I will keep on until all options have been exhausted, because that's me, Imogen. I'm a girl who fought for survival on her first day on the earth, and sometimes, more so recently in fact, it feels like I have been fighting every day since. That's it really.*

One

May 1989

Isla lay on her side, staring into the semi-darkness of the small room. She pulled the sheet up over her shoulder and wriggled her head against the pillow, trying to get comfortable. The mattress was too hard and the regular squeak of shoes pacing the linoleum floor outside, along with the beeps and bells of machinery in the adjoining rooms, meant her sleep had been disturbed. Her throat was sore and her eyes ached from all the crying. She was exhausted by it and sick of it, this never-ending well of tears. She screwed her eyes shut, trying to escape into the oblivion of sleep. It was, as ever, elusive.

It had been another bad night; along with her physical discomforts, nightmares and jumbled thoughts, which wrenched her from her sleep, she pictured her mum Mary's face when she'd heard the sad news, a couple of weeks back. She had been sorry, yes, but her words of comfort were tinged with a tiny glint of *I told you so*, thrown in for good measure. It was this sliver of self-justification, mirroring the night Isla had broken the news of her pregnancy, when the whole of Pilton must have covered their ears at her mum's yelling, that was more than she could bear.

Every time she thought about her little girl, the tears sprang anew; this seemed to be the instant reaction whenever she considered her daughter's future.

Upon discovering her pregnancy, and after the initial stages of disbelief and shock, Isla had dreamt of all the things they would do together; this baby and she would get their own place, they'd enjoy holidays by the sea, walks in the park, the first school play and the creation of clumsy, colourful paintings to adorn the kitchen walls... It was these vivid images of herself with a rosy-cheeked cherub on her lap that had given Isla the courage to tell her mum and dad, admitting in the process that not only had she and Duncan McGuire, the boy from two doors down, had sex, but they had also been a little lax about contraception.

She had won her parents over by painting them similar pictures of the future, ones that involved them and their grandchild: ripping open gifts on Christmas Day, playing in the snow on their trips up to the Cairngorms, or listening to the tiny child recite their lines in the first school assembly they attended. How lovely would it be to have a grandchild, a baby, while their own youngest was only ten? And who knew? It might be a little girl to give a bit of balance to a family dominated by rowdy boys, four children in all, of whom Isla was the eldest child and the only girl.

She bit her lip, tears threatening again. It was hard for her to picture any of these things now. Instead, if she looked towards the future, all she could see was a deep, dark hole into which all her hopes and dreams had tumbled. She worried that Duncan would no longer feel the same, fearing that their plans and all the promises he had made on cold, foggy nights would disappear down the deep, dark hole too. How long would he stick around? Of one thing she was sure, she didn't want him to be with her for any reason other than love. The idea of him feeling tied to her through duty was more than she could bear. If that were the case, she would rather be alone. The future felt bleak and, if she was honest, she didn't know if she had the strength to cope. It wasn't fair.

'Let's let the day in, shall we?' The chubby nurse bustled into the room and marched over to the window. She then twisted the rod that split the venetian blinds; sending a fractured white light across the cold, blue flooring. She cracked the window open just enough to let the buzz of traffic, creeping along the Crewe Road South, filter into the room.

Isla sat up in the bed and blinked. She had been thinking about their annual family holiday. Along with cousins, aunts and any neighbours who fancied the jaunt, the high-spirited group set off in a convoy of cars and vans with enough camping equipment to house an army. Rain or shine, for one week of the summer they played footie, built fires, barbecued fish and let marshmallows blacken over the coals as they dangled from twigs, while they all giggled at nothing in particular and berated their daddy en masse for the post-supper farts that he denied.

She was imagining herself swimming in the loch; something she'd never done in real life, preferring instead to dangle her feet in the water from a dock, to feel the warmth of the sun on her skin as it tried in vain to join up her numerous freckles. Her parents, Mary and Jim, and brothers would heckle from the depths, as they laughed and trod water with droplets shining like diamonds on their long soft lashes and plastering their strawberry-blonde hair to their pale scalps: *Come in, ya big dafty! Isla, come on, it's lovely!* they'd call. But there she stayed, rooted to the spot, too afraid of the sea monsters and kelpies that she was convinced lurked beneath the dappled surface.

One of the younger boys, Euan or Kurt, would then call her name: 'Isla! Help, Isla! It's got me!' before disappearing suddenly under the water, as if grabbed by the feet, only to break the surface seconds later, spluttering, laughing and high-fiving whoever was in striking distance. 'Oh, leave ma wee girl alone!' Mary would intervene, winking at her daughter and turning to laugh with her sons. What had her gran called it? *Running with the fox and chasing with the hounds.* Isla's mum had it down to a fine art. She went through life neither offending nor pleasing to any great degree.

In her daydreams, Isla had been confident, jumping with arms aloft into the cool loch, enjoying the feeling as she dived into a different world, pulling through the water with deft strokes that motored her along. She then lay on her back, staring at the sky, her body straight and her feet kicking, as her long, pale arms worked overhead, propelling her into the centre of the loch, which in this ethereal world held no terrors for her.

She wished she could be as fearless in real life. Wished she wasn't so afraid. How she would love to dive in! Isla had thought that becoming a mum might have given her courage and the confidence to strike out. That idea now seemed laughable.

'Did you get much sleep?' The nurse pulled the top blanket over the bed, making it taut, before tucking it around Isla's legs.

'A little bit,' she whispered, rubbing at her pale eyelids that felt full of grit, unwilling to admit that she had cried into her pillow until the early hours, struggling to breathe through the waves of fear that battered her senses and flooded her mind. *I can't do this... I can't... I don't know how I'll cope. My mum was right, I can't do this...*

Forgetting she was still recovering from the emergency caesarean, she pulled her knees up to her chest, planting her feet on the mattress, before wincing and carefully sliding them flat against the white sheet.

'Shit,' she murmured, through a mouth contorted by the sudden flash of pain.

'You're going to have to be careful. It's those little movements, small things, that can catch you unawares.' The nurse filled the plastic beaker with water from the tap and placed it on the nightstand.

Isla nodded. That's the story of my life, small things catching me unawares...

'Do you need anything for pain right now?' The nurse spoke louder than Isla was comfortable with. Did she not know how stressful it was to have the baby wake and start crying? Or how long it took to get her off to sleep again? Isla's eyes darted towards the plastic bassinet by the side of her bed. Thankfully, the baby didn't stir. She shook her head; she wasn't in pain, not physically, not any more. Her surgery had dulled to an inconvenience; gone was the sharp tug of trying to stand tall and the nervous hesitation when she had to pee. It was only these small, ill-considered movements that took her breath away.

'No, I'm fine,' she mouthed, letting her eyes dart towards the baby.

'Oh, don't you worry about her waking!' the nurse laughed. 'Have you ever listened to what goes on inside a stomach? It's a proper racket! That gorgeous little miss has been surrounded by noise – burps, shouts, hiccups and your very loud heartbeat – for the last nine months! My dulcet tones aren't going to disturb her.' She chuckled. 'In fact, in my experience, they quite like a bit of background noise. My eldest used to nod off to the sound of the Hoover. Which is funny, as he's sixteen now and I don't think he even knows what it looks like!'

But that's the problem: she wasn't surrounded by noise for nine months. She was born too soon, at just a little over twenty-three weeks, and only able to come home today, finally.

Isla smiled, knowing the woman was trying to be nice.

'Are you all set then? It's a big day for you.' Again, the nurse boomed.

'I think so.' She nodded, thankful once more for all the medical team had done for her and her new baby girl, unable to forget the hurried surgery, the feeling of panic in the air, the sight of her tiny baby lifted lifeless and floppy from her body, as machines beeped loudly and alarms sounded and voices were raised with an edge of adrenalin-fuelled tension to them that no years of practice could erase.

'She's a pretty little thing,' the nurse cooed.

'Yup, takes after her mum!' Isla laughed.

'Then she'll do just fine.'

Isla looked around, knowing that this would be the last morning she would spend within the confines of this little space, and weirdly, as desperate as she was to get home, back to her mum's, she was also sick with nerves about having to leave its security, where an expert lurked around every corner.

'It's odd, isn't it, that this room is so full of significance for me? These four walls, this bed... the place where my daughter was born, and yet there'll be another baby born here tomorrow, or even later today, and for those few hours it will be their special place.'

'That's kind of how it works, a bit of a production line.' The nurse coughed, as if remembering that this woman was a customer of sorts. 'I hope, of course, that it never felt like a production line. I hope that you've had a good experience here.'

Isla nodded. She had.

'It'll be okay, you know.' The nurse smiled at her reassuringly.

Isla nodded again. *Will it?* She wished she could be so certain. A thought popped into her head, an idea she had had about her child becoming successful and travelling around Europe, visiting all the cities that Isla herself had yet to make it to, and she did so by car, driving around in an open-topped Beetle... but there'd be no driving, not for her little girl. Isla closed her eyes and sank back on the pillow, finally feeling the pull of sleep. She decided to nap when the nurse had finished her pottering.

As if on cue, the baby let out a tiny mewling noise, calling from her crib. Isla instinctively pulled back the covers and swung her legs gently around in an arc, as she had been instructed. Lifting her daughter from the crib, she cradled her in one crooked arm. 'Morning, little one. Morning, darlin',' she cooed.

'Have you named her yet?' the nurse asked, curious.

'Imogen. She's called Imogen.'

'Well, that's a lovely name and one that'll carry her through life. You know, she can be anything she wants with a name like that.'

Isla stared at the woman, swallowing the thought that her name wouldn't be the thing that held Imogen back.

'Is there anything you want to ask me? I know you have had plenty of instruction and you're a dab hand at the bathing, nappies, feeding and whatnot, plus you've the numbers of your designated Health Visitor and they are on hand twenty-four, seven.'

'Yes.' Isla nodded. She had plenty of names, plenty of numbers, but she knew that wouldn't help in the early hours when her mind ran riot and she felt like crumbling.

'Is there anything that is worrying you right now?' The nurse sat on the chair next to the bed and folded her hands on her lap, like a friend settling down for a cuppa.

Isla placed her little finger in her daughter's mouth; her bottle would be along any minute. 'I was thinking about something last night before I fell asleep.'

'Uh-huh?' The nurse leant forward.

'How...'

'How what, hen?' she prompted.

'How will she know I'm her mum? How... How will she know it's me if... if she doesn't know what I look like? If she can never see me?' Isla swallowed the tears that threatened again and focused on her daughter's closed lids where fully functioning eyes would have been had she stayed nestled inside the noisy womb for just a little bit longer.

The nurse gave a small laugh as the door behind them creaked open. She placed her finger over her lips. 'Ssssshhh...' she whispered, indicating to the person hovering in the doorway to wait, before turning back to Isla on the bed and instructing: 'Close your eyes. Tight.'

She did as she was told.

'Who just arrived?'

'What?' Isla was confused.

'Come on, without looking and without our guest making a sound' – the nurse spoke in the direction of the door, turning it into an instruction – 'who is it standing in the doorway?'

Isla cocked her head, concentrated and smiled, inhaling the scent that had arrived with the visitor. 'It's... It's my boyfriend. It's Duncan.'

'How do you know?' the nurse whispered, looking from the man in the doorway back to her patient.

Isla beamed. 'I... I can feel it's him. I can feel him...'

'Exactly,' the nurse whispered as she tiptoed from the room.

★

Duncan stepped forward and rested his large hand on Isla's shoulder. She placed her cheek against the back of it and opened her eyes, something her wee girl would never be able to do.

'Didn't know if you'd be coming in.' She smiled.

Duncan's voice was gruff with emotion. 'Of course! I love you, Isla, and I love our daughter – and who knows what's gonna happen? Not you, not me, but that's got to be the best start, right?'

Two

May 1992

'Have you got any matches, Dunc?'
'My arse your face?' Duncan laughed into his beer and elbowed his mate Harry in the ribs.

'Charming! I cannot imagine talking in front of my mother-in-law like that!' Isla's mum, Mary, tutted and then winked at him, to show she got the joke, all was well.

'And anyways, I'm not your son-in-law, not officially, though not for lack of asking! I think she's trying me out, to see if I'm good enough for weddin'. We are still actually living in sin, in case you hadn't noticed,' Duncan announced loudly, playing to the crowd of one, as Harry felt his face colour.

'Oh, I have noticed, Duncan McGuire, and for the love of god, I don't need reminding!' Mary patted her bleached hair and went to rifle in the kitchen drawer; she was in need of a box of matches to light the candles on her granddaughter's Princess Belle birthday cake.

'Try Euan. He smokes, you know, in secret!' Duncan shouted after her. His mate snorted into his pint and sprayed the living-room carpet with the sticky foam. They might have been old enough to drink and for one of them to be a dad, but they were still teenage boys at heart when a rude joke and the chance to make the other snort laughter into their beer was the mark of a good time.

'Does he indeed?' Mary narrowed her eyes towards the garden where her fourteen-year-old son stood by the edge of the bouncy castle, his job to ensure that no toddler fell out, got injured or trampled on.

She stepped through the back door of the kitchen and marched across the hard mud and balding grass, where Mitzy the Staffie wore away any new growth with her frantic digging, and the football constantly being kicked around the small space finished the job. Euan stood with his back to the house, one hand leaning on the inflated wall. Mary tapped her son on the shoulder; he reeled around to face her. Both were taken by surprise, he by the sudden appearance of his irate mother and she by the tears that filled the eyes of her teenage boy.

'What on earth's the matter, love?' she cooed, as her previous spike of anger and desire to interrogate him evaporated.

'Nothing.' He drew breath sharply, embarrassed, and swiped at his face with the back of his sleeve.

'Well, it sure doesn't look like nothing.'

Euan shook his head. 'I just wish...'

'You just wish what?' She placed her hand on his arm.

'I just wish she could see, for one day, like the other kids. It's so unfair, Mum.' He looked back towards the bouncy castle where Imogen jumped high in the air, squealing as she landed, arms and legs entangled with the other children's. They were all of them clambering and giggling, each trying to stand on the wobbly base before being pulled back down by other grabbing hands in search of stability, rendered weak by the hilarity of the absurd situation in which they found themselves.

'She's having the time of her little life.' Mary smiled.

'Aye, but she just asked me what her dress is like,' Euan said, swallowing hard, 'and I didn't know what to say, because every description I could think of was a colour or a comparison, all useless to her. She doesn't know pink, she doesn't know marshmallow. I find it hard...'

'What's going on?' Isla shouted. Neither of them had heard her approach. 'Why are you upset? Is she hurt?' Without waiting for her little brother's reply, she placed her hands on her hips and began shouting into the melee, 'Imogen! Imi! Come out this minute before you get your head kicked in by one of those boys! I mean it, come off now!'

'She's fine, Isla! She's having the time of her life!' Mary tried to placate her, placing her hand on her daughter's forearm. This was Isla's stock response: to remove Imogen from any potential danger, to cushion her from life, keep her safe.

'She's under a ton of kids!' Isla pointed at the jumble of arms and legs. 'How do you know she's having the time of her life? She might be suffocating! Imogen, I mean it, come out right now!' she screamed. She looked at her mother. 'Have you seen the size of that Gary Bridewell? He could squash her or knock her out!'

Gradually, heeding the instruction, the birthday girl wiggled free from the crush, a froth of pale pink tulle and netting gathered around her, and made her way to the edge of the castle. 'What's up, Mum?' She tilted her head to one side, laughing every time a child behind her jumped, sending her teetering this way and that like a drunk.

'I... I... don't want you to get hurt,' Isla explained.

'I'm not hurt. It's brilliant!' Imogen exclaimed, before hurling herself back into the throng, unaware and uncaring that some of the children she bounced and fought with were twice her age and size. Her giggles could be heard above the yells.

Isla retrieved the large bowl of sweets that she had plonked on the floor and began handing them out. She caught sight of her little brother's face. 'What's up then, Euan? Are you okay?'

Mary ruffled his hair. 'He's just having a moment, wishing that Imi could see her dress.'

'Ah, you lovely thing.' Isla smiled at him. 'It's funny, isn't it, how it's the little things that get you? I was washing her hair in the bath the other day...' Isla pictured the moment: herself elbow-deep in suds as she massaged the foam into her little girl's scalp, then ducking as her daughter splashed in the bath, showering her in bubbles. 'Imogen asked me to describe the bubbles. I did my best and then we got talking, so I asked her what she thought about the world, and she told me it was big and noisy... and she's right, it is... and then she told me she thought it was the colour of laughing and happy. How great is that? Big and noisy and the colour of happy! Really, that's all you need, anything else is just detail.'

She winked at her kind little brother before returning her attention to her daughter, diving in and out of the gang of children littering the floor of the bouncy castle.

'Imogen's fine, you know.' Mary placed her hand on her daughter's arm. 'You have to let her be.'

'I know.' Isla rummaged in the bowl of sweets. 'I can't help it, though. I feel afraid for her. I want to wrap her up and hold her tight, for ever.'

'All mums feel that way.' Mary looked at Euan, her sensitive, secret smoker of a son.

'Yes, but I have better reason than most, don't I?' Isla held her mum's gaze.

'It's a reason, aye, but whether it's better or stronger than anyone else's, I don't know. But I do know that you have to let her have the freedom to fly. Only then will she come home to roost. You have to have more faith, Isla. For goodness' sake, let her be! And then do us all a favour and marry that boy of yours.'

'Imi's being mean! She just shoved me!' Duncan's wee cousin yelled.

Gary Bridewell laughed loudly. 'Shove her back, twice as hard!' was his advice.

Mary reached in and grabbed her granddaughter by the arm. 'Be nice, Imi. Remember, you catch more flies with honey than you do with vinegar!' Her gran patted her head.

Euan bent close, enabling him to whisper conspiratorially. Imogen could smell his soap, a sweet scent that clung to his skin and surrounded him in a slightly sickly aura. 'Aye, what your gran says is true enough, Imogen, but don't forget that when you come across a nasty wee wasp, sometimes you have to swat the irritatin' bastard!' He chuckled before wrapping her in a fierce, but brief hug. Imogen smiled, happy to be held in this warm embrace, and equally embarrassed by her uncle's use of a curse. She wriggled free and made her way back into the centre of the fray.

'Ow!' Gary Bridewell, the great lump of a lad, jumped from the bouncy castle, holding his hand over his face. A thin trickle of blood seeped from beneath his cupped palm.

'Good god, Gary! What have you done?' Isla rushed forward and prised the boy's fingers from his face.

'Imogen kicked me in the head!' he wailed.

Isla looked at her mum and laughed.

Three

Imogen sidled on to a padded bench in Café Chocolat and placed her handbag in the space beside her, along with her cane. She slid the screen on her mobile phone and held it up to her ear. She had a new message. The text-to-voice app spoke its robotic tone in her ear: *Your appointment for next Thursday with Dr Randolph is confirmed for 4 p.m. We look forward to seeing you then*

'Who are you talking to?'

Imogen looked up at the sound of Jenny's voice. It was slightly laboured, out of breath, as if she had been rushing. Imogen closed her phone. 'No one, I was listening to a text. Have you been running?'

'No, just didn't want to be late so I legged it up the escalator,' Jenny huffed as she sat down opposite her friend.

'You smell nice.' Imogen inhaled the scent, liking the earthy notes that danced up her nose like fragrant music.

'Do you know, you are the only one who ever notices? And, yes, it's new, Beyoncé's Heat.'

'Ooh, hoping to get Shay a bit hot under the collar?'

'That'll be the day.' Jenny sighed. 'The actual Beyoncé could prance around the front room naked, but if the footie's on, I wouldn't fancy her chances much. Unless she'd brought a kebab with her, of course, that might just swing it.'

The two girls laughed.

'You're not still replaying Logan's message, are you?' Jenny sighed.

'No!' Imogen answered, a little more indignant than she should have been, embarrassed by the fact that she had done just that earlier in the day. 'I'm so over him. You're right, anyone who doesn't want to be with me is not someone I want to be with.'

'That's ma girl.' Jenny sounded proud of her.

'In fact, I've started to feel angry. I can't even think of that word he used without getting mad.'

'What word?' Jenny teased.

'You know the one.' Imogen smiled, refusing to rise to the bait.

'Oh, you mean when he said, *I think it's best we go our separate ways, I can't cope with the...*'

'Liability!' the two girls said together then giggled in unison at this admission made by Imogen weeks ago. 'I mean, for god's sake, Jen, there's him calling me that and it's him who still lives under his mother's roof, with her wiping his nose for him every five minutes!'

'You're better off without him, mate, bloke's an arsehole.'

Yes, but an arsehole I quite liked, and an arsehole who left me because he couldn't cope... Imogen decided to keep this to herself.

'What'll we have?'

Imogen listened as her friend flexed the stiff cardboard of the menu.

'Usual for me, hot chocolate.'

'With fresh cream and extra marshmallows?' Jenny asked, smiling. 'Of course. You all right, honey? You look a bit... I don't know, nervous.' Her friend knew Imogen back to front and inside out, could tell from her body language or the slightest nuance of her behaviour when something was amiss.

'I guess I am a bit,' she confirmed.

'Oh, god, what have you done? What madness are you embarking on now? This isn't another bloody holiday you've booked, is it? Or some stupid stunt? The last time you looked like this you were about to go abseiling for that charity day! I nearly shat myself just thinking about it. And watching you was worse!'

Imogen laughed. 'No. Nothing like that. And I still don't know what all the fuss was about, I wasn't even scared!'

'That, mate, was because you couldn't see that you were one hundred and fifty feet from the ground with just a wee bit of rope keeping you from going splat!' Jenny shuddered at the memory.

'You might be right.' There was a pause while Imogen considered how best to continue. 'I do want to tell you something...' She swallowed nervously.

'Oh, for god's sake, spit it out, the suspense is killing me!' Jenny banged the table. Imogen jumped and the old couple on the next table looked up.

'I want to have a baby.'

'You what?' Jenny thought she might have misheard.

'I want to be a mum, Jen. I really do. I want to have a baby.' Imogen smiled and listened out for her friend's response.

There was a silent interlude while Jenny processed her friend's words and Imogen sat waiting. If they hadn't been best friends, it might have been awkward.

'For real?' Jenny needed it confirming.

Imogen nodded.

'Fucking hell, I think I preferred you jumping out of buildings on a bit of chewing gum!'

Both girls laughed with relief at the joke that broke the tension and at the mental image it created.

'It's true, Jen. I want this more than anything.' Imogen's voice was low and serious-sounding.

'How long have you felt like this?'

Imogen shrugged. *How long had she had the desire, the need, to hold her baby in her arms?* 'Always, really. I always thought I'd be a mum, eventually.'

Jenny exhaled, letting out a deep breath. She drummed her fingertips on the tabletop. 'Well, yes, eventually. But... how can I put this? You don't have a fella, and the last time I checked, they were quite important in the whole process.'

'So that's where I've been going wrong!' Imogen laughed. 'I know. But there are ways around it.'

'Oh, god, not Immaculate Conception? Have you been listening to Father Frank?'

Imogen chuckled again. 'No! But there are clinics. I'm going to see a doctor next Thursday, to talk about IUI.'

'God, you're serious?'

'Yes!' Imogen felt her smile slip; she wanted support, reassurance, not to have to convince her mate that this wasn't some kind of wind-up.

'Christ, Imi. I think this might be madness.' Jen's tone was level.

'Don't say that.'

'I've known you since we were five and I've never lied to you and I'm not about to start. I don't know how you'd cope with a baby and I worry that it'll be too much for you.'

'For god's sake, do you know me at all? When have I not coped? When have I ever failed at anything I've tried to do?' Imogen thought of the day she and Jenny had waited patiently in line for their turn at archery on a school trip. She recalled the way the ranger had gently placed his hand on her arm, saying: *Are you sure you're wanting a go?* his tone part condescending, part concerned. Imogen had turned her head towards him. *'Course I'm wanting a go!* she'd yelled. *Whaddya think I'm standing in the queue for?* She smiled at the memory. 'I do the things that everyone else does without a second thought – and you have always supported me, always told me that the last thing people notice about me is that I can't see – and now you're giving me this crap?' She felt her bottom lip start to tremble.

Jenny was silent. 'That's because I've always thought you can do anything, but this?' Imogen heard her friend's voice change direction, as if she was speaking to the floor.

'...this is something much bigger than going bungee jumping or flying off on holiday on your own!'

'Do you think I don't know that?' Imogen fought to keep the tears from her voice.

The waitress padded over Imogen heard the flip of her pad and the scratch of her pen on the paper. 'What'll it be, ladies?'

'I'll take a tea.' Jenny smiled at her.

'And for you, darlin'?' the kindly woman asked as she scribbled.

Imogen shook her head. 'Nothing for me, thanks. I have to go.' She felt her cheeks flush and a horrible hot, swarmy feeling wash over her.

'I thought you were having a hot chocolate?' Jenny sighed.

Imogen bent to the right and felt for her cane and her bag. 'I don't feel like it, Jen.'

'Oh, don't be like that!'

'Like what?' Imogen snapped.

'You know, a bit off with me, just because you don't like my response.'

'You're right; I don't, because your reaction makes it sound as if I haven't considered all the consequences! Do you seriously think I don't know how hard it might be? But it's hard for all new mums, and that's what I want to be – just another new mum. I thought you of all people would get it.' Imogen shuffled along the bench seat and squeezed out between the tables, using her uncanny knack of sensing the objects in her path and navigating around them expertly. Mikey, an old boyfriend, used to call her Batgirl because of this very talent.

'It's not that, Imi...' Jenny's voice tailed off.

'What is it then?' she said curtly, fastening her coat buttons, wanting to leave.

'I just... I just don't think it's fair on a baby.'

'What do you mean?'

'I mean just that! Aren't you worried that the little one will end up doing more than a child should? That it might end up looking after you?'

'I...' Imogen couldn't find the words. Her heart beat too fast for comfort and her pulse raced; she felt quite light-headed.

'It's not like you've got a partner who could help in any way. I'm afraid it might not be the right thing to do. I'm only saying what I think.' Jen's voice trailed off.

Imogen abandoned her buttons and turned her head in the direction of her friend. 'Do you know what, Jen? I think you should look a bit closer to home. Your mum's a junkie and yet she had five kids! And your own life's a bloody mess, and there's you and Shay hanging on to your relationship by a thread. And you think *my* baby would have it bad? I have a safe, stable home, with enough love to keep a child happy, and the wherewithal to provide for it.' Imogen walked across the café towards the door.

Jenny hung her head, stung by her friend's words and shocked by the way their discussion had deteriorated into this exchange. She expected it with Shay, but with Imogen? Never. Then Jenny did what she did best: came out fighting.

'Yes! You're right! My childhood was less than perfect, that's how I know what it's like to have a mum that you can't rely on, a mum who is preoccupied with her own struggle. It's not fair on a child!'

Imogen noted the tremor in her friend's voice; she was clearly hating their first serious altercation as much as Imogen was, but that aside, her words cut just the same. Jenny still wasn't finished. 'And how dare you say that about Shay and me? I don't know what the hell's got into you but you need to take a look at yourself!'

Imogen shook her head at the irony of her friend's ill-considered comment and left.

Jenny's words were still ringing in Imogen's head into the early hours. It wasn't only falling out with her best friend that had unsettled her so, leaving her feeling out of sorts and a little confused; self-doubt had crept into her mind too, causing her to question her own motives. She lay in bed, feeling on the bedside table for her glass of water from which she sipped, imagining a tiny baby asleep by her side in a cot. Imogen smiled. Even the thought cheered her. *I can do this. I know I can*. It was her last thought before falling asleep.

The next day, on her way to see her parents, Imogen thought about the quarrel with Jenny and her stomach churned at the prospect of losing her best friend; even the thought of not having her to turn to made her feel sick. As the bus drove her to her parents' house, Imogen was feeling anxious.

'How's ma wee girl doin'?' Duncan kissed the top of her head before taking a chair at the kitchen table.

'Great, thanks, Dad.' She sat down with him at the table and he poured her some tea.

'I'll just get your gran settled and then I'll be back.' Isla touched her daughter's arm before going into the next room. She was carrying a small floral laminated tray on which teetered tea in a china cup and a matching side plate with a slice of bread and butter and two Garibaldi biscuits on it.

When she returned, Isla took the seat next to her daughter. 'Did your dad read you Euan's letter?' Imogen's uncle had written from Canada where he had been living for the best part of ten years.

'No.' She shook her head and lifted her mug in both hands, tentatively bringing the hot liquid towards her mouth, testing the temperature against her bottom lip before taking a sip.

'I'll fetch it in a bit. He's doing great, happy as Larry.' Her mum yawned; switching between shifts at the Krispy Kreme doughnut factory always took its toll.

'I don't know who this Larry is, but half his luck! Does he ever have a bad day?' Duncan chortled, wheezing with laughter.

'Doubt it.'

Imogen heard the familiar mix of love and joviality with which her mum had addressed her dad for as long as she could remember. It made her happy, always, and she could see that when a relationship worked, it was a lovely way to live. Her parents had married when Imogen had been five; her mum said she'd wanted to be sure! It made them all laugh even now, but Imogen knew that she wasn't prepared to watch the years pass by, waiting to find her Mr Right. Or, worse, try to hang on to someone like Logan, who resented her disability and could only hurt her. No, she wanted to crack on with the important job of having a baby.

'I met Jen yesterday in town,' she said.

'Oh, right, how is she? I saw her mum a couple of weeks back. She seems to be doing better.'

'We had a bit of a row actually.' Imogen felt her shoulders sag; the fact that they had fallen out was still shocking to her.

'Never! You two are thick as thieves, always have been! What on earth is there to fall out over?'

The fact that her mum's voice had gone up a couple of octaves revealed that she was equally surprised.

Imogen placed the mug on the table and pushed her hair back from her face. 'I had some news for her and I thought she'd support me.'

'She's always supported you,' her mum interrupted. 'She's your partner in crime that one!'

'Yes. Yes, I know, but not this time apparently.' Imogen swallowed.

'What was your news?' her dad whispered. He was not a man who enjoyed change and Imogen knew he'd be running through all the dire possibilities in his head. Duncan was happiest knowing that his routine was unchallenged and his family and friends all lived within strolling distance.

Imogen felt their breath coming in her direction and the silent crackle of anticipation in the air.

'I told her I wanted to have a baby.'

'Well, of course you want to have a baby. You've said so before and it's a shame things didn't work out with Logan, but when the time is right you'll meet someone else and it'll happen.' Isla laughed with relief, having anticipated bad news, as she often did.

'No, Mum.' It was Imogen's turn to interrupt, unwilling

to rake over the reasons why things hadn't worked out with funny, amiable Logan, who had been polite to her mum, taken an interest in her dad, and had on occasion treated Imogen herself like a child who needed minding, resenting every moment and fearful of a future where she might depend on him more. It still hurt to recall it. 'Not *when* I meet someone… now. The time is right for me and I'm taking steps to make it happen. I'm going to see a doctor about having IUI. My GP says there's no reason the NHS would fund it. It's not as if I have tried to conceive and can't, it's just that I *want* to get pregnant and this is the best way for me. That's fair enough. I have the money saved for a couple of shots at the title and so I'm going to take it.'

Her parents were silent. She took a sip of her tea and heard her mum swallow. 'So, is anyone going to say anything?' asked Imogen.

Her dad cleared his throat. 'What did you and Jen fall out over? I don't understand.'

Imogen bit her lip. It wasn't easy for her to repeat her friend's remarks. 'She pretty much said that she didn't think it was a good idea and that it wasn't fair on the child.'

Her parents remained quiet. She sat up straight and took a deep breath. 'Am I to take it from your silence that you agree with Jenny?' She tried to keep the emotion from her voice, keep her distress in check.

Isla reached across the table and held her daughter's hand. Imogen heard the unmistakable sound of her weeping.

'Why are you crying?' she whispered.

'I'm crying because I'm happy for you and proud of you, and because you and Jen are closer than sisters and I don't like the idea of you having a fall out.'

Her dad's chair scraped across the floor and Imogen heard

him rip sheets of kitchen roll from the stand on which it lived and hand them to his wife before resuming his seat.

Isla blew her nose into the tissue. 'We are always here for you, love. No matter what, always. And we'll support you through this, but I do think I might be a tad young to be a granny!'

'That's what your mum said too, as I recall,' Duncan said into his mug.

Four

'**R**ight.'

Imogen sat up straight at the sound of this one-word greeting, issued as the man blustered into the room. She heard the slam of the door behind him. It made her jump.

She could tell a lot about people and their understanding of her condition by their awareness of the impact sound had on her. The clues lay in small things, like whether they thought to announce themselves or chat a bit more, giving her at least a chance to process who this was and their intention and mood. Introductory words did that for her and were vital in the same way that a first visual impression was for the sighted.

Imogen was skilled at discerning the way people felt from the smallest of clues; a slight foreshortening of a consonant in an otherwise jolly introduction, for instance, was often a clue to veiled aggression, and laboured sighs with a faint hum between words could signal pain, but were usually the result of sadness. People were so used to painting on a smile to fool the eye that they often forgot to disguise the voice too, or to measure their breathing or monitor their laughter, and she had learnt to speak this hidden language.

His footfall was heavy. She felt the slight quaking of the wooden floorboards reverberate up the chair legs and send a quiver through her... or maybe that was just her own nerves. She heard the creak of his chair as he lowered himself behind the desk, heard breathing that was slightly laboured. He was unfit, probably overweight, with a gruffness to his tone that she didn't encounter in anyone youthful. She listened to the spittle paste his tongue to the roof of his mouth and noticed how it gave way with a slight sucking sound as he began to speak. It made her swallow. Then there was the sound of a computer mouse sliding over a surface and the flutter of papers as a sticky finger leafed through them. The faint ticking of his watch punctuated his movements. He clearly figured it was okay to multi-task. Why not? It wasn't as if she could see him.

'I have looked at your file, Miss McGuire, the results of the questionnaire you filled in online and notes of the conversation you had with my assistant, Miss Wells.'

'Oh, good.' The questions had been probing, in-depth. Imogen smiled as if she had passed some kind of test and was whizzing through to the next round.

He continued as though she hadn't spoken: 'Having considered your position very carefully, I'm afraid to say that this has been a wasted journey for you.' He didn't bother with any pleasantries and the fact that he didn't look at her while he talked spoke volumes. Imogen had keen radar when it came to the way sound reached her ears, able to sense the direction from which it came and in some way assess the objects from which it bounced. He didn't offer her the courtesy of facing her but instead spoke with head down, looking at his keyboard or notes, distracted.

Imogen heard the tap of his fingers on the desktop, she couldn't decide the reason why; irritation or impatience, maybe both. She sat up straight and gave her practised smile, the one Jen had helped her with. *Oh, Jen! I wish you were here!*

In her early teens, Imogen had sat in front of her friend and given a number of smiles, asking her to judge them. She had gone through a whole range that went from comfortable, open-mouthed, tongue resting on bottom lip, to a full gurn. After nearly an hour of uncontrollable giggles, Jen had placed her hand on her friend's arm. 'Stop! That's the one, that's your best smile!' This had come at the end of a long afternoon spent hanging out. They had listened to S Club Juniors and sung along badly, before Jen had tried out several hairstyles on her friend, tugging at her scalp as she twisted and backcombed to achieve the desired result.

'You have, like, the best hair in the whole wide world!' Jen had told her.

'Do I?' Imogen had beamed.

'Seriously, it's so thick and shiny, and it always looks like you've just washed it, and it's got that little wave thing going on. Feel mine, it's so thin!'

Imogen had done as instructed, letting her friend's wisps of cobweb-like hair slip across her fingers. It felt fragile, insubstantial compared to her own that had weight and could be twisted around her fingers in a strong knot. She'd shaken her head, liking the feel of her thick mane shivering against her shoulders.

Now she recalled the tone of warm affection in her friend's voice as she'd given Imogen such valuable advice, selecting for her the facial expression with which she now greeted anyone she met. It was a hybrid, a cross between the most comfortable open-mouthed smile, with cheeks relaxed, and a more careful one with closed mouth and head inverted slightly. What would she have done without a friend like Jenny? It didn't bear thinking about.

The doctor continued, quickening his speech, as though keen to get this meeting over. 'I am afraid to say that I do not think I am the doctor, nor this the clinic, to help you. This seems to me to be all about you wanting to become a mother and not something that is necessarily in the best interests of the child. I have to consider the wellbeing of any baby, and I can't say I think it would be fair to encourage the birth of a child to a parent whose life is already... challenging.'

'Right.' Imogen uttered the one word and stopped smiling. She let the fringe of her scarf slip through her fingers, liking the feel of the soft silky fronds against her skin and taking comfort from the repeated gesture. She thought again of Jenny's hair. Jenny who had battled anorexia, Jenny who had fallen apart when her mum had been in and out of rehab, Jenny who limped from counsellor to counsellor, trying to find someone who might be able to explain her lack of interest in life while she was all the time bending over backwards to accommodate her pig of a husband...

'I think everyone's life is challenging. I don't think mine is necessarily more so than others'.'

A snort of laughter preceded his response. 'I think being blind might be considered a challenge of greater rather than lesser proportions.'

Imogen kept her voice level. 'I guess the question is, in comparison to what? There are quadriplegic mothers and mothers who contract terminal illnesses who would swap with me any day, I bet. Being blind helps to put things into proportion for me.'

She could sense that he was now facing her and a silence indicated that all background activity had ceased, as though he'd finally seen fit to give her his full attention.

'It's nothing personal.' Dr Randolph gave an awkward cough, clearly not willing to discuss the matter further.

'But it is, isn't it?' Imogen kept her voice steady.

'I'm sorry?'

She heard the annoyance in his tone.

'It is personal, it has to be.'

And then it began again, the clicking of a mouse, the movement of paper. The slight sigh.

Imogen wasn't done. 'It *is* personal because you are talking about me. This is my life, not some hypothetical question or virtual request or result from your questionnaire. I want to become a mum and I am asking you to help me.'

'And I have explained to you, Miss McGuire, that I do not think I am the doctor, nor this the clinic, to do so. It's all well and good to talk about quadriplegia or terminal illness, but the reality is, life cannot be governed by what may or may not happen. When tragedies occur that is one thing, but you, in full knowledge of your difficulties, are choosing to bring a child into the world. As I have stated, I don't think it's in the best interests of any child.'

Imogen felt by her leg for her satchel and her cane. She gathered the bag on to her lap and looped the leather strap over her head and one arm. She then unfurled her cane and stood up. 'Do you know, after careful consideration, I think you are right, Dr Randolph.'

She heard the scrape of his chair and the slight creak of his bones as he stood up. When he spoke, she detected something spicy, like salami, on his breath.

'Well...' he paused, voice tinged faintly with victory '...I am actually rather glad to hear that.'

Imogen gave her practised smile. 'Oh, no, don't get me wrong. When I say I think you are right, I mean you are not the doctor, nor this the clinic, to help me. But will it stop me?' She turned and walked towards the door, tapping against the wooden floor until she felt the door beneath her cane. Reaching out, she turned the handle and felt a breeze hit her face as the door opened. She turned back in the direction of the man and his big fat desk. 'Will it fuck!' With that, she walked off into the hallway, her uncle Euan's words ringing in her head: *When you find a nasty wee wasp, sometimes you have to swat the irritatin' bastard!*

Five

A month later, as Imogen sat in another warm waiting room, her expectations were low. She felt a yawn creep up on her and hid the stretching of her mouth and her tiredness behind her hand, in case anyone watching should think she was anything less than enthusiastic about the project.

'Hello, Imogen.' The man stood directly in front of her. 'I'm Dr Hamilton. Sorry we are running late, it's been one of those days!' He laughed. 'Actually, I'll let you into a little secret... I always say that, as though what my clients are experiencing is an anomaly, whereas in fact around here it is *always* one of those days!'

Imogen felt her shoulders relax. Dr Hamilton sounded nice. He sounded kind and human, and this made her feel it might just be possible.

'Please, come on through!' He waited for her to stand and touched his arm against hers, allowing her to walk alongside him until he stopped, opened a door and went inside. She followed him. In here it was cooler, the air more pleasant.

'Okay, chair about two feet directly in front of you.'

'Thank you.' She had already sensed the object using her Batgirl skills.

'I'm just going to open the window, bring up your details on the computer and then we can have a good chat. Did you want something to drink? Tea... coffee? Soft drink?' She listened to the bar of a window being secured and the rustle of clothing as he took his seat behind the desk.

'A glass of water would be great.' Nerves made her tongue stick like a magnet to the roof of her mouth.

He stood up and walked to the back of the room; there was the unmistakable glug of a water cooler. He held the plastic cup against her shaking hand, not letting go until she had it secured.

'Are you okay, Imogen?'

She nodded. 'I think so, a bit nervous.' Her tummy flipped as she recalled Dr Randolph's words: *I don't think it's in the best interests of any child...*

'Of course, but try not to be. Easy for me to say, I know.'

Positivity washed over her like a wave.

'How have you reached this decision, Imogen? Is it a recent desire you have felt or has it been something you've wanted for a long time?'

Imogen got comfortable in her chair. 'I don't remember one defining moment when I held a child or heard one cry and felt my womb pulse with longing, nothing like that.' She spoke calmly and eloquently, from the heart, telling him about her childhood and how this longing had pretty much always been with her. '...more so recently; in fact, it feels like I have been fighting every day since. That's it really.'

Dr Hamilton had sat quietly throughout her response. 'I see.' He adopted a more business-like tone and her stomach shrank, and then just like that he delivered the words that made a kind of music play in her ears, the words she had feared she might never hear. 'I think we can do this, Imogen. I think we can help you become a mum.'

'Really?'

'Yes.' He was smiling; she could hear it in his tone. 'Really.'

'I don't know what to say. Except thank you!'

'Ah, don't thank me yet! You've got a lot of hard work to put in and it's not an easy road to choose. There will be highs, lows and discomfort, in fact you might not be thanking me at all once we get started, but I think that's all part of the journey, don't you?'

She nodded.

'There are no guarantees, Imogen, but what is it they say: *you don't know until you try?*'

Yes, that's exactly what they say.

'And we will try very hard.'

Imogen beamed. This felt like it was the start of her adventure. Finally... finally it was happening!

Six

'So how does it work?' Isla was curious, casting the question over her shoulder as she filled the kettle.

'How does what work?' Granny Mary crept into the kitchen and took a place at the table, pulling her cardigan close as she did so, keen to catch up on whatever she had missed.

Isla sighed. She had been hoping for a private conversation with her daughter, happy that Duncan was out of the house. She'd forgotten her mother might be eager to join in. 'The whole... injecting a baby thing.' She deliberately kept it vague, already wary of her mother's reaction to the whole idea, not wanting to invite any more loaded statements about her views on single mothers and how it had been so very different in her day.

Mary let out a small chuckle. 'Oh, goodness me! I don't want to say the wrong thing, Imogen, and you know I love you to the moon and back.'

'I do.'

Mary laid her hand on her granddaughter's arm. 'But couldn't you just settle down with a nice man and do it the way everyone else does, with a good night out and a bit of hanky-panky?'

'Mum!' Isla laughed, muttering, 'Here we go...' under her breath.

Imogen chuckled. 'Don't think I haven't thought about that,

Gran. I'm not sure I want a relationship, not right now, but I do know I want to be a mum and this feels like the best and safest bet for me. The world's a different place now, you don't need to be half of a couple to raise a child successfully.'

'Well, that's not what I think, but I suppose I might be a bit old-fashioned. What about that Logan boy? He was nice enough.'

'Aye, but I don't want nice enough. I want fabulous, funny, great. Logan would have driven me nuts with his *màthairing*, and the fact that he was involved unwillingly would have driven us apart eventually. Better it happened sooner rather than later. I don't want to be with anyone who doesn't want to be with me,' she repeated the mantra. 'Besides, if I want to be smothered I can just come and sit here with yous two!'

Mary huffed. 'I'm curious though, Imogen, what exactly do they do? Put a baby in a test tube and whoosh it up your flower?' She spoke with calm confidence, as though they were discussing the weather.

'For god's sake, Mother!' Isla was quite unsettled to be holding this whole conversation in front of her.

'Not quite, Gran, no. Although that sounds easier!' Imogen told her.

'For the love of god, do we have to go into this much detail?' Isla queried, busying herself in the fridge, searching for something for tea. She pulled out a couple of tomatoes and a box of eggs. 'Who fancies an omelette?' she said, trying her best to distract them.

'I don't need too much detail, but just give me it in a nutshell.' Gran folded her hands in her lap. Both of them ignored Isla's question.

Imogen was happy to explain the mechanics to her gran. 'It's quite complicated, and a bit of a slow process, but in simple terms, they gave me three blood tests just to check my hormone levels and then, when they were at the right point, they gave me another injection that I had to administer myself at home, to stimulate the hormones you'd normally get when having hanky-panky.' All three of them tittered at this use of her gran's expression.

'Is that how the doctor phrased it?' Isla quipped.

'Yes.' Imogen smiled. 'Then I went back in to have the actual insemination, that's the whooshing, test tube and flower bit, and now we just wait. And it's killing me!' She placed her elbows on the table and her head in her hands.

'How long do you have to wait?' her gran asked.

'Two weeks. I had another injection after the insemination to top up my HCG, which is the pregnancy hormone.'

'Flippin' 'eck!' her mum summed it up quite nicely. 'And what happens if this doesn't work? What's Plan B?' Isla didn't want to appear negative, but she knew it was her job to prepare her girl for any disappointment that might be lurking around the corner.

Imogen raised her head and drew breath. 'Then I cry a bit and soldier on, and I have enough money left for one more round!' She tried to sound nonchalant.

The two women stared at their daughter and granddaughter in silence. Imogen felt the need to fill the void. 'So that's it in a nutshell.'

'Well, I'll be...' Granny Mary uttered. 'I still think a good night out and a bit of hanky-panky might be easier, and it's good for you too. No offence, Imogen!'

'None taken, Gran.'

'Do you feel like it's worked? Do you feel pregnant?' her gran asked with an obvious hint of excitement despite her reservations.

Imogen considered this and, in an almost subconscious gesture, placed her hand on her stomach below the table. 'I don't know. I think I do, but that could just be that I want it so badly I'm imagining it, the sickness, the boob tenderness and all that stuff. I think it's too soon to tell and so if I'm feeling these things then it's probably just a trick of my mind.'

Isla walked over to the table and hugged her around the shoulders, laying her head against Imogen's.

'On the other hand, I do have cramp-type period pains, which is either something taking up residence in my womb or just what it feels like, an impending period, and that's the hardest thing, waiting to see which!' Imogen placed her hand over her mum's.

'We could do a pregnancy test?' Her gran offered the idea as though it might not have occurred to Imogen.

'Aye, we could, but because I've had the injections of the pregnancy hormone, that could lead to a false positive and I don't want to go through that. I'm only just keeping calm as it is.' She decided not to confess to the nights of praying, wishing and hoping; hours that she had spent lying on her bed, hands on tummy, hoping beyond hope that this little miracle might be occurring inside her, beaming at the thought that it just might be happening this minute and then sobbing uncontrollably at the thought that it might not.

'Tell you what,' Isla huffed, 'I've gone right off eggs for tea.'

And all three of them laughed at the wonderful absurdity of the situation.

Imogen was still chuckling when an hour later she opened the gate in front of her house and fished for her key in her satchel.

'Imi?'

She raised her head, instantly recognising Jenny's voice.

'All right?' Imogen smiled. Hearing it brought her nothing but a wonderful sensation of relief.

'Thought you might fancy a cup of tea?' Jenny's tone was shy, sheepish. No matter, Imogen was just delighted that her best friend had taken the first step and was now building a bridge between them.

'Yep, as long as I get to make it. Your tea tastes like pish!' Imogen laughed.

'Firstly, you are the only one who complains about my tea-making skills, and secondly, have you ever tasted pish? How would you know?'

And just like that, they were back to normal.

Seven

Imogen opened her eyes and closed them again immediately. Her alarm hadn't gone off, but judging by her semi-wakened state, she figured it was about 6.30 a.m. She often did this, infuriatingly cutting her night's sleep short by half an hour or so while lying in anticipation of the infernal beep of her clock. Lying back on the pillow, she prayed for sleep to return, asked to be whisked back to the sweet oblivion of slumber. For if she could slip into the ethereal world, for just a bit longer, then she wouldn't have to admit to the reason that she had woken or face the reality that had jolted her from sleep on that quiet Tuesday morning.

Rolling into a foetal position, she tucked her arms around her shins and sank into the mattress, curled up like a little ball. She whimpered with distress. Who had she been trying to kid? It was going to be harder than she'd thought simply to 'soldier on'. Sadness came over her in waves as she awoke fully and had no choice but to accept that the dull ache in her stomach was confirmation she was having her period.

Imogen wept, deep, slow tears that were drawn from an inner well of despair. She so desperately wanted to be a mum and this, a cherished attempt at conception, had failed.

*

'These things happen when they're meant to.' Jenny tried to offer solace as the two girls sat on the bus that would take them into town.

'Yep, I know.'

All these weeks later Imogen still found it hard to talk about and, despite their reconciliation, the fact that her best friend had been less than supportive of her plan at first seemed to irritate her more now that the process had failed.

Jenny reached up and held Imogen's arm as she took the steep step down from bus to pavement.

'Shops first or hot chocolate?' Jenny queried.

'Shops, I think, we need to earn it.'

'What do you need?'

'Lip gloss and boring stuff like bin bags.'

'Ooh, the glamorous life we lead!' Jenny laughed.

The two of them sauntered into the chemist's where a young assistant with a badge announcing her 'Trainee' status appeared to be on a spring as she constantly bobbed up and down enthusiastically. 'Can I help you?' she asked, grinning.

'Uh-huh, we are after lip gloss, possibly with a hint of colour?' Jen turned to consult Imogen.

'Yes, something warm... not too harsh.' Imogen described the effect she was after the best way she could.

The girl turned to Jenny. 'With your colouring, I would recommend orangey tones. You could carry it off, with your pale skin.'

'Oh, it's not for me, it's for my friend here.'

'I see.' The girl stared at Imogen. 'I didn't realise...'

'Didn't realise what?' Imogen was curious.

'Didn't realise you might want to wear make-up.'

'Why's that?' She cocked her head, keen to pick up on the unspoken nuance behind the girl's words.

'I... I dunno. I just thought that as you can't see, you might not bother, because...'

'Because what?' Jenny prompted.

'Because you don't know what it looks like.' The girl's enthusiasm for her job was fading fast. Imogen made a noise that was somewhere between a snort of laughter and a chuckle of disbelief. 'I like to look my best.' She smiled, deciding it wasn't the wee girl's fault, she was curious, that was all.

'Yes, of course!'

Imogen heard embarrassment in the rushed response.

Jenny leant forward. 'I tell you what, hen, you'll be wanting to change your own lip colour to puce. It'll match your cheeks!'

Imogen heard the girl swallow.

'Ah, my friend is only teasing. Thing is, you probably wear make-up so that other people see you in a certain way, isn't that right?' asked Imogen.

'Uh-huh, yeah,' the girl agreed.

'Well, it's the same for me. Imagine you didn't have access to a mirror all day... you'd still want to look good, right?' Imogen's tone was soft.

'Yep. It makes me feel more confident.' The girl's voice was small.

'There you go.' Imogen smiled at her.

'How do you know what colour to go for or how to put your make-up on?' the girl asked, a little sheepishly.

'They're good questions and the answer is: with a lot of practice! My mum and friends have always told me what suits me or if I've made a howler... been a bit over-generous with the blusher brush!' Imogen listened to the girl 'humph' as if in recognition of similar experiences. 'Plus there are great tutorials online now. So I get to have a lesson, which is good.'

'Can you see anything at all? Is it like when I close my eyes and I can see a sort of glow of colour and nearly make out shapes, even though my eyes are closed?'

Imogen liked this candid approach.

'No, that would be very useful to me, but it's more like trying to look out of your finger when it's behind your back. No sight at all. Nothing.'

'Wow. That must be difficult.'

In some ways. 'Not really, not when there are people like you around to help me pick my lip gloss!'

'Oh, right, yes!' Taking the hint, the girl went back to her previous perky self as she led the duo down the aisles to find the make-up.

Jenny and Imogen made their way outside, laughing together.

'Cheeky mare!' Jenny chortled.

'Ah, bless her, she was very young. And, to be honest, she's only asking what most people wonder. It's not the strangest thing I've been asked.'

'What was then? Oh, god, I'm curious now!' Jenny pulled on her friend's arm and stepped in close.

'God, the list is endless! How do I watch a movie or TV is always a favourite, and I was once asked: *How do you know if someone is sexy!*'

'How *do* you know if someone is sexy?' Jenny laughed. 'Seriously?'

'Yes, seriously! I mean, it's not like you can look at them and get that phwoaaaar moment!'

'You are terrible!' Imogen laughed.

'Why am I?' Jenny feigned coyness.

'Because you should know that it's not only about how they look, Jen! Or it shouldn't be. It's about that super-sensory experience sight is only a small part of. I mean, surely the way Shay looks is just a small part of it for you?'

'Christ, Imi, you're right! I do close my eyes when I want to feel sexy, I have to... to superimpose Brad Pitt's head on to the useless lump!'

The two girls laughed and held on to each other through their giggles. 'So this super-sensory thing... is shagging you like sleeping with a superhero – does it set your spidey senses tingling?'

'Oh, my god! Mikey Thomson used to call me Batgirl! Maybe that's why!'

The two of them laughed even harder.

When the laughter subsided the girls stood facing each other on the pavement with a keen wind blowing from the Leith and whipping a chill about their ears.

'I'm sorry, Imi.'

'What for?' Imogen knew to what her friend was alluding but wanted to have this conversation, needing to know why Jenny had acted that way. There was a slight pause while she considered her words.

'For not being more supportive, for feeling a wee bit jealous...'

'You never have to feel jealous of me! I'm your best friend!'

'I know. I know, and I'm sorry. I just always thought I'd have a bairn and you'd be there and it'd be great, and then you were rushing ahead into it and Shay and I still haven't fallen...'

'Oh, Jen, you should talk to me always. I can help you figure things out.'

'I know. Although this doesn't take much figuring out: to get up the spout requires shaggin'.'

'Not always!' Imogen interrupted.

'No, good point, not always. But in our case it would

definitely help. There's a bit of a drought in that area at the moment. But I know how badly you want this and I'm sorry.'

'Don't say it again. Anyway, the second round seems to have gone pretty well.' So far Imogen had avoided talking to her friend about her recent trip to see Dr Hamilton, preferring to keep the details to herself. It was as much about self-preservation in case of failure as anything else.

'I'm glad.' Jenny sounded sincere.

'Perhaps you should do as Granny Mary says: have a good night out and then a bit of hanky-panky!' Imogen suggested to her friend.

'Oh, god!' She shuddered. 'Actually I think what we might need is some time apart. It's like he doesn't see, Imi, takes me for granted. I'd like to go away for a long weekend and let him miss me, then maybe when I get back, who knows?'

Imogen stopped walking and jumped up and down on the spot, as if she had borrowed Chemist Girl's springs. 'Let's do it! Let's go away for a weekend! We could go and book it now!'

'Who do you think I am – Kim Kardashian? I can't just pack up my negligee and waltz away for a weekend. I've got work and Shay and I are not exactly flush at the minute.'

'We can do this! I saved up more than I needed for my treatment, but not quite enough for another go, so let's do it. Let's go to the travel agent's and see what they've got. I would love to treat you to a weekend away. It would do me good too...' Imogen gripped her friend's arm, keen to get going.

'For the love of god, are you serious?'

'Yes! Lead on, Kimmy!'

The girls fell through the door of the travel agent's and took up seats in front of a bemused middle-aged man who wasn't used to this level of commotion.

'Can I help you, ladies?'

Through their nudges and giggles, they just about managed to say, 'We want a weekend away, the cheapest you've got, as soon as possible!'

Eight

Jenny and Imogen were catching their breath after six hours of wandering around the rain-soaked streets of Amsterdam. Not that the weather could in any way dampen their spirits. They were abroad, having fun, and nothing as insignificant as rain was going to get them down! They had taken in the maze of canals, trodden the cobbled streets, giggled in the red-light district and consumed a gargantuan lunch of pizza – eaten in the street, huddled under a large umbrella, in the drizzle.

'Imi, I'm knackered, I need a kip!' Jenny leant on a lamppost and flexed one trainer-clad foot.

'You're such a lightweight. There's loads more on our list!' Imogen ribbed.

'I know! And I want to see it all, I do, but can we have a break?'

'Tell you what, you go back and nap and I'll go see a couple of museums alone and then come and collect you when you've had your beauty sleep. Or else meet you somewhere?'

'You're making me feel bad, but I am seriously wanting ma bed!'

Imogen laughed. 'Don't feel bad, go back and chill out. I'll call you in a couple of hours and either you can come find me or I'll come back to the hotel.'

Jenny didn't need persuading. 'Are you sure?'

'Sure I'm sure!'

'Don't talk to any strangers!' Jenny yelled as she abandoned her friend and made her way along the crowded street, dodging the cyclists who criss-crossed in front of her.

Imogen sat at a table in a bay window and felt the glow of winter sunshine warm her skin through the dappled glass. At last the sun had found its way through the clouds. The earlier deluge had left pavements, boat decks and handrails along the canals with an almost phosphorescent glow and there was a clean sparkle to the air. The barista arrived promptly with her hot chocolate and a generous slice of the house speciality: *appeltaart* with whipped cream.

'There you go. Enjoy!' He placed the tall conical glass by her hand and the plate and fork a little further on to the table.

'Thank you. Smells delicious!' She inhaled the rich scent of buttery pastry, warm, cinnamon-laden apples and the sweetness of scorched powdered sugar. Her mouth watered. Imogen gripped the spoon in her right hand and used her left to feel the edge of the plate. Digging into the tart, she scooped up a large mouthful towards her face and felt the satisfying cloying sensation of cream against the roof of her mouth, as the sweet apple and divine flaky pastry melted on her tongue. She savoured the taste before chewing the tart slowly.

'Excuse me, is this seat taken?'

He was American. His voice held the slightest tremor that belied his confident baritone. His coat smelled of wet wool; he must have got caught in the earlier shower.

'No, that's fine! Help yourself,' Imogen said without thinking, and had to use her napkin.

'That looks good.' He slid into the chair opposite her; she heard it scrape along the wooden floor and then listened as he removed his coat. He dropped it in a heap on the floor; she felt the weight of it, as it lay partly on her foot.

'It tastes good, not sure what it looks like!' Imogen smiled.

She felt his breath coming in her direction, as if he was studying her.

'Oh! Sorry. I didn't realise you were blind.'

'That's okay; it's not your fault. Nothing to feel sorry about.' Imogen beamed, delighted that her lack of vision hadn't been the first thing he had noticed about her.

'Whose fault was it?' He slurped noisily at his coffee.

She swallowed the last of her vast mouthful of tart and sipped her hot chocolate before she replied. 'No one's, not really. I was very premature.' She shrugged and placed her drink on the table, raising her hands and letting them fall against her thighs. 'It just happened.'

'Who are you here with?' he asked. She heard his thick hair graze his collar, as if he was turning his head left and then right, possibly to see if anyone was approaching or watching them.

'No one. I mean, not right now. I'm here with my friend Jenny, but she's buggered off for a nap. Bit of a lightweight.' Imogen dug in for a second mouthful.

'You're here on your own?' He sounded surprised.

She nodded.

'Well, that's really cool!'

Imogen could tell he was smiling.

'Yep, it's actually just my sight that I'm missing. My legs work fine so I can walk from A to B. And I have a tongue in my head, so if I get lost...'

'Ouch!' he laughed. 'That is me *told*!'

They both laughed.

'Was that rude?' Imogen lowered her voice.

'Nah, not really, more... assertive. On the offensive scale it was a paltry three out of ten at most.'

She liked the way he sounded.

He reached out and took her hand so that he could shake it. 'I'm Owen. Owen Jackson from Chicago.'

She let her hand be waggled up and down. 'I'm Imogen McGuire, from Pilton, Scotland.'

'Yes, I gathered that from your accent. Good to meet you.'

She removed her hand and folded it into her lap, suddenly too self-conscious to scoff the rest of her cake in front of Owen Jackson from Chicago.

'Are you visiting here?' He leant forward, placing his forearms on the table. She heard the tap of a ring against the tabletop.

'Yes.' Imogen licked her lips, fearing that there might be stray blobs of cream lurking on her face. 'Just for the weekend.'

'Me too. My last city, a stopover really, and then home. I've been away for a couple of weeks, seen lots of Europe, it's been awesome,' Owen confirmed brightly, as if this weekend visit was the common ground they had been searching for.

'Did you get to Scotland?'

'No! Sadly not. I was in London and then had a few days on the Sussex coast, which was beautiful. I wanted to get up to Edd-in-borrow but didn't make it.'

'Oh, Edd-in-borrow? I think that's near me.' She laughed.

'Amsterdam's amazing, right?' Enthusiasm poured from him. Imogen nodded.

'It is. Still quite a lot on my to-do list, but so far, great!'

'Have you seen the Van Gogh Museum yet?'

She smiled at his pronunciation, Van Go – making the artist sound more like a commercial vehicle-repair garage. 'No, not yet.'

'Well, I'm heading over there right after this, if you... I don't know, if maybe you'd like to...' Owen coughed.

Imogen heard his feet shuffle under the table and his chair creak as he shifted his body weight. He was nervous.

'Are you asking me to come with you?'

'Yes.' He breathed out in relief.

Imogen felt a swell of happiness in her chest, tinged with nervous anticipation. 'I just have two questions?'

'Sure, fire away!'

'That ring on your finger... it's not of the wedding variety, is it?'

'No!' he laughed. 'Not at all. My dad bought it for me when I graduated.'

'Just checking! And secondly, how old are you? You might be sixteen or a hundred and four. Usually I'm fairly good with guessing ages from voices but...'

'Oh, this'll be good, guess then!'

'Oh, god! I am suddenly doubting my ability, but if I had to guess, I'd say you were thirty-four.'

'Thirty-four? No way! I'm twenty-four.'

'You should take it as a compliment! Your voice has gravitas... authority.' She giggled.

'If you say so.' Owen was mollified by the compliment of sorts. 'I guess it's harder to judge voices you don't know so good. Strangers, I mean.'

'It is. My friend told me not to talk to strangers, but you don't seem strange.'

'I'm not!' he almost pleaded.

'Yes, but even if you are, you're going to say that, aren't you?'

'I... I guess,' he stuttered.

'I'm only teasing you, Owen from Chicago, and besides, we're not really strangers, I know lots about you already.'

'You do?' He was curious.

'Yep. I know you have a heavy coat, quite unsuitable for travelling in, especially when it's wet. I know you have spent longer on the Sussex coast than I have, 'cos I've never been, and I know you graduated from college and that your dad was so chuffed, he bought you a ring.'

'All true!' He let his hands fall on to the table.

'See, we are not strangers at all, and so why not? I'd love to go to the Van Go Museum with you. You can be my guide.'

'Oh, god! I didn't think... I mean, is there any point in taking you to an art gallery?'

'Jesus H. Christ, sunshine, that's nearly a nine!'

'I am so sorry! I'm nervous, I guess. I don't know anyone that's blind and I swear all the words sitting on my tongue right now are about seeing and sight, like *did you see this* and *look at that*, and I'm really conscious of not letting them pop out!'

'That's funny! It's okay, I'm messing with you. I love art galleries. Usually I listen to the audio guide and it's like a good book!'

'Great!'

Imogen could hear genuine joy in his voice and it gladdened her heart. They finished their drinks in a calmer manner, both thinking about the afternoon that was about to unfold.

They stood on the pavement facing the canal. 'How do I...?' He grabbed her elbow and then felt for her hand.

'Neither!' Imogen laughed, shrugging herself free. 'Can I hold your arm like this?' She placed her hand on the underside of his raised forearm. 'Is that okay?'

'Yes! It's great. Not great that you have to... or that you can't...' he faltered.

'You have to relax, Owen!' she laughed as they slowly navigated Paulus Potterstraat, he nervous of going too fast and she too shy to ask him to speed up.

'You're tall,' commented Imogen as they paused at a pedestrian crossing.

'Yes, talk, dark and handsome, as a matter of fact.'

'Is that right?' She smiled at him.

'Well, tall and dark is true.'

'So what do you do in Chicago?' She was curious to learn.

'I'm an underwriter for an insurance company. Mainly, I just study computer files and pass them on or else refer them. It's boring, really.'

'Sounds it.'

'What about you, Imogen? Do you do anything?'

She stopped walking and faced the tall, dark stranger. 'That is also a nine! Jesus, what do you think I do... sit home all day and get my nails done?'

'I... I don't... I didn't mean to...' Owen stuttered.

Imogen howled. 'I'm messing with you again.' She patted his arm. 'I actually work for a charity, aimed mainly at teenagers who are blind or visually impaired, making sure they are aware of all there is available to assist them and trying to help with the isolation of blindness.'

'Is it isolating?' His voice was steady now, serious.

'It can be. In a world that's always busy, it can sometimes feel as if you are lost. Not only unable to see the world, but like it can't see you.'

Owen was silent. 'I don't believe that anyone can't see *you*.'

'Oh!' His compliment threw Imogen a little off balance. Her heart hammered in her chest. 'Thank you. I can hear a tram coming!'

They both stood listening. 'I can't see one.' Owen looked left and right along the street.

'I felt the rumbling in my feet,' she explained, 'just like I can feel the bikes whizzing past me. The way they cut through the air and the vibrations they make are quite particular.'

'Oh, yes, you were right, here comes a tram now!' Owen sounded surprised, as if she had summoned it, a kind of magic trick.

'Are all your other senses heightened, to compensate for your lack of sight?'

Despite his sincerity, Imogen doubled over with laughter, recalling her recent conversation with Jenny. 'Yes, that's me, a regular superhero, like Spidey Man!' She batted his arm. 'No, I just have regular senses like anyone else, though I suppose mine may be a little finer tuned.'

'You're a funny girl,' Owen concluded as they crossed the street.

Imogen wasn't sure if he meant funny ha-ha or funny weird.

The Van Gogh Museum was busy. Owen checked his heavy coat and Imogen's jacket into the cloakroom and then they wandered around the corridors and into the brightly lit galleries where masterpieces hung. Owen gave cursory descriptions of many of the paintings and any sculptures that they came across and was equally keen to tell her about the crowds they navigated, making their way to the Kurokawa wing where a small group stood gathered around the painting they had all come to see.

'There's a tour group in front of us but I think they're on the point of leaving, then we can get closer.'

Imogen gripped the arm of this stranger she trusted. Her

heart beat in anticipation, picking up on his sense of excitement. There was a burble of conversation, sighs and exclamations of joy all around her. Slowly, the sound seemed to drift to the right as people made their way into the next room.

Owen walked forward and the two of them stood in silence for some seconds. Imogen wanted to ask questions but was wary of shattering the peace, destroying the almost reverent atmosphere.

'Wow, Imogen! I'm staring at Van Gogh's "Sunflowers"! I am actually here, looking at this painting that is smaller than I imagined and worth tens of millions of pounds, can you believe that?' Owen turned to her to ask.

'It seems a lot. I think IKEA have prints for about a tenner.'

'I bet the ones in IKEA don't have security guards. This one does: two miserable-looking men in each corner of the room and cameras winking at us from the roof and the wall.'

'Are you saying nicking it's out of the question?' Imogen smiled.

'It's... It's beautiful,' he whispered, ignoring the question.

'Describe it to me.'

Owen Jackson coughed to clear his throat. 'I hope I can do it justice.' He took a deep breath. 'The picture is not perfect, or fragile like real flowers. The ones here are not even delicate... in fact the flowers are clunky, misshapen almost. The paint is thick and you can see the lines where a brush or a knife has been at work. But for those reasons it feels... I don't know how to describe it, new, fresh, like he's just finished it and walked out of the room and... even though we are in rainy Amsterdam, the colours are so vivid, so real, that it's like standing in the South of France in front of this bright burst of yellow and ochre, so real you can feel the heat of the midday sun on your skin. And the vase is simple, as if painted quickly because he had to capture the flowers before they wilted, and that makes me feel unbelievably sad, that something so beautiful is so transient and he's long dead, not just walked from the room, not at all...'

Imogen stood deep in concentration, her head turned in his direction. It was a second or two before she spoke. 'Thank you, Owen. Thank you very much.' Her voice was small. She knew that she would never forget the magic of this painting and the way her companion had made it real for her, painted the sunflowers in her mind so vividly that she too was lost in the picture.

Owen turned and bent forward. Without thought or forewarning he grazed Imogen's cheek with a kiss.

'Oh!' She was a little taken aback as her tall, dark guide snatched this moment. It was a sweet kiss, firm and full of promise, and while they both recovered from the intensity of the contact, Imogen's phone buzzed in her pocket.

'Hello.'

'Imi! I'm awake! Where are you? I'll come and find you and we can tear up the town.' Jenny whooped with newfound energy.

'Actually, Jen, I won't be free for a while. I'm just... er...' She wondered how best to phrase it.

'You just er-what? Is this code? Do you need me to call the Polis?' Jenny was only half-joking.

'No, I'm fine. I've met a nice guy. He's stood in front of me now so I can't say too much, but I thought I might hang out with him for a bit.' Imogen felt Owen squeeze her arm in approval.

'Are you joshing me? We come all the way to bloody Holland, I turn my back for five minutes and you've pulled a bloke?'

'I'll give you a call in a bit, Jen. Is that okay?'

'It'll bloody well have to be. I think I'll go back to sleep. I was only up 'cos I thought you'd be alone and I felt guilty. If you're sorted, I'll have another forty winks!'

'I'll see you later.'

'Be careful, Imi, and keep your phone on.'

Imogen returned it to her pocket. 'That was my friend Jenny. You probably gathered that, she's got a voice like a fog horn.'

'She's protective of you.'

'Yes. I've known her a very long time.'

'It's good to have friends like that.' He kicked at the floor, indicating by his forlorn tone of voice that maybe he didn't.

Imogen listened to Owen shuffling from foot to foot. 'What would you like to do now?' She wanted him to make the decision, wary of coercing him.

'Whatever you'd like. We can go get some food, seek out coffee, another gallery, a canal walk?'

'All good. I'll leave it up to you!' Imogen smiled.

Suddenly Owen clapped loudly, making her jump. 'I have it, I know exactly where I want to take you!'

'Lead on.' Imogen slipped her arm through his. This was turning into a very good day indeed.

They walked along, chatting and listening to each other in the way that two people do when they meet and feel a connection that is hard to describe. There was something new about this for Imogen. Often, when meeting a stranger, conversation was awkward, stilted, as she had so little in common with them and no shared history to fall back on, but with Owen it felt quite the opposite. There was so much to talk about because they knew so little about each other. It was exhilarating.

'Do you have brothers and sisters?' she asked.

'Yes, two. One of each, both older. My sister's married and

has two kids and lives in North Carolina and my brother is in the US Air Force, making us all proud, putting on the uniform. He's away on tour right now.'

'You must miss him.'

'I do, yes. And my sister's kids. They are two of my very favourite people.'

'You sound broody!' laughed Imogen, thinking how his tone mirrored her own, an insight into her longing to be a mum.

'No, not really. I love them but I can't have kids of my own... mumps when I was younger... It's just how it is. I'm kind of reconciled to it.'

Imogen squeezed his arm at the revelation. She heard the tone beneath his practised words and could decipher the echo of regret.

'What about you, any siblings?'

Imogen shook her head. 'No. Just me and about a million cousins! People often ask if it's lonely being an only child, but our house was always jam packed or else we were at my gran's, who lives close by, and *her* house was always packed, so no, not lonely at all.'

'My mum passed away when I was ten so our house has always been kind of quiet. I don't remember it being busy and full of her laughter, not really, but my dad tells me it was like that once.'

'You must miss her too.'

'Very much. Even now.'

Imogen heard the catch in his voice. 'I didn't mean to upset you,' she said quickly.

'No! Not at all. I just don't really talk about her much and, when I do, it gets me.' Owen clapped again, a habit of his. Again she jumped. 'Hey, no time for regret, it's our anniversary!'

'It is?' She laughed, a little nervously.

'Yes! I have known you, my new friend, for three hours exactly!'

'Wow! Happy Anniversary.' She smiled at him. 'And can I ask, do you kiss all your new friends?'

'Only the pretty ones.'

'Oh, well, lucky me!' she giggled.

'God, that sounded like I do it often. In fact I have never done that before. I just got caught up in the moment. I hope I didn't offend you.'

'Offend me? No. As my gran says, a bit of hanky-panky is actually good for you.'

'Hanky-panky? Now that's something I don't hear every day!' Owen chuckled.

Suddenly Imogen stopped walking, as if concentrating on something that lay ahead. 'Oh my word!' She inhaled deeply. 'That... That is quite possibly the most incredible scent I have ever experienced!' She breathed deeply, walking on towards the source of it. 'Oh, Owen!' She swayed, as if intoxicated.

He held her arm and guided her forward. 'I knew you'd like it. Welcome to the world-famous Bloemenmarkt... the Amsterdam Flower Market!'

They stepped out, Owen holding fast to Imogen's arm. 'So the market is here on the Singel Canal and it floats! The stalls are on houseboats,' he explained.

'That's amazing!' Imogen sighed, still quite overcome by the beautiful scent of flowers, whose rain-kissed petals had only benefited from a light touch of drizzle where it fluttered in beneath the canopies.

'It's an explosion of colour, rainbows in front of my eyes, all shades from hot to cold! Here, it's a lily.' Owen let go of her arm and bent forward to pick a pale, long-stemmed lily from a bucket. He held the flower beneath her palm. Imogen let the silky-soft petals brush the underside of her hand. It tickled a little. She raised the flower to her nose and inhaled the peppery, warm scent.

'Lovely,' she said, running her finger along the smooth, pointed outline of a petal.

'Try this one.' He removed the lily and placed a shorter, stubbier stem in her hand. Imogen ran her hand up the stalk, which was covered in fine hairs that felt a little resistant when she brushed them the wrong way. Her fingers tentatively touched the cluster of long, sharp petals that were almost quill-like. She sniffed her fingers; now slightly sticky with residue, they smelt sweet, sickly, and reminded her of fruit that was spoiling. 'Ooh, I'm not sure about that one! What is it?'

'Haven't the faintest idea, but it looks very exotic. Its colour is fiery and I can picture it growing somewhere hot and dusty.'

Imogen handed it back and wiped her hand on her coat.

'Okay, this one is easy.' Owen opened her fingers and placed not one, but two slender, twig-like stems in her palm. Imogen ran her fingers over the knotty hubs that held the most delicate, paper-thin, trumpeted petals in a neat row, clinging to one side of the stem. She raised them to her face and took a deep breath. 'Freesias!' Their smell was sweet, honey-like and pretty. 'I love them!'

'They look incredible too, they're a glorious deep, dark purple, the colour of a bruise or a rolling, thundery sky, and yet despite their darkness, they are delicate and beautiful.'

Imogen stood still, taking in the majesty of the market. Listening to the happy burble of the visitors who all sounded equally enthralled to be in such a place. It had been a long time since someone had gone to so much trouble just for her.

'Thank you, Owen. Thank you for bringing me here.'

'Oh, my pleasure! It's quite a sight, I shan't forget it.'

She could hear the happiness in his voice.

Me either...

As the two of them stood beneath the nearest canopy, rain began to fall again in earnest, pooling in pockets of canvas before falling in a rush, splashing down on the pavement below and sending spray up over their feet.

'Come on!' Owen gripped Imogen's arm and hurried her into the street, where a cab had pulled over to drop off a fare. He practically bundled her into the back seat before climbing in beside her and giving the driver the address.

'Where are we going? Should I be worried? Because if you are kidnapping me, I should warn you, you'll be very unlikely to get much of a ransom and you have clearly never met my friend Jenny, who would beat the shite out of you!'

'I'm not kidnapping you, I just thought we could go back to my hotel.'

'Flippin' 'eck, that's a bit forward, isn't it?'

'No! Oh, god, no! I didn't mean like that or... for that! No!'

She heard the embarrassment in his protestation.

'I... I just thought we could get dry and there's a nice bar so we could have a drink and maybe some... some soup!' he stuttered.

'Phew, well, thank goodness for that, Owen. Thank goodness we are going for soup because I'm not that kind of girl.' Imogen gave a mock tut. 'Soup sounds good.'

She felt his thigh muscles unknot with relief as they sat close side by side while the cab trundled across the city.

'I've had the best afternoon. Thank you.' Imogen turned her head towards him.

'Me too, absolutely brilliant.'

'You could be a guide, you know.' She gave him the best compliment she could think of.

'Really?'

'Yes, really, you are very considerate and original – who knew that freesias could be the colour of a bruise or thunder, but still smell so sweet!'

'I enjoyed it too. It's funny, it kind of made me look at the world in a different way, because you can't. I haven't had to think about how to describe things before, not in that way. I'm glad I did good.'

'You really did, you have a knack for it.' She patted his thigh.

The hotel lobby was a little sterile; the soft carpeting and groups of high-backed sofas meant it could have been any hotel in any city in the world. One of a large chain, it was soulless and efficient. Conversation was conducted at little more than a murmur, the temperature was carefully regulated and there was a tinkle of piano music in the background that Imogen thought might be more appropriate in a lift.

'So' – Owen removed his heavy coat and placed it over his arm – 'shall we get a drink?'

She nodded. 'That'd be lovely.'

They wandered to the bar area where foreign visitors sipped glasses of wine or swigged from cold bottled beers and all commented on the lousy weather, as though they had expected the Netherlands in winter to be tropical.

'What would you like?' whispered Owen close to her face. He was sweating a little; it heightened his natural scent and wasn't unpleasant.

'Glass of white wine would be great.' She folded her cane into her handbag.

'Shall we get a bottle?' he asked tentatively.

'Why not? We're on holiday after all, we should do things we wouldn't normally do at home!'

Owen clapped again. This time however she didn't jump. She was getting used to him.

With two squeaky-clean wine glasses and the opened bottle on a tray, they navigated the tables and sofas, looking for a good place to sit.

'It's all a bit busy.' Owen twisted to the left and right.

'We could take it to your room?' Imogen felt bold and scared, all at the same time, her cool delivery masking a pulse that raced nervously.

'Oh! Well, yes, sure, we can if you are comfortable with that...'

She heard him swallow; he was nervous too. 'Of course. I mean, it's only a glass of wine, right, and maybe we could watch some crap TV?'

'Yep, crap TV sounds good.' He smiled as they made their way to the lift. On his floor they giggled their way along the narrow corridor.

'Here we are.' Owen put down the tray and retrieved the key card from his wallet.

Imogen pulled out her phone and texted Jenny: *If you are awake, don't wait up! I'm safe and having a blast. Will make it up to you tomorrow! I LIKE Amsterdam! xxxx*

As the door closed behind them, Imogen found herself in a large room. Owen walked forward and put the tray on a hard surface, table or desk. The sound was muted, as if the walls were soft. The air felt warm against her face.

'This feels nice,' she whispered.

'Sorry, it's a bit dark, I'll find the light switch.'

'Owen, it doesn't make any difference to me.' She placed her hand on his arm.

'Oh, god! I'm stupid! I'm sorry, Imogen.' Once again he sounded mortified.

'Don't be sorry, you have no idea how happy it makes me that you forget.'

'I think you are amazing...' he breathed.

Imogen ran her fingers through her hair. 'I find it odd that people think I'm amazing or brave or any other adjective they want to throw at me, when I only do what everyone else does every day of the week, without praise or recognition.'

She knew that he was staring at her and felt the heat of a blush creep over her cheeks.

'But that's just it. You're amazing *because* you do what everyone else does every day of the week, when you can't see.'

Imogen shrugged. 'I guess.'

'So were you born with any sight? Have you ever been able to see?'

'No.'

'Then what do you dream about? I mean, how do you dream?' He was curious. 'I can't imagine not dreaming in pictures, not seeing things while I sleep or not seeing colour.'

Imogen smiled. It was rare that someone who didn't know her well was so forward with their questioning. She could tell by his tone that he was genuinely interested.

'I dream in sounds and feelings and smells and touch. It's just like it is for me every day, like real life, only I'm asleep!'

'Okay, I could have guessed the asleep bit. Duh!' he laughed.

'Oh, rude!' She folded her arms across her chest. 'That was nudging a four!'

Owen reached out and ran his hands over her arms before pulling her close to him.

'My life isn't great, Imogen. I'm quite lonely a lot of the time. Meeting you has made me feel alive! I feel happy! I never would have thought this was right here, waiting for me in Amsterdam.'

'I think you never know what's around the next corner, never know what twists and turns life might throw at you next, but you should always be ready to face whatever comes at you.'

He kissed her very gently on the mouth. Imogen pulled back and touched her fingers to his chest, feeling the buttons of his cotton shirt. 'I was thinking, Owen.'

'What?' he breathed.

'I might quite like to be a girl like that, just for an hour or so. It sounds like more fun than having soup...'

They laughed together as they tumbled towards the large, soft bed. When their faces touched, she felt the pressure of metal against her nose.

'You wear glasses?'

'Yes.'

She listened to the clatter as he threw them on to the bedside cabinet.

'You look beautiful,' he sighed.

'Oh, well, I do now you've taken your glasses off!'

'Trust me, you are beautiful with or without my glasses.' He kissed her neck.

'And you feel wonderful and smell wonderful.' Running her hands over his shirt, Imogen was helping him with the buttons.

'Is this okay?' he whispered, anticipating what might come next.

She nodded. It was more than okay. This was living, this was an adventure.

Nine

'Did you have a good time?' Duncan asked as he scooped up the girls' bags and guided his daughter and her friend out to his van in the airport's short-stay car park.

'Mmmnn.' Imogen smiled, wary of giving away too much to her dad.

'We had a great time. One of us rather more so than the other!' Jenny jabbed her friend in the back.

'One of us was too tired to keep up the pace,' Imogen retorted, laughing.

'Thank goodness one of us *was* too knackered to keep up the pace, or one of us might have been a right royal gooseberry!'

Duncan shook his head in confusion as he loaded their bags into the back of his van. 'I haven't got the foggiest what the two of yous is talking about, but as long as you had a great trip, that's the main thing.'

The girls squashed into the front seat together in the way they had been doing since they were small.

'We did, Dad. We really did,' Imogen told him.

Duncan beamed, happy that their friendship was fully restored.

After dropping Jenny off at home, where a rather animated Shay waited for his wife on the doorstep, and enjoying a cup of tea at her parents' kitchen table, Imogen lay on her bed and switched on her laptop. And there it was, his name, repeated in a slightly robotic sound alert from her Inbox. Owen Jackson. Owen Jackson.

It became part of her daily routine, reading and replying to his daily email. With a six-hour time difference, their lives ran half a day adrift, with him waking while she was in the middle of her working day and Imogen settling down to bed at night as he was hitting the gym or still sorting through computer files in a dimly lit office.

'So how's lover boy?' Jenny asked as the bus sat in traffic on the Ferry Road. The air was a thick fug of wet clothes, steamed-up windows and the smell of fast food wafting from the teenage boy a couple of seats back, who was tucking into a fat burger.

'Okay. Yep.'

'Okay, Yep? That's it?' Jenny elbowed her friend.

'Ow! What else do you want?' Imogen laughed, rubbing her side.

'I want the juicy gossip, to hear his declarations of love and to know what plans you are making for a re-match?'

Imogen was quiet. 'There are no plans, Jen, and certainly no declarations of love.'

'Aaaw, don't say that! I'm already saving for flights to Chicago and I've picked my wedding outfit from the catalogue!'

'Very funny.'

'Don't look so grumpy, this is supposed to be exciting! Don't you still email each other every day?' Jenny was not going to let it drop.

'We do, aye, but...' Imogen didn't know where to start.

'But what?'

'I don't know. It's difficult, being so far away. It's hard to progress, move forward.'

'Oh, honey, I know, but if it's worth having...'

'No,' Imogen interrupted her friend, 'actually it's not. It's not worth having. And if I'm being honest, it's started to feel like a bit of a chore. We say the same things over and over, I tell him about my day and he tells me about his, and we ask the same questions.' She sighed. 'There are only so many times you can read what someone has had in their sandwich for lunch and what the weather might do tomorrow! When you are with someone in person, you can chat about where you are, what's happening, make plans, but this... this is different. We are stuck in one day in Amsterdam. One beautiful, brilliant, magical day in Amsterdam, but I think that's it. I think that's all we were meant to have and staying in touch feels like we are trying to eke it out, make it more than it ever should be.'

'Shit.' Jenny sounded disappointed. 'I thought it might be the real deal. You were so happy!'

'I was. I am! I don't regret a thing. But that doesn't mean I have to keep playing boyfriend and girlfriend just because, for one day, I was happy and we had great sex in the Amsterdam equivalent of the Premier Inn!' Imogen hadn't meant to shout but the titters running through the bus passengers and the cough from Burger Boy told her that her voice had carried a little further than she had intended.

Jenny laid her head on her friend's shoulder as the bus finally moved forward. 'You're right. It doesn't.'

'Thank you for understanding. I'm going to tell him tonight, just get it done.'

'I found you much more exciting when you were my interesting, exotic friend with a fabulous Yankee boyfriend. Now you're just back to plain old Imogen from West Pilton.'

'Sorry to disappoint you. Anyway, I thought I was your adventurous friend who hung off a building on a piece of chewing gum?' Imogen laughed.

'Suppose so.' Jenny sighed; it was going to take a little while for her to recover from the disappointment and to erase the images of herself tripping the light fantastic around Chicago on a visit.

Imogen laughed, but her tummy still flipped at the prospect of the conversation she was going to have to have with Owen.

Imogen curled her feet under her on the sofa and pulled her fleecy dressing gown around her shoulders. This moment had dogged her thoughts all day. Her palms were sweating and her breath came shallowly. She dialled the number and waited. Owen's voice was a sharp reminder of his loveliness; he was happy to hear from her, his tone welcoming and comforting, like the warm back seat of a taxi on a rainy day.

'Hey, Imi! Well, this has just made a pretty bad day a whole lot better! I've left the office, I'm strolling along North LaSalle and it is c... c...c... freezing!' he laughed.

'It's midnight here and just as cold.' She kept her tone flat, not wanting to mislead him any more than she maybe already had. 'Owen, I need to talk to you.'

'Oh-oh! That sounds ominous, is everything okay?'

Imogen shook her head to erase the memory of the flower market and that wonderful time together. This was no time for sentiment, however. Far better for them both in the long run to be brutally honest. 'Not really, no, the thing is...'

★

'Only me, Mum!' Imogen called into the kitchen as she stepped into the hallway of her childhood home.

'Kettle's on!' came Isla's stock reply.

Imogen shrugged her arms from her coat and felt for the square newel post on which she hung it. Her fingers lightly brushed the spindles of the staircase to her right, as they had countless times before, helping her to navigate her way around her childhood home. 'Hiya,' she called.

'Hello, darlin'.' Isla came over and wrapped her daughter in a brief, but tight hug. 'How's you?'

'Great, tired, the usual.' Imogen gave the summary as she took a seat at the table and yawned.

'Work busy?'

'Yep.' She rested her head on one upturned hand, her elbow firmly planted.

'Good god, Imogen, if you're that tired, why don't you away to your bed?' Isla poured the hot water on to the teabags and gave them a little squeeze with the teaspoon against the side of the mug.

'Sorry, Mum. I've just no energy!'

'Have you got a bug?' Her mum swept her daughter's brow with the back of one hand. 'You feel all right to me.'

'Don't think so.' Imogen yawned. 'I'm getting my period and I'm just blurgh... you know, sore boobs, bloated, yuck. I'll be fine in a couple of days.' She stretched her hand across the table to reach for her tea.

'Imogen?'

'Uh-huh?' She sipped her drink slowly.

'Don't quite know how to say this, but there's no chance you could be pregnant, is there?'

Imogen snorted laughter into her tea, then sat very still. 'Do you know, Mum, I've not considered that. I've just assumed that this attempt will fail like the last time because I don't think I could cope with the disappointment, daren't hope! And I've been so busy.'

'I know. It's just that...'

'What?' Imogen placed the mug on the table and turned towards her mum, trying to pick up clues from her breathing and movements.

Isla coughed. 'You look rosy... well, blooming some would say. And your boobs might be sore, but they're also bigger. A lot bigger!'

Imogen cupped her chest and felt the spill of flesh over the top of her bra. *Oh my god!*

Her mum continued, 'And the tiredness. You could be.'

Imogen sat still, thinking of the evening she had spent cloistered in a hotel room with a tall, dark, kind, bespectacled stranger who was incapable of having children, never suspecting for a minute that the procedure she had had weeks earlier might have worked!

'Oh my god, Imi! This could be it!' Her mum trod the line between letting her own excitement get the better of her and not building up her daughter's hopes.

'I don't know.' Imogen swallowed and reached again for her tea, keen to rid her mouth of the metallic taste that had plagued her for a few weeks now. 'Oh, god, Mum! I just don't know.'

It was three days later, as Jenny stood in the hallway, that Imogen tried the words out for the first time.

'You are fucking kidding me?' Jenny yelled as she jumped up and down on the spot.

'I'm not.'

'Oh, my good god! But I thought... How? When?' Jenny lunged forward and squeezed her friend.

'The second attempt, just before Amsterdam!'

'Holy shit! Oh my god! No way! You are going to be a mum! Oh my god!'

'I can't believe it either, Jen. Turns out my gran was right. A good night out and a bit of hanky-panky to relax me *was* all it required, in a way.'

'Shit! Have you told Owen?' Jenny cut to the chase.

'No. I don't see the need. I'll not see him again and it's nothing to do with him. It hasn't really sunk in.'

'I can't believe it! I'm going to be an aunty!'

Imogen turned and made her way into the lounge, letting her fingers trail over the familiar surfaces and openings, the dimensions of which were imprinted on her brain like a map. The girls flopped at either end of the sofa.

'You're going to be a mum! How do you feel?'

Imogen exhaled. 'Tired, excited, nervous, shocked, and not necessarily in that order.'

'Did you do a test?'

'Aye, four tests, just to be on the safe side. My mum was with me, it was hilarious!'

'Have you told your dad?'

'Yep, that night. It wasn't like we could keep it a secret with my mum squealing the place down and planning her knitting.'

'How far are you?' Jenny sat forward.

'Eleven weeks.'

'Blimey.'

'I know. And what's scaring me more than anything is that if this baby was as premature as I was, it means it would be born in just about that time again.' Imogen pulled the sleeves of her jumper over her hands.

'Shit!' Jenny summed it up.

'Yep, shit.'

'When's the last time you spoke to Chicago Boy?'

'It was the night I ended it, about six weeks ago now. I'm definitely not going to tell him, Jen. What would be the point?'

Her friend placed her hand on Imogen's leg. 'The point would be that he mattered to you and it would be good for this baby to have as many people involved in its life as possible. I think he'd be a better role model than Shay!'

Imogen pictured Owen walking home from work, the way he had sounded when she had ended it, the crack in his voice, his clear disappointment. It didn't make her a very nice person, but she had been a little gladdened by his response, happy that he had cared.

'It's got to be about my choices too, Jen. Plus I genuinely don't want to hurt him. I'd hate him to feel that we might have a future. That wouldn't be fair to him. The important thing is that I'm fine, and this baby and I will be fine.' Imogen smiled at the thought of her little one, nestling safe and warm inside her. Every ounce of her body was filled with happy anticipation. *I still can't believe it!* she thought.

'But you said the reason it wasn't working was that you couldn't move forward, couldn't progress, because you were too far apart. Surely something like this opens up a whole new topic of conversation, and that will help things progress!'

'I said that was one of the reasons, Jen. Christ, you are taking this break-up harder than either of us!'

'I just remember how you looked, in Amsterdam, so happy. And that's what I've always wanted for you.' Her friend touched her arm.

'I know and I love you for it, you daft mare. But I'm happy *now*. I am. This is what I have always dreamt of! And getting hooked up with a guy I don't know, just for the sake of a neat ending, it's not fair on anyone. Least of all him.'

'I'm not sure if you are really brave or really stupid.' Jenny lay back on the sofa.

'I think we both know that anyone who dangles off a building on a bit of chewing gum is a bit of both.'

'You're probably right,' Jenny laughed. 'And if it's a girl, don't feel embarrassed about naming her after me. I won't mind at all.'

'No, that'd be too weird, having my child and my best friend with the same name. Anyways, it might be a boy.'

'Well, Shay wouldn't mind either!'

'I don't think so,' Imogen laughed.

'You dissing my man's name?' Jenny thumped her friend on the arm.

'Oi! You can't do that to me, I am with child!'

'With child? You dafty!' The two girls collapsed in giggles on the sofa.

Ten

It was the early hours of the morning, the heating was yet to kick in and the place felt a little damp. With her twenty-week scan picture stuck to the fridge for all to admire, Imogen ran the cold tap in the kitchen. She had slept poorly and her dry throat suggested she had been snoring, open-mouthed. Gripping the tall tumbler in her palm, she turned to make her way back to bed.

It happened in a flash. The glass slipped from her hand and shattered with an ear-splitting crack. Imogen took a step forward and felt the bite of a shard in the soft sole of her foot.

'Ouch!' She instinctively stepped backwards and this time the pain was sharp and instant in her heel.

Tears sprang to her eyes as she stood marooned in the kitchen, surrounded by slivers of glass. Turning carefully and trying to ignore the pain in her feet, she reached forward, sliding her hand along the work surface until her fingertips touched upon the phone in its charging station. Thank goodness she had replaced it and not, as was her habit, left it languishing on the sofa or in the bathroom. Her fingers shook as she pressed the pre-set digit that linked her to her parents.

'Hello?' her dad's voice croaked, as he tried to shrug off the veil of sleep.

'Dad... I...'

'What is it, darlin'? Are you okay?'

She heard the note of alarm in his voice and wanted to reassure him through her tears. 'Dad, I'm okay, but... but can you... can you come over?'

'I'll be there in a minute, Imi. Hang on.'

'What's wrong? What's happened?' she heard her mum's panic-stricken query as her dad fumbled to replace the phone in the darkness.

Imogen started to shiver. She had thought she would be returning to the warmth of her bed and had neglected to grab her dressing gown. It was cold in the kitchen and she was too afraid to move. Her cotton nightie shook with the tremors in her body. She ran her palms over her tummy.

'It's okay, little one, no need to be afraid. It's all okay.'

Only minutes later, she heard the sound of a key in the lock and her parents rushed in. 'Here we are, darlin',' Isla soothed as Duncan flipped the light switch.

'I've hurt my foot and I'm too scared to move!'

'Oh, honey! I can see. Stand very still,' her mum instructed, calmly, firmly.

Isla went into overdrive, crouching on the kitchen floor, collecting the larger shards of glass, sweeping the smaller fragments into the dustpan and finishing with a good vacuum around the space. Duncan overrode the boiler setting and put the heating on before nipping upstairs to fetch his daughter's dressing gown, which he placed around her shivering shoulders.

'There, that's the last of it,' Isla soothed. 'Dunc, can you fetch a chair from the table?'

He duly grabbed a dining chair and placed it by his daughter. Imogen sat and wrapped her arms around herself, feeling the warmth slowly return to her body. Isla lifted her right foot and placed it on her own lap, tending to her cuts, cleaning and cooing, as though her daughter were still a child.

'Thanks, Mum.'

'That's what we are here for. Any time you need us, you just shout and we will be here, always.'

'You frightened us half to death!' her dad chimed in.

'Sorry, Dad.'

'It was fairly comical. I'm only glad it's still dark out. There's your mother and me in our nightclothes and coats, running around the streets like we'd lost our marbles! And what's even funnier is that the sun is coming up soon and we'll have to walk home like this! I think we'll make out we were sleepwalking.'

They all laughed.

Isla placed her daughter's foot on the floor. 'There. And the other one.'

Without warning Imogen slumped forward into her mum's arms. 'Oh, Mum!'

Isla held her daughter and stroked her hair. 'Shhhh, it's okay. Don't you cry.' She looked at her husband; this was a rare display of emotion from their child.

'I'm scared!' Imogen whispered.

'No need! No need, it's all cleared away, nothing to hurt you now. It's fine.'

'I'm pregnant!'

'Yes, darlin', we do know, and if we didn't, we might have noticed.' She placed her hand on her daughter's full belly.

'I'm pregnant, Mum, and all I can think about is what would it have been like to have a baby crawling on the floor when that happened?'

Isla and Duncan were silent.

'How do I keep them safe, Mum? How do I keep my little one safe if I can't always stop myself from getting hurt? What am I going to do?' Her sobs were loud and unrestrained. 'How am I going to do this?'

Isla pulled her into a sitting position and held her by the tops of her arms. 'Now you listen to me, Imogen Claire, all new mums feel this way to a certain degree.' Isla sniffed. 'When you were born I was petrified, we both were.'

'That's the truth,' her dad chimed.

'The only blind person I'd had any contact with before that was the old man who used to stand outside British Home Stores, playing a harmonica and collecting coins in his upturned cap on the floor. Another man used to walk him there in the morning and then collect him later in the day. He was a poor soul and I...' Isla swallowed her own tears. 'I thought a terrible life awaited you. A little life. I was so scared of bringing you home for the first time, scared stupid! I couldn't imagine how I would care for this baby who couldn't see, how I would teach you about the world and how I would keep you safe. But the truth is, it was me who had a lot to learn, me who was taught. I watched you blossom into the most amazing child... strong, wilful, determined, inquisitive... your blindness never came into it. I have watched you overcome every obstacle that has ever blocked your path.'

'We're so proud of you, Imogen.'

She smiled to hear the tremor in her dad's voice. Her mum continued, 'And there was one day when things changed. Actually that's not true... more accurately, it was the day that I changed. You were ten and we'd gone on the family jaunt up to Loch Katrine. I'd always been so afraid of getting in the water because you couldn't see the bottom and the odd bit of weed or a branch might touch your leg. I used to watch the boys and Gran and Grampy bobbing around, having a laugh.' She sighed. 'But that day we arrived and unpacked the car and your cousins and all were in the water, screaming and splashing around, while we set the tents up. I watched you step out of your jeans and throw your T-shirt over your head. In your blue swimsuit you walked slowly to the edge of the grass. You didn't know I was watching you. And when your feet touched the plank of the dock and you felt the wood beneath your toes, you ran!' Isla stopped to mop at the tears that streaked her face. 'You ran, Imi! With no idea what lay ahead or how deep the water was or even when the dock ended, you ran!

'I watched you, powering along the dock with your head back and your arms held high, and as soon as your feet reached the end of the jetty, you lifted your legs and hurled yourself through the air.' Isla fought for breath. 'It was magnificent! You had no idea where you were landing or what lay in wait, but you didn't care. I stood staring at the water and it felt like minutes, but of course it was only seconds, until you popped your wee head above the surface like a seal. I called your dad...'

'She did, grabbed my arm and said, *You won't believe what she's just gone and done!*'

'I couldn't believe it. You were so brave, braver than me, fearless. I realised then I had to let you fly, my fearless girl. I knew on that day that you could do anything. And now you are having a baby, and this child will truly be the luckiest bairn alive to have you as its mum.'

Imogen beamed at her. 'Thank you. Thank you, Mum.'

Eleven

It was ten o'clock on a cold, rainy Thursday when Leah Mary McGuire arrived in the world, weighing a very respectable seven pounds and two ounces. Screaming and crying, with legs flailing and fists clenched, she was a little battler, just like her mum.

Isla and Duncan sat staring at their daughter, who held their granddaughter tightly in her arms, running her fingers through the baby's shock of dark, curly hair. Imogen was a natural.

'How are you feeling?' Isla whispered.

'You don't have to whisper, Mum, they are surrounded by noise the whole time they are in the womb, us talking isn't going to wake her!' Imogen laughed.

'Yes, I've been told that before,' Isla sighed.

'I'm feeling fine. Tired, obviously, bit sore, but good. No, better than good, amazing! She's a great little feeder. Not quite got the hang of sleeping at night time yet, but that'll come.'

'Has Jen been in?' Her dad whispered too.

'Has she been in? I can't get rid of her! She's obsessed. Talks to Leah as though I'm not here, making plans and telling her all the places she'll take her. Just hope I'm invited too!' Imogen thought about the moment when she'd asked her best friend to be her daughter's guardian, should there ever be the need, and the reply: *Of course I fucking will! Who else is going to do it? I'm her aunty and I love her.* Imogen smiled at the memory.

'Oh, talk of the devil!' Duncan smiled as his daughter's mate poked her head around the door.

'Hello, all! How are we?' Jenny made a beeline for the bed and kissed the little girl on the forehead.

'All good.' Imogen beamed. A smile was never very far from her lips these days. It was as if she existed in this blissful bubble, where all she needed was to be close to Leah, inhaling the warm scent of her and feeling the softness of her skin against her own.

'Isla, Duncs, this is going to sound really rude of me...'

'That doesn't usually stop you, Jen!' Duncan chortled.

'Ha! Right enough. But would you mind if I had a word with Imi on my own, in private?'

'Oh!' Isla grabbed her bag and sat up straight. 'No, sure.' She prodded her husband and touched her hand to her daughter's leg under the cover. 'Be back in a wee while.'

Imogen waved, listening for the door to close. 'What's going on?' she asked curiously.

'Oh, god. Here we go.'

'You all right, Jen?' She could hear her friend pacing up and down and huffing.

'Don't speak! Just let me talk.'

Imogen heard her take a deep breath.

'I don't always agree with you, Imi. But I always respect your wishes, you know that.' Jenny spoke quickly, nervously.

'True, that's why we get on!' She wondered where this might be going.

'The thing is, I've done something.'

'What?' Imogen's voice was stern. 'Oh, god, what have you done? I'm thinking you've registered her for karate classes or changed her name by deed poll to Jenny!'

Jen sat on the edge of the bed and ran a finger over Leah's

tiny, button nose. 'No. It's worse than that. Probably worse than all of that put together.'

'You've killed a man?' Imogen laughed to hide her rising fear.

'No again, but you might kill me. All I can say is, it was an accident. Kind of an accident. I started a ball rolling with the best intentions and it kind of came back very quickly and hit me in the arse... more like a crap boomerang than a ball, really.'

'For god's sake, Jenny, that's lots of kind ofs! Just spit it out!' Imogen was starting to feel nervous and Leah shifted in her arms, in tune with her mother's emotions.

'I might have accidentally sent out a message to all my Facebook friends that my mate Imi had given birth to a beautiful wee girl.'

Imogen laughed with relief. 'Oh, don't worry about that! Folk are sure to find out soon enough when they see me wandering around with this little bundle. Don't worry about it. So you broke the news? That's fine. You're forgiven.'

'Well, thank you. But that's not the end of it...'

'Oh, god! Go on.' Imogen felt her heart rate increase once again.

'The thing is, I forgot that one of my Facebook friends is Chicago Boy – I added him when you two were... you know.'

'Right.' Imogen swallowed, wondering how Owen might feel about the news and whether he might get in contact. 'Well, it can't be helped. I'm sure he won't even see it, and if he does, then he'll probably just be glad he had a lucky escape!'

'He did see it.' Jenny was adamant about that.

'Oh.' Imogen held Leah a little tighter as she squirmed in her mother's arms.

'He's outside.'

'I'm... I'm sorry?' Imogen thought she must have misheard.

'Chicago Boy, Owen, he's outside.' Jenny repeated.

'Out... outside the hospital?' Imogen felt her pulse race and her head swim.

'Outside the room,' Jenny clarified.

'Shit!' Imogen managed.

'Aye, shit.'

Imogen turned her head at the sound of a light rapping on the door. And before she had time to think, to remonstrate or plan, she heard the tread of his soft-soled shoes on the shiny floor. 'Hey, Imi.'

She had forgotten the pleasant note to his baritone voice. 'Hey, Owen.' He stepped into the room and with him came the unmistakable scent of freesias.

'I think I'll leave you two to it.' Jenny crept away.

Owen Jackson from Chicago pulled the chair towards the bed and sat down, leaning forward to get a better view of Imogen's baby and to steady his shaking hands on the mattress.

'So,' he offered, sounding calm.

'I had a second round of IUI just before Amsterdam, in case you were wondering.' Imogen spoke softly, feeling a wave of emotion that she hadn't expected.

'She's beautiful!'

'Wow!' She loved hearing this.

'Wow indeed. Why didn't you tell me you were pregnant?' he whispered.

'It was a lot to take in, a lot to think about, and we were done and I figured I didn't want to make it any more complicated than it needed to be.' She spoke the truth, quietly.

'What's her name?'

'Leah... Leah Mary.'

'Mary was my mother's name.' He smiled.

'And my gran's.'

'I brought you flowers.'

'I know. Thank you.' She smiled gratefully, listening to the rustle of cellophane as he placed them on the table. The sweet smell of freesias invaded her nose. 'Would you like to hold her?'

'I think so. I'm a bit nervous.'

He sounded it.

'Well, I am too. You'll be fine, just hold her snugly and close to you. She'll be happy.'

Owen stood and placed his arms under the body of the child and lifted her to his chest, where he cradled her against him. 'She's so tiny!'

'Not really, about average.' Imogen tried to calm the nerves that fluttered in her stomach.

'There is nothing, absolutely nothing, average about her.' His voice was thick with emotion. 'Oh, my! Hello, Leah. Hey there, little girl!'

'Describe her to me.' Imogen smiled as her hands toyed with the edge of the blanket.

'Oh, Imogen.' Owen paused. 'She has long fingers with tiny nails that I can see dancing over piano keys or holding a bow against a cello. Her skin is pale like buttermilk, pure and soft. Her eyelashes, thick and dark, sit like tiny sleeping bugs on top of her rosy cheeks. She looks like goodness, she looks like happy, she looks like you.'

'I forgot you have that wonderful knack of helping me to see things.'

'As compliments go, that's about a ten. I've missed you, Imogen.'

'I've missed you, Owen, but you have to know that I am not looking for a man, not looking for any more than I have right now. Being a new mum is a big adjustment.'

'I know. But the thing is, I love you, Imi. I do. I've tried not to since you called it a day, but I can't help it. I can't stop thinking about you, missing you. I've been so miserable. The only thing that's made me happy is reliving that one day in Amsterdam. I want to be near you because I think I'll be less miserable being near you in Scotland than far away from you in Chicago. I'm not asking for anything other than that we be friends and take it from there. I want to be with you, Imogen, only you, and if I can't be with you, then I'll be happy to be close to you, for now.'

Imogen felt the flicker of love in her for this kindly man who had travelled halfway around the world to hold her baby. 'I think Leah will be very lucky to have someone like you in her life. We both will.'

'That sounds like you might be willing to give us a chance?'

'I guess I am.' She smiled, it really was the very best start... 'But we have to take it slowly, Owen. One day at a time.'

He reached forward and kissed her forehead, holding Leah tight. 'I know, because you are not that kind of girl, right?'

'That's right.' She laughed.

Owen looked at the woman who held his hopes and dreams in her hands. 'Someone once told me that you never know what's around the next corner, never know what twists and turns life might throw at you, but that you should always be ready to face whatever comes at you.'

'They did.' She remembered.

'And I'm ready to face this, Imogen. I won't abandon you or Leah, not ever. I'll never let you down. I'm going to stick around and see where this twist and turn might lead us. I have a lot of love to give and who knows what's gonna happen? Not you, not me, but that's got to be the best start, right?'

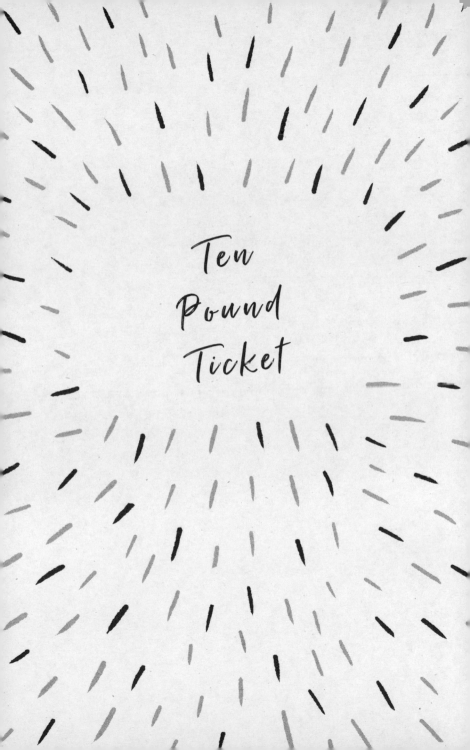

Ten
Pound
Ticket

One

Susie Montgomery held her son Nicholas close and stepped out of the bus and into the bright wintery day. She closed her coat over him, shielding him from the cold, until all that was visible was the top of his head. The sky was blue and the ground sparkled with a light dusting of diamond-like powder frost. She walked past Tilbury's war memorial; the week-old poppy wreaths dazzled red against the pale palette, the paper petals lifting and settling in the wind.

Susie needed somewhere to stay and had no idea where to begin; after all, she'd never had to consider her future before. Since leaving secretarial college, with her framed Pitman certificates confirming her proficiency in shorthand and typing, she had coasted from party to party, from boy's bed to boy's bed. She had lived in comfort under her parent's detached roof, certain in the knowledge that, like all the other seventeen-year-old girls she knew, her future was bright, happy and secure. It was 1962: life was good and out there, ready for the taking whenever she chose to take it. But that was before.

Now she skirted the square, protecting her baby from the November cold, swaddling him inside the front of her astrakhan coat and carefully moving her long tawny hair to ensure it wasn't pressed against his delicate nose and mouth. Her eyes darted around until she spied a sign for bed and breakfast in the window of The Anchor.

Susie stepped through the saloon doors and into a warm, welcoming fug of tobacco smoke and laughter. A large open fire blazed in the rusty grate, and two tarnished horse brasses hung on either side of it. The low ceiling, once white, was now stained yellow, and the concrete slabs around the bar looked sticky, thanks to years of slopped bitter and a dirty, ineffective mop. The walls, at least, were cheerful; covered with ornaments and knick-knacks – Susie spotted a door knocker pinned up next to a bronze bed pan, while overhead a cluster of postcards from British seaside resorts hid the cream-and-scarlet wallpaper from view.

The laughter stopped as she entered, and all eyes swivelled towards her. She was not only a stranger in this local bar, but she was a woman too. She looked around for a friendly face. An old man sat near the door, sipping his half pint but he kept his cap pulled down low over his eyes. A large black mongrel lay slumped across the hearth, greying hair peppered its muzzle. It was short of breath and she could hear the snuffles it made while it lapped at a saucer of beer.

Susie took a deep breath; she had never been in a pub like this before.

It was some moments before the barmaid and landlady, one in the same, trotted over from behind the bar on her black patent high heels.

'Yep?'

Susie stared at the network of lines that crept from the woman's thin mouth, evidence of puckering up for a cigarette, probably sixty times a day for as many years. Her red lipstick bled into these tiny tributaries. Her foot tapped with impatience, she had customers to serve.

'I saw your sign. I'm looking for a room, for a couple of weeks, for my son and me before we get on the boat to Australia.'

Susie pulled her coat open to reveal her little boy, who was still sleeping. His cheeks were pink against the fur of his mother's coat.

The landlady clapped her hand under her chin, showering ash from her smouldering cigarette down her front. She softened instantly as she took a shine to Nicholas; it was hard not to, he was angelic, beautiful and new. She poked a nicotine-stained finger into his sleeping face.

'Ah, look at him, he's a darling! Does he look like his dad?' The woman drew on her cigarette and eyed the little gold curtain ring on the third finger of Susie's left hand. She nodded and tried to smile.

'And you're off to Oz? What, is his dad already out there?'

'Yes that's it, we're meeting him there.' Susie delivered this to the sticky floor.

Two old men, drinking pints of Mild in the corner, suddenly laughed loudly at the precise moment she finished her sentence. They were laughing at a joke, a comment, something entirely unrelated, but for Susie, it was as if they laughed in recognition of her lie. She felt the stain of a red blush over her neck and up her face as she fought the light headedness that threatened to make her faint. She silently pleaded; *please I have nowhere else to go, please.*

The woman's mouth twitched sideways, and Susie held her breath. Happily for Susie, this lady knew what it felt like to need a bit of luck.

'I'm Sandra and I've got a room you can have for a while, it's not flash...'

Susie felt her shoulders sag with relief. 'I don't need flash.' She was adamant. 'Is there a phone box I could use, though? I just need to make a call.'

The stench of ammonia filled the cubicle. A little chrome

ashtray was overflowing with cigarette butts that had spilled into a soggy heap on the concrete floor. Someone had obviously tried to light a fire in one corner if the layers of half-charred cardboard were anything to go by, and a greasy newspaper chip wrapper fluttered against her knee-high leather boots. Nicholas remained asleep while she juggled the purse in her right hand, balancing it on the front of the phone, and searched for the correct change. Susie winced as she pictured the cash she had once frittered so easily on her social life. If only she had been more prudent, saved for now, when a healthy bank balance would make all of the difference to her son's life. She looked at the three pence in her palm. This was the sum total with which she could talk to her mother, very possibly for the last time. Tears pricked at her eyes. *Get a grip, Susie.*

The black receiver slipped in her palm. She was shaking with nerves, and Nicholas was wriggling, making small mewling noises as he tried to get comfy in her arm. The mouthpiece smelt of alcohol gone sour. Her breath fogged the air in front of her as she waited for the pip pipping noise to tell her the call had been connected.

She pictured her mother standing in the square hallway in front of the ornate gold mirror, patting the hair-sprayed curls around her temple and checking the tangerine-glow lipstick across her thin mouth before picking up the telephone. Her tan leather shoes would coordinate nicely with the pale, khaki carpet. No element of design or decoration was left to chance in the Montgomery household, from the faux fauna in the Adams-style recess, to her mother's cloying scent – 4711 by Maurer & Wirtz – which always hung around her in a pungent cloud.

Susie balanced the receiver under her chin and against her

shoulder, and pushed the coins into the slot. She had only a few minutes before her call would run out.

'Mum, it's me… I haven't got much time, I wanted to phone and say goodbye.'

'Susie? Where on earth are you and what do you mean goodbye?'

'I… We're going away.'

'Apparently so. I've had a rather awkward conversation with Sister Kyna at Lavender Hill Lodge. Why on earth have you discharged yourself and reneged on our agreement? Susan, this is totally unacceptable, especially after what you've put me through. Is this how you repay Daddy and I after all we've done for you? We had an understanding. You would spend time in London, do what was necessary to sort the situation and then come home! Where has this madness come from?'

'I suppose it's come from the fact that I became a mother. I'm a mother and you are a grandmother whether you like it or not—'

'Not! Thank you very much.' Her mother couldn't help but interject. Susie pictured her generous chest heaving with disapproval as her fingers agitated the double row of pearls.

Susie sighed. It was, as ever, pointless trying to reason with her mother, 'I couldn't do *what was necessary* as you call it, not when it came to it. I couldn't hand my babies over, I couldn't do it! I'm not asking for anything from you and Dad, I just didn't want to disappear without you knowing where we were. We are going to Australia, Mum.'

'Australia?' Her mother's voice had gone up several octaves. 'Don't be so bloody ridiculous! Australia! What in God's name will you do there with no money, no husband and a bastard baby?'

Susie bit her lip at the shock of hearing her little boy referred to like that, but arguing now seemed pointless, even if she could have summoned the strength. 'I'll probably die a slow lingering death, Mum, but at least I'll have my son with me.'

'Oh for goodness' sake, listen to yourself, Susan! Not only are you being overly dramatic as usual, you are ruining your life and throwing away any chance of happiness that you might have. And, I might add, ruining things for me in the process. Have you not considered me at all? Do you think I haven't imagined what it would be like to become a granny, showing our friends the latest Cine on the dining room wall of our heir apparent's first steps? Of course I have, and in my head it always starts with a big white wedding, not that there's much hope of you wearing white, not now. You'd be one of those ghastly brides in ivory, which we all know is only one step away from an empire line and a large bouquet to hide a bump. It sets tongues wagging before you've even said "I do..."'

Susie tried to interrupt, but her mother was in mid flow. 'James Tenterden is still single and he's an only child. His father has a very weak heart and I've heard that his mother is ailing. I've already described their house to you, they have a stunning Victorian conservatory and the best collection of hand-cut crystal this side of London and he *likes* you! You could still get out of this, Susie, go back to Battersea, drop off the boy and come home; I'd even send you a car, how about that? I could arrange a little soiree; invite James, nothing too flashy, home-catered if you'd prefer and you could take it from there.'

Susie laughed in disbelief, she half-wished she hadn't called; at least then she could have imagined her mother's words might bring comfort and homely advice instead of prattling on about hand-cut crystal and a home-catered soiree. She raised her hand to the tiny scar on her temple and tried to block out the terrible memories it evoked: *Please! It can't be too late... tell them I have changed my mind, give them another baby!* Her screaming, while her heart was breaking and her spirit cleaved in two. Nicholas stirred in her arm, and Susie hardened her resolve.

'Goodbye, Mum. And just so you know, I'm going to try my hardest to make things right. One day, my family will be whole again.'

She clicked the phone back into its cradle and pictured her mother having to lie down on the pink floral counterpane with a large gin and tonic to restore her well-being. It didn't matter, none of it did. Nothing was as important as keeping Nicholas. And at least they had found somewhere to live.

Following Sandra up the echoey steps to the room above the pub that was to be hers, Susie's heart sank. It stank of mould and was decidedly grubby. Someone had used the laminate top of the bedside table as an ashtray; it was pitted with scorch marks and sausage-shaped cigarette burns. The sheets on the single trolley bed were greasy and the thin pillow carried an odour of hair oil, sweat and cigarettes.

'You'll be all right, love,' was Sandra's parting shot as she gave a small smile and closed the door.

'I really hope so.' Susie's reply drifted up to the stained ceiling, spoken into the silence.

Susie sat down stiffly on the single bed with her legs stretched out and her coat over the two of them. She hummed against Nicholas's fluffy head, inhaling his intoxicating scent and kissing his tiny cheek and nose. It was easy to forget her squalid surroundings when she had that little face against her own. 'I love you.' She spoke this often, barely more than a whisper, but always a confirmation, as if worried that he might forget, even for a second. She cuddled her son against her chest; tucking the white, crocheted blanket under his bootied feet, cradling him as he fed, lying in a sleepy heap against her chest.

She reached into her pocket, and pulled out the pamphlet for what must have been the thousandth time. The cover depicted a big grey ship, and a smiling family sitting on board in deck chairs. Their trouser hems were rolled up to reveal bare shins and they all wore jaunty sun hats to shade their eyes as they smiled into the camera. An advert told of the ship's paddling pool, 'perfect for toddlers'. Another boasted of the 'Italian-themed buffet,' which would be served two nights a week on board.

Nicholas reached out, blindly batting at her arm with his tiny fist, and Susie smiled at him. Perhaps the journey wouldn't be so bad after all. And at the end of it lay a new country, and a new start for her and her son, far away from her hateful mother, and far away from Lavender Hill, where the memory of the birth and what came afterwards was still fresh in her mind. It was as if a piece had been torn from her and until she could glue it back, she would for ever be broken. Susie closed her eyes for a second; it was easier not to think about it.

'Well, my little one. This is going to be an adventure for us, isn't it? Who knows, we might just love it out there! Maybe swamp life is for us. We'll go for long walks and go fishing, we'll grow our own vegetables and you will become a big, strong boy. Maybe you'll ride a horse in those big open fields. It's just you and me, kiddo, that's all we've got. We might be a tiny family, but we'll look after each other always. This is our new beginning.'

Baby Nicholas wrinkled his nose and rubbed at his face as a single tear trickled from his mother's eye and splashed onto his fat little cheek.

Two

As Susie stepped off the boat, clutching little Nicholas to her chest, her first shock wasn't the vast emptiness of her surroundings, or even the red dust that clung to everything it touched. It was the furnace-like heat that assaulted her nose, her mouth, and crept across her skin. When she was on board in the middle of the ocean the heat of the Antipodes had been masked by the sea breeze. Now they were docked, it was like standing still in an oven. She looked around at the battered vessel that had taken them on the final leg of their voyage and felt a pull of longing for her cramped but cosy cabin. This boat trip was the last bit of certainty on her journey, and the temptation to go back to their familiar berth and stay there was huge.

'What do you think, Nicky? Is a life on the high seas for us?' He twitched his nose. 'No, I quite agree, a bit of dry land is in order, our pirate days are done!' She peered down at the jetty, surrounded by murky, green depths, and shuddered. 'Come on then, this is Darwin, our stop.' She spoke aloud to rally herself and, taking a deep breath, she prepared to take her very first steps on a new continent.

She stepped gingerly along the wobbly planks of the dock, juggling to keep hold of both her small suitcase and the baby. Her heavy coat hung over her arm. It had been her pride and joy for two years, warding off the November chill of home.

Here it would be useless. The irony wasn't lost on her that she was hauling her lambskin coat halfway around the world to return it to a sheep station, but it felt important, somehow, to hang on to it.

As she trudged down the jetty, every pore weeping in protest, her eyes filled with the salty sweat from her brow and her clothes clung to her damp skin. Nicholas howled. He didn't like it one bit. Susie was relieved that she had fastened his bonnet before disembarking – and more relieved, still, that Sandra had handed her the bonnet as well as a bundle of baby clothes as she left all those weeks ago.

It had been a cold, rainy morning when they had boarded the boat. As they'd pulled away into the choppy waters, Susie had considered how strange it was that she had lived in this country all her life and yet the only person who was sorry to see her go was the landlady of a pub she had stayed in for only a couple of weeks. Sandra's eyes had clouded as she hugged her and Nicholas to her breast in farewell, and pushed Susie onto the boat, as far away as possible from the other families whose nearest and dearest had come to wave them off, crying on the quayside with damp hankies held under their noses and headscarves tied tightly under pale, wobbling chins. Susie stood squinting into the squall, trying to take a mental snapshot of the place she was leaving behind. The pain in her heart was raw as she watched through an open porthole the dock at Tilbury getting smaller and smaller, each mile taking her further and further away from everything and everyone she knew.

The picture on the front of the pamphlet looked like a holiday snap, but it turned out that being crammed together on riveted decks with a great many excitable wives and squealing children, with nothing more than a shuffleboard for distraction, was no holiday. There was no beach within easy strolling distance, no donkey called Daphne to ferry people up and down a flattened stretch of dung-laden sand. No promise of lemon ices in cones, no amusement arcades at the end of a pier. There was also no hint of the interminable sadness that would assault her at the oddest of moments, as the ship ploughed on day and night like a hot knife through butter. Susie filled her days walking with her boy in a borrowed pram around the decks, trying to seek out the sun and avoid the wind. She stopped to admire other people's babies and to chat to their mothers, though she found that she envied the women their large, noisy families, shrieking with glee in the paddling pool, stuffing their faces happily at the Italian buffet. Most of all, though, she envied them the little gold bands that sat snugly on the third finger of their calloused left hands. They were a symbol and a currency that bought them a place in a world she didn't have access to. Every time Susie looked at her ten-pound ticket, she was reminded that she did not belong to a husband, or even to herself. She belonged to her new employer.

She became so used to telling the story of how she was meeting her husband, already in Australia and working on a sheep station, that she almost began to believe it herself. The night the ship had crossed the equator, and everyone had put on party hats and celebrated with pizza and whisky, she had got into conversation with one of the waiters. He said, 'I heard your husband's on a sheep station; I reckon I might have met him, it's not Jim, is it? Jim from Somerset, came out a few months back and he said his wife and little 'un was going to follow?'

'Yes,' Susie stammered. 'That's him, Jim. Jim from Somerset.'

'Well I never!' He placed his hands on his hips. 'What a small world!' He had been delighted at the connection.

Now, clutching her baby to her chest and surveying the vast

expanse of land in front of her, Susie fought the overwhelming desire to cry. One night on board she had actually dreamt of this fictitious husband; he was standing on the dock when she arrived, waving furiously and holding flowers. And however silly it was, she felt his absence keenly as she looked around. There were no buildings on the horizon, no clutch of tourists or local shops around the dock and certainly no Jim from Somerset waiting with his floral gift.

Everything was barren. The soil was so dry that it would be a miracle to get anything to grow here. Susie swallowed the tears that threatened to form, as the image of her vegetable garden withered in the heat. She scrunched her eyes shut and tried to focus on something that might lift her spirits, a friendly sign, a wave, a café, anything. But, with the exception of the odd spiky tree, nothing sprung from this barren landscape. To think that she had thought Tilbury grimy! What wouldn't she give for a cup of tea in The Anchor right now, with a view of the war memorial and the easy banter and laughter of the public bar.

Two rough-looking men, unshaven and wearing leather trousers despite the heat, stood with arms folded across grubby vests and patched shirts. They looked like tatty cowboys. They watched, smirking, at the procession of sickly, pale men with shirt sleeves rolled high – some even wearing ties – which wobbled down the jetty towards the quayside. Wives in wide-brimmed hats fought to keep their smiles in place as their children, lips quivering and eyes wide, trailed behind.

As Susie stepped onto the wood, Nicholas wriggled inside her grip. She moved to grab him but her sweat-covered hands were ineffective against his shiny skin, and he lurched backwards, falling out of her hands towards the water. She screamed, and, on impulse, dropped her suitcase and coat and grabbed at his fat little leg, squeezing it as tightly as she could. Nicholas howled as she gathered him roughly back into her arms, her belongings tumbling into the slimy water around the pontoon. She sank down on the jetty and cradled her baby into her neck, this time unable to stop the tears. She could not erase the thought of his head making contact with the splintery planks of the dock, of him bouncing up and sinking down into the murky water.

'Oh my God, Nicky, I am so sorry! I am so sorry, sweetheart.' She whispered it over and over again, apologising for so much more than the pain in his leg, hoping he might one day understand, terrified that he might not. She cooed and kissed until his crying calmed to a whimper, until his tears had stopped, and both of their bodies had stopped shaking.

One of the smirking unshaven men sauntered over. 'You're lucky, crocs'd've had him in one bite. A tasty little snack like that.'

She caught the smallest of winks through her drying tears. The man jumped down into the water and retrieved her sodden case, leaving her coat to sink in the filth. Susie imagined a snapping crocodile taking a bite, and tears pricked her eyes. She shook her head and swallowed. She would not cry again. She had to be strong for Nicky.

'I'm Slade Williams. Mitch sent me to fetch you. Christ, the fuss he made about sending someone to pick you up! You'd think he didn't even want the extra labour.' Slade was tall, with a long body, wide shoulders and a small, bald head. Susie thought his face looked like a weasel. 'Anyway, it's not as if you coulda made it on yer own, could you. Only been here five minutes and you can barely stand up!'

It was true. All those weeks at sea meant that every step Susie took was hindered by an extra bounce as if bobbing on water. Her legs couldn't work out how to stop accommodating for movement beneath her, even though there wasn't any. Susie smiled weakly and followed Slade to a huge red truck with over-sized chrome bumpers. In the back, an open flatbed was littered with packs of food pellets, a couple of pitchforks and bales of twine. Slade hurled Susie's luggage onto the planks, and Susie winced as she considered the sodden contents: her precious baby clothes, nappies, underwear, her school copy of *Pride and Prejudice* and miniscule amounts of shampoo and soap.

Slade, clearly unused to the company of women and babies, made no effort to help Susie climb up into the cab, but when he saw her struggling to reach out for the creaking door, he went bright red, and ran round to close it for her, muttering under his breath something about 'bloody women's lib, always trying to do everything themselves'.

The cab of the battered truck bounced along, throwing up a plume of red dust in its wake. Susie held Nicholas tight; he had cried himself into an exhausted slumber, and she was fearful that he might go flying if she let go and equally fearful of his reaction when he eventually woke up. She waited until she felt slightly more composed before deciding to make conversation with her small-headed driver.

'It's very good of you to come and fetch us, I'm sure you have other things that you should be doing. Is it far?'

''Bout two hundred and seventy miles.' He delivered this with a sideways smirk through his lipless mouth.

'Two hundred and seventy miles?' She stared at him in disbelief, she had thought that it would be a jaunt of twenty minutes or so, a bit like fetching a relative from the train station at home, giving you just enough time to pop the kettle on, flick a duster and flush the loo before they arrived.

'Where do you think you are, love?' Slade said, not unkindly.

Susie gulped. 'How long will it take to drive?'

'Six or seven hours give or take.'

'Gosh, really?'

'Yes, gosh really!' He attempted to imitate her voice.

She laughed with embarrassment. He grimaced.

'Don't laugh too soon. Reckon you're in for a bit of a surprise at Mulga Plains.' He shook his head ruefully and muttered, 'What the boss was doing employing a useless bloody pom *girl* is beyond me.'

Susie felt the first flutter of fear. She held Nicholas a little tighter and looked out of the window at the open plains beyond. In the distance, a mountain range nudged the sky. She wanted to find it beautiful in the way that the new or exotic can often be beautiful. But try as she might, it only looked threatening, alien and *vast*. The odd house or farm building they passed looked untended, abandoned. Sheds, fences and gates were all shabby, peeling and dry as tinder. It looked as though it would take just one strike of a match for the whole country to go up in smoke. Susie closed her eyes and pictured the rolling green patchwork hills of home. She saw the fields dotted with hayricks and swaying crops, the higgledy-piggledy Dorset villages, the horses cantering through the mist of the Downs. She heard the sea in a storm. She remembered the sound of the rain as it lashed against the window on the wildest of days, and the picture-postcard views of cliffs, beaches and dunes that framed each memory of her childhood. Picnics, bathing suits that became immodest when wet, her mother's huge hats, the way she even wore orange lipstick on the beach as they tucked into pork pies, bottled pop and crust-less sandwiches before chasing a ball on the wet sand. She thought about the way her fingers stung in winter as she shaped snow into small balls of ice and threw them at a wall to watch the splat. The particular smell of bonfires in the autumn as damp leaves hissed and sizzled when forked onto the pyre. And Christmas morning, that single magic moment, when she walked into the sitting room, the fire was lit and the tree glowed, laden with gifts. What would Nicholas's childhood look like? Susie opened her eyes and looked in the wing mirror. A rolling wave of red dust made it seem as if the car was being chased by fire; as though she had entered hell itself. Well, maybe she had.

Susie felt the cold creep of realisation that she was entirely alone. Everywhere else she had ever travelled in her life, she had made a friend. At Lavender Hill Lodge, despite being in the depths of her misery, she had befriended her roommate Dot Simpson. *Even* in Tilbury, she only had to ask and Sandra was there with a willing ear and a cup of tea. And on the boat to Darwin, though she had remained aloof, she was surrounded by English families, who if the need had arisen would have come to her aid. But out here, she didn't have a single friend. Anything could happen and no one would care. It was the first time in her life that not a single person was looking out for her.

Nicholas shifted on her lap, reminding Susie that whatever she might think, she wasn't *quite* alone. She stroked his little face, and resolved once more to be brave for him. This was their world now, and that was that. His face felt clammy; it was scorching inside the cab. The air vents on the dashboard and doors were open, but the air that rushed in was hot, like sitting under a hair dryer. She considered opening the window wider, but thought better of it. She didn't want any more of the red dust inside the confined space, she could already feel the grit crunching between her teeth and irritating her skin.

Slade pulled a soft packet of cigarettes from his top pocket and shook one into his mouth. Susie watched as his dirty black thumbnail rolled the flint of his lighter and his cigarette sparked to life, revealing it to be a foul-smelling concoction that made her eyes water. The baby spluttered and coughed as he wrinkled his nose, before finally waking and instantly crying.

Slade stared at the bundle on her lap. 'Ah, little fella's woken up, has he?' He spat into the foot well and grinned.

'Um...' said Susie. Nicholas's wails were growing louder. 'I don't suppose you could – you know – I mean, I don't think he likes it much.' She looked meaningfully at Slade's cigarette, hoping she hadn't just mortally offended someone she had to spend the next seven hours with. Slade frowned at the offending object, as though noticing it for the first time, and promptly threw it out the window. Susie exhaled, thanked him, and turned back to Nicholas, unbuttoning the top of her blouse and holding his little face to her breast. A slow blush crept up Slade's neck. Susie fixed her eyes on a point in the distance and stared straight ahead, trying to look indifferent and calm, acutely aware of Slade's sly glances to his left.

Suddenly, Slade shifted in his seat, leant forward and reached out towards her breast and her baby. In his hand was a tin billycan, chipped, dented and grubby.

'Here.' He thrust the can towards her, his eyes averted.

'Not for me, I'm okay, thank you.' She raised her palm.

'You may be okay now, Missy, but you won't be soon if you don't have some water. If you conk out, d'you think I'll make a good substitute nursemaid?'

Susie fumbled with the large can, trying to get a grip. She placed the spout on her lips and tried to ignore the smell of cigarettes that lingered around the opening. She swigged the water, which tasted vaguely metallic.

'Thank you.' She handed it back to her driver and watched as he took several large glugs.

*

Several hours later, the truck pulled up inside the gates of Mulga Plains sheep station. If Susie was still holding on to any shred of hope that everything would be okay, she let go of it at that moment. Maybe she should have begged her parents for the money, maybe she should have told Nicholas's father of the situation and asked him for help. Instead, the pride, stubbornness and scrambled brain that was the gift from Mother Nature for many pregnant women, had led her to this. Susie knew with a thudding certainty that her plan for a life in the sun with her baby had been a very grave mistake.

Three

It might have been 1962 in England, but here in Willeroo it felt more like 1862. The sheep station was accessed through grand, ornate wrought-iron gates, each forged with the name Mulga Plains in their design. They were imposing, huge and gave the impression of a well-kept ranch and a happy farm, both of which were entirely false. In fact the gates were the only element of grandeur about the place and made the disappointment of her surroundings more acute, like removing the ribbon on a fancy box of chocolates and finding dirt.

The main house looked like it had been added to in a haphazard fashion over the years. The original grey stone structure had been extended with the addition of large, timber-walled rooms with flat roofs and wire netting over the windows to try and stop the invasion of bugs. It was ugly and sprawling, grey, brown and uninspiring. A wide veranda wrapped around the front of the house, and was dotted with benches, upended chairs and card tables that held well-thumbed decks and empty beer bottles. It looked like the aftermath of a raucous boys' party. Susie was soon to learn that this was a normal, nightly occurrence. Her eyes widened at the sight of two shotguns resting like weary warriors, propped against a table. She instinctively held her son tighter.

She climbed down from the cab while Slade fetched her case, which had thankfully dried out in the hot sun, leaving only a residual tidemark where it had been submerged in the murky water. She pictured her dad's hand on the same handle as they arrived in neat hotels on the English Riviera. She'd barely been patient enough to wait for her parents to unpack before running down to the beach with a bucket and spade. That memory belonged to another girl, from another life.

Slade marched around the back of house. She trotted in his wake, his boots kicking up a crimson cloud. Susie swatted her hand around the baby, trying to remove or at least distract the determined flies that buzzed around them. The things were everywhere, stamping on her arms with dirty little feet, settling wherever skin was revealed, collecting at eyes, mouth and nose: any place where they could nestle and feed. Susie opened her mouth to flick out a fly and several more landed on and around her tongue. She gagged and spat them onto the floor. Nicholas too was covered. She brushed his face and covered it with her palm. She wondered with a pang if she would ever get used to these filthy creatures. Clearly here, the profusion of bugs and flies were simply part of life.

Slade stopped outside a low building with a sloping corrugated iron roof. The walls were sheets of plywood that had been tacked together, and the front door, transplanted from a more solidly built house and quite incongruent, didn't fit or shut. Susie wished Slade would get a move on. What was the use in pausing outside this shed when she wanted to get to her room, to get the baby washed, changed, fed and settled? It had been a very long day and she was exhausted.

'Here you go, love, home sweet home!' Slade kicked the door with his heavy boot and watched as it swung and fell open at a strange angle.

Susie laughed in disbelief.

'Is this where we're staying?' She couldn't hide the edge of hysteria in her voice.

'Yup.' He looked abashed at her discomfort.

'But, I... we...' She felt breathless. Her head spun as she considered how she would live in the shed with her tiny baby, how would she wash his clothes, his nappies, keep him clean, cool and boil his water?

'Are you sure this is where Mr Gunnerslake wants us to sleep? Is it a temporary measure?' She tried to hide the quiver to her voice.

'Temporary? Don't think so.' He shook his little head. 'This not quite what you expected, love? It's bound to be a bit different out here, you know, and there's a lot that live in worse. If you'd a come three days ago, there wasn't even a door.'

Susie clutched her son to her chest. 'Why is it so horrible here? I haven't done anything wrong and yet everything feels like a punishment!' Susie didn't know how she summoned the strength to find her voice.

'Well, given your situation, I reckon you did do something wrong. What kind of girl comes halfway around the world with her trouble? How bad is it that she can't stay in her own country and with a little 'un?' He spoke fast, out of the side of his mouth, and avoided looking her in the eye.

Susie's bravery evaporated. Everyone knew what she had done, what she was. But she straightened her shoulders and gathered her last ounce of strength.

'I want to see Mr Gunnerslake. I want to see him right now. I don't think for one minute he can mean for us to sleep in here, surely to God. Are there no rooms in the house?' As she pictured the state of the veranda and the guns carelessly abandoned on the porch, she wasn't sure that the house would be that much of an improvement.

Slade frowned. 'No love, no rooms in the house.'

'He does know that I have a small baby?' Susie refused to believe that anyone with this information would think this was acceptable.

'Oh, he knows all right, had one of the boys give it a bit of a sweep for you.' He made as if to say something else, but he stopped himself. Instead, he nodded once in her direction and strode away.

Susie took a deep breath and poked her head inside the cabin. She felt around the nearest wall for a light switch, but even before she felt the blank wall she knew that there would be no electricity in the shed. As her eyes adjusted to the dust-filled gloom, she spied a mattress on the floor. Judging by the assortment of unidentifiable stains and the wide indent where springs had collapsed and sagged in the middle, she wasn't its first occupant. In the corner was a white hand-painted cot with a vinyl-covered sponge base. At least she would be able to scrub and bleach it. A square window, without glass, was covered with green netting. It was her only source of light.

For the first time in many years, Susie prayed.

That first night at Mulga Plains would remain indelibly etched in her mind. The cold creep of fear plucked at her muscles and shook her bones. She stripped Nicholas in the diminishing light, trying to keep her tone soothing and reassuring as she struggled to replace his soiled nappy in the darkness. She forced herself to ignore the scuttling sound in the corner of the room, the gnawing hunger in her stomach, and the flat, single note that reverberated inside her skull.

Susie was too stunned to cry, so instead she tried to sleep. She wouldn't have thought rest would be possible, but eventually anaesthesia gripped her and, six hours later, she awoke to Nicholas's stuttered cries. Once she had fed him and rocked him back to sleep, she wiped down her crumpled shirt and trousers, tucked her hair behind her ears, and made her way around the path to the main house. Beyond the garden, the landscape was flat and vast. Acres of red dust and spiky trees stretched in every direction under a big sky that held the vaguest tinge of pink. It might have been beautiful, were she able to study it with different eyes. Slade was already up and sitting at one of the card tables on the terrace, forking fried eggs into his mouth. A cigarette smouldered on the table edge, which he drew on between mouthfuls.

'How was your first night?' he asked. He had the decency to look abashed as tiny flecks of food flew from his lips and landed on the table.

'I want to see Mr Gunnerslake.' Susie pulled back her shoulders, trying to feign composure and courage.

'Bit late for Mitch, he's already up and out. But he asked me you to show you around.' Slade pushed his oily plate into the middle of the table, and Susie watched as it was instantly descended upon by a gang of flies. As she stepped up onto the veranda she stifled a scream. In the corner, with his back against the wall and his knees drawn up to his chest, was the strangest-looking man she had ever seen. He wore a maroon T-shirt with a ripped sleeve, and khaki trousers that had been cut off at his calves. His skin was dark, and he had large, bloodshot eyes beneath hooded lids and a prominent brow. His nose was broad, with flattened nostrils that flared over thick, plum-coloured lips. His hair hung in beautiful, glossy twists, and his feet with their pale, dry soles were bare. He was fascinating. Susie raised her hand in a small wave, but he didn't respond.

She followed as Slade strode ahead into the main residence of Mulga Plains.

'Who's that? On the terrace?' she enquired.

'That's Elouera.'

She had hoped for a bit more. 'What does he do?'

Slade grimaced, 'Anything Gunnerslake tells her to. And for your information, he is a she, we call her Loulou.'

Susie opened her mouth to speak, but decided against it.

As they entered the house, her nose wrinkled at the musty tang that lingered in the air. She looked up, seeking windows that could be flung open at the first opportunity. The central hallway and main part of the house smacked of faded glory. Gold brocade wallpaper bore the marks of greasy skin that had rubbed along it. Smudged handprints covered the walls, evidence of someone trying to right themselves after a drunken stumble. A large wrought-iron light fitting hung in the double height hallway and held an ornate latticework of cobwebs. It was clearly years since anyone had wielded a feather duster in there. The doors that uniformly lead off the square hallway were unpainted dark wood, with tarnished brass handles. The bottom third of each door was spattered with all manner of liquid. Susie made out sploshes of what looked like soup, and drips of beer that had run down and formed a sticky fly-covered pool on the floor. One door had the perfect, neat imprint of a large boot stamped on it.

Thick, heavy curtains with braided, tasselled edges and co-ordinating tie-backs, hung at the filthy window. Susie prodded the fabric, regretting it instantly as a cloud of dust billowed into the space, filling her lungs and sitting on her hair and lashes. The heavy mahogany sideboard took up one whole wall of the dining room. Under a thick layer of grit, ornate soup tureens and matching serving dishes gleamed dully. The delicate gold-leaf pattern and filigree work around the rim was beautiful. At some point, this house had been occupied by someone who took pride in their possessions. Susie felt sad for whoever it was.

The kitchen at the back of the house was functional but large, easily big enough for her to ensconce Nicholas in a play pen or a makeshift bed, meaning she could keep him close when she was working. A huge dresser housed all manner of crockery, none of it matching, but much of it pretty, if slightly old-fashioned. It reminded of her Grannie's collection, which she had last seen nestling on shelves in the cellar at home, alongside abandoned croquet sets and rusting bikes. Here, the delicate pink floral-painted teacups and pale glazed milk jugs seemed incongruent to their surroundings. The cooker was a wood-burning stove that she could tell would, on the hottest of days of the year, make the room insufferable. Luckily there was a large, shuttered window that opened up like a hatch to the outside world. The fierce oven seemed to have two settings, roasting or off. She was sure it would take her a good few weeks to master it, not that she cared much if every chunk of meat she served was dry and singed.

Thankfully, the laundry room was in a spare block only yards from her own cabin. It was a long low building, housing an industrial-sized twin tub and oversized ceramic sink with a washboard placed across it. Washing lines had been strung like fat spaghetti across the roof space and back again. In the corner, a tap dripped fresh water. Susie smiled, she would be able to clean their dirty clothes and boil up Nicholas's nappies, and she would be able to fetch water to drink. Above the tap, on a scrubbed shelf, two paraffin lamps and four fat candles made her stomach leap with the knowledge that she would not need to be in total darkness tonight. For the first time since she arrived, Susie felt a glimmer of hope. Perhaps her stay wouldn't be as bad as she had thought.

Two days later, Susie stood in the kitchen admiring her handiwork.

'What do you think, Nicky? That's a bit more like it, isn't it?' Nicholas lay in the empty tea crate, lined with a thick, fringed velvet tablecloth that Susie had found in a drawer and which she had washed twice. She had scrubbed the entire room from ceiling to floor, and although it now stank of bleach, it was at least dirt free, without a cobweb to be seen. Susie jumped as she heard the sound of heavy boots treading the wooden floor outside. Slade had clearly been avoiding her since she'd arrived, so it was unlikely to be him. She turned towards the door to see a small, offensive-looking man in his early seventies, wearing snug jeans and a grubby shirt. Thick hair hung to his shoulders in grey, wiry loops, framing small, bright eyes, like chips of amber glass. His tight lips housed teeth that were neglected. The stubble on his face was dark and reached from the top of his cheekbones to the base of his throat.

The man walked forward and stood with his arms a few inches proud of his body; his legs too, slightly bowed, didn't meet between the thighs. The man looked to be full of gaps.

'I'm Mitch. You Susie?'

In any other circumstances Susie would have made a joke, *No, I'm another English girl who happens to be standing in your kitchen while you look for this Susie.* But there was something about his fixed expression and twitchy fingers, which told her he was not a man who liked humour.

She nodded.

'Find everything you need?'

'Yes, thank you, Mr Gunnerslake. I'm getting there. It's good to meet you; I wanted to say thank you for our sponsorship.'

He didn't respond. She tried to be more direct in an attempt to engage him. 'I've got a couple of questions if that's okay?'

He shrugged.

'My son, Nicholas, is a baby' – she pointed towards the makeshift cot in the corner – 'and our cabin is so hot and as far as I can make out, the only water is in the laundry, which isn't that close and in the dark it makes it tricky to get to and from, are there any rooms available in the house? We don't need much space and he is a very good baby.' She added the last bit in case the fear of Nicholas crying at all hours of the day and night might have been a concern.

'Keep him away from the machinery; it's no place for kids.'

Susie opened her mouth to speak, but was unsure how to respond.

'There's fourteen mouths want feeding twice a day including my Jackaroo, a handful of Abos who run my stock, ringers, boremen, and Slade my manager, who I believe you've met.' She nodded resignedly. Slade had evidently passed on her requests, and if Gunnerslake had any mind to help her out, he would have already done so. 'Supplies come in twice a month, make a note of what we're low on, give it to Slade. You get meat daily, with over three thousand head of sheep, there's always some available if you get my drift. We don't eat nothing fancy. Meat, veggies, potatoes, pie, stew, that kind of thing. Loulou'll help you with anything; just tell her what you need.'

'Okay.' Susie tried out a smile. 'I'll do my best!'

Mitch looked her over, studying her cropped trousers and vest. 'There's plenty of clothes and whatnot in the linen press on the landing. My wife's old stuff. She's dead.'

'I'm so sorry.'

'Don't be.'

She waited until he left before going up to the landing to see what clothes she could use. This was the first and last time Mitch Gunnerslake would show her an act of kindness or generosity. Susie felt a flutter of excitement as she lifted the lid on the large wooden chest to reveal the dust-covered florals and cottons. At home they would have invited ridicule; here, it was different and she rummaged through, extracting anything that might prove useful.

As she made her way back to the kitchen to sort through the jumble of dresses, shirts and trousers that filled her arms, she stopped in the doorway. Loulou was there, facing towards the open hatch, with her back to the door. Susie approached quietly. The woman was humming and singing, but not in a language that she recognised. As she turned, Susie felt her pulse quicken. Nicholas was lying placidly in the strange woman's arms.

'Get off him! Get away from him now! Don't you ever touch him!' She raced forward, shouting, dropping the clothes on the floor, intent only on getting her son away from this woman who looked and smelt like a vagrant. Snatching at her son, she pulled him into her, and he yelled instantly and powerfully. 'It's okay, Nicky, it's okay. Mummy's got you. I've got you now.'

Elouera stared at the floor, and quietly walked out of the kitchen.

Susie calmed her son, feeding him before he fell into a deep sleep. It was only as she watched him dozing that she replayed what had happened. Elouera had been singing to him, comforting him and he had been quiet, happy in her arms. Susie ran her fingers over her scalp.

Making her way back to the cabin with her booty under one arm and Nicholas in the other, Susie stopped before entering. Someone had placed an empty jam jar, half filled with water, by the front door. In the water sat a single, rose-like bloom. It had long mauve petals and a clashing red base that formed a hub of colour in the centre of the flower. It was so delicate against the ugly backdrop of her cabin it took her breath away.

'Oh, Nicky, look! Someone has brought us a flower.'

Susie marched around to the terrace, hoping to find Elouera in her usual corner, but there was no one around. She ventured to the left of the house and beyond the gardens, where there was a collection of huts and stores, stables and an open-sided barn of sorts. Stepping gingerly among the ramshackle collection of buildings, she felt her courage fading as she ventured further in, treading over piles of litter and trying not to inhale the stench of human waste. About to give up, she trod a path back towards the main driveway, when a flicker of motion drew her eye. Following the flash of maroon, she discovered a basic hut, approximately eight foot in diameter, made out of a corrugated iron sheet, which had been propped on two wooden posts at the back, and two oil drums stacked on top of each other at the front. The floor was covered with newspaper, and a folded bedspread made an inadequate bed. Elouera was sitting on the floral cover, her legs hunched up in their usual position. She didn't raise her eyes, so Susie crouched down until the woman was forced to look at her.

'Elouera, I've come to say sorry for shouting at you earlier. I was frightened, that's the truth, and I've come to say thank you for my beautiful flower. It's the first time anyone has done anything kind for me since I arrived.'

The woman ignored her.

Susie continued. 'I wish you understood me. I could do with a friend out here and I hope that I haven't blown it. Thank you for comforting Nicky, I'm really sorry I shouted at you. I was scared, that's all.'

She held out her sleeping son, whose little arms and legs dangled like a rag doll over her hands. Elouera reached out and received the bundle. Her mouth opened in a smile, revealing crooked, brilliant white teeth. It transformed her face into something quite beautiful.

'He can sleep anywhere!' Susie laughed.

'They'll sleep when they need to, they all do.' Her voice was a deep baritone.

'Oh! You speak English!'

Elouera smiled. 'Yes. Call me Loulou.'

'Okay, Loulou, I'm Susie. Elouera is a beautiful name.'

'It means *from a lovely place*.'

'Gosh, I wish I had a name like that, I think Susan means a flower or a lily, I'm sure that's what I was told.'

'Well, that's good too.'

Susie smiled. 'Although I must admit, I don't feel like this a particularly lovely place; in fact I think I'd like to be anywhere else!'

'I'd like to go to New York.' Loulou smiled.

'Oh, me too! I think I'd like to traipse around the shops and listen to some jazz.'

Loulou shook her head. 'I've seen pictures and a movie, once. I'd like to go to the top of the highest building and see how far I could see, up among the clouds.'

Susie nodded; she guessed when your world was as flat as Willeroo that would be incredible. She tried not to show her shock at the woman's surroundings, but it was hard. She had never seen such privation. It made her feel grateful for her own cabin, which in comparison was relatively sturdy.

Nicholas raised his joined hands in a cherubic stance under his chin, 'Ah, look, you're a natural.'

'Should be, I've had six of my own.'

'Six? You don't look old enough!'

'I've grown-up grandchildren as well.'

'Where are they?' Susie felt her cheeks flare, unsure if it was okay to ask.

'Gone.'

Susie nodded, unsure if she wanted to enquire further. 'I bought you a present too.' Susie unfurled the magenta floral dress that she had earmarked for Loulou, it had a white lace collar and delicate pearly shell buttons. Loulou gathered it into her free hand and placed it on the floor without studying it, seemingly uninterested, far too occupied with the tiny infant that filled her arm and slept soundly in her grasp.

'White babies look like grubs. Is that what you are, a little grub?' Loulou spoke to the sleeping infant.

Susie smiled, she knew love at first sight when she saw it, grub or not.

The next day, as Susie toiled with a mound of spuds that she was peeling for supper, Loulou appeared in the kitchen, resplendent in her new dress, which hung beautifully on her frame and reached down to the floor. She was beaming.

Four

Seven months passed and Susie fell into a routine of sorts. She had jazzed up her cabin with the addition of drapes made from old candy-striped sheeting that she had hemmed and tacked over the window. A row of glass jars suspended on wires from the ceiling held stubs of flickering candles that bathed their room in a golden glow, making it feel almost cosy. The floor was covered with makeshift rugs: multi-coloured rags that she had found abandoned in an old wardrobe, and in the corner of the room, opposite the cot, rested a white painted shelving unit which she had appropriated from the laundry room. On this, she stored all of her and Nicholas's folded clothing, the small amount of toiletries that Slade fetched for her when in town and her precious copy of *Pride and Prejudice*, which had recovered surprisingly well from being dropped in a swamp.

Her heavy workload and the constant need to boil and cool water for Nicholas meant she was exhausted and if it hadn't been for Loulou, always on hand to hold the baby or serve the food, she didn't know how she would have coped. In some ways she was grateful that her mind was constantly preoccupied with the work. The constant grind left little room for thinking about home, the life she had left behind, and, most importantly, Abigail. Only at night, when her mind emptied, would Susie lie in the darkness and wonder if Abigail, like her brother, could now sit unaided, grab for objects and gurgle as though speaking. Did she too have a tooth and was she too able to shuffle from her tummy onto her back and then flounder like a stuck turtle? Susie swallowed these thoughts and tried to feel relief instead, that her little girl was not being forced to live in the same conditions that she and Nicky were. It pained her to admit it, but maybe her child was better off with parents who would tuck her up every night in a pretty nursery in the suburbs, rather than here with her twin who lay covered in bugs and grime. It wasn't always easy to convince herself, though. Susie did not know anything about Abigail, and a black cloak of realisation engulfed her when she considered that she never might.

One day Nicholas fell ill. Six hours earlier he had started refusing food and then he'd vomited until he was spent. Now he lay in her arms, wailing as his little bunched fists beat the air over his head and his legs bent up towards his tummy as if in pain. 'It's all right, darling, it's okay, Nicky, it will all be okay.' Susie rocked him on her hip and spoke into his scalp, where his hair was stuck to his head with sugary sweat. She tried not to panic. Loulou had gone into town with Mitch and was not due back for a couple of hours. Mosquitoes and flies that a couple of months ago would have sent her spiralling around, squealing as she tried to swipe them from her child, no longer registered; it was simply part of life at Mulga Plains. At this time of day, the heat was so intense that it was dangerous to enter the oven-like cabin. Instead, she had erected a shelter of sorts; an old green, jacquard floral cover that she had found in the storage cupboard on the landing, and had skewered it onto four old lengths of wood at each corner before placing it in front of the cabin. There were three sofa cushions on the ground, on which she could lay Nicholas for his nap or sit and read to him when she had the chance.

Neither of these things was possible today, he had a fever, he was screaming and Susie was scared. She hadn't been up to the house to start supper and quite frankly today they would have to whistle, her little boy was her priority. The sound of hooves alerted her. Mitch cantered up and stopped short of the door, his horse kicking up a red plume that engulfed both her and her baby.

'Mitch, where's Loulou? I need some help, I need to get him to a doctor, he's not well.' She tried to keep the hysteria from her voice, struggled not to give in to tears. She longed for home, where she would have been able to bundle him up and take him to a cottage hospital to be treated by a bossy nurse in a starched white pinny.

'He got a fever?' he asked as he calmed his horse with the flat of his hand upon her flank.

She nodded.

'Diarrhoea, vomiting?'

'Yes, yes all of that, since he woke up this morning. I'm so worried about him. I don't know what to do.'

Mitch Gunnerslake spat on the floor. 'He don't need a doctor, he's got what Slade has got, been puking his arsehole up since last night. He'll be right, plenty of boiled, cooled water that's the key.' With that he turned the horse and prepared to trot off.

'Where's Loulou? Is she not with you?' Susie called after him, realising how much she had come to rely on her friend, the only one she had in this place.

'She's walking the last few miles back, needs to learn a bit of respect that one.'

Susie opened her mouth to ask questions and give vent to the anger that boiled in her veins, but he was already cantering off, leaving a plume of dust in his wake.

The knowledge that Slade was also sick calmed her. 'Okay,

okay.' Susie tried to gather her thoughts. 'Did you hear that, Nicky darling? It's just a little bug. It'll pass, you're not the only one, it'll pass and Mummy will be right here to make you feel better.'

She kissed his pink face, and it seemed to do the trick. Nicholas cried himself to the point of exhaustion and fell into a deep slumber in her arms. She pictured her own various childhood ailments, everything from mumps to sickness, all of which had been treated with a clean, freshly laundered bed and a mug of hot lemon barley. The memory of laying her head on a sweet-scented pillow slip made her tears pool. She cried into the still heat that shimmered on the horizon for a mother whose kindly nature existed only in her mind.

The next day, Nicholas had cooled, and Susie went in search of Loulou. It was unusual not to see her for twenty-four hours. As she approached her quarter, she noticed that the floral heap that lay on the new makeshift bed was dangerously still. The mattress was one of the many items that Susie had secretly taken out of the house, placing it quietly under the lurid bedspread on which Loulou had slept for most of her life.

'Loulou? Hello? Elouera?' She called her by this name sometimes, the formality made her friend laugh. Loulou groaned and rolled slightly to one side. Susie bent down and looked into the face of her friend. Susie gasped and cried out. Loulou's eyes were swollen shut, her bottom lip cut and bloodied and one of her very white teeth was missing. She had been beaten. Her feet looked like shredded meat; goodness knows how far and over what she had had to walk to get home.

'Oh my God! Loulou, who did this to you? What happened?'

Loulou didn't say anything for a moment. Her dress looked dirty and was spattered with blood. 'This was Mitch, wasn't it? The fucking bastard.'

Loulou rolled back over into a little ball, and Susie, touching her friend on the shoulder, quietly left the room.

As Susie approached the veranda with Nicholas on her hip, she could hear Mitch and his buddies raucously singing 'If You Knew Susie'.

Although it was late morning, Mitch sat on one side of the table, swigging from the neck of a bottle of brandy. She correctly guessed that this was not a very early start, but a very late finish, the residual celebration from the night before. His three whiskered comrades slumped over their deck of cards and propped weak necks up on scrawny elbows. Susie fought her gag reflex as she got close enough to take in their collective stench. It was a peculiarly masculine smell of sweat, sex and alcohol that had the power to make her feel nauseas and petrified at the same time. He may have been in his seventies, but she had seen Mitch land a punch on a cattle hand and the boy had toppled like a wafer. He was fast and mean: two traits that worried her deeply.

'Here she is!' Mitch grabbed at his crotch and ran his tongue over his lips. It was always this way when he had been drinking. Susie had done her very best for the last seven months to keep out of his way. She cooked, cleaned, fetched and carried like a silent mouse trying to evade capture. She slipped in and out of his stinky bedroom with the greasy sheets in her arms in a giant bundle to be washed, dried and returned to the mattress before his grey, curly head hit the pillow. She swabbed the wooden and lino-covered floors with a mop dipped into a tin bucket, opening the windows and doors to allow the heat of the day to dry them. She toiled over potatoes and hunks of meat, often skinning and preparing it herself so that Mitch and the hands had something to eat after a long day. She was a skivvy, but not just any skivvy; she owed the meagre bread she put in her mouth and the roof over her head, indeed the very price of her passage, to this miserable old boozing bastard who had sponsored her arrival. She was trapped.

'I need to have a word with you, Mitch.' She gathered her son into her chest, partly to hide her form, which her boss insisted on staring at, but also to try and stop her body from shaking.

'Well, what a coincidence, I need to have a word with you, in fact two words: get upstairs!' He laughed loudly until he wheezed and banged the tabletop with a flattened palm.

Susie stood firm, trying not to lose her nerve. 'I need to talk to you about Elouera, she's been badly beaten. How could you do that to another human? She's in a mess!' Susie swiped at her tears, unable to get her friend's damaged face and shredded feet out of her mind.

'Is that right?' He stuck out his bottom lip and scratched his chin.

She nodded.

He was silent, seemingly considering her words. 'I have a dog, you seen her?'

Susie nodded again. She had seen the muscle-bound retriever that flew around the yard and leapt at her master's whistle. He pointed a wavering finger at her. 'If that dog disobeys me, I beat her. I beat her hard and guess what? She stops disobeying me! Sometimes it's the only way.'

Susie felt her jaw drop open. 'But Elouera isn't a dog, she's a person! And you are a despicable bully!' She drew breath to continue, but it was pointless. Mitch was face down on the table and out cold.

Usually when he passed out, Susie would slip back to her little hut where Loulou and Nicholas waited for her. She would hold her son tight and tell them both stories of a green and pleasant land that was far away. Her son had no idea what she was talking about, but was soothed by her tone and her presence. But right now, she didn't feel like telling stories, didn't feel like doing much at all. Her heart and head were heavy at the thought of Loulou's suffering. Just when she thought she had been in this strange place long enough to bear it, some fresh hell emerged and she was proved wrong. Suddenly, an image of the Dorset beach at dusk swept through her mind. It was a stone's throw from her parents' house, and she would often wander down barefoot, enjoying the cool breeze that blew across the dunes as the weak, pale sun sank into the frothy ocean. Oh, how she missed it.

Every day, Susie planned for escape. But it wasn't easy. Without money, she couldn't bribe any of the hands to drive her and Nicholas to safety and without a vehicle she would die within twenty-four hours of leaving this godforsaken place, which was a good day's drive from anywhere. That was assuming she could have got to a port or town without encountering the hundreds of men whose very livelihood was dependent on Mitch Gunnerslake and to whom they were all fiercely loyal. Without money to board a boat or pay for her passage, it was hopeless.

As night approached, she gathered Nicholas and, wrapping herself and her boy in one of their throws, she sat by her friend's side on a pile of newspaper, feeding her sips of water throughout the night. Loulou spoke only once, in reply to Susie's incessant questions. What she said was truly shocking.

'I am nothing and it's not the worst thing that's happened to me here, not even close. You can't think about it, or it will drive you mad. Trust me.'

'You are not nothing; you are my friend, my only friend. I don't know what I would do without you.'

'Slade...'

'Slade what? Did he do this?' Susie was eager for an insight, but Elouera fell silent, slipping into a deep sleep.

As the dawn broke, Loulou sat up and attempted a smile. Susie had never been so happy.

Five

Susie awoke to the sun of the Northern Territory beating down mercilessly on her tin roof and realised that today was a special day: it was Nicholas's first birthday. She thought about how much she had changed since giving birth to her precious son and coming all the way across the world in order to find him a better life. Susie smiled ruefully as she felt the sharp bite of her hip bones against her mattress on the floor, noted the concave hollow of her stomach and the edge to the reflection of her cheek bones. Her curves had been flattened, her bust gone, her muscle lean. She didn't mind the changes; in fact, with Mitch's advances growing coarser all the time, they suited her just fine.

These days, Nicholas was walking on the wobbly legs of a drunk, stumbling from point to point with his eye on what he could grab next to steady himself. He was a sweet-natured baby, who liked to kiss his mummy's face and could almost say 'yes,' 'moo' 'Loulou' and 'sheeps'. They weren't entirely clear, but he said them with such regularity and in response to most questions, that she and Loulou knew what he meant. He made his mother laugh and she was thankful beyond words that despite the conditions in which they lived, she still found joy in everything her baby boy did and said.

Susie lay still, thinking of that day twelve months before, when she had been cleaning in the hallway at the mother-and-baby home. She could remember every last detail with perfect clarity. She had reached up with a feather duster and removed cobwebs and specs of dust, visible only to the eagle eyes of Sister Kyna, from the wall lights. She remembered carefully removing the fragile glass cloche from a candle bulb as she had been instructed, using the duster to scoot around the fluted edge. Reaching up to replace it, her body had convulsed without warning, her hands jerked and the delicate glass shade hit the tiled floor, shattering into a million fragments. Her roommate Dot had rushed over, and Susan remembered the sound of the glass as it crunched underfoot. Dot had placed her hand on Susan's lower back as she bent over, trying to ease the pain. Things had happened fairly quickly after that, a warm cascade of viscous water ran down her leg and splattered on the black-and-white floor, before she was marched to the infirmary.

She remembered the harsh strip light of the maternity ward and the rubberised doors that swung back and forth. The waves of pain that swept her body and took her breath away and finally, the sound of her babies, her twins crying in unison, it sounded like music. *Oh, Abigail, happy birthday my darling girl. One whole year and I miss you as much now as I did then. Remember me, Abigail, please remember me.*

Susie cried all day. She couldn't help it. This was not the birthday that she had dreamt of for her son. She had a vision of him sitting like a little prince among new clothes, fresh nappies, with one of those liquid-filled teething rings that you popped in the fridge, a mini xylophone and a plastic ball rattle on a stick attached to a sucker that you spat on and stuck to a high chair tray, all the things she wanted to buy him. Every time she looked at Nicholas, she saw the gap next to him where his sister should have been. Even when Nicholas was presented with a cake that Loulou had made, an iced sponge cake with one proud blue candle, Susie could not stop the tears from falling. She pictured a similar cake, with a pink candle, being presented by strangers to her little girl.

That evening, she and Nicky went for a walk. She had got into the habit of taking him down to the small lake at the back of the main house, behind the garden, where a big fat tree trunk made the perfect bench on which to sit and talk. Their daily jaunt was taken just before Nicholas's bedtime, when the sun was sinking and the pinky hue of the sky threw a pretty veil over even the hardest of days. With his podgy hand in hers, they would totter along the five-hundred-yard-long track, twenty minutes there and only ten back, as he hitched a ride on his mother's back. She chatted to him as she always did about England, grass and cricket in the park, about going to the beach and the tasty, prize-winning carrots that her grandpa grew on his allotment. Nicky listened with eyes wide, occasionally chewing the corner of the birthday card clutched in his hand, on which Elouera had drawn a big red heart – a reminder that he was loved.

Nicholas sped up and raced ahead as far as his chubby, little legs would allow, their seat was in sight. He dropped the card in his excitement, and Susie took her eyes off him for one second as she bent to pick it up. When she straightened, Susie swallowed the scream that hovered in her throat. Her son had stooped and gathered up a snake that he now held in both his hands.

Ignorant about the species in this strange land, she had no idea if this slithering creature could kill her son with one well-placed bite or was as harmless as a shrew. Her heart hammered in her chest just the same. She wished Loulou was with them. Studying its olive-green body, she looked for clues as to its nature. It had large eyes and what might its pale-yellow throat and belly mean, was that a good sign? A bad one? Would a sudden movement make it strike? Fuck. She didn't know anything. Her hands shook and her voice warbled. 'Nicky, listen to Mummy, put that yucky snake on the ground and let's go and find a bun! That's a good boy. Put it on the floor and let's go home!'

Susie watched as the reptile's long, thin, tongue darted out towards her son's hand, seeming to taste the air around it.

'Fuck! Drop it, Nicky! Now!'

Nicky was nonchalant as he bent down and rested his fat bottom on his haunches, before purposefully placing the creature in the dust. It wound off at speed, leaving an S-shaped track along the scrub, and came to rest under a large spiky tree near their bench.

Susie ran forward and scooped her son up, kissing his face. 'Oh, Nicky, oh my love, I can't stand it, I can't stand the idea of anything happening to you! I can't! You mustn't pick up snakes. Never. They might hurt you!'

Nicholas wriggled free of her restrictive grip and waddled back towards the water, he was not about to waste their journey by going home without throwing sticks into the pond. He turned to see if his mum was following. 'Fuck!' he shouted, with more clarity than she had heard him use in his speech before. Susie howled with laughter. 'Oh, that's perfect. Bloody perfect,' she whispered towards the heavens.

The next day, like every other, Susie woke early and toiled in the kitchen, percolating coffee on top of the stove and whipping eggs in a large bowl, while she fired up the oven. Mitch, Slade and the Jackaroo were seated on the terrace, waiting as usual. As she tipped a hot omelette from the metal skillet onto her employer's plate, she felt Mitch's brawny hand snake over her buttocks, gripping what little there was to grab.

'Reckon I'll get rid of the boys early tonight, give you and me a bit of time alone, how's that sound?'

The Jackaroo snorted laughter through his nose, and Slade looked flustered. He lowered his face and stared at the cracked tabletop. Susie tried to free her tongue, which had stuck to the dry roof of her mouth. Her hand was shaking, causing the spoon to bang against the edge of the skillet. Mitch laughed. 'What's a matter, love? You want flowers first?'

She shook her head. She didn't want flowers first, she just wanted to go home.

'That's just as well. And it might be good to remember that you were a fucking good-for-nothing in your own country and you're a fucking good-for-nothing here, you just talk different. You's on my land now and that tin roof over your head can be taken away with the click of my finger, d'y'understand?' She nodded, too terrified to speak and achingly grateful that baby Nicholas slept soundly; his crying would only have inflamed the situation.

Mitch spat. 'Reckon you need breaking in and reckon I'm growing a little lonely in the big house all by myself. What d'you think, girlie, that I pulled you all the way from England so as you could fix me soup? Your duties go way beyond that and you've been shirking up till now. Don't think I don't know your game. Hiding away with the boy in your little shed. I've stopped by once or twice, watched you sleeping all pretty in your undies. Out for the count you were, didn't hear a thing, but I watched you.' He ran his tongue over his top lip. 'And your sweet little boy.'

Susie swallowed the bile that leapt in her throat, the very idea of him watching her, of being close to her, was bad enough, but now was he threatening Nicholas? It was more than she could bear. Slade busied himself, cleaning under his nails with a paring knife that he kept in his top pocket. His cheeks were bright scarlet.

That afternoon as Susie took a break and lay on her mattress with Nicholas sleeping soundly in her grasp, she contemplated the night ahead of her. She thought about what was to come, tried to imagine Mitch's skin against her own, and tried not to think about the smell of him or the way his eyes shone when he grabbed at her flesh. She sniffed up the tears that clogged her mouth and nose and cried harder than she had in a very long time. The thought that Mitch might come to the room tonight and force himself on her was almost too much to bear. She wiped away her tears. 'Think, Susie, come on think!'

She hadn't meant to fall asleep but a full two hours later she was woken up by a commotion outside; shouts, the sound of horses and the Jackaroo's voice raised, as a blanket of panic settled over Mulga Plains. Placing Nicholas in his cot, she smoothed her hair and wiped away the residue of her tears. Walking out into the sun, she shielded her eyes as the late afternoon rays pierced her vision with their glare.

Slade ran towards her, with his small head wobbling like a pea on a drum, his question left his mouth when he was within ten feet. 'When's the last time you saw, Mitch?' His cheeks were flushed, he sounded breathless, a little hysterical.

'I don't know, earlier, I gave him his lunch on the deck, he ate it and then I came back here. Why, where is he? Is everything all right, Slade? What's going on?'

'No, it ain't. I've just been in to find him. Thought he was crunk, out cold, but he's not.'

Susie considered this. 'Well, he's probably gone out with one of the hands, he'll turn up, Slade.'

'No you dozy Pom, it's not that he's missing. I know exactly where he is.'

'Oh. Well, I don't understand, I thought you couldn't find him.'

'I found him all right, but here's the thing, he's dead!'

'He's what?' As the strength left her legs, she needed it repeating.

'He's dead!'

She flung her hand to her mouth; her heart beat loudly in her ears. She felt elated, relieved and guilty all at once. Then, slowly, the fear crept in. What would happen to her and Nicholas now? With no sponsor and no job, what exactly would happen to her and her son?

Six

Mitch's death left Susie in a state of flux. Rather than provide her with instant sweet relief, she instead felt anxious, frightened. She was torn between enjoying her new-found freedom away from the pawing hands of the deceased and the daily fear of what might happen to her and Nicholas now.

Without her defined role, she tended to hover, awaiting her fate in a different way than before. She cooked for the visitors and ranchmen, staying in the background and waiting until rooms were empty before scuttling in like an old retainer, clearing crockery and sweeping crumbs from the table. At least with Mitch gone, the guests ate in the dining room and not on the veranda where the heat of the sun was enough to make her faint as she looped from table to kitchen and back again, carrying trays, plates and bottles.

It was on a hot, hazy morning as she balanced the unwieldy bowl of liquid on the edge of the card table, when she looked across the terrace and saw the car pull up. This was not unusual, for the last few days, many a vehicle had kicked up dust as it stopped in front of the gates and poured forth people from all over, neighbours from a few miles away and suppliers from the other side of the state. All were keen to pay their respects to the sheep station owner who had provided them with a living and was at present laid out in his best and only suit on the dining-room table. She had avoided setting foot in there since the funeral home had delivered him earlier that day and this was how she would remain until he was buried tomorrow. The thought of witnessing him dead was almost as repellent as seeing him when he was alive.

Susie noted that many of the visitors were just as keen to enquire about his will as they were to drink and reminisce about good old Mitch who had in death, for many, lost his vulgar air. Indeed the man to whom they referred bore no resemblance to the hard-drinking, foul-smelling creature that had manhandled her until her heart beat in her throat with naked fear. It was strange how death could do that to a person.

She rolled the long white sleeves of the shirt up over her elbows, revealing her muscular forearms. She noted how tanned her skin was against the pale cotton – without a mirror or the time to study herself, she assumed her face was similarly coloured; certainly the ends of her hair had gone from chestnut to blonde.

Dipping the cloth into the metal bowl full of soapy water, she wrung out the excess before wiping it over the windowsill and submerging it again beneath the bubbles. Bringing the cloth out and wringing it once again. Susie watched as the back door to the shiny cream Holden opened. She wondered which land owner or supplier would lumber out and remove his hat and loosen his tie. She would of course offer cake and a cup of tea or something stronger, steering them towards the parlour where they could sit with the other mourners and Mulga Plains staff, who hadn't sobered up for the best part of a week. They were eager to greet any new arrival, as it was a good excuse to top up their glass. And yet, the man who stepped out from the back of the car was not a land owner or supplier. He was a smart-looking man with pressed white trousers and a blue jacket. Looking closer, Susie was shocked to see that he was wearing the uniform of a naval officer.

He looked to be a couple of years older than she was, tall and straight-backed, with thick, dark short hair visible beneath his hat. His skin was weathered, and under neatly arched brows, his blue eyes were cold and clear. Most importantly, he wore the uniform of the British. Susie had seen this cap, badge and shirt countless times in the harbours and seaside towns in which she had grown up. *Home…* He reminded her of home. A pang of longing twisted in her stomach. Ironically, he was just the sort of man that her mother would approve of – the sort of man with clean fingernails and a commanding stature. The sort of man that she would always have run a mile from.

She felt flustered at seeing him and as she turned, she caught the edge of the precariously balanced bowl, sending the water cascading over the deck and the metal clattering against the timber with an almighty crash. She crouched down and mopped ineffectively at the soapy pool that gathered on the floor. Tuning to her right, she came face to face with the shiny toes of two black, polished shoes.

'Hello down there!' He had the merest hint of an Antipodean twang to his vowels.

She shook her head, too nervous to speak. He reached down and with his palm towards her, urged her to stand. She placed her hand inside his and stood slowly. His eyes flitted between her face that was upturned towards his own and her braless form that was perfectly visible beneath her wet shirt.

'Any more water in that bowl and I'd be ditching the car and heading back for one of my ships.' He smiled, an odd half smile that used only one side of his mouth. She glimpsed his white, even teeth, and Susie smiled back before immediately casting her gaze downwards, ashamed by her appearance. He was not to be deterred. 'I'm Phillip, Phillip Gunnerslake. Mitch was my uncle. Haven't been to this old dump for years, I've just arrived with my wife.'

'I'm sorry,' Susie whispered, although what she was apologising for wasn't quite clear. She stared at him; noticing the tiny rivulets of sweat that gathered on his top lip. He pushed his dark hair away from his forehead and seemed not to notice her, casting his gaze around the terrace. Her heart hammered in her chest and her face flamed. She hoped he couldn't read her thoughts.

'I don't know your name.' Phillip asked with indifference.

'I'm just, Susie...' She reached out, trying to grasp the sud-covered bowl in her wet hands, but it slipped further out of her reach.

'Do you need a hand there, Miss Susie?'

He spoke slowly, and smiled his strange half-smile again.

'Phillip!' It was almost a scream. He practically leapt from the terrace. The woman, seemingly his wife, was a generous-hipped redhead who stood with her hands on her waist and several suitcases around her feet. 'Are you going to help me with these or do break my back doing it alone?' The woman's English accent would, under different circumstances, have been a balm, but her nasal tone irritated Susie. She wore a lemon-coloured paisley mini dress with matching coat and pillbox hat. It was more suited to a wedding than a funeral, Susie thought, but then who was she to comment, she was wearing men's clothes that smelt of moth balls. The woman's hair had been curled and set, the dry ends were starting to frizz in the heat.

Phillip gritted his teeth and barked a short laugh. 'No drama, Joanne, I'm coming.'

*

The night was pulling its blind on the day when Susie slunk back to her little shed after the drunken ceremony that had been Mitch's funeral. Her print frock, one of Mitch's wife's, was soaked with sweat and clung to her back. Susie had been glad of the gift, it would have been worse to skivvy for these people in her usual shirt and trousers. Nicholas was awake, sitting up in his cot, chatting to himself as he often did; Loulou was by his side. She stood, ambling towards the house in the darkness, ready to get back to washing dishes in the kitchen, trying to keep up with demand from the funeral guests outside.

'Hey there, little man! Here I am.' Susie lifted him from his cot and wrapped her arms around him. It had been over an hour since she had last seen and fed him. 'I missed you!' She covered his face with kisses. Nicholas clapped, which was his new party piece.

'You are so clever! Look at you clapping, my clever baby.'

Slade's drunken voice bleated from the doorway, taking her by surprise. 'Well, let's face it, he's probably a darn sight cleverer than his mother! How did you get things so wrong, if is this the best life you could manage for that boy?'

Susie placed Nicholas in the cot and walked outside. In her time at the ranch, she had learnt how to keep these brutes away from her son, using every diversion tactic possible. Nicholas didn't murmur, he was now accustomed to being raised up and plonked down at regular intervals. It made her heart ache at how adept he was, asking for so little of her time, tolerating the hours of abandonment.

'Please go away, Slade.'

He laughed. 'That's it, give me orders why don't you!'

'You are a nasty creature.' She was certain that Loulou had been going to name him as having some part in her attack. 'Don't think I don't know what happened to Elouera. You may think you've got away with it, but these things have a habit of coming back to haunt you. I don't know what I've done to make you treat me so badly, I really don't, but you've been awful to me since the day I arrived and I've done nothing to deserve it, I've only ever cooked for you and tried to keep out of your way.'

'You think I'd hurt Loulou?' He took a step closer. 'You know nothing! Think you can judge me, Miss High-and-Mighty? Think you've got it all figured out, don't ya?'

'No, Slade, I think I've far from got it all figured out, but I've got the measure of you!'

'No you haven't. Not even close. And if you think the gallant naval officer is the answer to your prayers, you better think again. I saw the way you were looking at him.'

'I don't know what you're talking about!' Susie felt her cheeks flush.

Slade chuckled and shook his head. 'I think you do, but that's not what I came to tell you. I heard good old Phillip list you today as part of the fixtures that go with Mulga Plains! That's how's he sees you, a thing, for sale along with the gateposts and the creaking old refrigerator!'

'What are you talking about?' She shook her head in confusion. He wasn't making any sense.

'I'm talking about the will, which was read this arvo, and there you were, listed along with Loulou.'

Susie sank down onto the red dusty floor, not caring for her pretty cotton dress.

'Don't be ridiculous! That's not true. It can't be.' Loulou's words sprang into her mind. *I am nothing and it's not the worst thing that's happened to me here, not even close...*'

Slade lowered his voice. 'Oh, but it's true all right, I seen it with me own eyes and you want to be careful, Missy, without

Mitch here to keep the dingo's off his property, things he owns might get a little damaged, d'you get me?'

Susie felt a quake of fear that started in her gut and spread to her limbs. Standing, she tried to feel strong, she could not be threatened by him, she had a little boy to protect. 'I think there must be some mistake...' She spoke to the ether, wondering if she was listed alphabetically and what might come before and after.

'No. No mistake, I promise you.'

Phillip's voice cut through the darkness, 'And I promise you, Mr Williams, that if you don't get your things together and be gone by sun up, then it'll be more than dingoes that you'll have to worry about. Go now and go quietly.' Neither had heard him approach in the dusk.

'I ain't afraid of you, you gutless Pom!' he veered on Phillip.

'And neither should you be. I am a man of reason and as long as you are reasonable you have nothing to fear.'

'A man of reason? Is that right? All I know is that your uncle was ashamed of you, he told me that, and I can see why! Reckon you might be fooling others, but I'm not taken in by your shiny buttons and your slick haircut!'

'Thank you for that valuable insight, Mr Williams, the clock is ticking. I suggest you go and pack.'

Slade swayed where he stood, considering his best course of action. It was a relief to all when he broke into a run towards the lodging block.

'Are you really a man of reason?' Susie asked.

'Depends on what you mean by reason.' Phillip's voice was soft.

Susie let her head fall against her chest and she mumbled into it. 'I mean, you wouldn't call a person a "thing", would you? To be inherited like a... a... a piece of furniture.' Her body shook with the exertion.

'Don't cry. Come on. That disgusting bully is gone and he won't be coming back.'

'I think he beat Elouera, very badly, knocked out one of her teeth and cut her lip. I'm sure it was him. I won't ever forget finding her like that. She hasn't told me exactly what happened, but I expect he did worse than that.'

He turned away from her and stretched his arm out towards her, urging her to follow him wherever he was heading and if she had been alone, she just might have.

'I... I can't leave my son.'

'You have a son?' He sounded incredulous.

She nodded towards the cabin, where Nicholas now slept, unaware of the drama unfolding outside the ill-fitting front door.

'Yes, a little boy, Nicholas. He's fourteen months old.' *One of two, twins...*

He took a sharp intake of breath. 'Is Mitch his father?'

'Urgh!' She couldn't contain the involuntary shudder that swept over her from head to toe. 'No. I'm sorry, I don't mean to be disrespectful, but, God no.'

'Good. If he had a son, it would change things significantly.'

Susie sat down on the cushion and drew up her legs, hugging her knees towards her chest. She spoke quietly, as if only to herself. 'I had twins. My boy, Nicholas, and a little girl, Abigail. It's a horrible mess. I'm from Dorset. I've been here for almost a year. I got pregnant back in England and my mother arranged for me to go to a mother-and-baby home.' She broke off to gather her thoughts, to try and regulate her breathing, this was the first time she had spoken her story aloud. 'They took her; the nuns who ran the house were quite wicked. I changed my mind about giving my babies away the very second I looked at them, but it was too late for Abigail, they took her and I had to think fast to escape with Nicholas. I heard that they were offering the ten-pound ticket for people to come over and start a new life here. Mitch sponsored me and it all went wrong and now you have to help me. Please.'

Her sob was loud and unrestrained; she shook her head before laying it on her folded arms and concentrated on getting her words out.

'I am so very, very unhappy. I don't know how I keep going. I miss my home, I miss having handfuls of shampoo to soap my hair, I miss music, coffee shops, London, the coast, rain. I miss everything. If it wasn't for my son I would have curled up and died, I know I would. I can't think. I can't think about anything, not my past or my future, I can't. I have to just keep going because if I think about my life or what lies ahead, I think I might go crazy. I'm on the other side of the world to my little girl who doesn't even know I exist. My baby boy spends his life either asleep in a cot or waiting for me to come home and when I'm not with him, I am a skivvy, cleaning and cooking and waiting on the pigs while they drink and play cards. I think this is hell. I think that I have been sent here to be punished, I really do.' Her tears dripped from her face and splashed on her arms.

Phillip reached out a finger and stroked her arm. Susie's hair stood on end. He had such a commanding presence, she almost felt afraid of him.

'What will happen to us now?'

'Well, Miss Susie, that depends on you.' Phillip placed his hand on her back, rubbing in small circles; she could feel the heat of his skin through the thin material of her frock.

It felt wonderful to feel human contact. She felt her spine unknot beneath his touch. 'I don't understand.' Her voice was barely more than a whisper.

Phillip leant closer and gave her the softest kiss on the lips. 'Let's just say that if you're nice to me, I'll make sure that everyone's nice to you.' He looked at her affectionately. 'Remember, you have your whole life ahead of you here. You might as well make the most of what you've got.'

She closed her eyes, confusion whirling in her brain, as he moved his hand down to her breast.

'No! No... I can't!' Standing up she stepped back and held him at arm's length. 'Phillip, I don't know if I can do this, I want to, I do, but you're married... I can't afford to make any more mistakes.'

She cried then as she lowered her arms to her side.

'Oh no, please no more tears.' His voice had taken on a different tone, harsher.

'I'm sorry,' Susie mumbled as she sank back down onto the cushions under the awning and lay in silence, allowing her racing heart to settle. Phillip lay next to her and stroked her skin. She savoured the weight of his palm as it skimmed her body, drawing the ache from her bones and healing her spirit.

'Now, why don't we try that again?' He rolled onto her, pinning her under his weight, pushing her down into the cushions as he fumbled under her vest, his breath coming in short, heavy, beery bursts as his tongue snaked into her mouth.

Susie tried to wriggle free. 'Please... stop... no! Don't talk to me like that!' She didn't know where she found the courage, but knew that she had to lay a marker, if he was going to be her new boss, she had to make a stand or things for her and her son could get a whole lot worse.

'I'll talk to you anyway I please. Slade was right, you come with the property.' A glob of spit landed on her cheek, as she felt her insides turn to ice.

She heard his zipper being opened and closed her eyes as he

whispered into her ear, 'I reckon old Mitch had the right idea, dirty old sod, and I think you'll make my visits here that much more palatable. Don't worry, I'll leave Joanne at home next time. Be a good girl and don't make a fuss, I'd hate to have to give you the same as Mitch gave Elouera.'

'You bastard!' she managed through her tears and had her arms not been trapped beneath his body, would have beat him with her fists.

As Phillip grappled at her dress, Susie felt her mind drift away from what was about to happen to her. She thought about her bedroom at her parents' house and wondered whether it looked the same as she had left it, the candlewick bedspread, the books, her guitar... Suddenly there was a crack and Phillip slumped forward. A guttural sound escaped from him, as if the breath had been knocked from his body. Susie scrambled out and saw Slade standing over Phillip with a plank in his hand.

'Slade!' Susie cried as she reached for dress, shaking.

'It's okay. It's all going to be okay. Get your stuff together; we haven't got long. I'll bring the truck round, you're going home.'

'Going home?' She hardly dared speak the words. 'How?'

'Mitch was a wealthy man, not that you'd think so, judging by how he lived, but he was, very wealthy. I took what was needed and I've arranged for tickets. You need to pack up your things and prepare to go, I don't know how long he'll be out for.' He indicated Phillip face down on the cushions, 'We're meeting a mate who will take you on and you'll be back in Pomland before you know it.'

'Really?' She blinked up at him.

'Really.'

'I'm going home!' She beamed. 'I'm going home and I can find Abigail, I can go and get my little girl! I... I don't... I...

What can I say, but thank you, Slade.' Susie sobbed, allowing all the sadness that had pooled inside her for the last few months come to the fore.

Slade disappeared into the darkness as Susie gathered up the sleeping Nicholas and shoved what came to hand into her suitcase. She waited, wondering if it was all a trap, not sure who to trust. The sound of the pickup engine was like music as it cut through the chirping night song. Slade helped her into the front seat, where a beaming Loulou was already seated.

'Loulou!' Susie fell into her friend, holding her tightly.

'Slade been looking after me, patched me up. I'm going across country to stay with my daughter.' She nodded matter-of-factly.

'Slade, I don't know what to say to you. I'm sorry…' Susie watched a small flicker of a smile on his thin mouth.

Slade spat into the foot well. 'Ah, cut it out. Don't start going all sweet talk on me.'

Nicholas sighed and carried on sleeping, unaware.

'Make good choices for him.' Slade spoke to the view from his window. 'You need to screw your head on right. There might not always be some nasty creature on hand to keep the boss drunk and out of your hair, or to leave you a welcome flower…'

'That was you?' Susie smiled.

Slade shrugged.

'Reckon Slade did a lot for us, Susie,' Elouera sighed. 'Reckon he might even have killed old Gunnerslake, least that what I think.'

Susie looked at the road ahead. 'Oh no, you didn't kill him did you, Slade?'

Slade shook his head. 'I didn't, never killed anyone. I couldn't.'

Susie closed her eyes. She pictured Mitch, moments before

he died, having his afternoon nap in his greasy sheets. It had only taken a moment to place a pillow over his open, snoring mouth. It had only taken a minute before he stopped struggling.

'He's telling the truth, Loulou,' Susie sighed. 'Slade didn't kill Mitch. I did.'

The two women interlocked their fingers, holding hands, as the dust kicked up a storm under the wheels of the truck, not that they noticed. They were looking forward at the road ahead, thinking of the new life that awaited them, a life beyond the gates of Mulga Plains. A new beginning.

Miss
Potterton's
Birthday Tea

One

'Your grammar is appalling!' Miss Potterton slammed the notepad onto the desk. 'I mean, I don't see what is so difficult about it. Did you not cover the subjunctive at school? In fact, no, don't answer that!' She held the magnifying glass aloft in her knobbly hand and closed her eyes, as if even the sight of the girl standing awkwardly in front of her was injurious. 'I am quite sure that your response would only depress me further.'

She sighed and blinked open her eyes to see the girl stooping down to gather up her anorak and the carrier bag containing her magazine and packed lunch. 'Wh... what... what's going on? Where are you going?' she shouted.

'I'm leaving,' the girl replied. 'I'll tell the agency that you not only want someone to clean, but they also need a degree in spelling!'

Cordelia Potterton winced. 'A degree in *spelling*! What kind of degree is *that*?'

The girl slammed the door behind her, sending a shiver through the dark-wood African masks collected by Miss Potterton's father and still hanging on the wall of the basement flat in Lexham Gardens, Kensington, where he had positioned them long ago.

'Good grief!' Miss Potterton gasped as she lifted the receiver. She pressed the numbers on the large-button keypad, repeating them out loud as she did so.

A voice on the other end sighed a morning greeting.

'Now, which one are you?' Miss Potterton asked curtly. 'You all sound the same. Is it Joanna or Katie?'

'It's me, Miss Potterton. Katie. And goodness me, this is nearly a personal best! It's only a quarter past nine and Martine was booked from nine o'clock!' The girl snorted her amusement.

'It really isn't a laughing matter. She was absolutely useless!'

'They usually are,' Katie muttered under her breath.

Miss Potterton gripped the phone, keen to explain further. 'I asked her to take dictation of a simple letter and she had the secretarial skills of a child! In fact, no, my sister and I would have done better when we were ten, and this girl was at least twenty!'

There was no response. Miss Potterton pulled the phone away from her mouth and gave it a rattle, as if that might fix the silence coming from the other end. 'Are you there, dear?' she shouted.

'Yes! Yes, Miss Potterton, I'm here.'

'I was told that the girl had been to university, a recent graduate, so I naturally assumed that she'd be able to jot down a simple letter to my MP. I feel very strongly about all these basement excavations that are going on. It can't be good for the foundations and I don't want to be discovered under a pile of expensive rubble one morning with a sign saying "I told you so" sticking up from the ruins.'

She drew breath. 'I assumed a university education would mean she was capable of drafting my letter, but no, apparently she studied *meeeja*, whatever that is. And she had the scrawl of a toddler with palsy.'

'And I'm afraid that's the problem. Martine is not a secretary. In the same way that Andrea was not a horticulturist—'

'It was a couple of snips to my bonsai...' Miss Potterton interrupted.

'Lynda was not a cat groomer—'

'Three measly claws that needed clipping!'

'And Katarzyna was not a hairdresser.'

'I couldn't see my Kindle! One swipe at my fringe with the nail scissors is hardly asking for a full perm and comb-out!'

Katie sighed. 'We are a cleaning agency. We hire out cleaners. Our staff are paid thirteen pounds an hour to *clean*!'

'And yet you charge me twenty-two pounds fifty!' Miss Potterton grumbled.

Katie mentally reloaded, cursing her misfortune at having answered the phone to this particular call. 'I tell you what I'll do, Miss Potterton. I shall pop another leaflet through your door detailing our charges, which are all quite transparent, together with the leaflet that lists the chores and tasks that our staff are happy to undertake. Things like dusting, ironing, cleaning the kitchen and bathroom, hoovering—'

'The term is vacuuming!' Miss Potterton shouted. 'Hoover is the brand and I find it most irritating that people think it is a verb.'

There was a moment of silence, during which Miss Potterton was sure she could hear counting.

'Hello? Hello?' she shouted.

'Yes, still here! Just, erm… just thinking how best to proceed.'

'It's quite simple really, Katie. I want a reliable cleaner for two hours, three times a week.'

'And trust me, I would like nothing more than to be able to provide that for you. If only to stop these calls.' Katie whispered the last part.

'What was that?' Miss Potterton shook the phone again.

'I said, thank you for your call!'

'So what do you propose, Katie?'

'That's the trouble.' Katie sighed. 'I'm running out of

propositions. Usually, after a client has refused one of our staff, we give them a strike, and after three strikes we don't supply them with cleaners any more. That's our policy.'

'Goodness me! How many strikes have I had?'

There was a pause while Katie placed the end of her pencil on the screen and counted.

'Twelve,' came the definitive reply.

Katie listened to the faint wheezing on the other end of the phone. At first she thought the old lady was crying, but then she realised it was actually the sound of laughter.

Two

Dr Ian Munroe dried his hands on a paper towel, balled it and lobbed it at the wastepaper bin in the corner. It missed.

'Bollocks.'

It felt shameful, emasculating, somehow, having to walk all the way over to the other side of the room and stoop low to retrieve it. Proof, if proof were needed, of his lack of sporting prowess. He scooped up the handful of stiff paper towel. This time it skimmed the rim of the bin, which was now mere inches away, and fell to the floor once again. With uncharacteristic aggression, he kicked the bin. It hit the wall and disgorged its contents under his desk. Stretching out his legs, he bounced his shoes on the paper-strewn floor, rather enjoying the sponginess beneath his feet.

He clicked the icon on his computer that meant the appropriate message would pop up on the waiting-room screen, then placed a mint on his tongue.

'Oh shit!' he muttered as he saw the name of his next patient. At almost the exact same moment there was a feeble knock at the door.

'Come in!' He searched for a tone that was neutral and professional but also welcoming.

The door remained closed.

'Come in!' He rolled his eyes and spoke a little louder.

The door opened a few inches and Mrs Coates popped her miserable face into the gap. 'Should I come in?'

Her sour demeanour had the most depressing effect on everyone she encountered, especially on Dr Ian Munroe, who was already feeling less than sunny today. She had what his late mother would have described as a face that curdled milk.

'Yes! Yes, please do, Mrs Coates.'

She crept apologetically into the small room and sat down warily, as though the chair were smeared with something unpleasant. She was just the type to complain a lot, about everything, thought Ian. The sort of person who would send food back after having eaten three quarters of her plate. And she probably spent a large amount of her time watching her neighbours, with the council number on speed dial, ready to report any suspicious non-food items being hurled into the little brown compost bin. She wasn't what you would call joyous.

Ian beamed at her nonetheless. 'So!' He did this, tried to rally her with invigorating enthusiasm, as though his tone and volume could sweep away the negativity that she emitted. He pictured her dourness as a physical thing, like little balls of miserable fluff that trailed behind her. 'What can I do for you today?'

'It's the cancer,' she muttered, head cocked to one side as she looked mournfully at the floor, her mouth set in a grimace.

'Whose cancer?' He darted his head forward, wondering how he had lost the thread so early on.

'Mine.' She pulled the thin blue hem of her raincoat up over her knees.

'But you don't have cancer,' he levelled.

'I didn't have it, Doctor, but I do now.'

'You do? Goodness me, Mrs Coates, I am so sorry to hear

that. I had no idea! You must have seen one of my colleagues.'
He decided to call her bluff. 'Let me take a quick look at your
notes.' He placed his gold-rimmed spectacles on his nose and
clicked and scrolled through several pages on his screen. 'Ah
yes, here we are. December 4th: suspected appendicitis, which
was just gas, is that right?'

She nodded regretfully.

'Then December 28th, we had Lyme disease symptoms, but
that also tested negative. January we didn't see you.' He looked
up at her, as this required an explanation.

'I was at my sister's in Fuengirola. We go there to save on
the heating,' she clarified without a smile. 'But I was admitted
to the local hospital with a suspected severe allergic reaction.'

'Suspected *and* severe?' He exhaled, intimating that she'd
had a lucky escape. 'What was it you were allergic to? We
should probably make a note.'

'They never found out,' she replied. 'But I've given up paella
and foreign sherry. Just to be on the safe side.'

Ian bit his lip to stop himself mentioning that, for Brits, all
sherry was foreign! 'Righto.' He looked back at his screen.
'February 16th: ankle pain when you coughed, but not when
you sneezed. March 3rd: double vision and diarrhoea. March
12th: double vision and constipation. March 20th: temporary
blindness and acute thrush. And so on and so forth. But I can't
seem to find your cancer diagnosis?' He placed his hands in his
lap and stared at her.

She held his gaze, with a glint of something resembling
triumph in her eyes. 'That's because I haven't shown it to
anyone yet. But what do you think of this!' She positively
glowed as she unbuttoned her blouse with what could only be
described as vigour, and there on her right breast sat a brown
lump.

'Goodness! Let's have a closer look.' Ian adjusted his specs and scooted his chair across the linoleum, carefully avoiding two paper towel mountains that threatened to get stuck in its wheels. He stared at her chest, then returned to his desk and retrieved a pair of tweezers.

Mrs Coates gasped and swallowed. 'Is it going to hurt? I mean, I can take the pain, and the treatment, and I'm even prepared to say my goodbyes, but I just need a minute to calm myself.'

Ian gave a tight-lipped smile as he went in with the tweezers. He gave the blob a small tug and dropped it into Mrs Coates' hand. 'Brown toast and Marmite!' He grinned.

'Oh, Doctor!' she trilled. 'I feel so foolish. I hate wasting your time. Thank you! I've been worried all morning. Thank you!'

'All part of the service, Mrs Coates. See you very, very soon, no doubt.'

As she left the room, Ian sank low in his chair and placed his head in his hands. 'Give me strength,' he muttered under his breath. 'Seven years of training and twenty-one years of practice for this – toast and sodding Marmite!'

When his phone rang, he reached out and, still with his eyes closed, gathered it under his chin. 'Dr Munroe.' His tone was clipped, conveying that he was both interested and harried.

'It's me.'

'Oh, hello, love.' He sat up straight and opened his eyes.

'I've made my decision.' There was no clue in her tone.

He swallowed. 'And?'

'I'm leaving you.'

Three

'Mum! Your programme's on!' Marley shouted into the kitchen from the leather sofa on which he reclined.

Tina bustled in with a mug of coffee and a side plate piled with three slices of Battenberg cake.

'Moveyrft!' She tried to speak but found it hard to make herself understood on account of the bag of salt and vinegar crisps dangling from her mouth.

'What?' Marley raised his head and stared at his mum.

'I said, move your feet!' Her crisp bag fell onto the deep-pile rug that created a cosy patch on the laminate floor. 'Jesus, lucky for you I'm only tiny, otherwise you'd have to sit up properly.'

The teenager tutted as he bent his knees into a pyramid and scooted his white sports sock clad feet along the cushion.

Tina plonked down at the end of the sofa and her son promptly laid his feet on her lap. 'Marley!' she screamed, before conceding defeat and placing a cushion on his shins to make a makeshift table for her plate and the crisp packet she'd retrieved from the floor.

'Is that your breakfast?' He grimaced.

'Yep.' She kept her eyes on the forty-two-inch curved screen, a present from Marley's dad and Lord only knew how he had acquired it. The vast thing made their tiny sitting room feel more like the local Odeon. She had hated it on sight, but had to admit to rather enjoying watching 'Enders on the monstrosity.

'Turn it up.' She nodded as she crammed half a slice of cake into her mouth.

'Ooh, look, Marl, this'll be good!' The show title flashed up on the screen. *I'll Prove I've Got What It Takes To Be A Dad, Even Though I Slept With Your Sister!* 'They might have your dad on it!' She laughed, shaking her head so her large gold earrings jangled.

'Very funny.' He blinked. 'You haven't even got a sister.'

'Lucky for me or he definitely would have!' She winked at him.

Marley was keen to change the subject. 'I can't believe you eat that junk. You need a healthier start to the day.'

'Oh good, does this mean you got that undercover job recruiting for All-Bran then?'

'Ha ha. I mean it! Just because you're skinny doesn't mean you're healthy.' He tutted.

'Marley, you've only been at college for three weeks, you're on your first module and already you've turned into Dr Bloody Hilary! And besides, I've done a job this morning, don't forget, so this is more like lunch.'

'It's just as bad for you even if it's lunch. I just want you to be healthy.'

'Aww, bless!' She smiled at her beautiful boy, who she knew spoke the truth. She couldn't imagine what his life would be like if she weren't around to smooth his path; they were a great team. 'Anyway, enough talking.' She sipped her coffee and pointed at the screen. 'That bloke in the wings looks like fat Barry from the chippy.'

They both squinted at the screen as Jeremy's voice cut

through their morning chatter. 'I'd like to welcome Barry from Hammersmith onto the stage!'

The audience clapped on cue as Tina sat forward and squealed. 'Flamin' Nora! It *is* fat Barry from the chippy!'

The two of them were transfixed.

'The dirty bastard!' Tina pulled open her crisp packet and they both laughed.

Four

Cordelia Potterton flexed her fingers as best she could. It irritated her beyond belief that her body no longer did the things she wanted it to and yet also did several things she would rather it didn't. Her mind was as sharp as a tack and for that she was grateful, but the weakness in her wrists meant lifting and twisting was almost impossible, the lack of dexterity in her digits made her feel like a clumsy child and the general softening of her physique was nothing short of maddening.

Eventually, she managed to button her coat over her slender frame, pulling it to straighten the shoulder seams that now sat a little askew on her bowed body. She had known that she would shrink with age, but when your starting point was six foot, this wasn't too lamentable. She had always stood a good few inches above Tom, not that this had mattered a jot, not to them. She'd expected to lose the odd inch here and there, bringing her down to a more average height, but what she hadn't banked on was the curve to her spine, the collapse of her hip and the sag to her shoulders, all of which had increased the shrinkage.

She placed her navy beret over her short, grey, razor cut, twisting it to a jaunty angle low over her right ear, then did her best to keep the slick of crimson lipstick on her lips, despite the wobbly hand that seemed to have a will of its own. Next she arranged her lime-green chiffon scarf in a pussy bow at her crêpey neck and collected her wicker basket, in which nestled a bunch of blue stocks, tied around the stems with a small twist of brown string.

Greta Garbo meowed and pawed at the thick brown tights beneath her mistress's vintage Jaeger houndstooth skirt before finally sitting on the toes of her rather clumpy tan brogues.

'What a ghastly racket. You sound quite frightful, Greta, and you know how I feel about clinginess. It smacks of weakness and dependency and we all know that for you it's just a ruse – you like your own company! You're only interested in me when I appear to be abandoning you.' She gave a throaty laugh and shifted her foot. 'I shall be no more than an hour. Nap or play with a ball, or whatever it is you do when I'm not here. You know the rules: no parties, and I've left Jenni Murray on for you for company.'

Bending to give Greta a brief, affectionate stroke, she felt the familiar swirl of giddiness and leant against the wall with her eyes closed. This was yet another aspect of being old that bothered her enormously. It wasn't that she wanted to dance or run again, although both would be fun, but she did want to be able to hear clearly, so that she could keep safe and listen out for burglars or the first crackle of a fire, and she would have loved to be able to bend over without the floor rushing up to meet her and every joint creaking in protest.

The doorbell rang. She turned to Greta Garbo and waggled her finger. 'Remember! No parties!'

Slowly she made her way along the hallway and opened the half-glazed front door.

'Morning, Miss P. Lovely day for it.' Len the cabby smiled and offered her his arm.

'If you say so, Leonard. I'm afraid my day has been rather difficult thus far. My cleaner just walked out without so much as a by your leave! So now I'm high and dry!' She tutted angrily at the memory. 'Such an inconvenience, and tomorrow is ornament day. I fear they will have to forgo the caress of a feather duster this week.'

'Oh, I'm sorry to hear that. People is unreliable sometimes. Mind how you go, now.' He pointed at the steep flight of slightly uneven basement steps as he guided her upwards.

'I'm afraid you are right, Leonard. People is.' She trod gingerly, with one hand on the metal handrail and the other looped through his crooked elbow. In his other hand, Len carried her basket.

'Ooh, they're beautiful. Stocks. They smell lovely, don't they?' He smiled.

She nodded and concentrated on putting one foot in front of the other. It took an age, but the reward was worth the effort. Looking around as her head emerged at ground level, Miss Potterton felt a surge of happiness at the fact that this was her home, this beautiful street in Kensington in the greatest city in the world! For her, the thrill never dulled. Her only sadness was that her advanced years and infirmity stopped her from gallivanting around the way she used to, no longer able to take advantage of the parks, museums and galleries that had been her sanctuary since she was a child. Not to mention all those deliciously bohemian dance clubs that she and Tom had enjoyed so much, the kind referred to in the more salacious social pages, where entry was via a secret knock on a rusting door.

'You all right for a minute while I get the walking stick?' Len asked, as he always did, before hurrying to his cab and opening the back door. 'Shan't be a mo.'

'Yes, Leonard, I promise I shan't run off.' Despite her flippant response, her eyes widened with the fear that, unsupported, she might wobble and fall.

With the special walking stick now retrieved – it was kept

exclusively for Miss Potterton's use, as she refused to give in and buy one of her own – Len returned to her side and so began the slow process of manoeuvring her into the back seat and getting her buckled up for the journey.

'Incredible to think, isn't it, that when I was a girl there were only two cars in this street and one of those was Daddy's. He had a Crossley. Its colour was Atlantic green. I can't recall the model, but it had a darling canvas canopy and studded leather upholstery. Very grand. I can remember street boys coming to leer through the windows and our driver, Mason, shooing them away from the paintwork that he'd spent all morning polishing. It was another world entirely. A man used to come and visit the street with a little monkey in a red-and-white striped waistcoat. He'd whistle and the ugly little thing used to flip over. Quite bizarre. Doubt it'd be allowed nowadays, it'd only want one precocious child to have its fingers bitten off and that would be the end of that.'

'That's health and safety for you.' Len nodded. He wasn't sure of the relevance but liked to join in. It was hard to think of something different to say when he'd heard the same anecdotes repeated more times than he cared to remember.

Miss Potterton liked that she didn't have to confirm her destination or make unnecessary small talk. Len had been driving her there once a month for the last twelve years, rain or shine.

The cars sat bumper to bumper on Kensington Church Street. 'It's a shocker on the roads today, world and his wife are out.' He spoke to the rear-view mirror.

She ignored him, gazing instead at the shop displays, the people that crowded the pavements, and the sky. This monthly trip was her window on the world and she didn't want to waste a second of it.

'Good Lord!' She inhaled sharply.

Len followed her gaze until his eyes fell upon a young girl who was covered in tattoos. Even her face was adorned with the stars and stripes of Old Glory.

'Shocking, isn't it, Miss P?' He shook his head.

She stared at the girl with her big eyes and dainty figure. 'I've always thought one should leave room in one's life for a small handful of regrets,' she mused. 'Do things while you can that will keep your cogs turning when your candle has nearly burnt out. But that seems rather drastic.'

'Can't see her heading up customer services or getting a job as the local bank manager!' Len chuckled.

'No, you're quite right. Lucky girl! Maybe she's smarter than she looks. Can't think of anything worse than being stuck in administrative mediocrity.'

Len blinked in response. 'I was just having a think about what you said earlier. One of my neighbours is a cleaner – smashing girl. Do you want me to have a word and see if she can fit you in? She might like the extra cash and it's not too far.'

'I'll think about it.' She was dismissive and Len wished he hadn't bothered, embarrassed at having made the suggestion.

When they got to Hampstead Cemetery, he indicated and pulled over, leaving the hazard lights on as he opened the door and helped Miss Potterton out.

The two wandered along the path arm in arm and at a snail's pace, with the bright autumn sunshine peeking through the canopy of trees above. Under his other arm, Len carried a lightweight fishing chair – something else that he kept in the cab especially for Miss Potterton's monthly outings. Both of them were silent, as usual, and almost reverent as they made their way between the various Gothic mausoleums, elaborate family graves and featureless statues whose faces and costumes had been eroded by centuries of wind and rain.

When they reached the spreading yew tree in the quiet north-eastern corner to the right of the gate, Len set down the fishing chair and waited. Miss Potterton shuffled forward and dropped the bundle of blue stocks onto a low grassy mound. Then Len took her arm again and eased her into the chair so that she sat facing a small cluster of graves.

'Be back in twenty minutes, Miss P. If you need me before then, just raise your arm. I'll be watching.'

It was as if she hadn't heard Len, who ambled back to the car with his hands in his pockets. She stared, transfixed by one of the weathered, moss-splashed gravestones.

Then she leant forward. 'Hello, my darling.' She smiled.

Five

Ian Munroe slipped out of his white coat and hung it on the back of the door before shrugging on his zip-up fleece, which sat snugly over his pale denim shirt. He smiled at his colleagues as he sidled out of his surgery and through the outer offices, avoiding the waiting room, where he would undoubtedly get waylaid by determined stragglers. But there was no escaping the receptionist.

'Ooh, Dr Munroe...'

He wondered if there was any way he could make it out of the front door uninterrupted – by whistling or checking his phone perhaps, anything that might convince her he hadn't heard. *Ten minutes in the car, that's all I want. Ten minutes in the bloody car!* It didn't feel like much to ask.

But Julie turned in her chair and reached out towards him as he passed. He had no choice but to smile and acknowledge her, particularly as she had grabbed his leg.

'I need you a mo.' She swivelled round and began searching for a document on her messy desk.

He could hear the seconds ticking by loudly in his head while she giggled at the chaos and peeled apart flimsy sheets stuck together with the residue of whatever sandwich she'd been eating and a smattering of biscuit crumbs.

'What it is, is...' She paused. 'Is I need a signature off you for Tyler Jackson's passport. His mum's been in and she said if we don't get it back to her today then Tyler won't be able to get his passport in time and he'll miss the geography trip to Latvia. He's cried himself to sleep for the last four nights apparently, worried he'll be left behind at school and will have to go into Mrs Alpass's class, and she's a right cow.'

She finally took a breath.

Ian had missed most of the detail but caught the gist. 'Ah, well, we can't have the little fellow upset.' He unscrewed the top of his fountain pen and signed the sheet Julie now brandished, on which she had pencilled a large X.

'Oh, he's not a little fellow. He's eighteen. Captain of the rugby team.' She blew a large pink bubble with the gum she was chewing so furiously and let it pop against her chin.

Ian always parked in the same spot in the corner of the car park. This was partly to hide his monstrous four-by-four under the large tree; he hated owning the most ostentatious car in the practice and would have preferred to cycle in, but Helen said that wouldn't be fitting. He also liked that spot because it offered the best view of the vast Asda megastore with whom the practice shared a car park, allowing him to people-watch while he ate his pasta salad or tuna and sweetcorn sandwich, depending on the day of the week.

As he settled himself into the capacious front seat, he swallowed, then swiped his finger over the screen of his phone. Time was of the essence, so he didn't have the chance to rehearse, which is what he would have liked. Instead, he was just going to have to go in blind and hope for the best.

'Yup?' Helen's tone told him she was in a hurry, made it clear that any call, even one from him, was a bloody inconvenience.

His heart raced accordingly. The only thing worse than knowing he was an inconvenience was knowing he was an inconvenience that she no longer wanted in her life.

'It's me.' He hated the quiver in his voice.

'Yes, I know it's you. As I've told you a million times, we have caller ID. Your name comes up with your number on the little screen.' Irritation dripped from her.

Yep, that's me: fucking stupid. I don't understand the phone, can't use the remote control, never made it as a surgeon and am not a patch on Julio, the suave, Spanish, tennis-playing dickhead who not only heads up his own team of plastic surgeons but probably also has a very large penis.

He shook the image from his head. 'Did you mean it?'

She prefaced her words with a sigh, a very bad sign indeed. 'Yes, Ian, I meant it. And it's not like this is news—'

'It's news to me.'

'Well, that says it all, really. The fact that you think we can simply waltz through life, watering the hanging baskets, taking a couple of holidays a year, having Sunday lunch with the family, getting the shopping delivered three times a week, having sex on Friday nights and special occasions, and expect that to be enough?'

Ian considered this as he pinched the top of his nose. 'I did, actually, Helen. I thought it was more than enough.'

'For you!' She practically spat the words. 'It was enough for you.'

'Yes,' he whispered. 'Enough for me.'

'Minty says she thinks I have been more than fair, she says she's amazed I've stuck it for as long as I have!'

Ian looked out of the window at a couple who laughed and stopped to kiss each other as they piled their groceries into the back of their van. 'I don't think it's fair that you've been discussing this with our daughter. Arraminta should not be asked to take sides, and by giving her details you'll make it very hard for her not to feel guilty.'

Helen laughed loudly. 'Minty? Guilty? Don't think that's likely! And she already knows the details. She's lived with you too – she knows how boring you are!'

'Yes, of course, I've been boringly working my nuts off to send her to that ridiculously expensive school and to get her a sodding pony that she lost interest in after five minutes and to keep our massive bloody house running and, best of all, to send you on numerous holidays, the last one of which is where you met fucking Julio!' He hit the steering wheel with the heel of his hand.

'And that, I'm afraid, is the problem. Julio says he thinks you somehow resent the life Minty and I lead.'

'I thought he was a plastic surgeon, not a bloody psychiatrist! And for his information, the only thing I resent is how unappreciative you both are. It makes me sick.'

Helen took a deep breath. 'We are mismatched species, you and I. Both wanting, no, *needing* different things. Julio gets me, Ian, he really does.'

'Is this about the vegan thing?' he asked, trying his best to understand. 'Because if it's that, then I suppose I could give it a go.'

'No! For God's sake! It's about so much more than you being willing to forgo a sausage.'

And just like that, he was back to thinking about Julio's penis.

Six

'What time you back, Marl?' Tina called from the kitchen where she was trying to re-create a Japanese flower arrangement she'd seen in a magazine, using the cut-price lilies she'd picked up at the market.

Marley came to the kitchen doorway with his large sports bag slung over his shoulder. 'Dunno. I've got college this afternoon and then me and Digsy are going to his to play FIFA.'

'Well, I don't want you out late. You've got college in the morning and you need to call your nan tonight. It's Wednesday.'

Marley rolled his eyes.

Tina pointed a blunted stem in his direction. 'Don't look like that. She looks forward to it.'

'I know, but... it's just boring. We say the same things over and over. *How your studies going? You eating good?*' He did a fine imitation of his West Indian grandma.

Tina suppressed her laughter. 'Boring for you, maybe, but for her it's a little lifeline and it makes her happy. And if you can make someone happy by doing something so small, then why wouldn't you?'

Marley shrugged. The doorbell rang and he raced down the flat's narrow hallway and opened the door to Digsy, who leant against the wall and waved.

'All right, Tina?'

'Yep. You?' She smiled at the cocky boy, whose manner and language hid a shy, sweet nature.

'I'm doing okay.' He beamed.

'Stay out of trouble and don't keep my boy out all hours!' She smiled again.

'What am I, his grandma?' Digsy sucked his teeth and let his body fall back while performing an elaborate arm gesture.

'No, cos his grandma knows that answering back gets you a clip round the ear!' Tina raised her hand in mock anger. 'And she'd know about it when Marley calls her tonight, like he does every Wednesday!' She looked at her son.

'Come off it! You love me, Tina!' Digsy shook his head, laughing as he adjusted his baseball cap.

'Good job, innit?' She winked.

'You still have to call your nan every week? No way, man.' Digsy smiled widely at his mate.

Tina could see this would be a rich source of ribbing later. 'Yes, Digsy, he does, because she lives over four thousand miles away and so, unlike *your* grandma, can't drag him to church every Sunday!' She grinned. That should even out the ammunition when it came to it later on.

Digsy was uncharacteristically quiet.

She smiled after the boys as they hurried off along the balcony and towards the lifts.

Almost immediately there was a knock on the door.

'What's he forgotten now?' she muttered. Opening up with a twist to her mouth, she was surprised to find Len, her neighbour, standing there.

'Oh! All right, Len! Thought it was Marley forgot something. What can I do you for?'

'Bit of a weird one, Teen, but I do a driving job for this lady in Kensington…'

'Ooh, very nice!' She cocked her head at him.

'I've done it for years. She's a bit of a character, and getting quite frail, although she'd have my guts for garters for even mentioning that. Thing is, she's been let down by her cleaner and she's a bit stuck. I mentioned you might be interested, so I just wondered, really...'

'Well, bless you for thinking of me. Where's she live?'

'In a flat. Lexham Gardens. It's between High Street Ken and the Cromwell Road.'

Tina mentally figured out the route, which was possible. 'How much?'

'Fifteen pound an hour.'

'That's good.'

'It's two hours, three times a week, starting tomorrow!' He laughed.

Tina did the sums. An extra ninety quid a week would be very handy, especially now she was saving for Marley's college and university.

'Do you know, I reckon I could fit it in, Len. If Marley can get himself off to college, I could do it. My other cleaning jobs are one full day, one early morning and two afternoons...'

'Oh, smashing! Shall I tell her you'll give it a go?'

'Yeah, go on, why not! I could do with the money, that's for sure.'

'She's quite hard work, but you'll soon get used to her.'

'I can handle meself.' She smiled. 'How's Lynne?'

'Good. Yeah, good. We're off to Tenerife week after next, for a bit of a break. So she's looking forward to that.'

'Oh, lovely!' Tina folded her arms across her chest. 'You been?'

'No!' She batted her hand at him. 'I've never been abroad. Haven't been on holiday since before Marley was born!'

'What? You'd love it, girl!'

'Oh, no doubt. Trust me, the reason I don't go is not because I have an aversion to drinking pina coladas in the sun!'

'Nah, course not. Anyway, I'll text you the details later. Her name is Cordelia Potterton.'

'Well, that's a name and an 'arf. Is it Mrs?'

'No. She's a "Miss".'

Seven

The clock on the radio chimed seven. Miss Potterton looked at the gold watch that now hung loosely from her tiny wrist.

'Seven o'clock,' she announced, tapping the face, happy that the two tallied.

Greta Garbo jumped up and sat on her lap in the lamplight.

'Hello, girl. Where have you been? Roaming the streets and up to no good, no doubt. You lucky old thing.' She chuckled and when her laugh turned into a wheeze, she sipped at her glass of water that sat on a lace doily within reach on the sideboard.

'I had a lovely chat with Tom today. Too little time, as ever, but I get dreadfully stiff sitting on that blasted chair in the middle of the grass. I'm sure I make quite an exhibition. I said how I'd sorted the stamp books out and that I'd sent a couple off to the Postal Museum in Bath. I do hope they can make good use of them. Tom will be delighted by that.'

She paused and stroked the top of Greta Garbo's head absentmindedly, her memories coming thick and fast.

'We had the most wonderful weekend there, in Bath. I think it was 1955, and I remember the sun shone – it really was the most glorious weather. I can see us now, like it was yesterday. We picnicked on the grass in the Royal Crescent. Gosh, do you know, Greta, I think we spent the entire day with shoes kicked off, sleeves rolled, just lying on that tartan blanket, holding hands and gazing up at the clouds. Not a care in the world, and no one paid us the slightest attention. I don't think I have ever been happier.'

Garbo licked her mistress's hand and stared at her intently, as if listening to every word.

'We took a stroll around Royal Victoria Park and there was a most impressive display of yellow roses. Tom picked me one and I pressed it, kept it by my bedside for years. I still have it. And I remember Tom saying, "Can we just stay here forever and ever…"' Miss Potterton sniffed her tears and fished for the white lace handkerchief that nestled up her sleeve. 'And by golly I wanted to. I really did.'

The telephone handset on the arm of her chair rang.

She sat up straight and coughed, answering slowly and deliberately. '589 8181.' She did this, gave her telephone number just as she always had, from the day they were first connected, way back between the wars. Their original number had been a mere three digits.

'Evening, Miss P, hope I'm not interrupting you. It's Len. Leonard.' Len spoke loudly and slowly, as if she was a little hard of hearing, which she was.

'Good evening, Leonard.'

There was a second of silence as Len hesitated, expecting a bit more of a greeting. 'Reason for my call is that I had a word with my neighbour, as I suggested when I dropped you home earlier, and she'd be more than happy to come and clean for you, or at least give it a go. I told her you'd like her tomorrow and she'll be with you about ten.'

'*At* ten, Leonard. Not *about* ten, otherwise it's jolly hard to keep track. Makes it confusing when you're chasing the odd minute here and there.'

'Righto, ten it is. Good night, Miss P.'

'Good night, Leonard.' She ended the call.

'No, don't thank me. My pleasure,' Len muttered as he replaced the receiver. He lay on the sofa staring at the phone, then smiled at his wife, Lynne, who was reading a guidebook to the Canary Islands.

'What you on about, talking to yourself?' Lynne looked up.

'Nothing, love.' And he settled back for a nap.

Eight

Tina knocked on the door and stood up straight, smoothing her dark, unruly hair back into its ponytail. She made sure to smile. If Miss Potterton was anything like her elderly nan, a smiling face would help put her at her ease.

It felt like an age before the shadowy figure finally made it to the door; then another few minutes passed as she fumbled with the bolts.

'Hello!' Tina leant forward, in case Miss Potterton was hard of hearing. 'I'm Tina! A friend of Len's. He said you would like me to clean for you?' Her smile didn't waver.

'You're early.' Miss Potterton narrowed her gaze.

'Yes! I don't like to be late, so I tend to go the other way. Sorry.' She wasn't sure if this required an apology but figured there was no harm in offering one.

'How old are you?'

Tina felt her cheeks blush. 'I'm thirty-four.'

'You look younger,' Miss Potterton replied, in a way that left Tina unsure as to whether that was a good thing or not.

'You're not one of those ghastly women who lie about their age to suit the circumstances, are you? Adding some years in their extreme youth and then removing them later on? I think that's the absolute height of vanity!'

'No, no. I've just got good genes.' Tina was confused by the woman's behaviour.

'Lucky you.' Her reply was curt.

'How old are you?' Tina stood as tall as she possibly could.

'What?'

'I was wondering how old you are, if we're going down that route.'

Miss Potterton opened the door a little wider. 'I am ninety-three,' she offered matter-of-factly, in a tone that, unusually, was not intended to elicit either wonder or praise.

'You look younger.' Tina spoke the truth.

'Good genes,' Miss Potterton replied.

The two women stared at each other, each wondering what the next move might be.

'You're very skinny.' Miss Potterton appraised her tiny form.

Tina laughed. This felt like a wind-up. She half expected Digsy and Marley to come jumping out of a bush and high-five the posh old lady.

'Yes I am, always have been, but it's not through lack of trying. I eat like a horse, and if you're worried about my ability to do the job, don't be. I have three other permanent clients and can get first-class references. I think I'm skinny cos I'm always on the go. You know, if I'm not working, then I'm cleaning up at home or racing round the supermarket.'

'You have a family?'

'Well, yes, just one boy. My son. He's eighteen.'

'Good Lord! And you are only thirty-four?'

'Yes.' Tina held Miss Potterton's stare, unwilling at this juncture in her life to be judged by her or anyone, especially for a predicament she had found herself in nearly two decades ago. The happiest, best predicament of all. 'What about you? Any family?'

'All dead.' She said this without sentiment. 'Bar a nephew and his frightful child – I forget her name, something ridiculous

– and an equally frightful wife. A social climber with a meanness of spirit, the worst kind. The sort of woman who would find it hard to take joy in other people's good fortune.'

They hovered for a second. Tina wondered who exactly this lady had lost. Parents? Definitely. Husband, kids? Possibly. 'Shall I come in then?'

'Yes. Do.' Miss Potterton turned her back.

Tina followed her inside and up the hallway.

'Wow!' She let her eyes rove over the walls, which were packed with gilt-framed oil paintings, black-and-white photographs of people and places, and even a tapestry of a grand-looking palace on the edge of an inviting beach, complete with palm trees.

The parquet floor was barely visible beneath a vast mahogany bureau stuffed with letters, magazines, balls of string and a dusty, pot-bound cheese plant. A brass umbrella-stand bulged with ivory-topped umbrellas, a couple of parasols with aged fabric shades and a clutch of walking sticks with a variety of handles.

No shortage of things to dust, is there? Tina noted, but she caught herself just in time and refrained from sharing this with her new boss.

The sitting room was just as full. French windows at the back of the room opened out onto a pretty walled courtyard, where tubs, pots, milk churns and any number of other receptacles fought for space. Some of them held flourishing ivy plants that climbed and clung, their variegated tendrils reaching this way and that towards the light. But there was plenty of room for some more cheerful plants, Tina found herself thinking. A chance to experiment with some of those flowering shrubs she was always admiring at the superstore, perhaps.

In the room itself, wide-armed leather chairs that would have looked more at home in a gentleman's smoking room circa 1930 sat next to side tables that listed under heavy glass paperweights, a bronze statuette of a lion, and books. There were books everywhere! But no TV.

As in the hallway, the walls here were so busy that only minute patches of the faded sepia water silk were visible. Tina's eyes became fixed on a framed piece of antique Chinese calligraphy and then on a photo of two young women standing on an immaculate lawn waving Union flags. They were wearing Land Girl uniforms – sensible, dun-coloured corduroy breeches and pullovers – and smiling broadly.

'Is that you?' she asked, pointing at the taller of the women. 'Doing your bit for the war effort? You and your sister?'

'It is. Me… and my friend,' came the clipped reply.

Heavy, fringed, plum-coloured velvet drapes sat at the windows and over the French doors, sun faded at the edges where the fabric met the gold braid and twists of tassel. In front of the doors was a round dining table with six pale-wood, ladder-back chairs whose seats were made of intricately woven bamboo.

'This is the most beautiful place I've ever seen!' Tina turned a full three-sixty, looking up at the crystal-drop chandeliers that hung at either end of the room and the ornate plaster coving and ceiling roses. 'It's like a museum! It's incredible!'

Miss Potterton was clearly delighted by her reaction. 'Well, yes, it's quite a collection. Most of it was my father's. It was spread over the whole house at one point, but it all got a bit too much, so the house was divided into flats and I live here in the basement. It's the space I wanted. I couldn't bear to have given up the courtyard.'

'I can see why. It's lovely! I love flowers and gardens. I don't have one myself, but one day.'

'It is particularly lovely in the summer. I take my breakfast out there and I do like to leave the doors open and feel the breeze. There's something quite wonderful about the warm London air rushing in as night falls.'

'I live in a flat too, but not like this. It's in a block, an ugly square block of concrete, and I daren't even leave my door unlocked, let alone open. It's a bit rough.' Tina laughed. 'But it's our little haven and that's all that counts, right?'

'We are not immune from crime here, you know.' Miss Potterton nodded.

'Do you have a panic alarm or MedicAlert or anything? My nan had one and it gave her peace of mind.'

'Quite. No, I have something much better than that.'

Tina tried to guess. 'Oh, what, a dog?'

'No. A gun,' Miss Potterton said levelly.

Tina laughed out loud.

Nine

The two women fell into a steady routine over the following months. Miss Potterton gave Tina a key so she could come and go as she liked, and Tina insisted that Miss Potterton keep her telephone number next to her big-buttoned phone in case of emergencies. Miss Potterton had pooh-poohed the very idea, but, later that evening, when she was alone, she held the slip of paper in her fingers and smiled, sleeping more soundly that night than she had in quite a while.

Tina whipped the duster around the bookshelves, lifting the objets d'art one by one, wiping them with the soft cloth and replacing them.

'Don't drop anything,' Miss Potterton called from her chair.

'I'll try not to.' Tina smiled.

'You are absurdly upbeat. Do you ever sit in a darkened room and howl?' Miss Potterton enquired.

'No, I haven't done that for a long while. I've learnt to be happy.'

'Oh God, you sound very much like someone who has found the love of Jesus. You're not going to lecture me, are you?'

Tina chuckled. 'No. It's much simpler than that. I was pushed around my whole life. My dad was a bit of a bully and Marley's dad was a shit, really. Oh, sorry!' She remembered who she was talking to, but Miss Potterton didn't seem to notice. 'One day, when my son was little, I was watching him playing and he picked up a dolly and shouted at it, "Get back in that kitchen, stupid girl!" And I realised that I had to set a different example for him, I had to be a better mum, a stronger mum, or he was going to turn out just like his dad and I was never going to get the respect I deserved and neither would any women that came into his life. So I learnt to respect myself and that made me happy.'

'And what did the boy's father think of this new-found confidence?'

'Oh, he'd already left by then – not that he was ever really there permanently. His visits have always been sporadic and are only ever if he is passing, which usually means he needs something, usually money.' She tutted. 'But Marley speaks to his nan, Lavender, once a week. It's a nice connection for him.'

'What does your son think of his father? Are they close?'

'I keep a lot of it from him; he doesn't know the half of it. And he's a different kettle of fish, wants to study the body and things. He's smart and who knows where that will take him?'

'You are proud of him.'

'I am.' Tina nodded. 'It's his birthday in a couple of weeks and he just wants books!'

'It's mine in four and I want books too!' Miss Potterton gave an uncharacteristic laugh.

'Oh wow! Ninety-four! That's quite an achievement. You should celebrate.'

'Do you think so?' Her tone was back to dismissive.

'Yes! Absolutely. You could have a tea party. I'd be happy to do it for you. When's the last time you had a birthday party?'

'Oh, good God!' She considered her answer. 'I think it was probably about thirty years ago, maybe longer.'

'What? That's shocking!'

'Not really. There are many more important things to be

shocked about, like the amount of hunger in the world, and the number of wars currently being waged, that kind of thing.' She picked up her magnifying glass and stared pointedly at the headlines in her copy of the *Telegraph*.

'Well, yeah, I know, but still, you should have a tea party at least, it'd be lovely!'

'I'll think about it,' Miss Potterton conceded.

'Or maybe just go out for a nice meal. There are some lovely places around here. You could go to Gordon Ramsay's.'

'Don't tell me you want to discuss fine-dining, Tina! Not given your penchant for family-sized buckets of nasty fried chicken. And you think all fish comes shaped as a finger.' She breathed onto her magnifying glass and wiped it clean with the corner of her cardigan. 'Besides, what would be the point of you going to eat chez Mr Ramsay when you'd struggle to find a babysitter for Marley?'

'I wasn't asking to come with you!' Tina ignored the insults, and she wasn't about to apologise to anyone for her love of fried food. She wiped her duster over the mahogany mask that hung on the wall. 'And anyway, even if I did want to go out, he's a big boy, as I said. Doesn't need a babysitter. But if he did, I would leave him with you. Wish I'd known you a long time ago!' she sang.

Miss Potterton lowered her magnifying class. The crossword could wait. 'You'd... You'd have left him with me?'

'Yes, of course! You'd get on like a house on fire. I'll bring him to meet you one day. He's good company, likes to nose through people's book collections, and he'd weed your courtyard in exchange for biscuits.'

Miss Potterton tensed her jaw. 'Does he know you are thinking of bringing him to meet a cantankerous witch like me?'

'Oh, Miss Potterton, you know I'd never say that!'

'Well, bless you, dear.' She coughed.

'No, I mean "cantankerous" isn't one of my words. I told him you were a miserable old cow.'

Miss Potterton raised the *Telegraph* until her face was obscured, keen to hide the wide smile that had spread across her face. 'Maybe it would be nice to have a party, but I'd have to give you strict instructions on food, etiquette, the guest list and so on. I can only imagine what would happen if it were all left to you. You'd probably just throw Mr Tyson-Blaine a packet of Garibaldis.' She winced.

'Ooh, I just might. And you can't have a tea party without a plate full of Fondant Fancies – they are a must. Do you know them? Little square cakes that are either brown, yellow or pink, and so sweet, they make your toes curl!'

'Oh, please, no! I could not entertain having such common, shop-bought confections on my antique table!' She gave a shiver of revulsion.

Tina smiled. 'And I was thinking I'd get them party blowers that make a little trumpet noise, and some pointy hats on elastic. I'll throw a few sausage rolls on a plate and maybe do cheese and pineapple on sticks.' She winked.

'Oh, dear God!' Miss Potterton fanned herself with the newspaper.

Ten

Helen's departure from the family home in Tunbridge Wells had left their solid Victorian villa feeling quite empty. It wasn't just the gaps on the wall, until recently occupied by her favourite pictures, or the space on the worktop where the microwave used to live, or even the two empty wardrobes where the empty hangers now clanged together like wind chimes, whispering into the breeze, *She's gone! Run away with Julio and his penis...* It wasn't even the deafening silence. No, it was more than that. It was as if the heart had gone from the house.

Ian dreaded coming back to the echoey hallway and its dusty staircase. He had to steel himself before going into their gloomy bedroom, where the pillow still smelt of her perfume and her toothbrush was missing from the pot that usually held two. He even missed her nagging, and her secret whispered calls to a certain Spanish lothario.

Above all, he missed getting Arraminta's news. Minty used to call regularly to speak to her mum, because Mum was fun and interesting and knew the names of her friends as well as all the answers to everything. He found it odd how Helen, who was very strict with Minty, had always been obsessed with her grades, and was pushy and often mean, seemed to receive the lion's share of their daughter's love, whereas he, who had only ever wanted her to be happy, was seen as weak. How did that work?

He stepped over the threshold and shut the front door behind him, considering whether a glass of wine might be the answer right now and deciding that in fact several glasses would be better. He could crack open that bottle of ridiculously expensive Valpolicella he'd bought yesterday, the one he'd read about in the *Decanter* magazine he'd snaffled from the surgery waiting room. He wouldn't be drinking Spanish wine for a good while anyway, that was for sure.

Dropping his briefcase on the hall floor, he bent to gather the mail, discarding the pizza flyer, taxi cards and parish newsletter in favour of the pale cream envelope addressed in an elegant if slightly shaky script, handwritten in navy ink. Sliding his finger under the flap, he carefully removed the stiff, gilt-edged card and read that he had been invited to his Aunt Cordelia's birthday party.

It was months since he'd last been in touch with his aunt, but he had many fond memories of the old lady. As a teenager, he used to enjoy going to her flat in Kensington. There'd always been something a bit unconventional about her, even racy, and though she'd never married, she was far from being a boring spinster. She used to like a flutter on the horses, he remembered. And when she'd been on the sherry, she'd tell risqué stories about the artists and writers she'd fraternised with in the 50s and 60s. He pictured his aunt and his mother, who was much younger, playing croquet in his youth, heard the satisfying thud of mallet against boxwood and the sound of their bickering over a point. To his acute embarrassment, he slid down until his bottom was on the welcome mat and with his back against the front door he cried. It had been years, decades, since he had sobbed like this and for the first time since his teenage years, he desperately wished he could see his mum.

★

Three weeks later, he was on the phone and about to hang up, when his call was finally answered.

'Yup?'

'Oh, Helen, it's me.' It was strange to feel so nervous when talking to the woman with whom he had exchanged vows and parented a child.

'Yes.' She sighed. 'I have caller ID. I think I might have mentioned it.'

He decided to ignore the comment. 'There's a lot of mail here for Minty and at least one in a brown envelope, probably another fine. I've left her a message, but if you speak to her...'

'Righto.'

'I'm driving up to London. Aunt Cordelia—'

'Finally croaked, has she?' Helen interrupted.

He drew breath. 'Actually, no, she's having a birthday party.'

There was a silent pause while she wondered why on earth he thought she might want or need to know this and he wondered exactly the same.

'Well...' She tittered. 'Enjoy!'

'Do you know, Helen...' He looked at the space where the microwave used to live. 'I was the only one who used the microwave, it's how I made my porridge every morning. But you know that.'

'You called to tell me you miss the microwave?' Her voice went up an octave, clearly amused.

'No, I don't know why I called, actually. Probably habit, and that basic human desire to know that someone is worrying about you while you travel, that someone might be concerned if you don't pick up the phone or make contact. It makes you feel connected, loved.'

'Christ, have you been on the cooking sherry, Ian?'

'Not yet, no. And I'm sorry I called, interrupted whatever

you were doing. I feel sad, Helen, you know, disappointed.' His heart hammered in his chest.

'Oh God, is this about the microwave again?'

'No.' He felt a wave of anger towards this woman, who thought she held all the cards, who was making all the decisions, making him feel like shit. 'It's about the fact that I feel you have treated me quite unfairly, I only ever tried to make you and Minty happy, I feel embarrassed that my very best efforts weren't good enough. And as much as I dislike Juan, I hope your interest in him doesn't wane as it did with me, because let me tell you, it is the very worst way to live. The worst.'

'Ian! I... I...' She was flabbergasted, shocked and angry all rolled into one.

He ended the call with a swipe of his thumb and, as he slammed the front door behind him and loaded up his boot for his trip to London, he laughed. He laughed out loud.

Eleven

Ian descended the basement steps and found the front door ajar. He walked the length of the hall, inhaling the familiar scent of the place and marvelling at the beautiful objects, things he didn't know he remembered from his childhood until the sight of them hurtled him back through time and space. There was a pen pot on the bureau that he distinctly recalled turning upside down and driving a toy car around. It brought a lump to his throat.

Tina stepped from the kitchen and into the hallway.

'I'm Ian.'

'Oh! Miss Potterton's nephew!'

'Yes, that's me. The GP from Tunbridge Wells,' he replied, rocking on his loafers, knowing this was how his aunt would have described him.

'How lovely!' Tina grinned.

'Oh, do you know it?' Ian was delighted to have found something in common with the attractive, bubbly woman standing in front of him, someone he wouldn't have immediately placed in his aunt's circle. They would have plenty to talk about; she was bound to have an opinion on the controversial opening of a Poundland on the high street, when most residents had been praying for a Waitrose.

'No... I've never been.'

'Oh.' He stared at her, a little flummoxed.

'But it sounds very nice. I was more saying lovely about your job, you being a doctor.' She pointed at him, as though this might be news to him. 'I've never met one before – well, apart from my doctor and a couple of other doctors. And Dr Kahn, who is my mum's doctor. And my son, who has made that his ambition, to be one, a doctor.'

'So you've met quite a few?' He squinted as he followed her over to the beautifully set table.

'Yes. But never one here. At your aunt's house.' She rearranged a pretty white linen napkin that had flopped open and twisted the crystal salt and pepper pot for no particular reason.

'So how do you know Cordelia?'

'Miss Potterton? I'm her cleaner. I've only known her for a few months. I think she's hilarious,' she whispered, tucking her white T-shirt into her jeans.

Ian gave a small laugh. 'I've heard her described as many things, but never that,' he whispered in return.

'I don't think she means to be funny, and I'm not laughing at her!' Tina raised her palms, keen to assert this. 'But I just find her way, and her words, so... I don't know, it's like she's from another time and she has absolutely no idea how things work nowadays. It's nice.'

'Refreshing,' he surmised.

'Yes.' She nodded. 'Refreshing.'

'It's funny, isn't it,' Ian said, 'how people who are fond of saying it "like it is" or who enjoy "being truthful" actually only ever say nasty things. Have you noticed that? Whoever heard, "I like to say it how it is and *that food was amazing*!"'

Tina laughed. 'Yeah, or, "I'm only being truthful, *but she looked fantastic*!"'

And just like that, the two were laughing, like they knew each other.

'What are you two scheming about?' Miss Potterton's voice boomed out as she made her way along the corridor to the sitting room.

Ian and Tina both stepped backwards, emphasising the conspiratorial nature of their chat.

'Nothing, Cordelia. We were just talking about Tunbridge Wells,' Ian offered cheerily.

'Urgh! I'm afraid the furthest outside of London I'm prepared to venture is Chiswick.'

Ian and Tina exchanged a glance, neither of them willing to introduce the idea that Chiswick was in London.

'Lovely to see you, Ian.'

'You too.' He presented his aunt with a wrapped book, which she set to one side.

Miss Potterton took a seat at the elaborately set table.

'This looks absolutely wonderful!' Ian placed his hands on his hips and surveyed the vintage china and silver cake stands, the ornate sugar bowl with matching tongs, the sparkling crystal champagne glasses and the purple and cream tulips that had been artfully arranged in slender bud vases. He noted the nine place settings. 'Who's joining us today?'

'We have a select and refined group of interesting minds, including some very high-profile local residents, who will provide witty repartee over tea.' His aunt nodded, a stern expression on her face.

'Oh gosh, don't know how witty I'm feeling!' He pulled a wide-mouthed face at Tina.

'Don't fret, dear. You were only invited to make up the numbers.' Miss Potterton smiled at her nephew. 'And talking of making up the numbers, where is that wife of yours?'

'Helen?'

'I am intrigued by your need to qualify. Is there another?' She tilted her head towards him to better hear the response.

'Ha! No, no! No other, erm…' He swallowed. 'She's busy. She's working, on her Spanish thing, so she can't make it, but she did send her very best regards and many happy returns of the day.'

'I bet she did.' His aunt spoke loudly but with her head turned, as though she were whispering.

'I'll remove her place setting and wiggle everything around a bit.' Tina smiled as she piled up the redundant side plate, cup and saucer. Holding the cutlery and napkin in her other hand, she whipped the lot into the kitchen, where Marley had the kettle full, the sandwiches wrapped and the cakes chilling, all ready for the nod from his mother.

'One down, I'm afraid.' She kept her voice low.

'Did they die?' Marley asked.

She stood in front of her son. 'What do you mean, did they die? Of course not! They're just stuck in Tunbridge Wells! What a thing to say, Marl!'

'What? Don't look at me like that! I just thought, you know, she's really old and her friends are all really old and so maybe one of them had died, which is sad, but also good.'

'In what way could it possibly be good?'

'Cos I can have their chocolate eclair!' He laughed.

Tina tutted. 'You can have one anyway, cheeky boy, and what about your healthy eating?'

'One eclair won't hurt, Mum. I'll just have to train a bit harder tomorrow.' He patted his flat, hard stomach.

'Ah, love, you might think you're chips and gravy now, but your dad used to be built like you and now he's got a proper belly. You want to watch that!' She winked.

'Tina! Tina!' Miss Potterton called from the sitting room.

'Yes?' Tina always bobbed a little when she stood in front of Miss Potterton. *Think I need to stop watching* Downton. She smiled at the thought.

'I think maybe we should set a pot to steep. People will be arriving any second and I would like to offer them tea the moment they sit down, plus I'm rather thirsty myself. And don't forget it's the Darjeeling.'

'Certainly, and I'll grab the door when they arrive.' She made her way back to the kitchen.

'Right, Marl, action stations. First pot of tea of the day.'

'Is she having a nice time?' Marley couldn't begin to imagine how it was possible to have fun when you were ninety-four.

'I think so, love, yes. She'll get more into the swing of it when her other guests arrive.'

'The Right Honourable Muir Tyson-Blaine!' He snickered.

'Ssshhh!' Tina placed her finger on her lips. 'Don't be rude, Marley. You are in Miss Potterton's home and these people are her friends and it is her birthday party.' She spoke solemnly.

'It must be odd having friends with titles. I can't imagine Digsy will ever have one,' Marley said as he fiddled with a teaspoon.

'You never know, love. I'll just pop back through, see if they need anything.'

Miss Potterton was in full swing. 'Well, that was the trouble with your mother, she was afraid of her own shadow! I'd have made myself quite clear, and that frightful man wouldn't have got a penny out of me.' She nodded, mid conversation with Ian.

'Funny, I was thinking about her only the other day, as I do on occasion. Thinking how I would really like a cup of tea with her and a bit of a chinwag,' he admitted.

'Oh, absolutely! I miss her dreadfully.' Miss Potterton placed her handkerchief at the corner of her eye. 'That's the thing about surviving the longest; you have to say so many wretched goodbyes. And doubly unfair when she was so much younger than me.' She sniffed. 'Ah, Tina, what's the time, dear?'

Tina looked at the clock and then her phone. 'I think my phone's running a little bit fast. It says ten past three.'

Miss Potterton sat forward in her chair and gripped the arms. 'Ten past three? Are you sure? That's utterly ridiculous. They're all late! I can't bear tardiness, I really can't! Tom always used to say, "Why do people consider their time more valuable than mine? How little must people think of me to make me wait." And I rather agree. Ten past, are you certain?' She craned her neck and then squinted at her watch face.

'I expect parking round here is a bit of a nightmare. Maybe they're struggling to find a space?' Ian offered kindly. Both he and Tina were wondering who Tom was.

'Well, no, Ian, that can't be right. Everyone is within walking distance or has a resident's pass. I don't understand it. I specifically said three o'clock. Didn't I, Tina?'

'Yes. Yes, you did.' She nodded. 'Tell you what, how about a nice cup of tea while you're waiting. I'm sure Dr Ian would like one – you must be gasping!' She smiled at him.

'That would be lovely. Yes, please.' He looked like a happy schoolboy who'd been offered seconds.

'No! Absolutely not!' Miss Potterton banged the arm of her chair. 'Can you imagine the embarrassment of Mr and Mrs Govington-Holmes or the Right Honourable Muir Tyson-Blaine if they arrived and we were merrily drinking tea, with festivities well and truly launched without them? How would that look? No.' She shook her head. 'We shall wait.'

She turned her head towards the hallway, her fingers fidgeting on the chair.

The expectation, as they listened for the reassuring ping of the bell or the light rapping of knuckles on the glass, gave the room a physical weight that bore down on them like a leaden cloak.

'Do you drive, Tina?' Ian made small talk.

'Only my son round the bend.' She smiled.

'Ha! Very good!' He laughed too loudly and for too long.

'No, never seen the point, really. Buses are good as gold from where I live and I wouldn't know where to start with a car, even if I could drive. I mean, it's not like I could get a car, so learning to drive always felt a bit pointless. My dad had a van. He was a delivery driver for Addison Lee back in the day.'

Ian nodded. 'I think it's admirable not driving a car. I hate to think what my gas-guzzling tractor does to the environment.'

'Oh God! Don't tell me Helen is encouraging you to go green and start riding a bike everywhere!' Miss Potterton tutted and ran her tongue over her lips, clearly parched.

'No! No, quite the opposite. I'd like a bike, in fact, but she was very keen we got the four-by-four – good for off-roading and narrow country lanes.' He looked at the floor.

'Do you do a lot of off-roading?' Tina wasn't exactly sure what that was, but she also wanted to make conversation.

'No, never.' He stared at her.

'But you live in a narrow country lane?'

Ian shook his head. 'Again, no.' He pictured the top-of-the-range monstrosity that Helen had convinced him was necessary, when all he really wanted was a bike, and a little Mini with cup holders for his lunchtime coffee and a good sun visor. 'In fact, I don't know why we got the bloody thing. Something else she talked me into.'

'Language, young man!' Miss Potterton remonstrated.

Tina felt the giggle rise in her throat and turned on her heel, making a hasty exit to the kitchen. She felt his eyes following her as she left the room.

'Mum, I'm getting bored.' Marley threw a sugared almond into the air and tried to catch it in his mouth. When he missed, he caught it in his hand and tried again.

'Not too much longer. What's the bloody time?' She pulled her phone from her back pocket and slid the screen. 'God, it's nearly half past! Please don't say they're not coming.'

She ran her palm over her face, wishing she'd never suggested the birthday party in the first place. Then she bent over the countertop and buried her head in her hands.

'Knock, knock!' Ian alerted her to his presence.

'Oh God! Hi! I was just having a think.' She was flustered and could feel two spots of colour rising on her cheeks.

'This is my son, Marley. Marley, this is Dr Ian.'

Ian walked forward and shook hands with Tina's son, silently admiring the boy's impressive Afro. 'Just Ian – don't worry about the doctor bit.' He smiled.

Marley nodded.

'Are you thinking what I'm thinking – that we might be a bit light on guests?' Ian held Tina's gaze.

'Don't! I'm hoping they've just got held up.' She blinked.

'Yes, possibly.' He nodded. 'But what do we do if they're no-shows?'

'We...' She looked around the kitchen for inspiration, staring at the beautiful iced fruitcake with the ivory bow and pearl detail. 'I don't know!' she squealed, dreading the thought.

'Who are we waiting on?' Ian asked.

'Oh, Gawd.' Tina hated having to recite the names, as if it was some kind of memory test. 'We've got Mr and Mrs Govington-Thingy, and Mr Tyson-Blaine, and the three ladies from the Residents Association, whose names, I'm embarrassed to say, I can't recall, because in my head I've been referring to them as Huey, Dewey and Louie.'

He stared at her as if she was bonkers. 'Right, do you have numbers for any of them?'

'Oh yes!' Her face lit up as she remembered. 'I've got Dewey's!' She rushed to a drawer and pulled out a circular from the Residents Association. 'Can I borrow your phone, Marl?'

He handed it over slowly, thinking of his depleting credit.

Tina turned away from them both; she didn't want to be watched while she made the call.

'Oh, hello, it's Tina here. I'm Miss Potterton's cleaner... Yes, cleaner. Anyway, the reason for my call is to see if you are able to come to her birthday tea today. We were expecting you at three and so...' She turned and looked at Ian and frowned. 'Oh, I see!' She listened some more. 'Oh really? Well, that's a shame. But thank you and sorry to have bothered you. Yes, I will. Thanks.'

She handed the phone back to Marley. 'Apparently Dewey had already called to say that she and her two mates were unable to attend. And she happened to know that the Govington-Doo-Dahs are on holiday. They also phoned, apparently.'

'And spoke to Cordelia?' Ian asked.

She nodded. The two stared at each other for a second or two. Then Tina clapped her hands together.

'Okay, this is what we do. Marley, you make a pot of the finest Darjeeling. I'll bring the sandwiches and cakes through. Dr Ian, you go and remove the plates and bits and bobs we don't need, and we will try and dazzle your aunt with our lovely food and distract her with our great company. Come on, Marley, shake a leg!' she urged. 'And we shall just have to hope that Mr Tyson-Thingy shows up as a kind of last-minute gift!'

'Right, so I'm on distraction and plate removal, got it! And yes, do hurry up, Marley. I'm *bloody* starving!' Ian spoke with gusto, as if he was having fun.

Tina laughed, noting his emphasis of the swear word. He was great.

She approached the table carrying a three-tiered cake stand crammed with delicate, crustless sandwiches.

'Good God, this is all rather lame! I've been to more atmospheric wakes.' Miss Potterton sighed.

'Okay, well, apparently, Mr and Mrs Govington—'

'Govington-Holmes!' Miss Potterton snapped in irritation.

'Yep, them. Well, they are on holiday.'

Miss Potterton sniffed.

'And the three ladies from the Residents Association are also now unavailable.'

'Unavailable? What does that mean? Makes it sound like I've missed my appointment.' She tutted again and then adjusted the pearls at her neck. 'Maybe it's time I admitted that I am just not as popular as I thought!'

'Oh, bless...' Tina whispered, feeling her heart twist, wishing that Miss Potterton was the type of woman who liked a hug, knowing it would make them both feel a lot better.

'The good news is...' Tina smiled brightly. 'That you get to enjoy the company of me and Dr Ian and Marley. And the good news for *us* is... there's more cake and sandwiches to go round. And I for one can't wait!'

Without waiting to be asked, she took a seat at the table and laid the napkin on her lap. She watched as Miss Potterton dabbed her eyes with her handkerchief. Disappointment was shitty, whether you were nine or ninety-four.

'Come on, Marley, where's that tea?' she called towards the kitchen.

'Does he know to add one for the pot?' Miss Potterton asked.

'Oh, don't you worry. He might not have attended many tea parties, but that boy knows about making tea!' She beamed.

'I would very much like to see your mother too.' Miss Potterton turned to her nephew as though they were mid conversation. 'She was such a kind soul.' Her voice was soft.

'Yes, she was.' Ian looked up at Tina. 'We were saying earlier how much we both miss her.'

'Oh.' Tina smiled as Marley arrived with the large silver teapot on a tray. His expression spoke volumes and it said, *I'm so glad my mates can't see me now...*

Twelve

'Champagne, Cordelia?' Ian held the bottle over the empty flute.

'I'm not sure I should – damned pills and whatnot.' She placed her gnarled hand at her neck.

'Doctor's orders! I'd say a couple of sips of this is almost medicinal!' He poured her a thimbleful. 'And it's a shame not to make the most of such a good bottle,' he added, peering at the label and making a mental note to add this to his wine journal.

'Marley?' Ian lifted the bottle.

'No, thanks.' Marley placed his hand over the top of the glass. 'I don't drink. I'm training. My dad used to say, "If you're training, you can't be drinking".'

'Oh good, more for us!' Ian laughed and returned to his seat. 'Is your dad an athlete too?' He pictured the suave, tennis-playing Spaniard.

'No, but he can talk the talk.'

'Ain't that the truth.' Tina dived in for another sandwich. No one was counting, but it was her fifth.

'I don't see him that much,' Marley said. 'You know, the odd text, or if he's in town... We don't really know each other, but it's cool, cos that's how it's always been, really, and your normal is your normal.'

Ian marvelled at Marley's maturity and his lack of bitterness.

The sadness was that the boy's dad was missing out on the chance to parent this driven, polite young man.

Tina sat up straight. 'Oh, Marley's dad's very clever. He's a musician. So he travels a lot.' She gave a tight smile.

Marley looked at his mum. 'He ain't a musician, Mum. And you don't have to keep saying that! He owns a guitar, but that doesn't make him a musician. I mean, you've got an oven, but you can't cook!'

Tina let out a loud burst of laughter that lightened the tone. 'S'pose you're right, love. He was pretty good back in the day. I guess he gave up on his dream and forgot to replace it with something.'

'That's why I've plans A, B *and* C. I don't want to end up just scoring a bit of dope and hanging around with my mates and sitting on the steps every night. Nah, mate, well borin'!'

Cordelia stared at the young man. 'I think you might actually be talking another language,' she shouted and reached for her second Fondant Fancy.

Tina winked at Ian. It seemed her common, shop-bought confections were going down a treat.

'So what are plans A, B and C? If you don't mind me asking.' Ian thought of Minty, who was usually to be found sitting on a beach, waiting for a life plan or a rich man to fall into her lap. He could hazard a guess as to which was more likely. *What a bloody waste.*

Marley leant towards Ian. 'I want to finish college and get my HNC in Sport and Exercise Sciences. If I do well, that might be enough to get me into uni, and I want to study physiotherapy or medicine, depends on how well I do and stuff.' He looked away, embarrassed to admit to his ambition, half expecting the same ribbing that he got from Digsy.

'So, a doctor?' Ian didn't look shocked or as if this was beyond the realms of possibility.

Marley nodded. 'That would be the dream.'

'But you didn't stay for A levels?'

'Nah, my school was proper crap and they'd kind of written me off and it felt too hard to try and change how they viewed me, so I thought college would be best, a new start.'

'That makes sense.' Ian nodded.

'And then I want to buy a house or a flat. So that's Plan A, really. In a nutshell.' He held Ian's gaze, shifting slightly in his seat, awkward at having shared his dream.

'Sounds wonderful, Marley. And what are plans B and C?'

Marley pulled back his shoulders, his chin jutting slightly as if to emphasise his resolve. 'If I fail, Plan B is to go back and repeat Plan A. And if Plan B fails, then Plan C is to go back and repeat A and B...'

'I get the idea.' Ian grinned at Marley's single-mindedness, the like of which he hadn't seen for a long while – if you didn't count Helen's determination to sod off with Mr Sausage Pants. Funny, usually when he thought about that, he felt angry, upset. Right now? He felt... nothing.

'I won't stop until I've made it happen and it doesn't matter how long it takes. I figure that getting to where I want to be is part of my job, and if I think I've already started on my journey, that spurs me on, you know?'

Ian nodded. 'Yes, I do know. I remember after my first three years of uni, when a lot of my friends were going off to quite well-paid jobs and I knew I had another few years of slog and studying ahead of me, it was tough. But reminding myself that I was on my way, that I'd already put in a lot of leg work, made it easier to carry on.'

'He's a good boy, works really hard.'

Marley cringed.

'You must be proud of him.' Ian smiled at her.

'I am. Not only because of what he'll achieve, but because he's lovely. I just want him to be happy. And I like him. I like spending time with him and I think that's the best compliment there is, really, that someone wants to spend time with you. I think that's love.'

Ian stared at her, trying to think of the last time he had wanted to spend time with someone or they him.

Miss Potterton smiled at the young woman who seemingly also wanted to spend time with her, and this thought made her very happy. 'I think the pot might need refreshing.' She reached over and placed the back of her liver-spotted hand against the cooling china.

'Oh, let me!' Tina jumped up and carefully scooped the teapot into her hands, carrying it like a precious thing into the kitchen.

Ian noted her slender form as she left the table. 'Your mum's full of energy!'

'She's always like that. It makes me laugh – and pisses me off sometimes. Oh! Sorry!' Marley hunched his shoulders and turned down his mouth as he apologised to their hostess.

Miss Potterton, however, was having a deaf spell. Conveniently.

Marley continued. 'I don't know anyone else like her – she's happy all the time. When the toast pops up, she makes this little noise like it's an exciting thing, and when she gets to pick up our chips, they call her order number and she waves the little slip of paper over her head like she's won something.' He shook his head. 'Even when things are shit...' Again he looked towards their hostess. 'She just seems to find the happy!'

'I think that's a really nice way to live.' Ian smiled at Marley.

'Tom was very much like that. A positive nature, always found the good. Whereas I could be a bit judgemental.'

'You, Cordelia? No!' Ian laughed.

'Hmmph.' She bristled, with the twist of a smile to her mouth. 'But Tom balanced me. And even now, all these years later, I still take the advice and try to temper my thoughts and views accordingly. We're always conversing, you know. On any number of topics. I find it most comforting that we can still talk. I find great solace in that.'

Ian stared at his maiden aunt. This new insight into her life was quite wonderful. He was glad that she'd had someone special, someone to help her find the happy. But who was Tom and why had they never married? Surely she wouldn't have got involved with a married man? He smiled at the thought, realising that everything he knew about her had come via his mother before she died and was therefore skewed by her views and his aunt's rather unforthcoming nature. He liked the idea of trying to figure out the puzzle of her in her ninety-fourth year.

'Where does the name Marley come from?' Miss Potterton asked rather abruptly. 'Was it a fondness for Dickens?'

'What?' Marley stared at her.

'Your name. Marley. Are you named from the novella? After Scrooge's partner?' She spoke a little louder, as if increasing the volume might help his understanding.

Tina scooted back into the room and placed the fresh pot of tea in the centre of the table. 'Oh no, Miss Potterton. Marley's one of his middle names.'

'What's your first name?' Ian asked.

'Bob,' he replied, and bit into a tiny crustless chicken sandwich.

'What's your other middle name?'

'Gibson,' he muttered through a mouthful of food.

'Don't eat with your mouth full.' Tina tutted.

'He asked me a question!' Marley pointed at Ian with the remainder of his sandwich, again speaking with his mouth full.

'So your name is Bob Marley Gibson?'

Marley nodded.

Ian chortled. 'Gibson as in the guitar maker?'

'His dad was a big fan.' Tina smiled and sipped her tea, which had cooled and was almost unpleasant.

'Of Dickens?' Miss Potterton asked loudly.

Tina and Ian laughed.

Ian noted Tina's slight shudder as she tasted her brew. He lifted the pot and poured hot tea into her cup.

The champagne and tea continued to flow through the afternoon. There was the singing of 'Happy Birthday' and the cutting of cake. Tina produced a batch of crumbly scones glued together with clotted cream and fresh raspberry jam, and there was gooseberry tart to follow.

At five o'clock Miss Potterton stood up. 'I should like a nap.'

Without a word of thanks or further discussion, she walked slowly from the table and made her way towards the hallway. Ian got up and took her elbow, guiding her along, leaving her at the entrance to her bedroom, much to the relief of them both.

'Is it okay if I push off, Mum?' Marley slipped his arms into his jacket as he asked.

'Yes, love, and thank you for today. You've been great.'

'Great to meet you, Marley, and I hope our paths cross again. If I can be of any help...' Ian shook the boy's hand.

Marley smiled. 'Thanks,' he replied, with the polite dismissal of a boy who had learnt not to rely too heavily on the word of any man who presented himself as a temporary role model.

Thirteen

Ian poured another glass. 'He's a nice boy, and he seems to love college.'

'He does. Mind you, I liked school, too – not that I learnt much.' Tina sipped her champagne.

'It's interesting, isn't it? I hated every second and learnt a lot. I went to this small private school for boys in the middle of the countryside, where I learnt how to pass A levels, read Latin and recite the periodic table.'

'Wow! I went to an inner-city school in Bow, where I learnt rhyming slang, winkle picking, how to sew on your pearly buttons and do the Lambeth Walk. General Cockney behaviour.'

Ian slumped forward, he was laughing so much. 'I'm picturing it! That's so funny!'

'I sometimes wonder what I might have done if I'd gone to a school where people had actually given a shit about my education.'

'What would you like to have done?'

She shrugged. 'Dunno. Suppose if I was starting again, if I was young and had all the time in the world, I'd like to learn floristry. I spend an awful lot of time looking at flowers and plants 'n' stuff, trying to copy arrangements and that. I've always had this little dream of having me own flower shop. I'd love that.'

'Well, it's not too late! You can do that any time!' Ian banged the table as if to emphasise his point.

Tina shook her head. 'Nah, too late for me. Even if I did do the course, how could I just start a flower shop? You need money and I've never had enough of that. Not that I want *a lot*, but enough would be nice. You kind of get trapped, don't you? Trapped in your life – working, setting the alarm, having a cup of tea, working some more... It's like you're on a hamster wheel, and sometimes just thinking about it can be exhausting.'

For some reason, Ian pictured Mrs Coates with her downturned mouth and her miserable demeanour. 'Well, my job isn't a picnic exactly.'

'But you're a doctor!' Tina said, wide-eyed.

'I am.' He nodded. 'But I don't remember having any choice. My father set the course upon which I was to sail and I just had to follow his coordinates and try not to let him down. It felt like the most enormous pressure, just to please him, and my choice never really came into it.'

'That's really sad.' She put her hand on his arm.

He liked the feel of her skin against his. He liked it very much.

She withdrew it as quickly as she had placed it there.

'What would you like to do, then, if you could do anything?' She cupped her chin in her palm, her elbow resting on the tabletop.

He liked the way her curls had worked loose and hung over her face but resisted the temptation to push them back for her.

'If I could do anything?' He looked up at the ceiling, as if that was where the answer might lie. 'I'd like to know about wine, maybe travel the vineyards of the world and come back with an improved understanding of the production process, what makes a wine great or terrible. And I'd like to open a vintner's, a specialist wine shop, with big oak barrels lining the walls, and flagstone floors. There'd be racks full of bottles of red, gathering dust, and fridges full of chilled whites, and great food to go with the tasting, like tapas... Maybe a bar as well, for real ale fans and anyone else who wanted to pull up a stool and enjoy a platter and a chat... Oh, and it would have to be near the coast.'

'Blimey, sounds like you've given it a lot of thought!' She laughed.

'I haven't really, not until this moment. But I'd bloody love that!'

'Well, it's not too late! You can do that any time!' She banged the table.

'Touché.' He raised his glass to hers as he mentally catalogued a million reasons that would prevent him from fulfilling this dream.

'I'd love to live near the seaside,' Tina said. 'I went a couple times when I was younger and I remember the way the air smelt and the feel of the sand under my feet. I felt free, with all that space and no concrete. Just that big patch of moving blue to look at. I think that would be my dream too, actually, to live somewhere where I can open me curtains of a morning and see the sea every day. And if I want to see it at any other time of day, then all I have to do is pop my head out and there it is!'

'That does sound pretty perfect.'

'I find you very easy to talk to.' She looked up at him.

'That'll be the champagne!' He sniffed, glowing at the compliment.

'Yes, probably.' She laughed.

'So do you have a partner now? After Marley's dad?' He tried to sound nonchalant.

She shook her head. 'No. He kind of put me off. I was proper crazy about him – Marley was on the button; he was a talker all right – and I was naive. I think I really wanted to believe that he was the one who might take me away for a different kind of life...' She stared into the middle distance.

'Is that what you wanted?' Ian thought of all the times he'd wished for something similar.

'I think so. But it turned out there were so many of us all under the same promise, he'd have had to hire a bloody minibus!' She shook her head at the absurdity of it. 'So what about you? What's Helen like?'

Ian sat back in the chair and placed his clasped palms behind his head. 'She left. We're done. She has someone else and I'm on my own without the microwave.' He reached for his glass.

'Oh God! I'm sorry. I feel awful. I wouldn't have asked...'

'No, no. It's fine. It's like you were saying: you are on that hamster wheel and you can't get off and then one day you're thrown off and while it might shake you, scare you, even, when you regain your senses and look at the life you were leading, you have to question whether you want to get back on. And I really don't.' He smiled at her.

Tina coughed. 'Can I ask you something?'

'Sure.' He leant forward, his arms on the table, as if this required his full attention.

'Why don't you buy a new microwave? They're only £24.99 in Argos.'

'Why the hell didn't I think of that?' He laughed, lowering his glass and staring at Tina as she mirrored his every move.

Her heart was beating so fast, she felt sure they could hear it all the way back in Hammersmith. He was going to kiss her! She was going to be kissed by a bloody doctor. Closing her eyes, she waited.

'Tina!' Miss Potterton's voice made her jump to attention. She shot off her chair as though the old lady had pressed an ejector button.

'Miss Potterton, I didn't hear you! Are you okay? Do you need anything?' she babbled, wishing her face would stop burning.

Ian smiled at her. 'More tea, Cordelia?' He lifted the pot in his aunt's direction.

Fourteen

'Good morning, Greta Garbo, how are we today? Ignoring me, I see. Well, that's fine, I happen to find you rather dull too.'

Miss Potterton placed one hand on the wall as she shuffled towards the kitchen. 'I think tea and toast with marmalade,' she mumbled as she made her way along the hall.

Greta Garbo meowed.

'Oh, I see. The mention of food and you're interested again! You fickle old thing.' She laughed.

'Too bad you weren't at home for my birthday tea yesterday, madam! It was most enjoyable, as it transpired. Despite the rather cosy turn-out.' Her eyes crinkled with pleasure. 'And those two youngsters seemed to get on well. I rather thought they would, actually...'

A sudden flutter in her chest stopped her short and she propped herself against the wall. It passed.

Settling back into her armchair, with her tea and toast cooling on the side, she placed the album on her fragile lap and opened the heavy cover until it rested on the arm of the chair. The stiff cardboard pages were interleaved with a thin sheet of tissue paper, covering the many black-and-white images, each held in place by tiny cardboard corners, stuck to the page. Cordelia ran her finger over an image of Tom, leaning on a shovel with a bunch of dirt-covered carrots in one hand, proudly holding them up towards the camera. She remembered the laughter; as the pose had to be held for quite some time to be captured. It seemed all they did was laugh, how she missed that.

Greta Garbo purred. 'Oh hello you. Look at this, Miss Garbo' – she pointed to a picture of a rubble-strewn street – 'the aftermath of the blitz, my beautiful city burnt and I was powerless, we all were. A frightful time.' She turned the pages, stopping at a black-and-white shot of a Soho street, in the sixties. 'Not as frightful, as this time. This for me was the worst. I lost my love, lost my hope. I think it was cancer, we were unsure, but with today's technology, I'm sure it would have been far more identifiable. Not that it matters. Death is death and that was that.' She took a deep breath and blotted at her eyes with her handkerchief.

The sound of the letterbox flap roused her. She closed the album and slowly made her way into the hall. She stood, staring at the front door, her smile broke and her heart filled with joy. For there, standing with one foot on the welcome mat, was Tom.

'Oh, my!' Cordelia Potterton put her hand to her neck, clutching at the double string of pearls that lay against her shirt. 'It's you!' she breathed.

Tom nodded, arranged the stack of mail in a neat pile on the bureau and placed the paperweight on top.

Miss Potterton took a step forward with her hand outstretched. Smiling broadly, she broke into a run, then jumped into the arms of the person she loved. Arms that had soothed her fearful heart during many a long, fretful night as their city had crashed and splintered under Nazi bombs. 'Oh, Tom! My Tom! How I love you.'

Fifteen

Tina hovered in the kitchen, not wanting to go and mix, unwilling to swap small talk with the hordes that were cluttering the sitting room and filling the hallway. She decided instead that she would make a sweep of the room every twenty minutes, offering to replenish a sandwich, cut another slice of cake or pour fresh tea. It wasn't as if she knew these people, though it had been lovely to see Len and his wife at the crematorium. She knew Miss Potterton would have been touched he'd made the effort.

'Oh, there you are!' Ian smiled as he rested his bottom against the kitchen sideboard. He folded his arms. 'You've done a great job here, Tina. It's a lovely spread – you've done Aunt Cordelia proud. And those tribute flowers you arranged for her coffin were absolutely stunning. You've got a real talent there.'

Tina nodded and picked up a cup from the drainer on the sink.

'Marley's been making conversation with Huey, Dewey and Louie, I see!' Ian chuckled. 'And everyone seems to be making the most of the free food and the chance for a get-together.'

Tina ran the tea towel around the rim of the cup, then popped it back on the shelf of the dresser. 'Yep, that's what I'm hearing. All them people who are standing in Miss Potterton's flat, scoffing her food, chattering away, and yet they couldn't even make the effort to come to her bloody birthday tea! I'm sorry, I shouldn't shout, but it pisses me off. It would have meant the world to her.'

Ian nodded. 'Yes, it would, but that's human nature, I'm afraid.'

'I don't like human nature much sometimes.'

'I don't like human nature much a lot of the time.' Ian raised his eyebrows in agreement.

Tina reached across him for the saucer.

'Her birthday tea was a great afternoon, despite the lack of guests,' Ian said, looking straight at her. 'I really enjoyed it.'

'Me too.' She felt her chest colour with embarrassment as she remembered their champagne-fuelled flirting.

'Marley says college is going well.'

She liked how he seemed genuinely interested. 'Yes, he's doing great. Studying hard, you know, getting on with it.'

'Still on Plan A then.'

'Yep.' She smiled. 'Still on Plan A.'

'I...' He hesitated, shifting his feet, awkward.

'What?' she whispered.

'I...'

'Dad!' The voice was loud, bossy.

Tina turned to take in the plump girl with the very high heels, jeans and sheer shirt that showed off her ample cleavage beneath her bolero jacket. Her hair was lustrous, long and curled. It looked either expensively coiffed or expensively stuck on.

'Can we go? This is the pits. I've shaken hands with a hundred old people who smell like wee and mothballs and then had to watch them eat sandwiches while they talk with their mouths open. It's disgusting! One man actually gobbed out a bit of cress that landed on my hand. Urgh!' She shivered.

The girl was pretty, but her words and her tone erased any attractiveness.

'That'll be you one day,' Ian replied.

'It bloody won't. I don't even like cress!' She shuddered again.

Ian and Tina exchanged a despairing look.

'I meant the getting old bit, not the cress bit,' Ian shot back.

'No, it won't. The day I start to lose my marbles or smell of wee, I shall throw a huge party, get pissed, say my goodbyes and take a private jet to Dignitas!'

'And guess who'll have to pay for that?' Ian directed his words at Tina, who looked away.

'I'm Tina, by the way. I was Miss Potterton's cleaner.'

The girl looked her up and down, gave a small-mouthed smile that didn't reach her eyes, and continued whining. 'Please, Dad, I need to leave!' She stamped her foot on the floor like a petulant three-year-old.

'Be my guest. Leave.' Ian held his palm out towards the door like an effusive maître d'. His tone was sharper than his daughter was used to hearing.

'But you drove me here!'

'That's right, and now you can get the train back, or the bus, I don't really care which.'

Minty stared at her father as tears of frustration glistened in her eyes. 'Mum's right, you are an irritating twat!'

'Oi, missy!' Tina's shout was almost involuntary. 'You can't talk to your dad like that! You can't talk to anyone like that! And especially not today. It's Miss Potterton's funeral.'

'I think you'll find I can do what the fuck I want, and I think you'll find it has fuck all to do with you!' The girl stormed from the room.

'Minty!' Ian yelled after her, furious.

He turned to Tina with his fingers tugging at his hair in embarrassment. 'I'm sorry she spoke to you like that.'

'I'm sorry she spoke to *you* like that! Flippin' 'eck, Marley wouldn't dream of—'

'I know.' He interrupted her. 'I know. And there are two things I want to say to you. Firstly, you were so much more than my aunt's cleaner; you were her friend. And secondly, I haven't stopped thinking about you since that afternoon. I can't get you out of my head and when my days have been gloomy or I've felt lonely, even just picturing you and the way you are has helped me find my happy.'

Tina stared at him, shocked that this lovely man, this doctor, no less, could feel that way about someone like her. She stepped forward and tossed the tea towel onto the sideboard. He took her small hands inside his own and bent his head, kissing her lightly on the mouth. Tina felt her heart leap into her throat and her stomach clench with nerves and excitement. It had been a long time since she'd felt a bolt of pure unadulterated joy shoot through her body.

'Ahem.'

They both turned towards the pompous-looking old man with the walrus moustache who was standing in the doorway, his large stomach bulging beneath his navy blazer.

'Afternoon! Muir Tyson-Blaine,' he boomed, as though this should mean something. And it would have, had he bothered to turn up to a certain ninety-fourth birthday party. 'Any chance of some more cake? We seem to have run out.' He nodded towards the sitting room.

Tina grabbed the packet of Garibaldi biscuits from her shopping bag and threw them at him. ''Ere you go, love. Get these in your norf 'n' sarf.'

Ian smiled at her. 'I think you lied to me – I think you actually learnt a lot in your rhyming-slang class.'

And the two laughed and kissed again.

When the last of the guests had been ushered from the premises, Ian switched off the lights and pulled the plugs.

'Can you still pop in, keep an eye, give the place a onceover? I want it kept nice until we know what's happening with it.'

'Yes, of course. I've got my key.' She smiled.

As they made their way into the hall, Tina noticed a small stack of mail piled neatly on top of the bureau under a paperweight. She gathered the letters into her hand and passed them to Ian. 'I suppose you'd better let the relevant agencies and whatnot know that she's passed on.'

He nodded grimly as he sifted through the letters. One in particular caught his eye. 'Gosh, look at this!' He held up the envelope and pointed at the large *ER* with a red crown above it. 'It looks rather official!'

'Open it!' Tina urged.

Ian placed his finger under the flap and pulled out a glossy card with a picture of Her Majesty on the front.

'What on earth…?' Tina was as curious as she was excited.

'I don't believe it!' Ian stared at her.

'What?' She did a little jig on the spot.

Ian read aloud: '*I am so pleased that you are celebrating your one hundredth birthday…*' He looked up at Tina. '*I send my congratulations and best wishes to you on such a special occasion. Elizabeth R.*'

'She was a hundred!' Tina blinked.

'She was.'

Tina remembered standing on the other side of the front

door and their first ever exchange. *'You're not one of those ghastly women who lie about their age to suit the circumstances, are you? Adding some years in their extreme youth and then removing them later on? I think that's the height of vanity!'*

'The sly old devil!' She laughed. Her laughter quickly turned into a torrent of tears. 'I'm going to miss her.' She sniffed.

Ian gathered Tina to his chest and kissed her scalp. 'And that, Tina, is the greatest compliment you can ever pay someone. To miss them. That's real love.'

They made their way up the steep steps to ground level and Ian looked up and down the street. 'Can't remember where I left the car!' He scratched his head.

'See, that's another advantage of not driving. I always know where I've left the Tube station.'

He laughed.

'Do me a favour, Ian, just drop me a little text when you get home. Let me know you got there safely. I know it's daft, but I'll worry about you when you're travelling.'

Ian stared at her, as his heart leapt with happiness. 'I will.'

Sixteen

'You sure you don't mind dropping me off, Len?' Tina leant
forward from the back seat of Len's cab.

'Not at all, girl. It's quite nice to be doing the journey, truth
be told. I don't 'arf miss old Miss P. She was one of a kind.
She used to call me Leonard. I never had the heart to tell her I
was called Len because me surname is Fairclough – it's an old
nickname from me army days, after that character from *Corrie*
– and not because I was christened Leonard.' He smiled.

'I never knew that. What is your first name then?'

'You'll never guess it!'

'It's not Rumpelstiltskin, is it?'

'No.' He shook his head. 'My mum was a right bookworm,
loved a bit of Dickens. It's Josiah. I'm named after Josiah
Bounderby in *Hard Times*.' He looked into his rear-view mirror
at Tina, who was crying into her tissue. 'You all right, girl?'

'Yep,' she managed. 'I just had a bit of a flashback, that's all.
Dickens, eh? It's a lovely name.'

Len indicated and pulled over by the cemetery wall. 'Right, as
I said, it's a little way round to the right of the gate. Follow the
path and you can't miss it. It's under the big yew tree. Next to a
family plot by the name of Jones, I think.'

'Thanks, Len. You sure I can't give you some petrol money?'
She jostled the bouquet of yellow roses in her arm.

'Nah!' He batted his hand. 'Don't be daft. I'll just take the next foreigner round the block a few times, make it up.' He winked at her, double-checked his mirrors and drove off.

Tina looked up and there he was. Her heart jumped and she felt a thin film of nervous sweat prickling her skin. He was wearing a white shirt, a dark green linen blazer, jeans and loafers. He looked lovely.

'D'you often loiter around graveyards?' she asked as she approached him. And just like that, they picked up where they'd left off, familiar and comfortable.

'I do today.' He leant forward and kissed her cheek, as though they met every day and this was how he greeted her. 'What beautiful flowers.' He ran his finger over the blooms.

She nodded. They were. 'I found an old pressed flower on her bedside table, it had a little brown luggage tag tied to it with a piece of string, it said, "yellow rose" and so I thought these would be fitting.'

Ian held her hand and guided her towards the gate. 'I got here early and decided to try and find the grave, which I did.'

'Oh wow! I'm dying to know more – no pun intended. Was he married, like we thought? Or did he die in the war?'

'Neither.' He smiled.

The two trod the path in near silence, conscious of where they were and wanting to show respect for the person they had both been very fond of.

'Here we are.' Ian crouched down and rested his hand on the top of the gravestone.

Tina bent down beside him and read the inscription. '*1912 to 1968*. That was young.' She looked across at Ian. 'Only fifty-six.'

He nodded. 'Read on.'

'*Here lies the body of Miss Thomasina Stanmore. Beloved daughter of the late Percy Stanmore and his wife Cecily, both formerly of this parish. May God keep you safe under his mighty wing.*' Tina couldn't stop the flow of tears that trickled down her face. 'Her Tom.'

'Yes. Her Tom.' Ian stood and watched as Tina placed the bunch of beautiful yellow roses on the grave.

'It's a shame they didn't get longer together.' She sniffed.

'There's a lot that's a shame about it.' He sighed. 'Shame we never met her, shame Cordelia never felt able to speak about her.'

'I hope they were happy.' She smiled up at him.

'Me too.' He placed his hand on the small of her back and guided her to the main road, where they decided to take a cab to Lexham Gardens.

'It still feels strange being here without her,' Tina said as she filled the kettle.

'Oh, she's here! She's everywhere you look!' He ran his fingers over the dresser in the kitchen, crammed with his grandmother's china.

'I wonder what will happen to the flat,' Tina said.

'Oh, didn't I tell you?' he asked, nonchalantly.

'No.' She shook her head as she reached into the ornate caddy with the slightly rusted lid and pulled out three tea bags.

'It's mine.'

Tina turned to face him. 'It's yours? Really? Well, that's wonderful! Will you live in it?' She felt her heart swell at the possibility.

'No. It's too big for me and too far from where I want to be.'

'Oh.' She swallowed her disappointment. 'It's only a little flat, really; not too big at all.' She silently chastised herself for trying to encourage him to move there, to be closer to her. As if.

'No, no, that's the thing. It's not just the flat. Apparently, she never sold the building when it was converted into flats, just had it divided up and then moved herself into the basement.' He looked straight at her, waiting for her reaction.

Tina stared back. 'She owns the whole building?'

'Well, no. She did. I do now.'

She tried to digest the significance of this news. A big, posh house in Kensington... 'What are you going to do?'

'Sell it, give some of the proceeds to Minty, to get her settled... And I was thinking of moving to the coast, somewhere I can open my curtains of a morning and see the sea every day. And if I want to see it at any other time of day, then all I'll have to do is pop my head out and there it'll be!'

'Are you taking the piss?' She felt shy and awkward. The kettle hissed as it came to the boil.

'No. I would never do that. I want to move to the coast and open a wine shop, with a bar and tapas and a florist's, a flower shop, where people can come for wine and eat great food and leave with a bouquet of beautiful yellow roses.'

Tina realised she was crying, again. 'You must think I'm a right wally. All I've done is cry today!'

Ian lifted her up and sat her on the work surface, so he could look at her eye to eye. 'I don't think you're a wally. I think you're amazing! I think you're the most amazing woman I have ever met. And I know that you're probably inundated with admirers...'

'Oh yeah, I have to carry a big stick to beat them all off with.' She smiled.

'...but I want you to pick me. I want you to come with me, live with me, work with me, and let me love you. Because you are my happy!' He was animated, bursting with all the possibilities.

Tina placed her arms around his neck. 'I missed you, Ian.'

'And that, Tina, is the greatest compliment you can ever pay someone. To miss them. That's real love.'

They both turned to Greta Garbo, who meowed in the corner.

Seventeen

Two years later

'I'm a bit nervous.' Tina paced the floor of the grand hallway and ran her palms over her bottle-green pinny with the *Vine and Bloom* logo embroidered on it in white thread.

'Don't be. This is going to be the best night ever!' Ian grabbed her by the waist and swung her round. 'And if we change our minds or fancy some different scenery after a few years, we can simply shut up shop and go have an adventure.'

'Hark at you, Mr Live-For-The-Moment! I don't know what's got into you.'

'I am perfectly happy knowing that the future is in safe hands, with Marl off at uni and all set to make a fine doctor, and Minty happy, engaged to that chinless wonder.'

'Don't call him that! It's mean!' She giggled. 'And we don't do mean.'

'No, you're right. But flippin' 'eck, he's hopeless!'

Tina laughed at how he had adopted her favourite phrase.

'I just want people to love what we've done to the place.' She looked around her, admiring for the millionth time the timber-framed walls, the wing-backed leather chairs in front of the humidor, and the vintage oak barrels that doubled as tables, just waiting for the first customers to stand around them and chat.

She walked over to the long chrome bar and double-checked

that the slate platters of cheese and cold meats were still looking fridge-fresh. Then she buried her nose in one of the flower arrangements that filled the vast concrete urns dotted about the room. She'd decided on large blue hydrangeas and huge bowers of foliage. It had taken a lot of research to find hydrangeas with a scent, but these ones really did look and smell wonderful. And this was only stage one! Later in the month she'd be opening her very own florist's in the orangery at the back of the vintner's.

'Mum!'

Tina whipped round and there he was – her boy. The same but different, as was always the case, however recently they'd last seen each other. It was a pleasure to observe him growing into the confident man she knew he would become.

'There you are!' She reached up and hugged him. 'God, I love you and I miss you!'

'You only saw me two weeks ago.'

'I know, but if I had my way, I'd see you every day.' An image of the two of them lolling on the sofa together in front of *The Jeremy Kyle Show*, back in their Hammersmith days, flashed through her head.

Marley rolled his eyes at Ian, who reached out, shook the boy's hand and then pulled him in for a hug. 'How are we doing?'

'Struggling a bit with pharmacology and excitable tissues.' He pulled a face.

'Ah, don't worry, we can go over that this weekend.'

'What we goin' over this weekend?' Digsy yelled as he waltzed in with his large suitcase.

'Pharmacology and excitable tissues,' Ian recited.

'I'm in!' Digsy shouted as he crushed Tina to him in a hug. 'How's your mum?'

'She's good, Teen. You won't believe who she's dating!'

Marley and his mum shook their heads, wondering who the latest in her long line of beaus might be.

'Who?' Marley barked.

'Fat Barry from the chippy! It's wicked, I'm getting all the free food I can eat, and so is the whole family! My mum, her sister!'

Marley caught his mum's eye and they both laughed until they cried silent tears.

'What you laughin' at?' Digsy looked puzzled.

After everyone had enjoyed a glass of wine and the boys had been settled into their rooms in the spacious chalets at the back of the new premises, Tina and Ian stood on the large terrace at the back of the building, drinking in the stunning view of the sea and welcoming their opening-night guests. It had taken them months to find the right place, rejecting some for not feeling quite right, others for lacking the magic they sought, but the moment they had set foot on this plot, with the galleried Dutch Barn, wooden floors and the apron of land teetering only feet from the cliff edge, they had looked at each other and smiled. This was what they had been waiting for.

They greeted their new neighbours and schmoozed the various dignitaries and members of the local press, explaining the concept of the new business and handing out cards, wine, dainty canapés and sweet posies for the ladies. The two of them kept catching each other's eye and beaming. They were both happier than they had ever thought possible.

The sound of Helen's voice carried on the wind and sent a shiver down Ian's back. She was accompanied by Julio, Minty and Mr Chinless.

'Welcome to our new venture!' He smiled, spreading his arms wide in greeting.

'Good God, Ian, it's miles from bloody anywhere!' This was Helen's opener, as she kissed him on both cheeks. The expression on her face could surely have curdled milk, he thought with a wry smile to himself and a nod to the memory of his late mother.

'Hello, Julio, thank you so much for coming!' Ian shook the man's hand and couldn't help but notice that he had lost most of his tan and a lot of his sparkle, the poor sod.

Minty and her man made straight for the wine and grub. Helen, meanwhile, was staring with lips pursed at the venerable old house on the cliff top. 'Aren't you worried about soil erosion?'

Ian noticed for the first time how her voice had a particularly annoying nasal twang. 'Well, as I've said to Tina, if we change our minds or it tumbles into the sea, we shall simply sail off and have a grand old adventure.'

'Honestly, Ian, you sound like a hippy. What next: tofu and tattoos?' She looked at her Spaniard and laughed.

'Here she is!' Ian beamed.

They all turned to watch the smiling Tina as she walked down the steps towards the terrace, bearing a fresh bottle of rather pricey Valpolicella in her hands. Her dark hair hung around her pretty face and her slight frame looked beautiful wrapped inside her *Vine and Bloom* apron. Ian noted Julio's eyes widening.

'Hello, Helen. You made it then!'

'Only just – this place is in the middle of nowhere.'

'That's why we chose it.' Tina laughed. 'And as Ian said, if we get fed up, we can just sail off into the sunset.' She laughed again.

'You have a boat?' This had clearly piqued Julio's interest.

'Yes.' Ian took him by the elbow and steered him to the edge of the cliff. 'There she is.' He pointed to the dock below them, where a luxurious sixty-five-foot pilot cutter was moored.

'She is beautiful.' Julio looked at the yacht enviously.

'Yes, she is. And I love her. She represents a whole new chapter in my life.' Ian beamed down at the boat as she bobbed on the water. The early evening sun glinted like diamonds on the water and her name, written in pale gold paint, sparkled: *The Cordelia Potterton.*

Ian was sure she would have liked that.

He looked down and noticed that Julio had exceptionally small feet – tiny, in fact. He placed his arm around Julio's shoulders and walked him back to the terrace, smiling. He might not be practising medicine any more, but he still knew the truth about men with very small feet...

A
Christmas
Wish

A Christmas Wish

Poppy raised her hands behind her head and slipped her shoulder-length hair into a pink scrunchie she had found nestling at the bottom of her handbag. She squeezed out a blob of fluorescent cleaning fluid and wiped down the work surface in the kitchen. Her tongue poked from the side of her mouth, as it always did when she was concentrating. Flipping over the sponge, she used the scourer to shift a little bump of spinach that had dried hard after making a break for freedom from the colander. What had Peg said? *'Don't eat it, Maxy, it's not real food, it's like grass!'*

She cast her eye over the sitting room, torn between enjoying the festive decorations and bits of tat that the kids had adorned her usually clutter-free surfaces with and the desire to put them away and give everything a good dust. They were going away but had as always put up a small Christmas tree in the window, a concession that the kids loved. Poppy pretended not to notice that the foil-wrapped chocolate decorations that hung from every branch were deflated and slightly crumpled, having been niftily emptied of their melting bounty. Peg must have engineered the heist, no doubt with Max roped in to spread the blame. She would find the right time to reveal her shock and horror that they had been robbed of the twelve sugary gifts. She smiled.

Poppy took pride in keeping her little house neat and

clean. A strict routine meant that clothes were washed, dried, ironed and returned neatly to drawers just in time for when they were needed next. A daily whizz with the Hoover, swish of the mop and flick of a duster meant their home rarely lapsed below show-house standard. The order in which she lived was proof of her success, having achieved all that she had dreamed of for her and Martin. She never wanted her children to experience the gut-wrenching embarrassment of wearing dirty clothes to school, going to class with the wrong PE kit and not being able to invite anyone home as the house was cluttered and filthy.

The tiny kitchen in the flat she had grown up in encapsulated all that had been wrong with her grubby life: cupboard doors bloated with damp and hanging off their hinges, and sticky shelves bare of food but stacked with pill bottles containing cures and suppressants for everything from constipation to hallucinations. The dull metal sink full of dirty, tea-stained cups and old fish and chip wrappers; and the blackened, encrusted grill sitting in its base amid a thick layer of soft, opaque bacon fat. Poppy could still smell the kitchen of her youth, even now. It was the sour odour of frying, grime and mould.

Standing back, she smiled at her sparkling work surfaces and gleaming cooker. '*You could eat your bleedin' dinner off that floor, girl!*' She heard her nan's words, even now, after all these years, making her laugh, giving advice.

'Mum?' Peg shouted and banged her palm on the table. Making sure she was heard the second time.

'Sorry, love, I was miles away. What?' Poppy leant on the back of the chair at the square pine table in the kitchen where Peg was toiling over her homework. A task, as Poppy had pointed out on numerous occasions that would take half as long if Peg would only speak less and write more.

'What's the difference between a wish and a prayer?' Peg asked. Her head cocked to one side as she twisted a pencil inside her dark blonde locks, her feet in their white socks kicking against the table leg.

'Is this your homework?' Poppy asked, thinking it a tad deep for primary year three.

'No!' Peg sighed. 'My homework is writing a page about why you mustn't punch someone, even if they are a boy and even if they are bigger than you.' Peg kept her eyes downcast.

'Let me think. A wish and a prayer? That's a very good question.' Poppy pulled out the chair and sat opposite her daughter. This required some thinking. She hitched up the long sleeves of her T-shirt and placed her freckly forearms flat along the surface. 'I guess the main difference is that a prayer is specifically aimed at God, meaning you believe there is a God and that he or she is powerful enough to answer your prayers. Whereas a wish is more general, like throwing what you want out into the universe and hoping that something good might come back.'

Peg considered this, tapping the pencil on her teeth. 'I'm not sure I believe in God.'

'Well, you are only eight, you have a lot of time to figure that stuff out.' Poppy smiled. 'Plus you could always hedge your bets and do both.'

'Am I allowed to do that?' Peg sat forward, wide-eyed. This sounded like a plan.

'Absolutely! I think that if there is a God, they wouldn't mind you sending out a wish along with a prayer; and if there isn't, then you are safe, aren't you?' Poppy thought about the times in her life when she had done exactly that, though she couldn't be sure that either had been answered.

'Mum, you are a genius!'

'Yes I am. And I need you to put your books away, gather all your bits and bobs into your rucksack ready for tomorrow and clear the table. Aunty Jo is coming round to babysit soon and I want the house tidy.' Poppy winked, stood from the table and went to plump the cushions in the adjoining open-plan sitting room.

Peg rolled her eyes, reminding Poppy of herself. 'I will in a minute. But I've got to do my wish and prayer first!'

'Oh I see. You are doing that right now?'

'Ye-s!' Peg managed to give the word two syllables, showing her disdain.

'Can't you do it in your head while you do your chores?' Poppy asked casually.

'No, Mum, I can't! This is important and I would actually like you to leave the room.'

'Oh right, okay.' Poppy nipped into the hallway that ran from the front door to the kitchen and listened at the door as Peg placed her elbows on the table and her forehead against her clasped hands.

'Hello, God and universe, it's Peg Cricket here. I shouldn't have punched Elliot in the face, I'm sorry about that, but he said I loved Jake and I don't love Jake, I love Noah. Anyway, I just wanted to ask you for one thing.' Peg took a deep breath. 'Can you send my daddy home?'

Poppy laid her head against the doorframe and swallowed the tears that threatened. She only allowed herself to cry in the bath or shower and never in front of the kids.

Peg wasn't done. 'It's just that I really miss him. He's a soldier and he's working away, fixing all the cars and tanks for people that do the fighting and stuff, and I haven't seen him for a long time. Please don't tell my mummy, but I can't quite remember what he looks like, not in real life. I've got photos of him, but it's not the same. Anyway, that's it, I don't want anything else, I just want him to come home, please. Thank you.' She was silent for a second. 'Although if having two things *isn't* against the rules, I'd like One Direction to come and sing at my school and pick me to go on the stage with them, but that really is it. Unless I can have three and if that is possible, I would like a pet guinea pig called Toffee. Oh, and amen, just in case, thanks. Bye.'

Poppy watched as her little girl placed her books, pencil case and woolly gloves into her multi-coloured school backpack.

'You can come in now, Mum!' she shouted.

Poppy sloped into the kitchen and reached for the cloth to give the table a onceover.

'How quickly do prayers and wishes get answered?' Peg looked her mum squarely in the eyes. Her tone matter-of-fact, certain, as if she was asking how long the post might take to arrive or what time the next bus was due.

'Ooh, I don't know. I think it depends.'

'Depends on what?'

'Well...' Poppy considered this. 'How many other prayers and wishes need answering. It's probably like Argos: at quiet times, the man out the back brings your stuff through very quickly, but at Christmas when he's flat out and people are going crazy trying to get all their shopping done, it can take ages!'

'Are you getting any of our presents from Argos this year?'

'Ah, it's not me that gets your presents, is it, silly billy! It's Father Christmas!'

Peg stopped in the hallway, hitched her bag up onto her shoulder and turned to her mum. 'Purr-lease! Who do you think you are talking to – Max?' Peg screwed her face up. 'I know there is no Santa Claus. Jade McKeever told me. Her older sister told her and she's thirteen and has got four bras. I know that it's mummies and daddies that get all the presents. But don't worry, I won't tell Max until he's at least five.'

Poppy nodded, grateful that she wasn't going to give her baby brother the devastating facts just yet. At two, he deserved to enjoy the magic a little longer than his streetwise sister. Poppy pondered the fact that Peg had received this information from a freshly minted teen that owned one bra more than she did.

'Will my wish and prayer work, Mum?'

'I hope so, little darlin'.'

Jo knocked as she entered the narrow porch, her gold earrings and bangles jangling as she did so. Poppy let her in and tried to hide her slight irritation as her friend and next-door neighbour dumped her cardigan and slumped down on the newly plumped and brushed sofa without acknowledging the perfect state of the furnishings. Jo flicked her dark hair extensions over the back of the sofa and dabbed at her lower lip, checking her lip liner hadn't bled into the gloss. It hadn't and still sat in a perfect line that matched the ones drawn over the space where her eyebrows used to reside. Jo was pretty, but her rather elaborate make-up masked her natural beauty, meaning you only saw the harsh lines and bright colours of artifice and not what lurked beneath. It fascinated Poppy, who only owned three items of make-up and was uncertain what to do with them.

'All right, Poppy? Blimey, what a day.' Jo was a Londoner like her. 'I went into Salisbury and it was absolutely heaving. I was elbow to elbow in Marks and Sparks, trying to buy socks and pants for Danny's stocking. I know he's going to be away, but I'm going to do the house up anyway. I'll fling up a bit of tinsel and watch any old crap on the telly. We'll have fake

Christmas day when he gets back in January. People were going crazy today, shoving stuff into baskets, barging their way through. I wanted to get on the tannoy and remind them it's just a couple of days of Christmas holidays and not the end of the bloody world. Honestly, the way they were going mad for food made me feel a bit sick. They're only shut for a day or so, no one is going to go hungry, are they?'

Poppy shook her head and sighed. It was always this way with Jo. Until she had vented her spleen and aired the backlog of all that she had encountered since they'd last met, there was no room for Poppy to comment. To try and interject meant a jarring of sentences and a clash of words, with no one getting heard.

'Anyway, when I got back, I'd only gone and missed a call from him. I couldn't believe it, bloody typical! He left a message saying he'd call back so I sat waiting for over an hour, you know what it's like, you don't want them to miss their slot. I was dying for the loo, but I didn't go. I thought knowing my luck I'd be on the bog when he called and I'd miss it. When he finally got through, it was patchy and there were people mucking about in the background, which really got my goat. They clearly didn't give a shite, larking around, but it was my chance to speak to him and I don't know when he'll call again, you know what it's like. It was a rubbish line. He sounded like his head was underwater and not just in Afbloodyghanistan.'

Poppy flicked her head towards the door and open-tread staircase, hoping Peg was out of earshot. Although she herself had grown up with swearing and easy banter as the norm, she had changed since she had become a mum and these days was conscious of everything that left her mouth, knowing how easily it could find its way into her children's ears. Jo didn't have kids and Poppy assumed this was why she was so cavalier with her language. Poppy pointed upstairs and gave a wide, false grin.

Jo snickered. 'Oh sorry, love, I forgot! Anyway, we spent a couple of minutes arguing because I could hear a woman's voice laughing and it really wound me up and then I put the phone down on him. So that was productive. Might have been better off if I had been on the bog and missed it.'

'Oh, mate, that's tough. Those phone calls are a mixed blessing, aren't they? You want to hear their voice and know that everything is okay, but you're under pressure to have this perfect, lovey-dovey phone call because you think you should, when really you just want to shout at them and say how lonely you are and angry that they are not here!'

Poppy knew that a woman's voice in the background would not bother her a jot. Martin loved her and she him; they were an item, unshakeable and this had always been the case. Her theory was that if he were going to be unfaithful or hurt her in any way, he wouldn't have to go to Afbloodyghanistan or any other dark, dusty place to do it. Each and every communication that she got from him filled her with unimaginable joy, from the odd brief email to the hurried, stolen phone calls; each second got stored away in her head to be endlessly replayed in the early hours when sleep evaded her. They were always the same words, stuttered, rushed and with an irritating delay, his voice, taut with emotion: *'I love you, Poppy Day, I love you and I... I miss you. Tell the kids I love them, I miss them too. Not much longer.'*

'You can't be lonely!' Jo's words focused her. 'You've got Peg and Max, you're too busy to be lonely.'

Poppy felt sorry for Jo, who filled her days with shopping and watching re-runs of American shows on the television. She had confided in Poppy after too much wine one night that she had desperately wanted to be a mum. But after years of monthly disappointments, she and Danny had decided to distract themselves by saving for a cruise every other year. Poppy mollified her friend with tales of sleepless nights, the expense and lack of spontaneity. She never confided that her greatest moment had been seeing the tiny, white-wrapped bundle handed to her husband in the delivery suite, watching his eyes glaze as he searched for the words, her heart swelling as he said, 'Look what we did! She's... she's so beautiful.'

Jo filled the void that kids would have occupied by cramming her wardrobe with new tops, all rather similar in shade and design, and stuffing her bathroom cabinet with toiletries that could keep her clean for a lifetime.

'True, they keep me busy, Jo, but it's not the same as having Mart home, someone to cosy up with.' She smiled at the thought of it.

'Urgh, pass the bucket. You're like a lovesick teenager! I thought it would have worn off by now. How long have you two been together?'

Since we were fourteen, more than half of my life, and he was my best friend long before that. She heard Mart's voice loud and clear, as if he was standing by her side and as if it was yesterday. 'I promise you, Poppy, that I will always be your best friend. It's like we are joined together by invisible strings that join your heart to mine and if you need me, you just have to pull them and I'll come to you.'

'Yeah, I know, a long time. He always says he'd have got less for murder!' Poppy felt the need to play down their commitment and happiness, aware that Jo and Danny didn't seem to have what they did, but also not wanting to put it out into the universe, as if they shared a precious secret.

Peg ran down the stairs, arriving with her little vanity

case full of nail varnish in garish colours and several sparkly lipsticks in various shades of pink.

'Hello, darling, I was wondering how long I would have to wait for my makeover!' Jo waved her bare nails at Peg. She had, as usual, come prepared.

'I'll just get set up.' Peg smiled, eager as a puppy. 'But we can't take too long, I have to practise my lines.'

'Lines?'

'Big day tomorrow, end of term school play!' Poppy grinned.

'Oh fab! What are you in the play?' Jo sat forward.

'I am sheep number six!' Peg nodded.

'Sheep number six, eh? That's always been my favourite sheep.'

Poppy watched as Peg removed the little glass bottles from the case and lined them up on the edge of the coffee table.

'What colour would you like today, madam?' Peg adopted her posh, lady-manicurist voice.

'Oh, I don't really know! I think I'll leave it up to you.' Jo matched her, sounding affected and formal.

'Are you going to a special party or a function?' Peg enquired.

Poppy laughed as she reached for her coat from the rack of pegs on the wall in the hallway.

'Actually, yes I am! My husband is taking me out for a very posh dinner at the flashiest restaurant in town!'

Peg put her hand to her chest. 'Oh, how lovely, is it the Harvester?'

Poppy smiled. It was the one place Peg had celebrated family birthdays and anniversaries.

'Why, yes it is!' Jo replied.

'I have been there,' Peg gushed. 'They have lovely ice cream!'

'Why, thank you for the recommendation, although I am trying to watch my figure.' Jo smiled.

'Don't worry about that! You are only a little bit fat, not *really* fat like some people. It's only your tummy and your bottom that are wobbly and you can always cover them up with a longer top!'

Poppy felt her cheeks flare and was rendered speechless. Jo didn't flinch.

Peg continued. 'I think today we need to do stripes, in pink, purple and blue!' She nodded as she selected the three colours of choice.

Jo looked over her shoulder at Poppy and mouthed 'HELP!'

'Right, you two, have a lovely evening,' Poppy offered, relieved the awkward moment had passed. There was a fine line between encouraging Peg never to tell a lie and letting her pursue her own brand of honesty, often funny sometimes brutal.

'We will!' Peg waved without looking up.

'Be a good girl for Aunty Jo.' Poppy wasn't sure her daughter was listening, so she turned her attention to her friend. 'Max is soundo and probably won't stir. If he does, his sippy cup is in the fridge and just cuddle him back off.'

'I think I can manage that.' Jo spoke over her shoulder as Peg placed her splayed fingers on one of Poppy's cushions and shook her little bottle.

'And I shall be back later to tell you exactly what your new teacher had to say, Peg Alessandra. So you might want to hide the big stick.'

Peg again spoke in the direction of her mum's voice without turning her head. 'Jade McKeever said Mrs Newman is a meanie poo-poo breath and I think she is too.'

'Peg!' Poppy shook her head as she buttoned up her warm green coat and tied her stripey scarf into a knot at her neck. With her feet snug inside her wellies, she set out into the cold December night.

She cautiously trod the path between the identical houses – army quarters, built in the 1970s, that she and the other service wives on the patch tried to personalise with fancy lamps, oversized Ikea pictures and wacky welcome mats. Nonetheless, in the half light of a winter's evening, they all looked the same.

The snow was at that horrible stage when it turns from crisp white powder to a thin orange-coloured sludge that clings to your feet and sprays up the back of your legs. Higher up on the slope of the fields though there remained a healthy smattering that almost sparkled in the moonlight. The night was still, the moon large and the air had the faintest aroma of wood smoke from real fires and damp earth. It was a smell unique to the countryside, so very different to East London, where she had grown up. The atmosphere here was untainted by the waft of fried food pumping from extractor fans along the high street, or the pungent, lingering scent of cigarette smoke and diesel, or the stink from the grime that smeared the buildings and sat in darkened heaps against the kerb.

Poppy gathered her coat at her neck and set off with a determined stride down the lane, her breath blowing smoke out into the night sky. They lived in the middle of Wiltshire and it was breathtakingly beautiful. As soon as she left the cul-de-sac she was surrounded by open fields with low barbed-wire fences, dense hedging and fat sheep. On a clear day, from the brow of the hill, she could see Stonehenge, a fact that thrilled and fascinated her. Each season she watched as the landscape was transformed from waving fans of yellow oilseed rape to rich brown furrows to the white snows of winter. It was a world away from the concrete block of flats in Walthamstow in which she had lived as a child, the place her nan Dot had entered as a bride in 1962 and had left six decades later when dementia and old age were victorious. When Martin had finished the basic training for his new trade, they had packed up their little family and moved from Bordon to Colchester then Hounslow before finding themselves in Larkhill, another world.

Poppy walked to the end of the road and turned left opposite the parade of shops that catered mainly for squaddies and their families. There was the obligatory newsagent's and a convenience store at which you could buy several varieties of lager and crisps but couldn't for love or money find a vegetable that hadn't taken on the characteristics of a gourd. There was a post office where loved ones queued with shoe boxes and padded envelopes whose contents weren't necessarily very original but were at least under two kilograms in weight and so would be delivered free to the BFPO address at which their other halves temporarily resided. An army surplus store provided bits of kit that made life easier for those who worked in trying conditions. And there was a chippy and two other takeaways.

The Turkish kebab shop owners had made a lovely effort for Christmas: in their window were two large blinking neon signs that said, 'Happy Chri tma !' Both 's's had long since given up the ghost. They had also hung blue lights that looked like icicles dangling from the peeling fascia. Whenever Peg and Max walked past they would hover on the pavement outside, squealing with excitement at what this meagre display represented, shouting, 'Happy Chritma! Happy Chritma!' over and over.

Poppy wondered what they would make of the ornate Christmas windows of Oxford Street if this was enough to send them into raptures. She remembered as a child going up West and pressing her nose against the windows, drawn by the sparkle, lights and scenes from a fairy wonderland. She used to wonder what kind of child got to go in stores like that.

Selfridges held particular fascination; it was the store in which her nan had worked as a young girl. Poppy used to try and imagine a youthful, laughing Dot walking through its revolving doors with the shiny brass push plates. It was sometimes hard to picture her nan in that way, when she considered the woman she became, trapped in a confusing world of memory loss, anxiety and fear, watching any old rubbish on television and wearing easy-fit elastic-waisted trousers.

Poppy carried on along the path, enjoying the sound of the patches of remaining snow crunching underfoot and seeking out the areas that were less well trod. She passed the Packhorse pub and made her way round the corner into the low-rise building whose bright lights and propped-open door seemed to beckon her inside.

The little school catered for the children of service families and the farming community as well as for the kids of a few city slickers whose country piles boasted indoor pools, games rooms and annexes above the garage. As she hovered in the corridor, Poppy felt her anxiety levels rising. *'Get a grip, girl. It's only a bloody meeting, you've been through worse!'* It was her nan's voice. She nodded.

Rows of pegs were positioned on the wall a couple of feet from the floor, each marked by a personalised sticker. She ran her fingers over Peg's space, imagining her daughter placing her coat and bag there every day. She smiled at the large yellow combine harvester that sat above her name; Peg had rejected princess crowns and sparkly rings, mermaids and puppies in favour of this hunk of farm machinery. She liked the way Peg looked at the world – differently.

Poppy peered through the little glass window in the classroom door and saw Freddie's parents sitting on the teeny chairs in front of Mrs Newman. All three were laughing loudly.

She couldn't hear exactly what was being said, but they were all clearly delighted. Well done, Freddie! Poppy knew for a fact that Freddie's dad had an indoor pool and an annex, because he had told her so the first and only time they had met. She watched now as he kept adjusting his long legs in their pinstriped trousers, pinching the crease above the knee as he shifted his position. Freddie's mum flicked at her platinum-blonde layers, adjusting them on the shoulders of her navy blazer. In Poppy's professional opinion, the woman would be better off going a couple of shades darker and opting for a softer fringe. She hadn't worked as a hairdresser since she'd had Peg, but old habits died hard.

She sank down onto the equally teeny chair outside the door. It wasn't the first time she'd been made to sit outside the classroom while all the fun was had on the other side of the wall. She remembered clearly when she was six and the whole class had been told to bring in empty, rinsed squash bottles and yoghurt pots to make puppets for the end of term concert. Little slips of paper with this instruction had been slid between the pages of their reading books a month in advance and reminders were issued weekly.

The problem was, there were no empty squash bottles or yoghurt pots in Poppy's home. There was hardly ever a cooked meal; the best she could hope for was toast and she didn't have the courage or foresight to mention this to anyone. Her reading book remained closed because when Poppy got home from school, no note would be read by her doting parents and stuck on the fridge as a reminder. Her mum didn't tuck her in at night or snuggle her up on the sofa for reading time, eager for her child to increase her vocabulary, encouraging her to jump to Biff, Chip and Kipper's next adventure. No, Poppy's prime concern would be trying to get her uniform a little bit clean for the next day. This she tackled by dabbing at any obvious marks with a dot of Fairy Liquid on a piece of wet loo roll, which, far from being effective, would simply disintegrate into little rolled worms that left a greyish smudge in their wake. She spent the hours between arriving home and going to bed making sure her nan had taken her tablets and her mum didn't fall asleep sloshed and with a fag on. Her head was way too full to think about end of term puppet shows.

The art and craft teacher, Mrs Greenwood, who came in one afternoon a week, had not given her a chance to explain. And even if she had, Poppy would have chosen silence rather than reveal the state of affairs at home in front of her classmates.

'Where are your empty bottles and pots, Poppy?' Mrs Greenwood had boomed as Poppy's classmates upturned their carrier bags and emptied their plastic booty onto the desks.

She stole a glance at Martin, who looked on sympathetically, before shrugging her shoulders and staring at the scuffed tips of her shoes, inside which her toes were bunched and hurting.

'I see. That's your response, is it? This is very disappointing. You have had weeks to prepare and this really isn't good enough! Outside, now!' She pointed towards the door. Poppy remembered the gold cross that dangled below her wrist from her gold bracelet. It twisted in the light and made her think of Jesus.

It had almost been a relief to go outside and stand with her back against the painted wall. Far easier than watching her classmates use generous dollops from the glue pot to add little felt jackets, heart and star stickers, googly eyes and hair made from wool onto their puppets, which were finished off with large sticks shoved up their jacksies.

It was these memories, sharp and bitter, there for perfect recall, which made Poppy feel waves of anger towards her mother. The thought of Peg or Max experiencing even a second of unease or discomfort made her heart constrict. She wanted to bubble-wrap them from the world for as long as possible, keeping them safe and happy inside her little nest, and this instinct made it even harder to understand her mum's total lack of interest.

Poppy stood and perused the school noticeboard opposite the classroom, where idling parents could read about what was going on in the school community. She leant towards it, studying the posters and flyers that detailed fundraising events, dates for the pre-school Nativity, slimming clubs with vacancies and mother and baby yoga classes. She squinted at the telephone numbers of enterprising mums who flogged candles and aloe vera products at awkward parties where you felt obliged to buy something after knocking back a glass of cheap plonk and a slack handful of salted peanuts.

The classroom door opened suddenly and Freddie's parents spewed forth like a laughing, chattering wave breaking in the hallway.

'Oh yes, let's do that! Call you soon!'

'Bye! Have a lovely break, Janine!'

'You too. Bye bye!'

Poppy swallowed the swell of sickness that washed over her as nerves threatened. *Janine*, so that was what the 'J' stood for. As a child she had always found it impossible to imagine her teachers having a first name; she just couldn't picture them being referred to as anything other than Miss or Mr. The other thing she just couldn't picture was what they looked like in their pyjamas.

'Ah, yes, Mrs...?'

Poppy had met Mrs Newman on a couple of occasions and yet didn't seem to have gelled in the woman's mind.

'Day, Poppy Day.'

'Of course, come in, Mrs Day.'

Poppy stuttered. 'Oh… sorry, actually it's Mrs Cricket. I'm Peg's mum. Poppy Day is my not married name.' She blushed. *Not married name?*

'I see. Please sit.' Mrs Newman stretched out her palm towards the chairs and gave the 't' such a hard sound, Poppy felt like a dog. 'No Mr Cricket?' Mrs Newman looked at the little chair next to her.

Poppy bit her lip, fighting the temptation to say, *'Yes, he is sitting right next to me; he is just very, very small!'*

'No, he's in Sy—' She stopped herself. What had he said? *'No specifics, just say "away".'* She gave a small cough. 'He's away.'

Poppy watched Mrs Newman inhale deeply as if preparing for battle.

'I see.' She shuffled the sheets of paper in front of her. 'Peg has been in my class for one term now…' She paused and looked up. 'May I ask, is Peg an abbreviation?'

'Not really. I mean, yes, it is, but not for Margaret or anything, which I get asked a lot. Her name is Peggy, but she's always been Peg.'

Poppy noticed the flicker of irritation around the woman's eyes. She continued as if Poppy hadn't spoken.

'If I am being honest, it has been a most challenging term.'

Poppy wondered if it would be okay to have the dishonest version, thinking it might be slightly easier to hear. 'In what way?'

Mrs Newman pushed her glasses up her nose, back to the point from which they had slid. 'Peg asks a lot of questions.' She smiled briefly.

'That's a good thing, isn't it? Shows she's interested.'

Mrs Newman gave a small laugh. 'Well, I can see how one might assume that. But let me assure you, it really isn't a good thing. Peg feels the need to question everything and I mean everything.' She proceeded to check the notes in front of her. 'This week's examples include, why are children seated alphabetically and not allowed to sit with their friends? Why are some of her classmates given two goes at being register monitor, when others are still waiting for a first go? And why are Shahul and Hamjid allowed to miss assembly when others who aren't sure that they even *believe* in God have to attend?' She placed the paper face down and once again looked at Poppy. 'The list is long, Mrs Cricket, and ever increasing.' She put her hands on the table in front of her.

'Why *are* they?'

'Why are they what?' Mrs Newman twitched her nose.

'Why are some children given two goes at being register monitor when others are still waiting for a turn?' Poppy understood her daughter's need to try and fathom apparent injustice and this point seemed the most ludicrous of all.

Mrs Newman removed her glasses and used one of the arms as an indicator, pointing in turn to herself, the wider classroom and Poppy, who found it incredibly irritating. She gave a snort before she spoke, as if surprised at this line of questioning from Peg's mother. 'I am not here to defend my teaching methods, Mrs Cricket, but as you ask, I use it as a means of reward. If a pupil is well behaved, attentive and courteous, I reward that behaviour with privileged duties and praise. It is a good lesson for life.'

Poppy thought about her own class in school. Harriet, who already had a pretty cushy life, a nice house, an attentive mum, good teeth and a fabulous lunch box, was also given treats at school, to which she was slightly indifferent. What was the big deal in being given a fun-size Mars when she had a whole cupboard of sweets and goodies at home? Whereas to a child like Poppy or one of her mates it would have meant the world. This she knew because she had been given a fun-size Milky Way once by a neighbour and had got at least six bites out of it.

She considered her response. 'I just think that maybe if you let one of the less well behaved, inattentive or discourteous kids be register monitor, it might encourage them to try harder. You might ignite that spark inside them to do better, if they can see they will be rewarded.' Poppy felt awkward. Maybe she had overstepped the mark – what did she know, a hairdresser from Walthamstow.

'Was there anything else?' Mrs Newman looked at the clock over Poppy's head.

She shook her head, positive that she hadn't yet eaten up her allotted time. Under pressure, she was now unable to think of a single one of the pre-prepared questions she had conjured on the way over. She knew she would leave having learned nothing about how her little girl was faring academically.

Mrs Newman stood, replaced her goggles and headed towards the door. There were no trills of laughter or suggestions that they get together *soon*. She reached for the handle and turned to Poppy.

'I understand that having a husband in prison brings its own set of difficulties, but if I made allowances for every child with a difficulty, chaos would reign and that is something I simply can't allow.' Her smile was brief and insincere and at such close proximity Poppy could smell her breath, which was most unpleasant.

Flabbergasted, she stepped from the room. *Prison?* Where on earth had she got that?

Then her giggle caught in her throat. Mrs Newman had thought Poppy was going to say 'inside' when she'd checked herself earlier.

Poppy fastened her coat and stepped out into the cold night air feeling deflated and frustrated in equal measure. She *wanted* Peg to question everything and knew how hard she worked. What did Mrs bloody Newman know? Questioning things and having courage had proved invaluable to Poppy in her life. Without that, she wouldn't have escaped the deprivation into which she'd been born; she wouldn't have known that she could.

Jade's mum and dad swung their car into the car park and jumped out, obviously running a little late.

'Hi, Poppy! How are you? We are *so* late, he's only just got in.' Jade's mum jerked her thumb at her husband, still in his uniform and rolling his eyes.

'I'm okay,' she lied, nodding, wishing that Mart had only just got in and had been by her side to face Mrs Newman.

'We can have a proper catch-up tomorrow after the play?'

'Yes, great.' Poppy nodded again.

'How did it go?' Jade's mum looked towards the school.

Poppy sighed. 'Not great. Mrs Newman is a meanie poo-poo breath.'

Jade's mum laughed loudly. 'So I've heard!'

Poppy loosened her scarf, shook the damp from her hair and strode up the path to her front door, stamping her boots to rid them of the residue of snow. As she put her key in the lock the telephone on the little table at the foot of the stairs rang. Jo answered it.

'Oh! Hello, mate... No, it's Jo next door. One sec, she's just coming in, Mart! Quick, quick!' She beckoned to Poppy with her brightly painted fingernails as she held the receiver out towards her friend, knowing that every second counted.

Jo grabbed her cardigan and shut the front door on her way out. These calls were precious, and she wanted to give them privacy. She'd pop in tomorrow for a catch-up and a cup of coffee.

Peg, hearing it was her dad on the phone, threw herself face down into the sofa cushions, kicked up her heels and screamed into the soft pillows. Excitement turned her into a mad thing. She jumped up and pulled her nightie over her head to reveal her knickers and ran around the room with her arms flapping.

Poppy had grabbed the phone from her friend and sat on the stair a couple from the bottom. 'Hello, love! All okay?' Until she had heard his voice and his words of reassurance she wouldn't be able to control her heart rate and irregular breathing.

'All fine, it's all fine.' Mart knew enough to give her the words she craved, quickly and without preamble.

She exhaled sharply. 'We miss you.' Poppy pushed the phone into her face, trying to get as close to him as possible, cupping it with both her hands.

'I miss you too, so much. Kids okay?' This was the nature of their calls: no time for pauses or detailed descriptions, explanations or plans; it was all about exchanging the basics, ticking the boxes of concern so that when the receiver was replaced, you knew all was well.

'They're great. Maxy's getting so big and Peg, well... here she is. Hang on.'

Poppy handed the phone to her daughter, who was now right in front of her, having restored her nightie. She was pogoing up and down on the spot, her fists tightly clenched, her hair flying with every bounce.

'Calm down, Peg. Here he is. Speak slowly so he can hear you properly.'

Poppy handed the phone to her little girl, who, like her mother, cradled the mouthpiece out of which would come her dad's voice. She beamed at her mum. 'Hello, Daddy! I miss you a lot. I made you a card and I got Maxy to sign it, but he just scribbled on it. I've got my play tomorrow and I've been practising my lines with Jo after I did her makeover and we are gong to Granny Claudia's in two more sleeps.'

Poppy watched and listened. She returned her daughter's grin and strained to hear the faint tinny echo of the voice she loved, coming from so far away.

'I *am* being good, Dad, and I'm looking after Mummy... Yes... Yes I will.'

Peg's eyes grew wide with the effort of keeping her tears in check. Her lips trembled and her cheeks reddened until finally she could hold back no longer. Fat, hot tears tumbled down her face, turning her eyes bloodshot and making speech difficult. She tried to carry on smiling and it was this combination of distress and bravery that tore at Poppy's heart.

'Yes.' Peg nodded, attempting another smile as her mouth clogged with tears. 'I love you too.'

'It's okay,' Poppy whispered as she stroked her daughter's arm beneath her nightie. 'It'll be okay.' *'It will. Everything will be all right, Poppy Day, I promise.'* It was her nan's voice once again in her ear.

Peg handed the phone back to her mum and walked slowly to the sofa, where she sat with her hands in her lap and her back straight.

'It's me again, love.'

'Is she upset?' Poppy heard Mart swallow as he asked.

'A little bit, but she's fine now, playing and right as rain!' she lied, not wanting him to worry later. She knew how important it was to keep his mind on the job; that was how you stayed safe, that and a whole heap of luck.

'I love you, Poppy Day. I can't wait to get home and take you in my arms.'

'I can't wait either. I love you, Mart. I need you here, not there. But not much longer, baby.' *Another eight weeks.*

'That's right, not much longer.'

The phone went dead abruptly, but they were used to that. It could be for a million reasons, most of them down to a failure in technology or a dropped connection. It no longer sent her into a blind panic.

Poppy held the phone for a second or two after he'd gone, letting his final words linger in the atmosphere and waiting to see if by some miracle he might still be on the line. Then she took a deep breath and walked into the sitting room, where Peg sat with a steady stream of tears beating the same path down her face, which was ruddy from crying. She sat next to her on the sofa and placed her arm along her little girl's back, pulling her into her chest with her spare hand, cradling her little head into her neck. She kissed her and held her tightly.

'M... mummy?' Peg stuttered through her tears.

'Yes, darling?'

'He's... he's not coming home.' Peg struggled to catch her breath.

'No, he's not, not yet.'

'But I wished really hard and I said a prayer and everything and that's what I wished for! I just wanted my dad back, but it didn't work. I thought he was phoning to tell me it had reached him, but he wasn't.'

Peg shook her head and wriggled free of Poppy's grip so she could face her as she tried to sniff her tears back from where they had come.

'I'm sorry, Peg. I know it's tough. I hate him being away as much as you do and if I could wave a magic wand and make it all better, then I would.'

Peg smacked the sofa. 'It's not even a proper Christmas without Daddy here. I hate the stupid army!' She sank back against the cushions and both sat in silence, ordering their thoughts and replaying the words Mart had spoken.

'What did Mrs Newman say?' Peg piped up as she remembered the reason for her mum's outing, forgotten in the excitement of her dad's telephone call.

'Oh, she said you were fabulous!' Poppy smiled. 'She said you could do anything you set your mind to and that you were a smart cookie. I am so proud of you, Peg.' These last words were the absolute truth.

Peg's face broke into a grin and she wiped away the residue of her tears and runny nose with the back of her hand. 'Do you think she might let me be register monitor next term, Mum?'

Poppy swallowed the emotion that rose in her throat. 'I reckon, if you pay attention and are very polite, she just might.'

'That'd be brilliant, wouldn't it?'

'Yes, darling, it would.' She smiled at her little girl. 'I know, as a reward for doing so well, why don't we treat ourselves to one of the special chocolates from the tree?'

Poppy jumped up and walked in an exaggerated fashion over to the window. She lifted one of the little packets and shook it next to her ear. 'What on earth…?' She gasped and placed her hand on her chest. 'Peg! I'm afraid I have some very bad news! Something terrible has happened. We have been visited by greedy little mice who have eaten all our tree chocolates!'

Peg sank back against the sofa, giggling.

Poppy placed her hands on her hips. 'But they are the cleverest mice I have ever seen! How did they manage to put all the empty packets back on the branches without me ever suspecting a thing!'

Peg now howled.

'Unless...' Poppy stroked her imaginary beard. 'Maybe it wasn't mice. Maybe it was Max! Where is that big stick?'

Peg laughed through her words. 'It wasn't Maxy. It was me, Mum! I ate them all, but I did give him two.'

Poppy flopped down next to Peg and gathered her into her arms. The two of them sat quietly for a moment. 'It'll all be okay, baby, I promise you.' She felt her daughter nodding against her chest.

As she made her weary-footed way to bed a few minutes later, Peg stopped halfway up the stairs and poked her head over the bannister. 'Jade McKeever said you'd sort Mrs Newman out.' With that she plodded on towards her bedroom.

Poppy was beginning to like Jade McKeever more and more.

She slipped down on the sofa and, hugging a cushion to her chest, closed her eyes. She didn't want to sleep alone in their empty bed tonight. *I miss you, Mart, I really, really miss you.* She remembered his first tour, when she slept in their bed alone in the empty flat. Then, like now, she missed retrieving the little pile of dirty linen that gathered on the floor seven days a week – the pants, jeans, T-shirt and socks, evidence of a life lived in harmony with hers. And in the half an hour or so before falling asleep, she wondered what her man was doing, where he was sleeping, what he was thinking. Holding his pillow, she imagined his protective arms around her. She would talk to him about her day, how she was feeling, ask about his. She would hear his response and it was as good as chatting – *'Goodnight, baby, sweet dreams'* – as if he was dozing by her side. It gave her comfort then and it still did.

Two days later, Poppy slammed the boot of their little Golf and then patted the door, as if a little TLC might make the difference between the engine finally going pop and it getting them to Oxford and back safely. Bags and brightly wrapped gifts and toys were stashed in the boot space and the back seat was crammed with everything the children might need to keep them occupied for the journey. Each had a piece of electronic wizardry, a book, pens, colouring pencils, their pillow and a little lunch box filled with healthy snacks and a few not so healthy ones to see them through the arduous hour and thirty minutes spent on the A34. Poppy took particular pleasure in making their little packed lunches, something she would have loved when she was little, instead of two slices of white bread glued together with lumps of hard butter and a thin smearing of jam, shoved inside an empty bread bag.

'You off, mate?' Jo called from her front door, tea towel in hand.

Poppy nipped up the path of the house next door. 'Yes, just leaving. You've got a key if there are any disasters, haven't you?'

Jo nodded.

'See you when we get back.' Poppy winked at her friend.

'You bet.' Jo smiled. 'Happy Christmas, Pop.'

'You too, honey. Have a nice relax, spoil yourself a bit and then come over for supper when we are home.' She felt a little guilty, leaving Jo on her own.

'Yeah, I'll be fine. My mum and dad are coming down at

some point and my sister will pop in on Boxing Day. I'll be fine!' She smiled with false bravado. 'I meant to ask, how did the play go?'

Poppy bit her bottom lip. 'It was...' She searched for the words that failed to materialise and leant on the wall. 'Oh God, Jo, it was awful. It only lasted an hour, but I felt like we were there for days. Peg, bless her heart, had to say, "I will follow the farmer anywhere. He is my friend!" And she put her heart and soul into it, as though she was at the Palladium. Her head teacher said they wanted to give her a bigger part but couldn't rely on her to stay on-script.'

'Bless her. Well, if her acting doesn't work out, she can always do manicures for a living.' Jo held up her stripey fingernails.

Poppy jumped into the car. 'All set, kids?' she asked as she tilted the rear-view mirror.

'Yep, prepare to move!' Peg gave the rolling hand signal her dad had taught her.

Max tried to copy her. Poppy laughed and pulled out, heading towards the A303.

As they drove past the parade of shops, Peg waved and shouted, 'Happy Chritma!'

Poppy giggled and she too waved at anyone she saw. 'Happy Chritma! Happy Chritma, Larkhill!'

The Cricket family made the journey to Claudia Varrasso's house regularly, but twice a year, once in the summer and again at Christmas, they went and stayed. In the warm months they would potter around the neat walled garden, collecting soft fruit and transforming it into golden, butter-coloured crumbles eaten with sloshes of double cream at the garden table, under the shade of the gazebo. After the feast they would paddle in shorts and wellies, bucket in hand, in the stream that ran along the bottom of the village. With their brightly coloured nets they fished for sticklebacks and other tiddlers, which they would examine, name and then set back in the water with a 'Bon voyage!'

At Christmas, the cottage always smelt of spiced apple and cinnamon. The gauzy summer nets that fluttered in the breeze were replaced with dark tartan curtains, drawn to ward off the chill of winter. The fire roared in the grate and their summer night-time tipple of Pimm's, drunk on the grass with the last of the day's rays warming their skin, was traded for ruby-red port that glazed their throats as they sat with feet curled under their legs on the wide sofa.

Poppy had first met Claudia Varrasso at the funeral of Miles, her journalist friend and Claudia's son. The two had stood entwined, united by grief, both having shared the love of the man snatched from them in his prime by an act of monstrous violence. They had formed a unique bond, forgetting they had not met until after Miles' death, sharing stories about him and acting as a salve for each other's loss.

Poppy, without her mother in her life and with her beloved nan dead, welcomed the feminine, educated Claudia as a guiding figure. For Claudia, whose hope of becoming a grandmother had died along with her son, Poppy and her children were a blessing that she had no right to expect, but one that she nevertheless received gratefully and with love.

'Are you looking forward to seeing Granny Claudia, Max?' Peg asked, between mouthfuls of sweets.

Max nodded enthusiastically without any understanding of her question; he had been daydreaming as usual. Poppy smiled at him in the rear-view mirror and felt a rush of love for her little boy who still hovered close to babyhood and yet showed hints of kindness and purity, traits of the man he would become.

'You know she's not our real granny, don't you? But she is

our kind-of granny because we are all she's got, that's what
Mum said to Daddy.'

Poppy grimaced, reminding herself that she needed to
censor a little more of what came out of her mouth what with
Peg so alert and always within earshot. Max nodded again at
his sister, as though he was keeping up.

'And we are all she's got because her son was Miles, Mummy
and Daddy's friend, but he got blowed up before we were
born.' This she followed by allowing her fingers to rise and
splay into an elaborate arc, accompanying the action with a
gurgling sound of explosion.

'Oh, gosh.' Poppy felt her heart skip at the casual way in
which her little girl referred to what still tore holes in her heart.
'We aren't going to mention that to Granny Claudia though,
are we, Peg?'

'Why?' Peg leant forward. 'Doesn't she know?'

'Yes. Yes she does know but...' Poppy gripped the steering
wheel. When she thought of that day, the moment she lost her
good friend, it was as if she was watching a movie, playing the
events over in her mind with a clarity that time had not smudged.
The girl she saw in her mind's eye, standing lost in the centre of
the action, did not even vaguely resemble her; she looked like
an actress on a screen. This somehow made it easier for her to
remember, in fact easier to remember all the events surrounding
that terrible adventure that had shaped the rest of her life.

She decided to deploy every mother's last resort: divert and
distract.

'Ooh, did I mention that I got a card in the post for you
from Cheryl? You can open it with your pressies on Christmas
morning.'

'Did she just send a card?' Peg enquired.

'Yes, Peggy Alessandra, and I've told you about being

grateful for everything you receive, no matter how small. It's the thought that counts, right?'

Peg nodded, her nose and mouth curled in disapproval. She turned to her brother. 'Yes, Maxy, you mustn't be disappointed if Cheryl only sends cards from Lanzagrotty and not a present. She is your *real* gran that we don't see. And in all honesty, would not have passed an inspection to rehome a pet let alone have a child – there should be laws against it!'

Poppy gasped. 'Where on earth did you hear *that*?'

'It's what you said to Aunty Jo. Is that a secret too?' Peg looked perplexed.

'No! And it's not that these things are secret, it's just…' Poppy blew out through inflated cheeks. Sometimes she simply ran out of the right things to say.

She watched as her daughter wound down the rear window with some urgency. 'Are you okay, love?' she asked, wondering just how many sweets Peg had gorged on.

She stared at the wing mirror, calculating how quickly she might be able to cross to the inside lane and pull over. Just as she reached for the indicator, Peg screeched into the afternoon air, 'Come on, you Spurs!'

'Peg! I thought you were going to be sick! Did you just wind down the window and shout that at the car we passed?'

'Yes! They've got a West Ham sticker in their window and Dad and Danny next door said that West Ham fans are a bunch of walkers and that I had to shout that out if I saw their sign.'

Poppy was torn between hysterical laughter and fury. *I'll bloody kill you, Mart!*

'Well, you can ignore Dad and Danny, and I don't want you shouting that at anyone again, got it?' Poppy could see Peg miming and mimicking her on the back seat. 'I can see you in my mirror!'

Peg huffed. 'I can't even speak now! I'm not allowed to mention anyone getting blowed up, I can't talk about Cheryl keeping pets and only sending cards, and now I can't mention Spurs. Jade McKeever was right.' She folded her arms across her chest.

Poppy was desperate to know what Jade McKeever was right about now, but didn't want to open another can of worms; she was lacking the energy and inclination for another battle with her daughter. Silence reigned supreme for twenty seconds.

'Can I get a pet?'

Poppy sighed. 'Oh, love, not that again! I've told you, no, not yet.'

'But why not yet?' Peg stuck out her bottom lip.

'Because you would lose interest in it after a week and it would become *my* pet and I would be the one that ended up cleaning up guinea pig poo on top of everything else!'

'I wouldn't lose interest in it, Mum. I'd love it! It would be so cute! Jade McKeever says you can get guinea pig outfits on the internet. Her cousin got some and she dresses hers up to look like Sherlock Holmes or a lady ballroom dancer.'

Poppy snorted her laughter. 'That is hilarious and I agree, tempting, but the answer is still no.'

Peg, indignant, considered her next course of action. 'I know, I'm going to Sellotape my mouth shut to stop words coming out and then I can't say anything wrong if I can't say anything at all.'

Poppy chortled. 'Don't let me stop you.'

She listened to Peg rummaging in the craft box, then heard sticky tape being pulled and ripped. She flicked her head to the back seat, where Peg was sitting with four pieces of tape crisscrossing her mouth. Poppy laughed, wondering how long her daughter could last without talking. It would be at least another ten minutes before they arrived; she doubted she'd last the rest of the journey.

A couple of minutes later, Peg resorted to writing notes in her pad and holding them up for Poppy to read in the mirror. The first was, *I need a wee*, followed by, *Put One Direction on*. This second instruction Poppy couldn't read, sadly, not even when Peg held the note directly under her nose and pointed at each word in earnest.

'No, sorry, Peg, still not got it!'

Peg beat her fists either side of her on the back seat as Max chuckled and copied her.

Poppy pulled the car into the driveway and parked on the gravel. It had been months since she had last been there; the carpet of petals from the climbing white tea rose that clung to the old brickwork of the cottage had given way to snow. Despite the chill of winter, she felt the same flicker of warmth in the pit of her stomach. It was like coming home.

A lamp shone from every window of the cottage and the small wooden front door was adorned with a vast ivy and berry wreath. The two bay trees that stood either side of the porch had been decked with lights and the whole scene looked like it had come straight out of a fancy Christmas card.

Claudia trotted from the house in her festive apron and her reading glasses, with her hair slightly askew, waving and clapping her hands until they came to rest under her chin. She kissed Poppy warmly on the cheek. 'There you are! Kettle's on. Don't ever get your squeaky brakes fixed or I won't know it's you and you'd have to wait a good minute or so longer for your tea.'

Peg stood in front of the two women as they embraced. She emitted a series of grunts and hums, very keen for her taped mouth to be admired.

'Why have you got tape over your mouth, sweetie?'

'Don't ask.' Poppy shook her head as they made their way inside the cottage.

'She makes me laugh.' Claudia beamed at Peg, who peeled off her tape and rushed forward to hug her not-real Granny.

'I did my school play and I was sheep number six!'

'Wow! That sounds wonderful. Did you have any lines?'

'Yes, lots, and I got them all right!'

'I can't wait to hear all about it.' Claudia laughed.

Peg ran into the sitting room and wound a length of tinsel around her neck and over her shoulders, like a feather boa. 'Look, Maxy, I'm on the X *Factor*!'

Poppy tutted. 'I have to admit, I wasn't laughing much a couple of days ago, at parents' evening.'

'Oh, that bad?' Claudia grimaced.

'Not *bad* exactly. I think it's my fault partly – I had such an unhappy time at school that I'm a wreck before I even go inside.' Poppy lowered her voice. 'Peg's teacher is a bit of a cow and I can tell Peg doesn't like her. But thankfully she has her friend Jade McKeever to teach her everything she needs to know, and Jade McKeever's word is law, apparently!'

Claudia smiled, then shook her head. 'Her teacher sounds like a silly woman. She probably doesn't get Peg and that's a great shame. A child like Peg is a gift in a class if you use their energy and creativity correctly.'

Poppy thought how she would have loved to have had a teacher like Claudia – not that her school had taught Classics or had even heard of it!

Claudia sighed. 'But if she doesn't know how to get the best out of her, then she will just try to control her, keep her down and Peg will feel boxed in and there will be tension.'

'I think you should go in my place to the next one.' Poppy smiled and sipped at her tea.

'With pleasure! I fought a few battles for Miles in my time.'

Poppy watched as Claudia's eyes clouded. She couldn't imagine losing a child. How could you begin to accept that all the dreams and plans you had for them were not going to come to fruition? It was a horrible thought. The worst.

'It *was* slightly awkward. She thinks Mart is in prison!'

'What?' Claudia roared. 'Oh, he'd love that! He's off doing his bit and meanwhile his reputation is being destroyed! Poor thing.'

'I know, but I didn't feel I could say!' Poppy chewed her bottom lip. 'Mind you, he may as well be in prison, we see so little of him. In fact it might be a bit easier, at least we'd get visiting rights!'

'You must be missing him?' Claudia asked, her voice soft.

Poppy nodded. 'I really am. I don't sleep properly and I'm always worrying, I can't help it. They say you get used to it, but I certainly never have. When he's home I don't like being in a different room to him, let alone this.'

'Poor love.' Claudia smiled.

'I need to try and be more positive.' Poppy rallied herself. 'And I'm great most of the time. I keep it together for the kids, but when they've gone to bed and I'm on my own, or if something happens, like having to deal with Peg's horrible teacher, I just miss him.'

'That's understandable, but you know he's safe, don't you? Has he called?'

'Yes. The night before last, in fact, which was lovely.' She smiled at the memory. 'I know Peg really misses him and that makes me feel even guiltier. It's like everything is on hold – we don't have a properly family life when he's away and it's like a double blow when he's not here for a birthday or Christmas. I don't know what I'd do without you, Claudia. If we didn't come here and get spoiled, we'd just be at home, going through the motions, I do try, but…'

'Oh I know, love, you don't have to explain. It's the same for me. I miss Miles most of all at those times; even decorating the tree is painful. I picture his little hands passing me baubles and ornaments from the box when he was little. Without him it all feels a little pointless, but then I think of Peg and Max and it gives me the lift I need to keep going.'

Claudia's words made Poppy feel instantly guilty. What wouldn't Claudia give to have her son alive and working away, knowing she would see him at some point, one more Christmas.

Poppy looked at the beautiful Christmas tree that sat by the side of the vast fireplace and dominated the room. It was fairly short but full. Each bushy branch held a red china Santa, a reindeer or a salt-dough star, painted and glittery, probably Miles' handiwork. Strings of fairy lights flickered in abundance and the effect was magical.

Tens of cards were strung up above the fireplace between two hooks, each held in place by a tiny festive peg. On all the coffee tables and in the deep-set windowsills were cream-coloured church candles that sat in ornate rings of velvety green spruce with minute pinecones and red berries threaded through them. A fire crackled in the grate and piles of logs and kindling were heaped up in deep willow baskets alongside the fireplace, ready to meet their fate over the Christmas period.

Poppy watched as Claudia arranged a plate of cinnamon-sugar cookies to accompany their cups of tea. It felt lovely to be looked after and she felt the tension leaving her shoulders.

She noted the streaks of grey in the loose bun that sat at the nape of Claudia's neck; they had grown wider and lighter since Poppy had last seen her. The lines creeping from the corner of her eyes and across her honey-coloured brow were deeper and had multiplied. It was the first time Poppy had thought of her as old.

She wandered over to look at the photographs of Miles that were dotted around the room. Miles as a child with his late father on a boat, wearing shorts and grinning into the camera with his sailor's hat over one eye. Another at his graduation, his arm carelessly slung across his mother's shoulders in a gesture that had now assumed unbearable poignancy. Poppy's favourite was a black-and-white shot of him caught unawares, laughing, with his index finger placed over his mouth; it was a side view, his dark curly hair falling over his forehead and his eyes crinkled, just how she pictured them. It had been taken shortly before he was killed. She touched her fingers to his face. 'I love this picture.'

'Me too.' Claudia nodded. 'He was a handsome boy.'

'He was.' Poppy smiled.

Max was curled up sleepily on the sofa. She gathered him up, not wanting him to doze off just yet or he wouldn't sleep through the night. 'Come on, Max, let's show Granny Claudia your dinosaurs.'

'Yes!' Max squealed. As ever, a man of few words.

'Granny Claudia, I want to fly a plane!' Peg gushed, worried her Granny Claudia was about to be commandeered for dino play.

'What, right now?'

'No!' Peg shrieked. 'When I'm big.'

'Oh!' Claudia winked at Poppy. 'That hasn't worn off then. I remember you saying that the last time I saw you.'

'Yep. I still do. I want to fly all over the place.'

'I'll be sure to tell you which airline she is working for, Claudia, so that you can book a different one.' Poppy grinned.

'I might not even work for an airline, Mum. I might join the army and fly attack helicopters.'

'I thought you hated the army?'

'I only hate them because they've got my dad! I think I would like to be a soldier and fly over the baddies!'

'I don't think so.' Poppy's smile slipped a little.

Peg stamped her tiger-feet slippers on the wooden floor. 'But you said I can do whatever makes me happy!'

'I lied.' Poppy placed Max on her hip and carried him into the kitchen.

Claudia sat at the table and took him from her, scooping the sleepy boy into her arms, inhaling the scent of his sweet, blonde scalp. 'Ooh, you've grown, little man!'

'He's a solid lump of gorgeousness!' Poppy bent and gently bit his chubby leg. 'He's the image of Mart. It's weird for me, Claudia. Mart and I were already friends when we were Peg's age! That's only a few years for Max and I can see him morphing more into his dad every day.'

Max gave a very broad grin and clapped. The two women chorused their approval. 'Yay! Clapping – you are so clever.'

'Ducks here!' Max pointed to the window.

'Oh you *are* clever! He remembers the ducks in the pond last time he came! We shall go outside tomorrow after breakfast and see what we can find, Max. After you have opened your presents and once Mummy and I have had a good catch-up.' Claudia set the toddler down on the floor and watched him race around the floor with the wobbly gait of a drunk, still woozy from impending sleep and clutching a triceratops in his hand.

Peg got on the floor and followed her little brother, corralling him under the kitchen table. She pulled him close to her and whispered into his ear. 'Stay close by me when we open our presents, Max. They might try to trick us. Sometimes they might give you an orange and a walnut and make out that is your only present, but your real presents will be close by so don't have a turn, just say thank you very much! And if they give you a little bell wrapped up, don't look sad, that means they are going to take you into the garage and give you a bike or a scooter. It's like a little clue and it makes them very happy, but you mustn't let on that you know. Jade McKeever told me that. Okay?'

'Okay.' Max nodded as he bit the tail of his dinosaur.

Claudia smiled as she tuned into Peg's mumblings. The two children scuttled out from beneath the table and made their way back to the sofa, where they flopped and put the television on.

'I've been so excited waiting for you to arrive. It's lovely to have you all here.'

'We couldn't wait to get here!'

Claudia pulled up the sleeve of her shirt and glanced at her watch. 'I've got a last-minute errand to run, do you mind if I pop out for a mo?' She stood, reaching for her handbag and car keys.

'Not at all. Shall we come with you?'

'No, no! You stay here, get settled. It's literally a little something I want to pick up for the kids.'

'Oh, you don't have to get them any more, really.'

'It's important and I want to.' She kissed Poppy's cheek as she passed.

It felt natural, nice. Poppy had learned to welcome the human touch that had been absent during her childhood; being constantly pawed and kissed by the children had worn away any last vestiges of awkwardness.

Claudia was back within the hour and quickly set about preparing more tea.

'How are you *really* doing, Claudia?' Poppy asked, quietly, sincerely.

Claudia placed the teapot on the work surface and turned to face the young woman who under different circumstances might have been her daughter-in-law, the kind of girl she'd hoped Miles might marry.

'Oh, you know.' She let her eyes narrow with the beginnings of a smile. 'Good days and bad days, same as ever. It's not going to change for me, Poppy. I think I am as healed as I can be. It actually doesn't bother me anymore that I'm a bit broken; I don't want to heal any more than this. It keeps him present. I'm resigned to waking up every day with these rocks of grief hanging from me, weighing me down. I think about him all the time. Even now, if the phone rings, I think, oh, that'll be Miles. Or I might wake up and think, naughty boy, he hasn't phoned me for an age. And when I remember, it's like I'm receiving the news again for the first time; the shock nearly knocks me over, every single time.'

'I think about him all the time too.'

Claudia squeezed Poppy's hand. 'He was lucky to have a friend like you.'

Poppy shrugged, awkward at the sentiment, not wanting to cry, not here, not today. 'And I was lucky to have him. He was a great friend to me and when I look at Peg and Max it breaks my heart, partly that he didn't get to meet them, but also because he didn't live long enough to have this life. He'd have been a great dad.'

Both women paused in silence to consider this fact.

'I'm hun-ger-reee!' Peg hollered from the sitting room, breaking the solemnity of the moment.

Both women smiled and Claudia immediately rushed to the doorway of the sitting room. 'Come and see what you fancy.' She held out her hand, into which Peg slipped hers. 'I have a larder full of goodies, all your favourite things!'

'Max too!' he shouted as he stood and ran over to grasp her other hand.

Claudia opened the stable door of the large food cupboard to reveal a haul that would put any well-stocked supermarket to shame. The shelves were bursting with Christmas biscuits, the tins of which were decorated with snowflakes and snowmen, leaping reindeers, Father Christmases and angels with large trumpets. There were boxes of chocolates and jars of nuts with red ribbons tied around the lids. Pickles, chutneys and relishes sat next to crackers awaiting lumps of soft cheese. Rows of glass jars held shiny strawberry jam, sticky orange marmalade and the clear, golden honey that Peg liked to swirl over a plump, warm muffin. Red-and-white-striped candy canes poked their heads from buckets, squeezed between fat, twisted pretzels and dainty iced cakes decorated with sugar-paste holly leaves and packed into cellophane boxes. Several large boxed panettoni, their soft bread stuffed full of juicy raisins and candied orange and lemon peel, stood ready to be eaten over the coming days, roughly carved into thick slices and slathered with butter and scarlet homemade jam.

'Wow! Granny Claudia! You got all my favourite things!' Peg beamed.

'What you would like, *amore mio*?'

'I'd like some chocolate and a piece of cake, please.' Peg glanced at her mum, who gave her a lopsided smile and swallowed the suggestion that she go easy on the sugar. It was Christmas after all.

'Would you like chocolate and cake too, Maxy?'

Max gave an exaggerated nod, making sure his chin hit his chest before being thrown back into the air.

'You ruin these children!' Poppy laughed, thinking that these were the memories her kids would recall in years to come, so very different from her own lonely musings on Christmas Eve. She remembered wishing, hoping, for a book from Santa but being given eyeliner instead, bought on the knock from the catalogue; she remembered curling her feet, chilly, into her nightie for warmth, waiting for the sound of her mum's key in the door and her drunken stumbling in the hallway as she issued a loud 'Sshhhh!' to whichever beau she was trying to smuggle in.

The four of them sat contentedly in front of the fire and ate sugar-coated treats washed down with tea and pop. Max actually licked the sugar and cinnamon crumbs from the empty plate. Darkness fell and, as was their tradition, Granny Claudia turned off the lights and lit the candles. They all snuggled up on the sofa and she read their favourite poem, peeping over the pages at their faces, rapt and shining in the flickering candle glow.

With the lines 'When, what to my wondering eyes should appear, / But a miniature sleigh, and eight tiny reindeer' ringing in their ears, Peg, Max, Claudia and Poppy slipped their thick coats, hats and gloves on over their nighties and PJs and ventured out into the back garden. This custom had also started a couple of years back and while they were still to succeed in spotting Santa Claus dashing through the night sky, the possibility that they might was magic itself. They pulled the two cold wicker chairs, lined with fleecy blankets, into the middle of the patio and the children sat on the laps of the adults as all stared at the sky, waiting to see if the sledge would break through the thin cloud. Peg gazed up, wide-eyed, with her head under her mum's chin. She was torn between wanting to believe and knowing it wasn't logical. They saw stars, planes, a couple of bats, but no Santa on his sledge. Undeterred, they returned inside, Poppy convinced that she might have heard the jingle of bells behind them and Max nodding in agreement.

Once the kids were tucked up in the twin room at the back of the cottage, Poppy soaked in a hot bath full of bubbles, letting the water wash away the last few days. She placed her hand over her heart and felt its steady beat beneath her fingers. She felt the pulse of her heartstrings and closed her eyes, picturing her man, god knows where on Christmas Eve. 'I miss you and I love you.' She let the tears slip down her cheeks; after all, she was in the bath and this was allowed.

With her wet hair wrapped in a warm towel and her dressing gown tied over her thick pyjamas, Poppy descended the stairs and found Claudia on the sofa, under a duvet.

'They are soundo. They've had the most wonderful night.'

Claudia smiled. 'I have too.'

'Are you sleeping down here?' Poppy asked.

'Yes, I thought might like to tonight. I shall watch the fire die and make sure Rudolf eats his carrot and the bearded chap gets his mince pie and brandy.' She winked at Poppy. The kids had left the snacks on a little tray in front of the fireplace and the first thing they would do upon waking would be to check for crumbs and bite marks. Even Peg.

'Ooh, if you see him, ask him if I can have a dishwasher. Tell him I've been really, really good.'

'I've told you I'll get you a dishwasher if you'll let me.'

'No.' Poppy shook her head. 'I'm only joking. I don't know what I'd do with one, in all honesty, and washing up is my thinking time. I stand at the sink and shove my hands in the suds and switch off, it's quite therapeutic!'

'I'll have to take your word for it, darling.' Claudia smiled. 'Fancy a nice drop of red?'

'Well, ordinarily no, but I can't have you drinking alone, can I?'

'You are too kind!'

Poppy sidled under the duvet at the other end of the sofa while Claudia went to fetch the fancy pants bottle of wine and two very large glasses. Sinking down, Claudia pulled the duvet over her legs and uncorked the bottle, sending the heavenly woody scent up into the rafters of the cottage. Poppy was no wine buff, but when she took a sip of this deep, warm red, her nerves tingled and her taste buds whooped with joy, warning her throat of what was about to arrive. She swallowed the rich claret and savoured the spiced berry aftertaste that lingered.

'This is lovely!' Poppy held the glass up to the firelight and studied the long tears that clung to the glass.

'Miles' father used to say, no matter how hard-up we got, there were two things he would never tolerate: cheap shoes and cheap wine. Typical Italian!' Claudia smiled. 'He was a lovely man. I still miss him, although the poor old thing has rather been pushed from my thoughts as Miles has taken precedence. He looked like his dad, exactly like him in fact, but his personality was more like mine, a little bit cautious, bookish. I was glad that I could claim part of him.'

'Ten years this year.'

Claudia took a large gulp. 'Yes. It feels both like a lifetime ago and yesterday, depending on my mood.'

Poppy nodded. It was the same for her.

Claudia stared into the fire. 'I keep thinking that there will come a time when he will have been dead longer than he was alive and I'm not sure I want to be here then. It will make him feel very far away from me.'

This idea made Poppy feel unbelievably sad. 'I think about the future too. I know that someday someone will want to tell Peg and Max our story and it's not like when I was a kid, when you had to scrabble for scraps of information – they will only have to pop a few words into a search engine and there it'll be, my life, my story, warts and all!'

'They will be so proud of you. They are already. You're a fabulous mum.'

Poppy beamed at the best compliment she could receive. 'I want to be.' Her voice was small. She pictured walking home from school and spying her mum drunk on the floor of the pub in the precinct, propped against the wall, her legs folded, her T-shirt vest slipped to reveal her bra and a small glimpse of her chest. Poppy shuddered.

Claudia continued. 'Oh, you really are and you will find a way to tell them. Give it to them in bite-sized chunks. It will happen organically, you wait and see.'

'I hope so. I'm glad Mart's happy, I really am. It's important to me that he is doing something he loves, but sometimes I just wish he'd get a normal job so we could have a normal life. No more moving, no worry and no separation. I'd love to stay where we are.' Poppy hadn't realised she was crying until the sob left her throat. 'I'm sorry, Claudia, I didn't want to fall apart, not tonight.'

'You don't have to apologise to me, ever.' Claudia held Poppy's wine-free hand.

'It's just that sometimes I feel a bit overwhelmed by the idea of packing up again – another new school, worrying how the kids will take to it, new neighbours, new city. I'm not saying I want them to live like I did, never going anywhere or seeing anything new, but in some ways it was quite comforting to go to bed at night in the place where we had always lived, everything familiar and knowing everyone around me. There must be a happy medium, surely. I want to stay in a house where the kids' heights are notched on a cupboard door and I want to live somewhere long enough to plant something and watch it grow!'

Poppy took another sip of wine. 'Oh God, listen to me, rambling on. I've got a lot to be thankful for, I know.'

'It'll all come, darling, you wait and see.' Claudia squeezed her hand.

Both looked to the stairs as Max started crying and appeared on the top step, quickly followed by Peg, who carried him down. She plonked him on the sofa and climbed onto her mum's lap.

'Well, this is a lovely surprise!' Claudia beamed. 'Couldn't you sleep?' She stroked the hair from Max's forehead.

'Maxy had a bad dream.' Peg lay against her mum.

'Oh no. Are you okay now, Max?' Poppy bent and kissed him.

'Damonsters!' His bottom lip trembled.

'Oh, darling, there are no monsters.' Poppy glanced at Claudia. 'And tonight you have got Peg right by your side, keeping you safe.'

Max nodded, somewhat mollified.

Peg sat up straight. 'That's true, Mum, but I don't sleep in the same room as Max *every* night, do I?'

'No, love.' Poppy looked perplexed, unable to see where this was heading.

'You know what Maxy needs?' Peg grinned as if the most marvellous idea had just occurred to her.

'What?' Poppy asked.

'A guard guinea pig! One that sleeps in my room, that I can look after and not lose interest in, but is trained to keep an eye on Maxy and keep him safe!'

Poppy and Claudia laughed until their tears flowed. It was partly the wine, partly Peg's unashamed sales pitch, but also because it was Christmas Eve and all emotions felt somewhat magnified.

An hour after the kids had been restored to bed, Poppy yawned. 'Do you mind if I leave you to it?'

'Not at all. No doubt we'll be up early tomorrow.'

'Probably.' Poppy smiled. 'Do you want me to sleep down here with you? I don't like leaving you on your own. Especially as you don't have a guard guinea pig!'

Claudia's eyes twinkled. 'What *are* you going to do with her? No, I'm fine, darling. You go on up. I like my own company, this is *my* thinking time. There is something quite magical about tonight, don't you think?'

Poppy bent low and kissed Claudia on the cheek. 'I do now.'

'Night night.'

Poppy poked her head into the kids' room. She loved to watch their chests rise and fall with each breath, their hair spread over their pillows like halos. She felt the familiar twist to her heart that threatened to burst with love for these two little people she and Mart had created.

It was 4 a.m., according to the display on her phone, when Poppy was jolted from sleep. She had heard a noise, possibly the loo door being closed or possibly the central heating in this old house whose sounds were so different from that of her own. Propping herself up on her elbow, she listened for any cries coming from the kids' room. When there were none, relieved and happy at the prospect of more sleep, she turned her pillow over and with the cool cotton against her cheek, fell back into a deep slumber.

'He's beeeeeeeen!' Peg screamed from her room, providing the alarm that woke the whole house.

Poppy checked her phone: it was five in the morning. She thought of her nan, who used to walk around the flat with a torn paper crown from a cracker stuck on her head, and Wally, dozing in his chair, his stomach full of turkey and Christmas pud, relieved that he hadn't been served his usual bacon. Then her thoughts turned to Mart, who would be waking up alone. 'Happy Christmas, my darling man, wherever you are.'

Poppy closed her eyes and twisted the little gold band on the third finger of her left hand, proof that someone wanted to be married to her – a fact that gave her a jolt of joy every time she remembered his teenage proposal. The two of them had been mucking around together in the concrete play area of the flats. Mart was leaning on a post, drawing on a fag and watching her on the swings. And she was swinging higher and higher, kicking her legs back and forth.

'Look, Mart,' she'd yelled, 'I'm going to do a looper, right over the bar!'

'Don't, Poppy, you'll hurt yourself.' He looked away.

'I won't, I bet I can do it!' Poppy pumped her legs, taking the rickety swing up higher until it was level with the bar.

He could hardly stand to watch as the chain squeaked and her legs blotted out the sun with rhythmical regularity. It happened suddenly – the seat wobbled and she flew through the air with a guttural shriek, landing in a heap by the bins. Winded, she sat up and held her aching ribs.

'Poppy!' Mart ran to where she had landed and crouched down, holding her hand between his palms. 'Are you hurt?' His breath came in short bursts.

She swallowed and composed herself, running a mental checklist and grateful not to have landed splat down on the tarmac. 'I think I'm okay!' She giggled with relief as a large bruise started to spread up her arm and thigh.

'You silly cow! You frightened me,' he snapped.

'I was only mucking about. You're not the boss of me.' She shook her hand free.

Martin Cricket cupped her face in his hands and spoke in a voice so low, she had to concentrate to hear. 'I never want to be the boss of you, but I do love you. I always have and I always will. If I even think about you getting hurt, I feel sick. I want to take care of you, Poppy Day, and I want you to take care of me. I want you to marry me and I want us to live together until we get old and die.'

'What?' Poppy shook her head. Maybe she was concussed.

'Will you marry me, Poppy Day?'

She had stared up at him and considered what it would be like to be looked after by this man she loved. Then she had smiled, knowing that this was where she belonged, right by his side. Nodding, she'd kissed his palm with a shaking hand. 'Yes, yes, I'll marry you.'

Peg thundered into the room and jumped on the bed. 'Happy Christmas, Mummy!'

'Happy Christmas, my darling.' Poppy kissed her daughter, who jumped off and lifted Max up onto the mattress. All three snuggled under the duvet, kicking their feet, bubbles of excitement filling their stomachs.

'Has Father Christmas brought you presents, Max?'

'Yes!' Max grinned. Poppy ran her fingers through his blonde hair, sticky with sleep and juice that had splashed from his sippy cup.

'There is a pillowcase full of presents at the bottom of my bed and Max has one too and I honestly think that Father Christmas left them for me, Mum! I really do.' She beamed at Poppy.

'Well, good.' Poppy didn't want to find out how the conversation might progress.

'Can we go downstairs and open our presents?' Peg now bounced up and down.

Poppy rubbed her eyes and scraped her hair into a scrunchie. 'We can go downstairs but I don't want us to disturb Granny Claudia just yet.' She was sure Peg's hollering could have been heard back in Larkhill, but wanted to give Claudia a moment alone on this joyous and difficult day. 'Why don't we tiptoe downstairs and give her another half an hour? Do you think we can do that?'

Both kids nodded, Peg with a slight look of irritation.

They threw on their dressing gowns and padded into the sitting room, where the Christmas tree lights were on and a fire roared in the grate. Claudia must have been up early – if she had slept at all. Peg bent down and gathered two little square boxes from under the tree; each had an oversized label attached to it, one saying 'Peg' and the other 'Max'.

Peg shook hers beside her ear and heard a faint tinkling. 'Who are these from, Mummy?'

Poppy turned the box over in her hand. 'I haven't a clue, darling.' She looked at the label: it was Claudia's handwriting. 'Put them back under the tree and we'll wait for Granny Claudia.'

'No, it's okay, Poppy, they can open those now.' Claudia's voice came from the kitchen. She beamed. 'Happy Christmas, my loves!'

'Happy Christmas! You're up early! Are you okay?'

'I'm more than fine.' Claudia enveloped Poppy in a hug and as she pulled away from her, took the scrunchie from her hair, allowing it to fall in a coppery curtain against her neck. 'You have beautiful hair, Poppy, you should show it off more.'

Poppy smiled, embarrassed, and tucked the loose tendrils

behind her ears.

'Can we open these now then?' Peg shook the little box; the suspense was nearly killing her.

'Yes!' Claudia clapped. 'Open them right now!'

Peg tore the paper to reveal a little brown box, then did the same for Max. She lifted the lid to reveal a shiny bell, the kind that sat snugly on handlebars. Peg stared at Max, dying to speak, but knowing she mustn't blow the surprise. 'Oh, a bell! That's lovely, thank you very much, Granny Claudia.' She smiled sweetly.

'Yougranicordiya!' Max grinned.

Peg gave a small cough, as if waiting to be led to her shiny new bike or scooter. She hoped it was a scooter, with silver wheels and a blue sticker and rubber foot pads, the same as Jade McKeever's.

Poppy stared at Claudia, slightly puzzled by the little gift. Although mentally two steps behind her daughter, she was starting to suspect there was more to this present than met the eye.

'It's going to be a chilly old day, who thinks we might need to fetch more logs from the garage?'

Peg nearly burst with anticipation. 'I definitely think we need more logs!' She jumped up and down on the spot.

Poppy shook her head, trying to keep up.

'What about you, Maxy, do you think we need more logs?'

He nodded vigorously.

'Be a dear, Poppy, take them out for me while I make some tea.' Claudia sniffed.

'Sure.' Poppy opened the side door and gasped as the wave of cold air filled her lungs. There had been a fresh fall of snow in the night and the garden looked like a winter wonderland. The birdbath, lights and wicker chairs had all been sprinkled with a powdery dusting. It was quite beautiful.

Poppy lifted Max as they approached the garage. Peg raised the latch and pushed open the side door. No one moved for a second or two, each paralysed with shock and surprise. Then the surge of adrenalin hit. Peg screamed and then she cried, unable to stop the sobs that built in her chest and escaped loudly. Poppy gasped as the tears rolled down her own face, and Max wriggled to the ground and toddled across the room.

It wasn't new bikes or scooters that waited for Peg and Max in the garage. There in the soft lamplight, with a tartan blanket over his legs and cocooned in the moth-eaten armchair that had never quite made it to the tip, with sand in his boots and dust on his uniform, sat their daddy.

Mart stood and rushed forward, crushing Poppy to him and with his spare arm around Peg as Max clung to his leg.

'I heard my girl needed me,' he whispered into her hair.

'She did.' Poppy placed her mouth against his cheek, inhaling the scent of him, confirming he was real.

'I'll always come when you need me, you know that.' Mart kissed her on the mouth and then bent down to lift his children, one in each arm. They stood just like that for a minute or so, happy to be reunited, a little family.

As they made their way back inside the house, Claudia stood at the back door, simultaneously crying and laughing. She hurried over to Poppy. 'I couldn't tell you. He swore me to secrecy!'

Poppy wrapped her in a hug, too emotional to speak. She stared at her husband, propped against the sink, holding a mug of tea between his palms. She shook her head, unable to take it in. He was in the kitchen! He had come home!

'How, Mart?' she eventually managed.

'They told me a few weeks ago that they might cut our tour

short. I didn't want to say anything in case it didn't happen – you know how these things work.'

She nodded. She knew, better than most.

Mart continued. 'I wasn't sure if I could get back, even when they did cut the tour. I didn't want to raise your hopes, or mine. I only knew for certain I was coming home when they confirmed there was a seat for me on a helicopter and then a plane and then another plane. It all happened very fast. I can't tell you how happy I was to touch down at Brize.'

Poppy smiled at him, sharing recollections of the place that held such strong memories for them both. It meant home, safety.

'When did you get here?'

'About four this morning. Claudia waited up for me. I kipped on the sofa until we heard you all.'

'Do you have to go back?' Poppy chewed her lip, hardly daring to ask.

'No, that's it. Back in Larkhill now – you're stuck with me.' He squeezed his wife's hand.

Peg hugged her dad tightly around his middle. 'I missed you.'

'I missed you too. You've grown, you both have!'

'I'm going to try and be register monitor next term, Dad.'

'That sounds good.' He smiled.

'Can I get a pet? I would really like a guinea pig called Toffee.'

Mart laughed. 'Well, I don't see why not.'

Poppy sighed and rolled her eyes at Claudia.

Peg reached up and pulled her dad's neck forward until his ear was level with her mouth, so that he alone could hear her whisper. 'I prayed and wished you home to me, Daddy, and it worked, didn't it?'

'Yes,' he whispered back, looking from her to his wife and son, smiling. 'It worked.'

Mr Portobello's
Morning
Paper

One

It was a crisp February morning as Sophia Perkins stood on the pavement with her hands in her cardigan pockets and stared at the shop on the opposite side of the road. Cars sped by and a bus pulled in a little further along, the wheeze of its brakes filling the air as a grease-spotted chip wrapper skipped along the kerb. This was it. The day she had been thinking about and planning for since she first spotted the 'To Let' sign almost six months ago. It had been the day after she had resigned from her job without any plan for her future – an uncharacteristically spontaneous act. Now she wished her mother and father could have been here to see this day. They had always been her most strident supporters as well as her best friends, and she missed them more than she could say; to lose them within months of each other felt cruel.

Quickly, she painted on a smile and swallowed the lump in her throat; this was no time for maudlin reflection. Plus, if her parents hadn't passed away, leaving her the contents of their house – namely books, books and more books – then she would not have had the stock that made opening 'Perkins' Book Emporium' possible. She smiled coyly at the rather grand name, the low hum of excitement in her gut warming her.

It had been her dream for a number of years to give up teaching English, to which she had dedicated a large chunk of her life, and open a second-hand bookshop. Sophia was a realist, as most of us are when middle age comes a-knockin', and she knew that of the many children who had passed through her classroom, only a select few would give her a second thought; possibly as they clutched their degree scrolls or sank into a soft chair on a rainy day with the comforting weight of a book resting in their eager palms. But most, she was sure, would not be able to put a name to the quiet English mistress who wore men's lace-up shoes because her feet were flat and square. Nor would they remember the last time they spotted her walking the corridors with her tawny hair scraped back into a loose bun, the top button of her floral blouse done up, her cat's-eye glasses sitting on the middle of her nose, and more often than not with a book in her own hand. She was and would remain as anonymous to most of them as they were to her. And what a pity it was!

It hadn't always been this way. She recalled wistfully the first time she stepped into a classroom, fresh out of college and with energy enough to motor all the wonderful change she foresaw. The students had fired questions at her:

Jude the Obscure? *Is that his surname?*
How long is this book?
Can I doodle in it?
Are you married, Miss?
Who do you support?
What does S stand for, is it Susan?

And Sophia had known there was no place she would rather be, happy to provide the fuel for these enquiring and humorous minds.

But over time everything had changed and it had become a very different story.

In the last few years of her teaching career, she had become acutely aware that the excited anticipation when she met a new school year was gone. And her belief that with the right books and encouragement, she could change the lives of these children in her charge was long buried. Too many times she'd seen her ideals proved wrong. So she wouldn't miss it, any of it. Not the endless hours of marking long after the school bell had rung, and not the bureaucratic middle managers who seemed intent of hindering rather than helping her to do the job she had trained for. Her will had been broken and she was sick and tired of trying and failing to explain to those more interested in the flash and strobe of a screen than the tightly packed black letters of a story typed on to a page just how magical the printed word could be and the many, many worlds they could transport you to.

There was one exception, one moment that stuck in her mind, one boy whose enthusiasm for her classes made him stand out. His name was Tyler, and he was a boy who had secretly wept, swiping the tears from his cheeks when Winston betrayed Julia, the woman he professes to love, in Orwell's *Nineteen Eighty-Four*. As she watched him shield his face from his peers, Sophia was not only moved by the effect it had on him, but also saddened that he lived in a world where his tears would be deemed shameful. This was a boy touched by literature and her hopes for his future life as a bookworm were high. That was until he sauntered in to class one day, late and clearly distracted.

'*Have you read it, Tyler?*'

'*Nah, Miss, I watched some of the film instead.*'

'*You watched some of the…*'

Words had failed her, and Sophia knew this was the precise moment that the last sprinkles of enthusiasm – all that now remained of the solid rocks of hope and aspiration she had felt when newly qualified, rocks that had been pummelled into a mere dust of indifference over the years – fled her body.

She had closed the book – *The Great Gatsby* – and nodded, dismissing the boy from her desk with a slight shoo of her hand. The same hand that immediately and without hesitation selected the slim silver ballpoint pen from her pencil case and wrote at the top of the piece of paper in front of her:

> Dear Mr Blandford,
> It is with some small measure of regret that
> I write to inform you…

Mr Simon Blandford. She especially would not miss the meek head of school; Simon was a lanky hill runner who wore the same mustard-coloured corduroy jacket with leather buttons in all weathers and nodded with a sage smile whether the news she was delivering was that someone had won an award, achieved an A* or had been arrested for intent to supply in the alleyway at the back of the canteen. They had come to blows only once, when Sophia, frustrated by his lack of support over the cuts in library funding, had shouted at the man, 'For goodness' sake! What does it take to see you riled, fired up, feeling alive!?'

He had, of course, neglected to answer, offering instead his usual sage and irritating smile. Now when she thought of the incident, Sophia felt a curious mixture of embarrassment at her uncharacteristic outburst, and exhilaration. It had felt good to stand her ground.

That day when she got home from school, her mother, the person who knew her best, had noted her melancholy and said, 'Hang in there, darling, these collapsing cardboard boxes full of literary treasures will one day line the shelves of your own shop and you will be able to sit among them as if they are your friends, and it will be glorious!'

And here she was on the day that dream became a reality.

There was much she liked about her new venture. She had no boss and no education board or local authority to report to, no contact with aggressive or disillusioned parents who thought they knew what was best for their little darlings, and conversely no frustrated conversations with the parents who simply didn't care; there were no reams and reams of health-and-safety paperwork to complete, likewise on-line forms of assessment. No endless nights of drinking coffee while red-ringing pitiful essays, which she knew for a fact had been scrawled hastily on the bus so as to avoid punishment. Those who executed the set task in this manner would sometimes smirk as they lay their sorry offering on a pile of similar papers, but they never fully realised the wonderful opportunity they were giving up. Oh! To be asked, nay, *told* to spend hours inside the heads of Woolf, Dickens, Hardy and Brontë! To be given *time* to dive into the pages and dance among the words and particular punctuation that turned each paragraph into pure poetry – poetry which fed the soul! But no. Most of her charges would rather scribble what they could glean second-, third- or even fourth-hand from the internet on to one side of paper ripped from a friend's book as the number 84 trundled through town. Job done.

Fools, the lot of them.

She knew that some of them, when they were older and their life was preoccupied with paying the bills and running like mad on the treadmill of life just to stand still, might just long for a day of reading...

This state of affairs saddened and angered her in equal

measure. And she had reached the conclusion that responsibility for these young minds was not hers.

Sophia also liked the welcoming tinkle of the little brass bell every time the green front door of her bookshop opened. She liked the stripped wooden flooring with its dips and gnarls, guessing at the many different heels that had trotted, skipped or even danced across the surface over the last four decades. Each set belonging to a pair of feet, attached to a person who walked the earth and had their own tale to tell – no doubt a tale of love, loss and longing: the universal themes. And a tale that ended in death because this was how all of our stories ended, whether we liked to acknowledge it or not.

She had once read a quote, that she had since heard attributed to Buddha, Gandhi and Stephen King, which had stayed with her.

The trouble is, you think you have time.

They bothered her, these eight simple words. They bothered her because she wasn't done, not nearly, and yet she was aware more than most of how time could simply... stop. As always when she thought of this, she painted on her smile and tried not to picture the lick of brown hair that hung over his right eye, the almost imperceptible cross of his front two teeth and the way his brows lifted as he listened. Each and every part of him was catalogued in her mind, there for perfect recall whenever the need arose. And the need had arisen a lot in the twenty-two years, four months, two weeks and five days since his time had just... stopped.

Sophia cleared her throat, shook her head and adjusted the floral Peter Pan collar of her blouse over the neck of her cardigan.

She also liked the brass step over which she had to tread to enter this magical world of stories, but most of all, she liked the smell of the place. Despite being a new venture, the building, contents and fittings were not, and it was these that helped create the comforting, nostalgic fug that brought to mind roaring fires, country walks, soft socks and afternoon tea. It was a heady perfume of dust, old leather book jackets, the faint scent of her mother's lavender soap, perfume and hand cream that lingered on the many, many pages, and the pervading aroma of the previous occupant, a man who had been in residence in this building for the last forty-odd years.

She knew a little about him: he was a portly accountant who wore a navy-blue pinstriped suit that had gone shiny in patches; a gold watch chain dangled in a loop from his waistcoat button to a neat little double-seamed pocket, and his brogues were brown with metal bits in the heels that made his every step click. And when the fancy took him, he could be seen sporting a rather lovely buttonhole that varied according to the season.

A dandy.

That's the word she thought best applied to the man. His name was Mr Portobello. This Sophia only found out when enquiring via the man's solicitor, a Mr Hayes, about the lease. She had seen Mr Portobello out and about – who hadn't? He was, as the phrase went, a real character; someone who stood out, a man everyone recognised, but knew little about. He kept himself to himself, but was one of those people who was like the local war memorial, the fancy library steps or the Gothic fountain in front of St John's, part of the fabric of the street, someone you expected to see, although usually didn't look at too closely. To comment on him, mention him, and be able to describe him meant you were part of that community: a local. She didn't know if he was aware of the role he played, but Mr Portobello, like other characters, familiar buildings, architectural quirks and local customs was part of the glue that gave the high street its community feel.

Mr Portobello, the solicitor had informed her, was one of a kind, as stubborn as he was smart and with a heart as big as the county. He didn't own a computer and apparently wrote daily in oversized ledgers with a stubby Montblanc while he smoked cigars – big fat Havanas, to be precise, rolled, he had assured her, on the thigh of a virgin. Mr Hayes had laughed loudly at the thought and, in truth, his manner had unnerved her a little. Right now, though, on her very first day of trading, she gave the solicitor no thought at all and was nothing but grateful to the enigmatic Mr Portobello and the lingering scent of his delectations, which gave a layer of something deep and woody to her beloved shop.

'*My* bookshop!' She bit her bottom lip as she turned the natty metal sign to read 'Come in! We're open!' before racing swiftly around to the slightly rickety stool behind the reclaimed wooden counter where the till sat. She thought it best to be in position when her very first customer walked through the door.

She fidgeted nervously, neatening up the clutch of brown paper bags with twisted twine handles that had been stamped with the words 'Perkins' Book Emporium' inside a fancy ornate circle. After much deliberation, she had settled on green ink, because it matched the front door and give her an identity of sorts, a brand. Plus, she knew of no book lover who could resist the lure of a green cloth cover. Green books were her very favourite. As were green doors.

Sophia smiled and let her eyes rove the wooden shelves that stopped a little shy of the deep plaster cornicing that itself carried the yellow tinge of cigar residue. In the centre of the ceiling a plaster rose took pride of place. It was a thing of such magnificent beauty! A hand much steadier and more patient than her own had picked out the cornucopia of flowers with fine gold lines and the merest hints of pink, olive green, teal and mustard. This beautiful work of art fascinated her and had done from the first time she saw it, making her wonder who had had the time, eye and patience to execute such a feat. A stunning six-armed oil lamp chandelier hung from it, the silver dulled to a burnished gold, supporting an opaque grass-green glass dome above. This also captivated her; it would not have looked out of place in a Viennese ballroom. Whenever she gazed at it, Sophia would hear the swish of full skirts, the trill of gentle laughter and the whisper of promises from moustachioed men, barely audible over the strident woodwind and delicate strings of a German waltz.

A grey-haired woman in a heavy scarf, who had stopped in front of the window and was peering in, interrupted her daydreams. Sophia felt a slight spike of adrenalin, a heady mixture of excitement and nerves. She willed her to come inside, whilst at the same time half hoping the woman might walk on, as the thought of actually entertaining her first ever customer was almost more than she could stand.

Ohmygodohmygodohmygod…

The woman took three steps to the left and pushed on the green door. The bell gave its satisfying little tinkle.

Right, Sophia, just as you have practised; you have seen this moment in your head a million times…

'Good Morning. Welc—'

'Have you got the, erm, the latest by whatshisname?' the woman interrupted, speaking quickly, as she stood on the brass step with her head inside the door and her body out in the street, hanging on to the door handle. Her manner suggested that to have stopped at all was the biggest inconvenience. 'The one about the dog?' she urged. 'You know, the dog and the thingy, erm, the, er, the blind man. The blind man who came from

Russia with the dog and they try and take the dog off him, as it's not allowed in his hotel, which his aunt owned before the war? That one. Set in Eastbourne. No, Bournemouth, or maybe Sidmouth. One of them, anyway.'

'Oh!' Sophia thought she might have read about something vaguely similar in the Sunday papers a little while ago; her fingers twitched towards the latest catalogue from which she could order more contemporary works. 'I don't actually have a copy here, but I could order it for you, or I do have lots of lovely thrillers if that's what you like reading—?'

'No, no, don't worry! Don't worry!' the woman again interrupted and shook her head, her nose and top lip raised as if actually offended. 'I'll order it online meself.'

'Thank you for—' Sophia flinched as the front door slammed. She raised her shoulders and her stomach bunched, half expecting the two etched panes of glass in her beloved green door to fall right out of their frames and on to the pavement. They didn't. Thankfully.

Okay, that was a trial run, Sophia, not your actual first customer...

She smiled and walked around the shop, pushing in spines of novels so they aligned with their neighbours, stopping to run her finger over a particularly fine cover or to pinch the dust from the top of a book, which must have slipped under the radar of her feather duster when unpacked.

The bell gave its little tinkle.

'Hello?' a friendly voice called from the front of the shop. Sophia rushed out from behind the bookshelves that bisected the two rooms to find a very smiley woman standing by her till in muddy wellington boots. She had left the sloppy imprint of her footwear on the wooden floor. Sophia tried not to notice; it would, after all, be easy enough to sweep up when dry.

'Hello, welcome to Perkins' Book Emporium. How can I help you today?'

'Oh! Goodness me!' The woman laughed loudly and took a while to catch her breath as she snorted. Sophia wondered if her greeting was a little too much. She'd have to work on it. She felt the blush of embarrassment rise from her chest up over her neck.

'Actually, I was wondering if I could help *you*.' The woman bent to lift a shallow cardboard banana box and plonked it on the countertop. 'My aunt's having a clear-out and asked me to take these to the charity shop at the top of the high street, but I saw your shop and thought, why lug them all the way up there when you might like them?'

'I'm not sure.' Sophia eyed the box. There might be gems in there that she could read and then sell, or it might be junk; she wasn't sure how best to proceed.

The woman reached in and pulled out a copy of *Little Women*.

'Ah, one of my favourites! Which Little Woman are you? I think I'm probably Beth, but of course we all want to be Jo.' Sophia felt a rush of affection for the characters she thought of as friends. She pushed her glasses up on to the bridge of her nose, aware she might be gabbling.

'I don't... I don't read myself.' The woman grimaced and Sophia stared at her. What was it with people? That phrase, 'I don't read...', was like saying, 'Oh, I don't breathe... I don't sleep... I don't eat... I don't dream... I don't wish...'

HOW COULD PEOPLE NOT READ? It was entirely beyond her.

'Well,' she said, recalling the much-practised response she used to give to pupils who were less than keen on books. 'I think reading is a habit; one you can get into or slip out of.

I personally can't sleep unless I've read a chapter or two of something! I can highly recommend it.'

'But that's what the TV's for!' The woman laughed again, good-naturedly no doubt, but it left Sophia a little disinclined to take the books; she almost wanted to punish the woman's lack of reading by making her walk to the charity shop at the top of the high street with her heavy load. 'There's a lot like this' – she held up the book once more – 'and a few leathery-looking ones as well.'

Sophia was first and foremost a bookworm and the idea of snaffling through a pile of leather-bound books to read or to discover an old favourite was an opportunity she could not pass up. Plus, as she had always told her pupils, it's nice to be nice.

'Well, if you want to leave them, I shall have a sort through and any I don't want I could take up to the charity shop for you?'

'You are a doll!' The woman pushed the box further on to the counter and placed Jo, Meg, Beth and Amy inside the dark confines before closing the lid. 'Shall we call it twenty quid?'

'Twenty quid?' Sophia was confused.

'For the books?' The woman nodded at the box.

'But you were taking them to the charity shop.'

'Yes, but you are not a charity, are you?' The woman put her hands in her pockets and her smile faded.

'No, but...' Sophia struggled to know what to say, the right thing to do. She had thought she was doing the woman a favour, but then again, she might possibly find one or two books to sell...

'Tell you what' – the woman took a deep breath – 'you seem nice, let's call it a tenner.'

Slowly Sophia made her way around to the till and pressed

the button to ping it open. She eyed her carefully selected float and pulled a ten-pound note from the little plastic section in the money drawer before handing it over to the woman.

'Cheers, see you again!' The woman left, and Sophia stared at the cardboard box, wondering what had just happened.

As she lowered it behind the counter, thinking she could sort through it later, the bell pinged again, and Sophia looked up eagerly. This time there were two strikingly dressed women, each wearing a flowing, black cotton embroidered frock with striped tights and heavy work boots, and they both had an abundance of curly hair – one ginger, one dark. They were make-up free save for dark-red lipstick, which meant you couldn't help but stare at their mouths. Bewitching. Witchy.

Sophia hoped her thoughts were quiet.

Double, double toil and trouble...

They advanced at speed in an over-confident manner and before they spoke, she sensed they were not here to buy, or even browse, books.

'Hello!'

'Hi.'

They both waved, despite standing right in front of her.

'Are you the manager or the proprietor?' the red-haired witch asked.

'I'm both.' This statement alone was enough to restore her flagging spirits somewhat.

'Smashing, we are from MABS.'

'MABS?' She had never heard of it.

'Mother and Baby Sing-along – held three times a week in the church hall at the back of St John's with squash, tea and a biscuit afterwards.' The dark-haired lady spoke up.

'Ah, right! Well, no wonder I've never heard of it. No baby! So no mother and baby sing-along for me,' she babbled, trying to ignore the brief look of abject pity the two women exchanged with heads tilted and bottom lips protruding. Sophia looked away, knowing they were right. It was a pity she was not a mum. It was a pity she had no partner, it was a pity that her fiancé had not done as the Green Cross Code man had advocated and looked both bloody ways! 'Anyway, how can I help you today?' she asked, managing to keep her composure.

The dark-haired witch spoke up. 'Can we possibly put a leaflet in your window?' She unfurled a small purple poster with the word 'MABS' written across the top in bubble writing, and a picture of a smiling toddler sitting on a mat, holding a plastic tambourine and looking a little nonplussed.

'Oh!' Again she was unsure of the right thing to do or say. These were the very things that she was unprepared for, and each interaction felt a million miles away from the selling and informing on books that she had envisaged during the lonely commute to and from school whilst planning her escape.

'Your neighbours on both sides have taken one, and Waterstones have one too, in their café. It's considered a community thing and makes people stop and read your door and then their eyes stray left or right and they see your books!'

'Right, yes, of course,' Sophia readily agreed. *I mean, if Waterstones have done it…*

'Brilliant.' As soon as Sophia had finished speaking, the dark-haired witch leapt into action, pulling out a mini tape dispenser and proceeding to fix her leaflet to the front door facing out. Irritatingly, it was at an angle. 'Thanks a mill, and good luck with the new venture!' She opened the door and held it open for her friend.

'Thank you!' Sophia smiled, remembering that today's browser or visitor might be tomorrow's customer.

'Your shops smells of…' The woman paused and sniffed the

air. 'It smells like my gran's old house.' And the bell gave its little tinkle as she closed the door behind her.

Whether intended or not, Sophia took this as the very best compliment. She looked at the small gold watch that sat on her wrist. It had been her mother's, and she ran her finger over the thin leather strap, feeling close to her.

It was ten o'clock.

Was that all? Only one hour of trading? It felt like an age since she had stepped over the threshold but she had yet to sell a single book. Was this how it would always be? She didn't know who she could ask. She set to with the dustpan and brush to remove what she could of the mud that lay in an ornate lacy pattern on the floor.

The bell rang and Sophia looked up in time to see none other than Mr Portobello, former resident of the premises, enter with purpose. He was a large man, tall and rotund, his thinning hair greased over his bald pate with what looked to be hair oil. He was still splendid in his navy-blue pinstriped suit, as if this were any other day, as if this were still his place of work. She jumped from her stool and went to greet him.

'Mr Portobello!'

'Yes, and you must be Miss Perkins.'

'Yes, Sophia, please.'

'And how are you settling in, Miss Perkins?'

'Well, first day today, as I'm sure you know. I'm nervous, excited and anxious. And please call me Sophia.'

The man gave her a sideways glance. 'You have a lot of books.'

'I guess that's a good thing, being a bookshop and all.' She laughed.

Mr Portobello did not.

'It looks smaller somehow, crowded, like this. I used to have just the one large desk in the middle of the room, belonged to my grandfather, and filing cabinets and so forth dotted around the walls.' Using his silver-topped walking cane, he pointed to the spots where they used to be located. 'Spacious.' He closed his eyes briefly and smiled. She supposed it must be odd for him to see the space he'd worked in for so long look so different.

'I'm having rather an odd morning,' Sophia confessed. 'A woman shouted at me from the step, asking for a book I haven't got, and another came in and I ended up giving *her* ten pounds, for what I'm not really sure, and then a couple of ladies came in to stick a leaflet on the door, and that's been about it.' She raised her arms and let them fall by her side.

'The day is young.' The man held her gaze.

'You were here a very long time, Mr Portobello.'

'Forty-three years,' he said. 'Hoped to make it fifty, but there we go. I do like round numbers.' He sniffed, and she sensed it better not to ask what had curtailed his career.

'I'm forty-three.' She liked the coincidence.

He looked her up and down.

'I was thirty-six when I took the keys to this place. Keen as mustard. I had been with a big firm in the City since qualifying; I was a bit of a whiz-kid, I don't mind telling you! And my wife thought it a good idea to go out alone.'

Nearly eighty, and married; two things I did not know about you...

'Turns out she was right. I rather enjoyed being my own boss. And my clients stayed with me, which was a gift, really. All those years.'

'What are you planning on doing with your retirement?' she asked softly. She pictured her father, who when he had left his post in the Civil Service had taken up fishing. Trudging up to the canal on the other side of Bank Street on fine days and Sunday afternoons with his collapsible canvas fishing stool, a rod and net in a long bag, a small gas burner and old tin kettle. He never caught a fish. But as her mother explained, 'It's not about the fish, darling. There's plenty of fish in the fishmonger's and I don't doubt they are a lot fresher than anything your father is going to catch in the canal. The journey gives purpose to his walk, and the stool and all his props legitimise his desire to sit by the water and get lost in daydreams and, occasionally, if he's lucky, people stop to chat – old and young – asking if he's caught anything or to talk about the weather, and the fishing gives them a reason to stop, and he likes that. It's never been about the fishing.'

'My father took up fishing.' She thought it worth a mention.

'Did he now? Well, good for him.' Mr Portobello shook his head, as if this concept were alien. 'I am taking each day as it comes and make a habit of coming up to the high street to collect this.' He waved the copy of *The Gazette* he was holding. 'I like to know what's going on.'

'Yes.' She smiled at him. 'And if you ever want any other reading material...' She let this trail as her eyes wandered over the wooden shelves crammed with books.

'I wish you every success in this little shop, Miss Perkins,' he said as he tucked his morning paper under his arm. 'There are three things to remember. Do not let others bamboozle or bulldoze you; always, always keep your receipts; and do what makes you happy. These are the first rules of business and the first rules of life! It really is that simple.'

'Right.' Sophia mulled over his words.

Mr Portobello turned on his heel and walked towards the door.

Click... click... click...

He paused with his hand on the brass door plate, reaching for it while turning towards her, as if memory could lead him to that exact spot for ever. 'I think the question, Miss Perkins, should not be what am I going to do with my retirement but rather what is my retirement going to do with me?' He chuckled, a throaty, mischievous laugh that she rather liked, before closing the door behind him and walking briskly down the high street.

Sophia sat with her feet folded underneath her on the vintage tapestry sofa in the sitting room of her cramped Victorian terraced house. Uncle Vanya the cat gave her a look of pure disdain from the silk cushion on which he was perched and it made her smile.

'You are so judgemental.' She shook her head at him. 'So what if I like these books? I don't have to think too hard; I can just dive in and switch off.' She turned the book in her hand, looking at the cover of the second in the *Twilight* series. 'Anyway, I bought these today in a job lot from a rather pushy niece who was helping out her aunt, so not only do I get a whole few hours of escape, but it was kind of a good turn. I forgot to get a receipt. Lesson learned.' She tapped her temple. 'And did I say that Mr Portobello came to visit me? I felt like he was checking up, and he was chatty-ish. Why am I talking to you?' She ran her hand over her face as the day's fatigue caught up with her. 'I think one day you might answer me and, frankly, I'd be very scared and a little bit thrilled. I sold two books, in case you are interested, both to the same man, and it was brilliant and surreal and also – and I can only say this to you as you are a cat and won't think I'm a total loon – I didn't want to hand them over. Not really. It was weird. He gave me the money and I put the books into one of my new snazzy paper bags and when he tried to take the bag I held on to it for a fraction longer than I should. He looked at me a little nervously and then when I let go we both laughed, with relief, I think.'

She looked to the mantel, where a photograph of her parents sat inside a small silver frame, the two of them sitting in front of their car, picnicking on the banks of a river, laughing, young and very much alive. How she envied them the love that had sustained them through a lifetime. 'It was because it was my dad's copy of *The AA Book of England and Wales* and an Agatha Christie paperback that has been hanging around since I was a child and I didn't want to let them go to that stranger. My *books...*' Sophia snapped shut the world of vampires and teenage love and clicked off the lamp before making her way up the creaky wooden stairs to bed. 'I guess that's something I am going to have to get over or we will both go hungry very quickly. And I love you way too much for that.'

Two

Sophia loved this time of year.

May.

When windows were flung open to allow the scent of peonies, sweet peas, ranunculus and other blousy-headed soft blooms to drift in. When flowers filled the beds of her small back garden, as well as the vases, window boxes, pots and jardinières of the paved frontages past which she walked to work. People, she noted, wore lighter fabrics; the floaty cottons and linens that had been relegated to the back of the closet during the drizzly months, now fluttered against their skin. They also moved with a slight saunter to their gait, as if warming up for a dance. It was like the whole town was alive with the promise of summer ahead and all that it might bring, happy to shake off the cold, grey winter colic that had dragged them down with ailments they had tried to stave off in chilly homes. The air itself carried the sweetness of the pink- and champagne-coloured petals, where bees buzzed and birds chirped, all, she suspected, singing out their joy to once again feel the warmth of the big yellow sun on their skin when it peeked through the gaps in the clouds that littered the sea-blue sky.

With her pale cotton cardigan over her arm, she put the key into the lock and pushed open the door of Perkins' Book Emporium, which had been trading for nearly three months.

The smell that greeted her made her smile; it always felt a lot like coming home. Her routine was steady, and she found comfort in it. For a woman who had spent the last couple of decades with her working day divided by a strict timetable, it was freeing, a revelation of sorts, not to know what the day might hold.

Business was, she found... unpredictable. There were days when she didn't take a red cent in the store, relying on online orders – which were themselves sporadic and which spiked and dipped depending on how many books she felt inclined to list on the internet. It was a chore she found both taxing and laborious, yet it was so thrilling when the word 'SOLD' appeared by the little image of the book. She would then take great joy in the careful packing, labelling and posting of said book, saying goodbye to it before shipping it off to various postcodes in places as far-flung as Bury St Edmunds!

And then there were the other days, full of endless possibilities; when a collector or a book lover would stumble in and inhale the scent of the place, whilst gazing lovingly at the many works of art; covers that invited them to select one particular book above all others, as if it called to them. She would watch as they homed in, taking it gently into their hands and opening it slowly, reverently, not knowing what wonders might be revealed. And on those days...? Well, it felt like the sky was the limit.

Only a couple of weeks ago, a man, a dentist who had been passing through the town, bought fifty books. *Fifty!* So many that he had to bring his car around and double park with the blinkers going, and the bus had to toot its horn for him to get out of the way, while they each carried teetering rectangular towers that reached to their chins, before gently piling them into his cavernous boot. He hadn't cared about the price, in fact had barely enquired as to the total, but had handed over his credit card with his eyes glued to the weighty tomes with titles like *The Victory of Irvine Melrose, Inside The Head of Lady Macbeth* and *Model Railways for Boys and Beginners.* She hadn't minded waving off part of her parents' collection to dentist man, not only because after three months of trading she had got more used to parting with them, but also because the way he held them, arranged them, touched them, told her that he would love and care for these books. She was confident he would not use them as a coaster for a wet-bottomed mug or fold back the corners of a page to hold a place or, worse still, crack a spine so widely that it left a crease – all things that should, in her view, carry a custodial sentence.

There was no need for her to worry about the gaps any sales might create on the shelves, as books seemed to find her. Not only did she still have a fairly ready supply on the spare shelves in the tiny, dusty basement stock room, but also people brought her books. They sent her books. And some even bartered for her wares: one for two depending on the title and condition of the books in question. Admittedly, it did little for the takings, but it was thrilling and wonderful nonetheless.

Financially, she was ticking over, taking enough to cover her rent and keep Uncle Vanya in fish, but not enough to pay herself a wage, not yet. Luckily, her inheritance more than covered her living expenses and she still had savings from her teaching days when she earned averagely and spent even less.

Folding her soft chocolate-coloured leather handbag into the lockable drawer under the counter, she looked up at the sound of the bell. It was the witches again. Her heart sank as she looked at the door groaning under the weight of leaflets and posters advertising, promoting and requesting attendance at craft fairs, school fetes, walking clubs, open days and the many, many charities looking for joggers/knitters/swimmers and cyclists that littered the glass. Not only did it look scruffy but also they blocked the view of the shop from any visitors who might pitch up after hours and want to peer through the glass door to see the shelves to the left.

'Hello there!'

'Hi!'

They waved as they raced forward and took up position side by side. Their dark flowy frocks had been traded for teal and green dresses in the same design, and on each there were bright flowers embroidered on the front panels. The striped tights were the same. Sophia raised her hand in greeting.

'We have a favour to ask.'

'Yes, I guessed as much, since I haven't seen you since the last favour when you stuck your leaflet on my door. Wonkily.' She pointed at the flat A5-sized notice that was still *in situ*. 'I remember it well, as it was my first day of trading.'

'Ah! Great!' They nodded as if enthused, but their eyes spoke of indifference, keen to get on with the job and make their exit. The red-haired woman unfurled a new leaflet and held it up for scrutiny. Sophia spied the tape dispenser sticking out of the edge of her beaded handbag. 'The thing is, St John's are chucking us out and we've had to move venue and we were wondering if we might be able to—'

'I'd really rather you didn't.' Sophia shook her head.

'I'm sorry?' The dark-haired witch looked at her quizzically.

'I'd really rather not.' She stood tall and did her best to control the quiver to her voice. 'I do appreciate you asking, but no, no, thank you. Not today.'

'We haven't even properly asked yet!' The red-haired one looked a little aggrieved. Her tone was quite sharp.

'Well, the thing is, I think I can guess what you are about to ask.' Sophia gripped the countertop to hide the slight tremor to her hands and planted her feet firmly on the ground, as if this might help keep her steady, because the desire to crumple was strong.

'But...' The women looked at each other. 'It's a community thing! Your neighbours either side have taken leaflets and Water—'

'Waterstones too; yes, yes, you said before, but I'm afraid I *don't* want another leaflet on my door. They clutter up the glass and I lose light. And customers can't see in.'

'But...' The women looked at each other again then back to her. Sophia held her nerve. This was her in action, not being bamboozled or bulldozed and standing firm.

'Well, I think it's a shame that someone so uncommunity-minded has moved into the high street. We support local businesses!'

'You haven't supported mine,' Sophia pointed out.

'Because... Because you don't have books we like!' the dark-haired witch blurted.

'Oh! Which books do you like?' she asked softly, genuinely curious to know. This had caught her interest, knowing for a fact the women had never let their eyes meander across the shelves or ventured further than the counter. But if there was something they wanted to read, something that would encourage them to step inside and actually buy a book, then she was keen to hear.

'Well, I don't know!' The woman was shouting now. 'I don't read! Who has time to read?'

'People like me.' Sophia smiled wryly.

'Yes, that's right.' The red-haired woman looked her up and down, her expression verging on sneering.

Sophia felt it to be a slight on her very existence – a woman who has time to read. A middle-aged, single woman who had missed her chance of love when her idiot fiancé had stepped from a kerb in a second of misjudged haste. A woman who had tried to teach kids, help kids, who in the main had rejected both. A woman who had been at the beck and call of her ailing parents for the last decade or so. And now, a middle-aged, single woman who lived with her beloved cat. No wonder she had time to read, she saw on their faces. Well, whether or not it was true, this middle-aged woman was her own boss and, like it or not, was not going to allow another leaflet in her window.

One of the women marched to the door and tore her original poster from the window; her execution of the task was poor and as they closed the door behind them Sophia was irritated by the four little purple corners of card that remained on the glass panel, fixed by four strips of yellowing Sellotape.

'Well I never!' she sighed. 'That was all a bit dramatic!'

She tidied the shelves and labelled a new arrival of *Treasure Island*, placing it next to *Moby Dick*, thinking the characters might be able to find common ground for a chat when the lights were turned off, and she closed up for the night. Things like that mattered to her. She would never, for example, place a book about sharks next to one about fish, unable to stand the thought of all the little fish quivering inside the cover, aware of their neighbour lurking dangerously close. Likewise, she separated left-wing and right-wing politics, imagining the unholy racket of heated debate that might keep all the other books awake at night. And between the histories of Israel and Palestine she placed a book called *Birds of the River Jordan*, thinking the water and its wildlife might calm things a little, help them find common ground.

These small acts were, she knew, a quirk, an oddity, but nonetheless they brought her comfort, helped her sleep and gave her a sense that all was at peace when she closed up for the night. She hadn't told anyone about this.

Not even her daily visitor.

As was now an established part of her day, on the dot of 10 a.m. Mr Portobello walked through the door. And as every day, Sophia pulled the rattan chair from behind the counter for him to sit in and placed it opposite her. His attire was splendid as ever, the navy pinstriped suit, his fob watch shining against his waistcoat, and today he sported a rather natty sprig of purple lilac, which he had pinned into his buttonhole. He looked dashing. She watched him run his finger along the inside of his white shirt collar, as if releasing some kind of pressure.

'Goodness me, that hill does not get any less steep.'

'Surely it's no more than a slight incline,' she teased. 'And good morning, Mr Portobello.'

'Good morning to you, Miss Perkins.' He placed his copy of *The Gazette* on the countertop.

'I do like your lilac.' She smiled. 'Very dapper.'

'Thank you.' He smiled with the delight that her compliments seemed to bring and ran his podgy fingers over the delicate cluster of star-shaped flowers.

'Do you know, the left-hand wall of the garden is groaning with it, the bricks almost listing under the boughs that carry the blooms in a waterfall of purple that even on the rainiest of days makes it look like summer. And the scent! Oh my word, that perfume… It's my very favourite time of the garden's year, closely followed by the arrival of the wisteria, which is interspersed with a snaking vine. Can you believe it? An abundance of riches! Grapes *and* wisteria! How very lucky am I?' He chuckled.

'You are very lucky,' she concurred. 'I should love to see that.'

'And you shall.' He nodded. 'You shall.'

It was the closest he had come to inviting her to his home, which she could picture perfectly and was a place she was extremely keen to wander around in. She found herself entranced by his descriptions of his world: the faded, clotted-cream-coloured plaster of the grand hallway, where there was an expanse of grey marble underfoot; the parquet-floored library with its ornate wrought-iron fireplace; the wide twist of the mahogany staircase that led to a half-landing and then continued up to the bedroom floor, and above that the attic. The attic... this the most mysterious and promising part of any house, and Mr Portobello's sounded more intriguing than most, crammed, as she had been told, with old steamer trunks and suitcases, hat boxes and a gentleman's valet on which he stored his old silk-covered top hat. The various luggage upon which, according to Mr Portobello, his children used to clamber so they could reach the window and fire a water pistol at their rather crotchety neighbour, Mrs Skelton, but they always missed.

'The angle was all wrong and the distance too great. Not that either myself or my wife ever told them this; we were always rather eager to have them out from under our feet!'

His children, Emily and Anthony, now grown up of course, lived in Australia and Kenya with their respective families. He missed them, but thought it a parent's job to give children the wings that enabled them to fly.

'And if this is one's philosophy, one can hardly moan when they have flown...'

Sophia thought about this phrase often, knowing her parents had not wanted her to fly, not at all. They had wanted to see her every day, talk to her, hold her, feed her; they had loved her so much that they needed to keep her within arm's reach, and in truth it had made her feel as safe as it had them. Odd, really, as now they had gone she felt anything but and could see that it would have been kind and generous to give her wings. In fact, at forty-three, she felt more alone and adrift than she ever had. It felt like her safety net had been cruelly ripped from beneath her. She was not prepared, not ready to be an orphan, not at this or any other age, but there was very little she could do about it. This was one of the reasons she lived softly and slowly, wary of the fall with nothing below to catch her. If only... if only they too had had the courage to give her wings and help her soar.

'How was your weekend?' She liked to hear of his life, to picture him in the large four-storey Palladian-fronted home at the bottom of the hill.

'Pleasant. I sat in the garden on Saturday, such a gift of a day! I rather lost track of time and it was only the rumbling of my tum that sent me back indoors. My housekeeper—'

'Mrs Waller.' She liked to show she had been paying attention.

'Yes.' He smiled at her. 'Mrs Waller left a rather lovely plate under a cloche in the fridge with all manner of cheeses and a jar of plum chutney, my absolute favourite. I found crackers in the larder and I must admit made rather a pig of myself; washed the lot down with an overly large glass of port.'

'That does sound lovely. I sat on the sofa and Uncle Vanya and I shared a tuna salad. He was, as ever, much keener on the tuna than the lettuce.'

'I don't blame him. My wife used to be very keen on salad herself; myself, not so much, which I am sure won't come as a surprise to you.' He patted his large stomach.

'I think it's nice not to cook sometimes – to just rip things and chop things and open a tin and throw it all into a bowl.'

'My wife was an average cook, said the chore bored her rigid!' He paused and chuckled that mischievous throaty laugh of his. 'She didn't mind cooking for a dinner party or a celebration, and at Christmas time she always went to town: golden roasted birds galore, sausage-meat stuffing, rich, thick gravies and crispy spuds basted in goose fat and covered in salt flakes.' He closed his eyes, as if able to still taste the food. 'But the humdrum, the everyday drudge of having to pull together three squares, well, let's just say it wasn't for her.'

'What was your wife's name, Mr Portobello?' She had wanted to ask for a while, but respect for his privacy had dictated she waited, until now.

'Her name?' He blinked, again as if the memory, or rather having to give the name of the woman now gone, was simply too painful, and this she more than understood.

Oh, darling! Darling, there has been the most terrible accident!

What is it, Mummy? Tell me now! Please! What's happened?

'Her name was Sophia.' He spoke plainly, and yet his response pierced her breast with its sorrow.

'My name!'

'Yes.' He nodded and looked at the floor.

It was a coincidence, bittersweet, wonderful and sad all at the same time. Having originally assumed it was a generational thing, she now wondered if this was why he insisted on calling her Miss Perkins.

'You must miss her very much,' she whispered, wary of stepping over the delicate framework that bound their friendship.

He drew in a deep breath and took his time forming his response. 'I miss all that she was and all that she could have been and all that she could have made me and our time together.'

'Oh, Mr Portobello, I think that is beautiful.' His words

were profoundly moving. Sophia looked out of the window at a woman with a stroller who walked by smiling, seemingly happy with her lot, and then at the two young lovers, hand in hand, who stopped to kiss and bump noses as if new to the coupling and still figuring out which part of their face went where.

'I had—' She coughed. This didn't get any easier. 'I was... I was engaged to be married. A long time ago.'

He stared at her and said nothing, as if it was not his place to do so, but rather hers to fill in the gaps.

'We met at teacher training college and he was wonderful and we just...' She paused and saw him sitting by the tree with *The Wind in the Willows* in his hand, too lost in the riverbank tales to notice her creeping up on him.

Hello, you.

And then that smile as he looked up and she knew that there was no one else in the whole wide world that he would rather be disturbed by.

Hello, you.

'. . . we just clicked.'

'And then you unclicked?' he enquired.

'No. And then he died.' The word still sounded monstrous to her ears and tasted sour on her tongue. *How could it possibly be?*

'Oh, my dear.' Mr Portobello shook his head, his eyes misty. 'That really is most terrible.'

'It was most terrible. It *is* most terrible.' She smiled, but her heart felt awash with sorrow.

'What was his name?'

'His name was Christopher,' she whispered.

You can call me Kit, or Chris, or Christopher; in fact, you can call me anything you like...

'You must miss him *very* much.'

She nodded. She did.

There was a beat or two of silence while both mentally readjusted to this change, where new knowledge meant they had to re-evaluate what they thought they knew about their friend. Letting the facts reshape the way they viewed the other. It was Mr Portobello who ended the silence.

'I didn't know Christopher, but I do know that had I been your friend then, as I am now, and I hope that's not too much of an assumption on my part or indeed an imposition—'

'We are most definitely friends, Mr Portobello.'

He closed his eyes briefly in acknowledgement before continuing, 'Had I been your friend then, I would most definitely have told you that life is not for the dead, it's for the living, and if you ever find yourself in the unfortunate position of being left behind, you have a chance – no, a duty – to continue living the very best life you can. It is imperative that you seek out happiness and not let yourself sink into the mire of grief. Because that, Miss Perkins, would be the biggest waste, as well as a fool's errand.'

'Why would sinking into grief be a fool's errand?' It was a hard thing to hear, but it was true that she had done just this: filling her days with busyness and filling her nights with recalling every small aspect of Christopher and wishing, wishing, wishing for one more day with him...

'Because it's utterly pointless,' he snorted, 'to step into a cage of your own making, and I should know.' He nodded slowly. 'It is a bizarre yet human trait that in the cake of life we let one small, dry portion dictate how we enjoy the rest of it, and the rest of it might be wonderful – lemony and zesty with flecks of icing and crumbly light sponge that makes your taste buds sing!'

Sophia laughed and was instantly maddened by the tears that sprang to her eyes.

'Oh! Goodness! I am sorry, I don't really... I don't really cry much.' She reached for her handbag in the drawer under the desk and ferreted inside, sniffing, until her fingers fell upon the lace-edged handkerchief that had been her mother's and with it she dabbed at her eyes and gently blew her nose.

'I didn't mean to make you cry!' He looked aghast. 'Quite the opposite; I thought thinking of life as a lemon cake might in fact lift your spirits. I know it does mine!'

She nodded and swallowed her remaining distress.

'It does, Mr Portobello, and I am thankful to you. Truly.' It felt good to see his smile restored. 'I know what you're saying makes perfect sense. My parents always taught me that there would be good days and bad days. In fact, glorious days and truly terrible days! But what I hadn't banked on was the fact that the terrible days would leave an indelible watermark across the glorious ones, thus reducing them to merely good, or that the stain of sadness might leach into every crevice, every crack, every spare thought. Spoiling things. It's unrelenting, and would turn something as lovely as lemon cake to salt on my tongue; it can dull the brightest sunset and means that music falls flat before it reaches my ears.'

'Well.' Mr Portobello stood and straightened his waistcoat before reaching for *The Gazette*. 'If I might give you one piece of advice, I would say, "Snap out of it!"' He spoke loudly, with his chin jutting.

'What?'

'I think you heard me, Miss Perkins. I said, "Snap out of it!" Enough! Choose to think differently! And if I might be so bold as to suggest, Christopher might not have been the love of your life.'

'*What?*' she asked again, with more energy; this was a preposterous thought as well as an unwelcome one.

'I said, he might not have been the love of your life! You were so very young! You were in love, but love fades, things happen, people change. Who knows? Maybe things with him would have cooled and you would have waltzed off into the sunset and bumped into the real love of your life when you least expected it and you would right now be living a different life, with a different man; one who filled your heart and head. Uncle Vanya would not be your only dinner date and you wouldn't be hiding here among your parents' books.'

'I'm not hiding, I... I...' She ran out of words. His truth hit her like a bolt to the chest, the force of which left her feeling quite winded.

I am hiding.

'Forty-three is not old,' he continued in the same strident tone. 'Eighty is old! I am nearly eighty, and you are not. You are almost half my age; you have a lot of life left and you need to think very carefully about what you do with it. And I am not suggesting you take up fishing. Life is precious, as both you and I know. You have time.'

He took a step towards the counter and she wondered for a split second if he might hug or kiss her. In truth, she welcomed the idea of both, missing the feel of her father's arms around her more than she could ever express. But then he turned on his clickety heels and walked out of the bookshop without looking back.

I have time...

Three

Sophia woke up one Monday morning in September and felt immediately that something was amiss, although quite what it was eluded her as she got ready for work.

'What have I forgotten to do, Uncle Vanya?' she quizzed him as she stood in the narrow kitchen of her home and used one of her granny's silver teaspoons to agitate the herbal teabag in the cup of hot water. He looked at her, and she swore he raised his eyebrows as if to say, 'How should I know?', which made her laugh.

'Is it a dental appointment? No. I'd have put that on the calendar.' She shook her head. 'Is there a book I was meant to post?' She tapped her chin, confident her system for logging and checking each order for dispatch was infallible. 'I can't put my finger on it...' She ran her palm over the waistband of her wool skirt and exhaled, wishing she could pinpoint the cause of her unease and therefore stand a good chance of putting it right. 'It's bothering me.' She chewed the inside of her cheek.

It was at half past eight as she was preparing to leave the house, tying the silk scarf at her neck, straightening the watch on her wrist, gathering her book bag and locking the front door, that it dawned on her.

'Aaah! Of course.' She stood on her step and adjusted her glasses as she watched several children from her street and the surrounds – some with their hands inside their mum or dad's, others clinging to older kids – walking as a collective with sullen expressions, shiny new shoes and backpacks weighing down their narrow shoulders; all unmistakably heading back to school after the summer break.

'That's it!' She smiled, throwing her keys in the air and catching them again, happy to have finally realised the reason for her unease. Here she was, the first week in September, and for the first time since she was four years of age, this week did not herald going back to school. It gave a lightness to her step and put a smile on her face. Sophia took a deep breath; she had stepped off the hamster wheel of the education system in which she had had to run just to stand still, and now she felt like she had slipped from the grip of something oppressive, had made her break for freedom and was giddy at the fact that she had survived. So far.

She walked briskly towards the high street, realising that what had been missing when she woke up that morning was the jitter in her bones at the prospect of the term ahead and the deep growl of uncertainty and worry in the pit of her stomach at the thought of a new school year. Two little girls walked towards her, each holding the hand of their mum. Their faces were alight with excitement, their hair in neat ponytails and their uniforms almost comically large on them as their hands disappeared inside the sleeves of their voluminous blazers.

'Nearly there, darlings!' their mum sang, with the faintest edge of nerves to her tone.

'I going to do sums and I going to do reading,' one of the little girls enthused.

Her sister took up the mantle. 'I'm going to play the drums and then I am going to do art and I am going to do gymnastics and then I am going to have my lunch!'

'Goodness me, that sounds like a very busy first day.' The

woman smiled at Sophia, and Sophia felt a pang of something very close to regret and similar to jealousy; what wouldn't she give to be greeting those eager little minds on their first day of school?

'Don't be so silly, Sophia!' She shook her head as she pushed open her green shop door. 'This is a good, good day!'

She hummed as she restocked the shelves, and she hummed when she popped to the bank to deposit the thin takings from the weekend and treated herself to a large posh coffee in a lidded cup and a slice of cherry Bakewell tart from the delicatessen on the corner, which she carried carefully in her book bag. She took up her spot on her stool by the till and ate her cake with her fingers. She felt... if not happy, then certainly happier than she had in a while. And now, powered by cake, she decided to give everything a jolly good dust.

The little bell above the door gave off its pleasant ring.

'Well, I must say, you are looking very chirpy this morning, Miss Perkins!' Mr Portobello smiled as she twirled on the spot with the feather duster in her hand. 'And what, might I ask, is the cause of such chirpiness?' He took his seat, sitting down hard. 'And, I might add, you look very well on it.'

'Why, thank you.' She gave a small curtsey. 'I am chirpy partly because I have had cake for breakfast, and the reason I had cake is because I woke this morning and realised that I am free, Mr Portobello! I am absolutely free!' She beamed.

'You are, my dear. Free as a bird and able to wander as far as you like. And in truth, I rather wish that you would! The world is big, and anyone with an interest in life, in people, should hear it beckoning, should feel the pull of the oceans and the hum of the wild; a rhythm that only well-travelled global souls can dance to.'

'Yes.' She paused and looked at the many, many books she

had spent time in, learning about the wonders of the Orient, sleeping among the snakes of a jungle, learning how to scuba dive, reading what it was like to feel the wind on her face as she raced down a mountain. Running her fingers over texts, drinking in the description of the exact colour of the water as it lapped an island shore; she had done all of this and more, but she rarely set foot outside of her postcode. 'But if I went exploring, you'd miss me, Mr Portobello. You'd miss our chats and you'd have nowhere to stop on your way home after collecting your morning paper. You'd be absolutely exhausted by the time you got to the bottom of the hill, and that would never do.'

'That's a very good point; you'd best stay put!' He smiled at her, but his eyes carried a look of what she could only describe as regret. 'I want you to *feel* life and not just read about it, Miss Perkins. I think you need to step outside of your comfortable bubble. Will you at least think about that?'

'I will,' she promised as she watched her friend leave as quickly as he had arrived.

It was a day when business was brisk and, in her happy mood, Sophia found it easy to talk to customers. She discovered that the more she chatted, engaged with them, the more they bought. She made a mental note to try harder to adopt this attitude every day, able to see a correlation between her customers' experience and her own happiness. It wasn't always easy when past sadness, longing and thoughts of what might have been pawed at her senses and made her outlook a little foggy. But Mr Portobello was right, and she would try.

The bell above the door rang at a little after 4 p.m. She looked up with a ready smile, her welcome greeting poised on her lips. Both, however, fell from her mind as the breath caught in her throat and nerves made her heart stutter. It was the last person she had expected to see.

But there he was.

Standing in the doorway was none other than the Head of the school, Mr Simon Blandford. Still, she noted, wearing his mustard-coloured corduroy jacket with the leather buttons.

He lifted his hand, as if this might be preferable to breaking the silent cocoon of awkwardness that enveloped them. It was most peculiar to be in such close proximity in this environment. Their paths had only ever crossed on school property, when every encounter had an underlying purpose or was merely a result of bumping into each other because they worked in the same building. And to meet that way, a little break in their busy days, had felt nice. This felt plain weird.

Eventually, he coughed and brought his hands together in front of him, as she had seen him do often at the start of morning assembly and before making any staff announcements.

She smiled.

'Good afternoon, Miss Perkins.'

'Good afternoon, Mr Blandford.' She took a slow breath and tried to quell the shake to her limbs, reminding herself that he was no longer her boss and she no longer had to feel the frustrations of his inaction or his overly calm demeanour.

'First week back at school.' She wanted him to know she had remembered.

'Yes.' He closed his eyes briefly and gave a half-tut/half-laugh. 'I definitely have more grey hair than I had when I left home this morning. And at least three more wrinkles.'

'I remember what that feels like.' She felt a flicker of sympathy for the man who she knew bore the weight of the whole establishment on his corduroy-covered shoulders.

'I've driven by a couple of times, but today I thought…' He paused. 'Today I thought, why not? Why not park up and actually go in and say hello?'

'Well, I am glad you did. Welcome to Perkins' Book Emporium!' She smiled proudly, as he looked around.

'You have a lot of books.'

'Yes, so I've been told, and as I said to that person, "It's a good thing, really, being that we are a bookshop and all."'

He laughed quietly, as his eyes jumped from shelf to shelf before settling on the ceiling rose and its marvellous chandelier.

'Goodness me! Who painted that?' He walked forward and stood beneath the ornate plasterwork, craning his neck to make out the detail.

'I don't know, but it's beautiful, isn't it?'

'My goodness, it really is!'

She walked from behind the counter and stood by his side, staring up. 'I know the gentleman who was here before me for a number of years. I really must ask him if he knows more about it.'

Simon squinted and walked in a small circle, as if to appreciate the view from all angles. 'It reminds me of something grand, opulent, makes me think of orchestras or...'

'Ballrooms,' she whispered.

'Yes! Ballrooms!' He turned to her and smiled enthusiastically, and for the first time she noted that his teeth, which were usually hidden behind clamped lips, were white and even, making him look more youthful than his jacket and thinning hair might suggest. 'That's it, ballrooms with candelabras around the floor!'

'Yes! And ladies with fine silk frocks in the colours of sugared almonds...' she picked up the mantle.

'And moustachioed men with stiff white collars and tails, whose drivers are sitting out in the cold in their fancy motorcars, blowing into their cupped hands and praying it won't be too much longer before they can get to their beds,' he added.

They both giggled and then he coughed, seemingly a little embarrassed by the shared and surprising flight of fancy, just as she was. There was a beat of silence, which was deafening.

Sophia made her way to the safety of the counter and stood behind it. She could feel the creep of crimson up over her neck and face. She adjusted her glasses.

'Did you want a particular book, Mr Blandford? Or are you just here to browse? Both are perfectly fine.'

'Oh!' He looked a little startled, as if neither thing had occurred to him. 'I, I don't know.' He put his hands on his hips and turned this way and that. 'I suppose I came to see you more than to hunt for a book.' He swallowed, and she saw the crimson bloom of awkwardness spread on his cheeks too, and thought they matched, like a pair of chameleons taking on the blushing face of their shared embarrassment.

She stared at him, unsure of the convention but knowing she had to say something. Anything! But her mind was suddenly blank. Why had he come here? Was she in trouble? Was there a long-forgotten form misfiled or wrongly numbered? Could they come after her now, after all these months, for an administrative error? She didn't know, but her heart beat a little faster nonetheless.

'So what has today been like, Simon, back at school?' She tried to keep her voice steady as she tried out his first name.

Simon cleared his throat and folded his arms across his chest. 'As you'd expect, Sophia.' He smiled. 'Day one, and I already have a staffing crisis and the whole place is hectic, loud, busy, chaotic...'

'None of those words sound very good.'

He laughed now, a proper unselfconscious chortle. 'No, I guess you could say that.'

'So why do you do it?' She looked down, knowing that if it

were not for the separation between them – the counter and her change of career – she would never have been so bold.

'Why do I do it?' He looked upwards again, as if this was where the answer might lie.

His voice, when he spoke again, was barely more than a whisper. 'I do it because I know what it's like to live in a house with no books.' He held her gaze. 'To wake up in a house where there is no breakfast and to go home to dark rooms without heating and where supper, six nights out of seven, is a piece of toast. And all I looked forward to, all I *had* to look forward to, was going to school, where the rooms were warm and I was around people and there were books aplenty. And I got to have a hot, cooked lunch.' He smiled. 'Glorious things like quiche with soggy chips and beans, followed by chocolate sponge and chocolate custard for pudding. Or even better, chocolate sponge with thick mint icing on it!'

She smiled, remembering enjoying that exact same pud at school too.

His words had shocked and surprised her in equal measure; she could not imagine the picture of home he painted, remembering her mother in her apron making fine home-made soups, which they would eat with warm home-made bread, the table set for tea, and in winter months, the fire blazing.

Simon continued, speaking plainly and movingly. 'I vowed that if I could, then I would do my very best to make a difference to these kids – kids like me. Because they deserve better. They deserve more.'

His answer had been unexpected, and Sophia felt a flush of guilt at her rather uncharitable thoughts about the man and wished she had taken the time to get to know him a little better.

'I guess I stopped believing I could make a difference,' she confessed.

He looked towards the floor and shook his head. 'You made a big difference, and the school is poorer without you. In every way.'

She blinked rapidly, not adept at handling compliments of this nature. She found herself wanting to explain her decision to this man in a way she hadn't felt at the time of her resignation.

'I lost all the enthusiasm I'd felt in the early days. I used to love what I did and I was so excited to get into the classroom. But it wasn't like that at the end. I was bogged down by the tasks surrounding the teaching when all I wanted to do was teach!'

Simon's eyes widened and he nodded, as if he more than understood. It gave her the confidence to continue.

'It all ended for me one afternoon – the day I wrote my letter of resignation.' She swallowed the emotion that flared, remembering the sad and unfitting end to a career she had thought she would always love. 'I remember one boy telling me he hadn't read the book I had set, but had watched some of the film instead, and it felt like the final straw. It all felt so utterly pointless.'

He looked away. 'So you gave up on him?'

It was her turn to let out a snort of laughter, but one of derision. 'Hardly. I didn't give up on Tyler, he—'

'Tyler Groves-Peterson?' he interrupted.

'Yes.'

Simon took a step towards the counter. 'He's hoping to go to university.'

'He is?' She felt her heart lift at the prospect.

'Yes, he's applying this year to read history.' He beamed, taking joy from the very suggestion. 'He's quite remarkable; works in his parents' restaurant for at least thirty hours a week, and yet his attendance is high. And I'm not saying he was right, but maybe watching snippets of the film was as much as he could manage so he could pass a test, engage with the story or not let you down. Maybe to sit and read the whole book was too much for him with all the other demands on his time, demands I have very little control over, sadly.'

'Oh God!' She ran her hands over her face. 'Tyler.' She pictured the handsome boy with the cheeky smile. 'If he had told me...'

'Sophia, nearly every child has their own story, you know this,' he chided her gently.

Maybe I needed reminding.

'Some of them won't ever reveal their true lives, but it's up to us, up to *me*,' he corrected, 'to help them find a way through. So they can be better, do better, because they deserve better.'

She nodded. 'I want to say, Simon, that I am seeing a different side to you today. And I'm sorry for the things I said on the day I shouted at you. That was wrong of me, unprofessional, and I regret it.'

He pushed his hands into his pockets. 'I remember you asked what it took to see me riled, fired up, what it took to make me feel alive.'

'Yes, I did.' She recalled the exchange with no small amount of shame.

'And the simple truth is, I have to keep calm for fear of giving in to the rage I feel at the injustice of it all.' He bit his lip. 'I am a peaceful man by nature, I seek out the quiet, I walk hills and wander dales, and that's what gives me balance. But each and every day for me is like swimming against a tide of obstacle-laden treacle and I never know what is going to come hurtling towards me next; I am almost constantly overwhelmed by the frustration I feel, and the stories I hear of poverty, neglect, sadness, which are commonplace, and yet these kids come into our school, *my* school...' He corrected himself. 'They come in every day and they try. And their efforts might often fall well short of what we expect, but the fact that they are in the building at all means we are in with a shout of making a difference. And I *want* to make a difference. I have to keep calm because, if I didn't, the ship might run aground. I am the captain who needs to keep a steady hand on the tiller when all around us are rocks and danger. People are relying on me. These children are relying on me.'

'Yes. I can see that.' For the first time, she saw it from his point of view and it humbled her.

'Anyway' – he smiled and took a deep, calming breath – 'I have already taken up too much of your time. I had best let you get back to your books.' He made for the door.

'Thank you, Simon, for coming in. I have enjoyed our chat.'

'Me too. And, Sophia?'

'Yes?' She stared at him as he looked into the middle distance, his mouth moving as if his brain were searching for the right words.

'Nothing. It doesn't matter...' He nodded, and the little bell gave its tinkle as he closed the door behind him.

Sophia placed her glasses on the bedside cabinet, pulled the pink candlewick bedspread up to her chin and settled back into the familiar comforting dip in the middle of her mattress, as she stared up at the ceiling. Simon's visit had unnerved her a little. Not only did she find herself reassessing her view of him, seeing his silence in a new light now: not as weakness, but actually as strength, because it took strength to stay calm in that environment, when all around the air crackled with high emotion. But also, for the first time since walking out of her classroom, she felt the slight pang of regret, wondering how her love of the profession had slid into this indifference, and feeling saddened by the realisation.

Good for you, Tyler. Good for you... Her tears sprang as she thought of the boy who had worked harder than most for a ticket to university; she wished him nothing but good things.

Uncle Vanya meowed from the end of her bed.

'I know. Pointless musings, but it's made me think, Uncle Vanya. What if Mr Portobello was right? What if Christopher wasn't the love of my life? And if I was wrong about him, what else have I been wrong about? Have I been closed off to other possibilities? Should I spread my wings and go and see the world? Is that what I should be doing? What if there is more out there for me? And should I have left teaching? Was I *actually* making a difference?' She sighed, remembering how it had felt when she heard of Christopher's death: like her heart had dissolved and a big piece of her had died too. 'I'm just tired. Go to sleep, beautiful boy. Dream of fish and playing with balls of wool.' She smiled and turned over on to her side, hoping for sleep to come quickly and quiet her busy head.

With her appetite diminished, Sophia skipped breakfast and headed for the shop. Looking now at the kids who walked slowly towards school with heads hung low, she wondered what their stories were, wondered if they had been working in family businesses or had made their own supper in a cold kitchen or had woken with tummies rumbling in want of food. Her stomach dropped at the thought.

I was so lucky. I am so lucky... Her mother's pretty, smiling face filled her mind.

She put the key in the door of the bookshop and stepped inside. Looking up at the plaster rose, she felt a flush of joy at the thought of her visitor the day before. He had surprised her, Mr Blandford; the surprise was in the realisation that there was much more to him than she had ever thought.

It was a shade before ten o'clock when the bell rang. She looked up, about to greet Mr Portobello, but it wasn't him. A smile broke over her face and she wrinkled her nose behind her glasses, surprised to see Simon Blandford step over the shiny brass threshold again. He came and stood in front of the counter.

'Simon! Hello! Well, this is a lovely surpr—'

'You!' He breathed heavily, as if he had been rushing, cutting her off mid-word.

'Excuse me?' She had lost the thread.

'I said, it's you!'

'What's me?' She frowned up at him and adjusted her glasses.

As he opened his mouth to speak Mr Portobello pushed open the door and looked from her to Simon and back again with a slow smile playing about his mouth.

'Good morning, Mr Portobello! Do come in! Please.'

'Good morning, my dear! Thank you, but no, I'm not staying, just on my way home!'

'But—'

Before she had a chance to encourage him in, he lifted *The Gazette* in a brief goodbye, winked at her, and made his way along the street.

She turned her attention back to the man who stood in front of her.

'I'm sorry, Simon, but I'm not really following. What's me?'

He leaned on the counter and she could smell his scent: lemony and clean. 'You, Sophia Perkins, are what riles me, fires me up, makes me feel alive! You! And my days are less rich because you are no longer in the corridors I walk or behind a classroom door I pass, and now there is no chance I might see you across the canteen or sit within sight of you in the staff room. These were the small things that for me were actually the very big things. They shone like jewels even on the most grey and testing day, and I miss it. I miss you. That's it.' He raised his arms and let them fall to his sides. 'That's all I wanted to say. I have nipped out and now I have to get back.' He looked at his watch. 'I don't expect anything from you, but I wanted to let you know because life is short. It's too short.'

She stared at him.

Her heart boomed in her chest, and it was while she sorted her jumble of thoughts, tried to put the words in her head into some kind of order and attempted to loosen her tongue from the dry roof of her mouth that he turned on his soft-soled shoes and left the shop, a flash of mustard corduroy disappearing out of sight.

Sophia stared at the space he had only recently vacated and felt her face break into a smile.

Four

Sophia spent the weekend in a state of agitation, realising it was one thing to be in receipt of such life-affirming information, but quite another to know what to do with it. There were so many questions!

How long had he felt this way?

Why had he not said something sooner?

What did he want to do about it now, if anything?

And most importantly, *what did she think about it all?*

She lay in the bath on Sunday evening, letting the warm sud-filled water turn her pruney, and decided that in the morning she would ask Mr Portobello, her friend and one of the wisest people she knew, his thoughts on the matter. He had, after all, lived a long and happy life with his Sophia, so what better role model for her now?

The following morning, wearing her favourite pale-pink jersey, she said a cheery goodbye to Uncle Vanya and skipped down the road, smiling at the bright morning and the gaiety she felt in her heart.

Small things that for me were actually the very big things. They shone like jewels...

Sophia replayed his words over and over and she had to admit the feeling was quite wonderful, like a thawing at her centre where, before, it had been uncomfortably cold.

She flexed her fingers and wiggled her toes, as if feeling was returning where there had been only numbness.

Yes, Simon, they were the big things for me too...

It was a quiet day in the shop, not that she minded, not that she noticed, because her thoughts were almost entirely lost to Mr Simon Blandford, who saw the beauty in her plaster ceiling rose and who had liked knowing she was within reach. It was the first time since she had lost her mother that she felt... wanted. Like there was someone on this big old planet who might be thinking about her and wondering if she was okay. It was a wonderful sensation, one she had almost forgotten: the absolute privilege of being in someone else's thoughts. It made her feel infinitely less lonely.

It was only when she glanced at her watch and realised that it was nearly midday that it became apparent that Mr Portobello had missed his ten o'clock appointment.

For the first time ever.

'That's odd. I do hope he's all right.' She spoke aloud into the ether, stepping outside and, with her arms folded, looking along the high street to the left and right in the hope that he might appear, knowing that if it were at all possible he would be along to collect his copy of *The Gazette*. She thought about last Friday, when he had popped his head in, seen Simon and had made a hasty retreat; she would tell him tomorrow in the strongest terms that he should never walk past; in fact, she would not allow it! And that he was always, always welcome.

Mid-afternoon, and the bell gave its familiar ring. She looked up, and would have been lying to say it was not with utter disappointment that she saw the witches enter her shop.

They had again returned to their black flowing frocks and she missed the teal shades with the bright flowers that had heralded the start of the warmer weather.

'So,' the red-haired one began, 'I think maybe we were a little hasty in ripping down our MABS poster on our last visit.'

'Yes, a little hasty,' her dark-haired friend concurred.

'Well, maybe I was a little curt in denying you permission for a second leaflet,' Sophia conceded. And the witches smiled.

'Could we interest you in this?' The dark-haired one whipped out a postcard from her pocket. 'It's smaller, therefore less clutterous for your window.'

Sophia liked the word 'clutterous' and decided to find a way to incorporate it into her speech.

'And Waterst—'

'Let me guess.' Sophia cut her short. 'Waterstones have said yes to one? And my neighbours either side?'

The women nodded, as if delighted that she already knew.

'All right then.' Sophia sighed. 'You can put this in my window, just to prove that I am community-minded *and* on the condition that I give *you* a leaflet the next time you are passing and you can put it up on the noticeboard where MABS meets, telling people about Perkins' Book Emporium.'

'Deal!' The red-haired witch beamed while her friend got to work with her tape dispenser.

She liked the way the women stopped and waved through the window before they left, friendly and welcoming.

It must be something in the air.

As she locked up for the night, she again hoped all was well with Mr Portobello and looked forward to seeing him in the morning. She imagined Mrs Waller was looking after him with a selection of cheeses placed under a cold glass cloche and possibly a hearty warm soup, because on the odd occasion when she was ailing, a good soup was the one thing that was almost guaranteed to make her feel better. Soup was her very favourite thing. Maybe he had the September cold that seemed to jump from child to child when they returned to school. And again, just like that her thoughts turned once more to Mr Simon Blandford, wondering what was to be done about the situation, if anything, and then realising that, should she decide something needed to be done, she didn't have the first clue how to get in touch with him other than going via school, which she would rather not do.

On the Tuesday morning at ten to ten, Sophia put the rattan chair in position and waited eagerly.

But Mr Portobello never came.

On Wednesday morning at ten to ten, she put the rattan chair in position and waited eagerly.

But Mr Portobello never came.

Thursday... Friday...

A full week! Still there was no sign of her friend. Her concern for his wellbeing was growing daily. She began to worry, thinking that it might be more than a cold that had befallen him, possibly a nasty bug or a virus. When you were nearly eighty, not only was it a little harder to shake something like that off, but the prospect of walking up the hill to the high street might not be a welcome one.

Sophia took her time over her Sunday-morning breakfast, thickly applying the right quantities of butter and marmalade to her toast and warming the pot with hot water for her cup of tea. Uncle Vanya sat on the cushion of the chair next to her and she let him drink milk from the saucer.

'I'm not sure what to do, old boy,' she levelled. 'I don't want to interfere or overstep the mark, and yet I feel concerned for my friend. It's so unlike him not to visit.' She bit into her toast. 'The truth is, I miss him.'

Uncle Vanya ignored her, far more interested in lapping milk from the floral bone china while she considered how best to proceed. Mr Portobello, she knew, had a full and busy life, and she didn't want to look like an interloper, particularly if he was unwell; it was, in her opinion, a fine line to tread, and not without awkwardness. Or perhaps one of his children had come to visit and he was spending time with them?

Sophia took an age to decide whether to make the trip, and then another age to decide what to wear, settling eventually on a sensible pair of shoes and thick woollen tights, a neat green kilt and an oatmeal and green Fair Isle jersey. The thought crossed her mind that Mr Portobello might not have mentioned her to his housekeeper, or indeed to his children, should they have made the trip over. She chewed the inside of her cheek, wondering how she might introduce herself.

'My name is Sophia Perkins and I am a friend of Mr Portobello.'

'A friend, you say?'

'Yes, he comes into my bookshop...'

Urgh, she hated the inadequacy of the words. Yes, he was her friend, but he was also her confidante, business adviser and the only living creature other than Uncle Vanya with whom she engaged in daily conversation. She hoped he might have mentioned her, making the whole horrible prospect of having to explain who she was and how they were connected redundant.

There were only a handful of grand houses at the bottom of the hill, and she knew it would be easy to find out which was his. Not only would she be confident that his neighbours would point her in the right direction, but the descriptions of his beautiful home were so vivid she was certain she would be able to walk straight to the front door, which, if she wasn't mistaken, was pillar-box red. He'd once told her that it was his wife's favourite colour, and one he had seen no reason to alter after she had passed away.

It was a crisp day, cold with a bright-blue sky and the chirp of birdsong above. Sophia smiled as she walked past the bookshop, feeling pride at the fact that it was hers and liking the clutterous nature of the window, where books were piled high in an enticing mix of titles. Who wouldn't want to potter in a shop like that? She thought of Simon and decided that when, *if*, she saw him again, she'd give him a guided tour. She walked down the hill with caution. Mr Portobello was right, it was quite steep in places, and her admiration at his daily effort rose. It was no mean feat to conquer this in all weathers every day and at the ripe old age of nearly eighty.

As she approached the bottom of the hill she took a second to stand and admire the row of stunning Palladian-fronted houses, standing close together with their columns rising up like proud sentinels, keeping watch over the pale exteriors.

Of the eight houses, three had red front doors.

'Just my luck!'

Sophia made her way along the terrace and approached the first house, but upon closer inspection found it not to be a house at all, but five flats. Five small rectangular holders with names scrawled or printed inside sat alongside each of the worn brass buttons. She stepped back from the front door. At least this narrowed her options. She felt a flicker of excitement at the thought of getting closer, deciding there and then not to overstay her welcome or even venture inside if Mr Portobello was feeling poorly. It would be more than enough for her to simply leave her name with Mrs Waller or whoever, so that he knew she was thinking of him. If nothing else, recent events had taught her what a comfort it was to know someone was thinking of you.

The second red door was, she saw, also not a house, but this time had been divided into three flats. As she studied the door a young woman with an oversized dusky pink pashmina around her neck pulled up on a bicycle and jumped off, her cheeks flushed, her smile bright.

'Can I help? I live here.' She nodded towards the building.

'Oh yes, please. I am looking for a friend of mine and I know he lives along here. Mr Portobello? He lives in a house, one of these houses.' She laughed, a little nervous.

'Oh well, that makes it easy.' The young woman undid her cycle helmet and ruffled her hair. 'There is only one house, the rest have all been divided into flats. I've never been inside, but I'd love to have a look!' She lowered her voice to a whisper. 'I can only imagine what these were like when they were family homes.'

'Is it the one with the red door?' Sophia pointed to the pillar-box-red paint along the street.

'No.' The girl shook her head. 'Actually, it's the grey front door at the very end. Big brass lion's-head knocker, you can't miss it.'

'Oh!' Sophia couldn't hide her surprise; she must have misheard Mr Portobello, whose descriptions could often be a little wordy. 'Thank you so much.'

Sophia tidied her hair behind her ears as she walked to the end of the terrace, and took a breath. She trod the three wide marble steps and lifted the heavy knocker, smashing it down against the wood, where it landed with an almighty thump.

She heard the sound of footsteps running towards the door and, eventually, it was pulled open by a woman with two small children – a boy and a girl – running around her feet.

Mr Portobello's daughter Emily, she suspected, and instantly her heart leapt. How ill must he be for his daughter to have made her way back from Australia?

'Hello, are you Emily?'

'No.' The woman looked at her quizzically, her tone sharp. 'How can I help you?'

'Oh, are you Mrs Waller then?'

'What *are* you talking about?' the woman fired.

'I'm so sorry.' Sophia felt her face colour. 'I'm not making much sense.'

The woman did not deny this.

'I am a friend of Mr Portobello's, and I haven't seen him for a few days and just wondered if he was under the weather or—'

'Look,' the woman interrupted, shaking her head whilst shooing the children further back into the hallway with her foot. 'I don't know who you are after, but there is no one here by that name, Mr Portywhatever or Mrs Waller. This is *my* house and I'd like you to get off my steps.'

'But I thought... Is there another house, or—'

'I'm sorry, I can't help you!'

The woman shut the door.

Sophia teetered until she tripped backwards, unnerved by the woman's rudeness. This made no sense! Could it be that he lived in one of the flats? Had they divided his beloved home up and, if so, which one was his and why had he not told her? She crossed over to the other side of the pavement and stared at the once-grand homes, their many windows shining in the sunlight. The prospect of going back along the terrace and scanning each name was not a task that filled her with joy. She sighed.

'You all right, love?' A woman with bleached blonde hair and dark roots, wearing a red-striped tabard over her blouse, rested her bottom against a low brick wall and inhaled deeply on a cigarette, the rest of the silver pack clutched with gold-painted nails against her chest. 'You look a bit out of sorts?'

Sophia smiled at her. 'I guess I am a bit. I'm trying to find someone, and I suspect he might live in one of those flats that I thought was actually a house, and the trouble is, I don't know which one! So I guess I'm going to have to go and look.' She wiped invisible dust from her palms.

'I've worked here for nearly twenty years.' The woman pointed her cigarette at the ugly orange-brick 1970s building behind her. There was a central concrete ramp, bordered by sturdy rails that led up to the wide double door, with criss-crossed safety glass, and a flat roof on which two fat seagulls perched. 'It's not like it used to be around here. Everyone knew everyone else and it was a community, you know?'

'Yes, same where I live across town. When I was a child I called the neighbours on either side of my parents aunty and uncle, but now there are tenants next to me who change every few months or so and the only communication we really have is via notes left under windscreens or pushed through letterboxes, and more often than not they are to complain about noise or stolen recycling bins. It's sad, really.'

'It is that.' The woman took another long, deep draw on her cigarette. 'Who is it you're looking for?' she asked casually, running the edge of her thumbnail over her bottom teeth.

'Someone you might have seen around, actually; he's a bit of a character, really, very dapper – Mr Portobello?'

'Mr Portobello?' The woman stood up and dropped her

cigarette on the pavement, treading it underfoot before lifting her mouth to fire a plume of smoke up into the air. 'Oh, love!' She stared at Sophia and took a hesitant step towards her, reaching out to lay her gold-taloned hand on Sophia's arm.

Before the woman said a word, Sophia knew what she was going to say... and she held her breath.

'Oh, sweetie, I am so sorry. Mr Portobello died. He passed away a week last Friday.'

'He died?' she repeated, struggling for air.

'Yes, my love. Very peacefully. He just came back from his morning walk, lay down and went to sleep. It's a blessing to go like that. The funeral was yesterday.'

'Yesterday?' She felt the bolt of sorrow pierce her chest.

'Yes.'

Sophia felt her legs sway a little and leaned back on the wall. 'I didn't know. I missed it! I missed his funeral!' she whispered, reaching now for the handkerchief in her pocket, and mopping the tears that trickled down her face.

'Well, how could you have known, my lovely? He was a very private man. Kept himself to himself.'

'How . . . How did you know him?' Sophia was curious.

The woman gave a small dry laugh, as if their connection was obvious, but it wasn't, not to Sophia. 'He lived here.' She pointed again to the low-rise building behind her, and for the first time Sophia noticed the sign behind the woman, which read 'Hawthorne House: Sheltered Living Accommodation for the Elderly'.

Sophia stood and shook her head emphatically, suddenly feeling relieved – this woman must have it wrong, 'Oh no, he didn't live here. No. Maybe it was another Mr Portobello.' Even she heard the absurdity in the statement. 'He... He lived in one of the houses! One of these houses!' It was her turn to point.

The woman looked at her kindly. 'You might be in shock, love. But I can assure you, there was only one Mr Portobello, navy pinstriped suit, liked a decent buttonhole, a proper gent.'

'I don't understand.' She stared at the woman. The facts would not sink in; it made no sense.

'He lived here at Hawthorne House for the last fourteen years, and before that he was in a flat the other side of the railway, as far as I know.'

'Are you absolutely sure?' Sophia asked in a last-ditch attempt to confirm what she already knew in her heart to be true.

The woman nodded. 'I should know, I was in his room every day; especially over this last year, to make sure he'd taken his medicine. He wasn't the best patient, found it hard to be looked after, poor old thing.'

It was odd to hear him described in this way. Sophia had never considered him to be a 'poor old thing'.

The woman took a sharp breath and narrowed her eyes as if something were occurring, a memory stirring from the depths, 'Oh my word!' she clicked her fingers. 'You're not his niece, are you, his niece, Sophia?'

Niece?

'I...' She didn't know what to say. She felt confused, alarmed and intrigued all at once. She swallowed the tears that gathered at the back of her throat and nodded. 'I am Sophia.'

'Oh, bless you.' The woman tutted at the tragedy of it all. 'Would you like to see his room?'

Again Sophia nodded, feeling out of kilter, walking as if there were another step and faltering on legs made of jelly.

'I really would.'

'Okay, well, it's being cleaned up and emptied tomorrow, we have a new resident coming in, so good job you came today. I'm sorry to be the one to have to break it to you; we had no address or details for any relatives and he never mentioned any apart from you, and that was only recently.'

No relatives?

Sophia paused on the path. 'But that's not right! He has children! Emily and Anthony! I thought they would have come over for the funeral, thought they might still be here.' She would have liked the opportunity to tell them how much their father had meant to her.

'How very odd; we were told Mr Portobello had no children, no next of kin. But as his niece, you obviously know differently?'

'No.' She thought of the implications of her words, shaking her head quickly. 'No, you're right, I think I must be in shock.'

The woman held her eyeline. 'I know he was married, but sadly she passed away when they were in their twenties. But I'm sure you know this already.'

In their twenties... Oh my, oh, Mr Portobello... Sophia received the news like a punch to the gut. It left her feeling winded and so sad for the man who knew more than most what it was like to lose a great love...

'Who... Who went to his funeral?'

'Oh, a lovely man, his solicitor, I think. Mr Hayes, is it? Mr Portobello left him his watch, I think that was the only thing of value he had. Sad, isn't it, really? Mr Hayes cried like a baby. He told me that in all the years Mr Portobello had the accountants on the high street, paying only a peppercorn rent because he'd been there for ever, he only had one client – just one, can you believe that?' She smiled at the thought.

'Who was the client?'

'It was Mr Hayes himself. He looked after the tax affairs of Mr Hayes and his few employees, and that was it.' The woman laughed. 'By the way' – she touched her fingers to her chest – 'I should have said, I'm Mrs Waller. I look after the housekeeping and run errands, deliver food, whatever needs doing, really.'

'Mrs Waller.' Sophia repeated. *Of course you are...* 'It's really lovely to meet you.'

She followed Mrs Waller up the ramp and into the corridor, where the windowless walls were bare and painted in a glossy magnolia. The air carried that particular odour redolent of many institutions – a nose-stinging combination of bleach, cabbage, decay and sadness. For it was indeed a sad smell, without warmth or personalisation. A smell that came from inside industrial kitchens and from cupboards where wholesale-sized bottles of detergent lived before it was sloshed liberally, no doubt from a grubby mop, on to the blue linoleum floor once a week. Every eight feet or so there was a door, some with welcome mats in front of them, and by the side of each doorway at head height sat a small whiteboard fixed to the wall with a name and number written on it.

Mrs Allworth 46
Mr Duke 47
Mrs Manson 48
Mrs Smith 49
And finally: *Mr Portobello 50*

She wasn't sure what it was about the sight of his name on the little whiteboard that caused her the most distress. Possibly the way it was so crudely written in a black marker pen, the first letters big – too big – and getting smaller, sloping to one side until the final 'l' and 'o' had to be written on a new line as the writer ran out of space. Sophia hated the fact that someone did not consider this an important enough task to simply wipe the board clean and rewrite his name with adequate spacing; it was lazy and disrespectful and all too bloody late now. Her sadness also came from the fact that she was not going to see him again – news that was still sinking in. Or it might have been that simply seeing his name and room number in a row of several others confirmed that this really was where Mr Portobello had lived. This was the truth; this was his grand Palladian home with a walled garden, marble floors and a parquet-floored library... The fact that he had lied to her every single time he had visited and the fact that he felt he had to was a lot to take in.

Mrs Waller pulled a large ring of keys on a jailer's loop from the front pocket of her tabard and held various keys up for scrutiny, trying to locate the right one. Sophia looked along the corridor, noting the scuffmarks on the wainscot and the digs out of the plaster that no one had thought to fill and repaint. Her eyes were drawn to a space at the end of the hall where walking frames and wheelchairs blocked an emergency exit, the items quite abandoned.

'Here we go!' Mrs Waller tried out a positive smile, as if she knew what Sophia was about to experience was going to be anything but. She put the key in the door handle and opened up the room.

Sophia walked in, and the first thing that struck her was the room's dimensions. It was small; small and chilly, but the unmistakable scent of her friend lingered still. If she still held on to a modicum of hope, now there was no doubt: this was Mr Portobello's room. She turned in a circle and the soles of her sensible shoes squeaked underfoot.

A single bed, stripped of its bedding, was pushed into one corner, and beside that a bedside cabinet with an orange, fringed lampshade sitting on a faux-onyx base. A walnut-veneered single wardrobe, not dissimilar to one her parents had owned, stood in the corner. She opened the door, running her fingers over the metal hangers that held five white, ironed and starched shirts. Her eyes wandered to a thick tartan wool dressing gown with a rope cord that had been hung on the corner of the wardrobe door. She hoped this garment had helped stave off the cold a little.

'He didn't have much.'

She had almost forgotten Mrs Waller was there, and her voice made Sophia jump.

'No, no, he didn't.' Sophia managed to speak around the boulder that had gathered in her throat. She had imagined him each night in front of a roaring fire surrounded by opulence and with a decent brandy in his glass.

Sophia walked over to the bed and fingered a green-jacketed book that lay on the bedside table. She carefully picked it up and read the title.

Mr Brown's Morning Paper.

It wasn't a book she knew, but she could tell from the age, condition, scent and script that it was probably much older than her.

'He was always reading that,' Mrs Waller added. 'I swear he'd finish it and go straight back to the beginning.'

'I would have' – she swallowed – 'I would have given him other books to read.'

'Oh, I offered to fetch him some from the library, but he was insistent; said he had all he wanted to read right there.'

'Do you think...' She hesitated, wondering if these things should be left for his children, for Emily and Anthony, before remembering with a jolt that there was no Emily and Anthony. 'Do you think I might be able to take this book?' She held it to her chest.

'That would be fine, lovey.' Mrs Waller walked closer. 'I

think everything in here will be going to charity. It's nice to think his favourite book is with you. He was a lovely man. A gent.'

'Yes.' Sophia took one last look around the empty, cold room. 'Yes, he was.'

A hot bath did little to restore her wellbeing, nor did her freshly washed warm pyjamas. She sat now on the sofa with Uncle Vanya on her lap, a recently finished cup of tea resting in the floral saucer on the side table. Opening the book about halfway through, her eyes fell upon a passage.

> *Mr Brown laughed his familiar throaty, mischievous laugh.*
> *'Do you know, the left-hand wall of the garden is groaning*
> *with it, the bricks almost listing under the boughs that*
> *carry the blooms in a waterfall of purple that even on*
> *the rainiest of days makes it look like summer. And the*
> *scent! Oh my word, that perfume... It's my very favourite*
> *time of the garden's year, closely followed by the arrival*
> *of the wisteria, which is interspersed with a snaking vine*
> *Can you believe it? An abundance of riches! Grapes and*
> *wisteria! How very lucky am I?'*

Her tears came quickly.

Sophia closed her eyes and wept. She wept for the loss of the man she had lived with inside the pages of this very book for the last eight months. There was much she did not know, much she could not figure out, but one thing she knew with absolute certainty: she would miss him. She would miss him every single day. It made her sad to think that his life was so thin he had to fall inside the pages of a book to find happiness and enrichment.

How she wished he had been honest with her, because then she could have taken him on some real-life adventures, to visit a garden with lilac or to sit in front a roaring fire... It also made her think about her own life, one that she knew she wanted to live, really live. It was time she acted on the advice that Mr Portobello had given her, advice that, for whatever reason, he had not taken himself. She resolved to wander far into the big world! She could hear it beckoning, could feel the pull of the oceans and the hum of the wild, a rhythm that only well-travelled global souls could dance to, and she wanted to be one of them. She wanted wings!

It had not been her intention, but she must have fallen asleep.

The ringing of the front doorbell woke her. Uncle Vanya leapt from her lap and hid behind the chair. Some guard cat, she thought, smiling for the first time that day. Sophia flattened her hair and adjusted her reading glasses, which had slipped down her nose. She opened the door wide, expecting to see one of the neighbours and wondering what the issue was now. Was her wheelie bin blocking their gate? Had Uncle Vanya again taken advantage of the previous tenants' sandbox and made a deposit? She took a deep breath.

It wasn't a neighbour that stood there, however, but Simon. He had his hands raised as if expecting a shoot 'em up.

'Simon!'

'Yes, I got your address from your old personnel file. I am sure I'm breaking about a million rules, but—'

To her mortification, just the sight of him brought the hot tears that she'd only just been keeping at bay to the fore.

'Oh God! I've made you cry! That's really bad! I'll go. I'll go right now; please pretend this never happened. It's a dreadful intrusion for which I am truly sorry.'

She reached out and grabbed the lapel of his mustard

corduroy jacket. 'Please don't go. I'm not crying because you're here; I'm crying because I'm sad, but seeing you' – she managed a smile – 'seeing you actually makes me feel happy, makes me feel better.'

'You're in your pyjamas!' he pointed out. 'And it's only 3 p.m. Are you sick?'

'I might be.'

'Can I get you some medicine or anything?'

She sniffed. 'What I'd really like is someone with whom I can share a large bowl of soup.'

Simon laughed and took a step over the threshold. 'That's me! I am a soup lover, nay, a soup aficionado!'

'I did not know that.' She wiped her eyes and closed the door behind him. 'And then later, after we've had soup, I want to travel somewhere wonderful and swim in a waterfall and see exotic birds and walk on sand and sit in the sun! I want to trek in a jungle and build a wall and jump off a boat into the sea!'

'Okay. Yes.' Simon nodded. 'That sounds great. Let's do all of that. But first soup. I have many specialties: carrot and coriander, spiced ginger and pumpkin, Stilton and broccoli; you name it and I can soup it! Where's the kitchen? Straight ahead?' He shrugged off his jacket and hung it on the newel post, as if he had done it a million times before. As Sophia took a step towards the kitchen, the unmistakable smell of cigar smoke filled her nostrils, and then, just like that. It was gone.

'Goodbye, my friend,' she whispered. 'Goodbye.'

Epilogue

One year later

Simon indicated and pulled the car into the car park. It was a bright September day.

'Can I ask you something?' Sophia turned in the passenger seat to face him.

'Ask away!' He smiled.

'Was this whole thing a ruse to get me to come back to school? To help with your staffing crisis?'

'Yes.' He nodded as he levelled up the steering wheel in his parking spot. 'You got me! I thought it would be cheaper, quicker and easier to sell my house, move into yours, merge our clutterous belongings, get married and adopt Uncle Vanya, who, by the way, I still think hates me—'

'Not at all! He loves you!' she lied.

'Yes, I figured all that would be easier than advertising and interviewing for the new English teacher I needed. Far easier to go through all of that and shoehorn you back into your old job.' He reached across and held her hand. 'How are you feeling?'

'I'm feeling good, nervous but good.' This was the truth.

It had been an easy decision. Simon's enthusiasm for his quest to make life better for these children was hideously infectious. That, and she realised that losing her parents had hit her harder than she had known. She had felt lost, adrift, lonely and fearful of the years ahead. It had seemed that the only possible course of action was to run away from all she knew: the school and everyone in it. Mr Portobello had been right, *hiding*...

Mr Hayes had helped with the transfer of the lease to the new tenants, and rather than finding it a chore, she and her husband had quite enjoyed packing away the shelves and shelves of books, stopping to read from anything that caught their eye and drinking endless cups of tea. She paused one afternoon to see Simon sitting with his shirtsleeves rolled up and his back against the bookshelves with a copy of *The Wind in the Willows* open in his hands, chortling to himself.

'This is really great, I'd forgotten.' He looked up at her.

She thought of dear Christopher then, and smiled, wondering how that fleeting moment of youthful joy had anchored her for so long to a place and time long gone.

Such a waste.

It had taken Mr Portobello coming into her life to make her see that she was stuck and Simon coming into her life to set her free...

'It is,' she beamed. 'Really great.'

When the fancy took them, and to ease the task, the two would take a break from book packing and dance to classic tunes, which came from the small transistor radio on the counter.

'Is this the most rubbish honeymoon in the whole wide world?' he had shouted above the music, as he twirled her beneath the beautiful green glass chandelier and the stunning ceiling rose, her heels making small dents in the wooden floor.

'No!' she had laughed, her head back, her hair loose about her shoulders. 'It's the best honeymoon in the whole wide world! Plus, we get to travel for real next summer and I just can't wait!' She squealed. Their South African adventure was booked. Just a year of school to get through first.

It now made her smile to drive past the shop with its radical shop fit, and she had to admit, she didn't dislike the new sign: 'MABS! The Home of Mother and Baby Sing-along!' She wished the witches nothing but success in their permanent home and had already planned on sneaking in with the key she had kept and covering the door, and possibly the whole window, with leaflets... she had yet to decide what they would advertise.

'Morning, Miss!' a boy called out as she made her way across the car park.

'Good morning, Marcus!' she responded, pleased to remember the boy's name. 'All ready for the new year?'

'No! I'd rather be on summer holidays! School sucks!' he answered honestly, and she laughed.

Simon had been right, it was exactly like riding a bike, and as she stepped into the classroom, which had been someone else's domain for the last academic year, it felt very much like coming home.

She wrote her name on the board for all to see, 'MRS BLANDFORD', wondering if the thrill of seeing it would ever diminish.

The students filed in. Some she recognised, some she did not.

'Quiet, please, everyone. Take your seats and get settled as soon as possible. Today is a very exciting day!'

The students looked at her, most with expressions of disbelief.

'Why's it exciting, Miss?' a boy on the back row asked.

'I am glad you asked!' She beamed. 'It's exciting because today is the day that you will dive into the world of F. Scott

Fitzgerald – we will be reading this!' She held up a copy of *The Great Gatsby*. 'Now, please take one and pass them along.' She popped piles of books at the beginning of each row and looked around the room as the students opened the books or turned them over and read the back; one girl, she noted, sitting in the back row, looked a little anxious as she ran her fingers over the front cover. Sophia wondered if she worked too many hours, cared for someone at home, whether that home was cold, kind, whether food was forthcoming, and she softened her tone.

'We shall be reading the text together in class, and homework will be writing about the text; what we have learned and what we think about it. If you have any questions about that, or if there is anything you would like to discuss with me, then please do so at the end of the class. We will go at your pace and, as a team, there is very little we can't overcome. Right, let's get settled.'

It was as she took her seat at the desk that the questions began to come thick and fast.

Why's it called The Great Gatsby?

What's a Gatsby?

How long is the book?

Can I write in it?

Is it true you are married to the Head, Miss?

And Sophia knew as she looked around at the inquisitive faces and heard the impatient finger-drumming of the students that there was no place she would rather be; happy to provide the fuel for these enquiring minds.

'Okay' – she clapped her hands – 'who wants to start us off?'

The same girl from the back row put up her hand. 'I'll read first.'

'Thank you for volunteering.' She sat back in her chair and listened as the girl began.

Sophia looked up towards the small window of the classroom door and knew what Simon meant. The prospect of seeing him in the corridor, glimpsing him across the canteen or sitting within sight of him in the staff room... well, these were the small things that for her were actually the very big things.

She also now knew that Mr Portobello had been right: life is not for the dead, it's for the living; and she understood that she had a duty to continue living her life. And she had done it; she, Sophia Blandford, had sought out happiness and not let herself sink into the mire of grief. Because that, she knew, would have been a fool's errand...

About the Author

AMANDA PROWSE is an international bestselling author whose 27 novels, 7 short stories and memoir have been published worldwide in dozens of languages. Her first children's picture book is *The Smile That Went A Mile*. Her chart-topping, number 1 titles *What Have I Done? Perfect Daughter, My Husband's Wife, The Girl in the Corner* and *The Things I Know* have sold millions of copies around the world.

To find out more about her work please visit her website
www.amandaprowse.com